The Lover With Five Names

Lila Mary

Published by Lila Mary, 2024.

THE LOVER WITH FIVE NAMES

First edition. January 23, 2024.

ISBN: 979-8223775713

Written by Lila Mary.

Table of Contents

PROLOGUE

The Nameless Lover knows what it means when the door closes like that. That crash of thunder, just from the latch clicking into place.

The Lover's throat bobs.

Edgorn's eyes were sharp with lightning as they ascended the stairs. His hand on the Nameless Lover's back was a smoldering ember waiting to ignite. Stomping upstairs after the evening ball, Edgorn shoved off the servants waiting to help him undress. His guards were ordered to wait in the antechamber of marble and gold just beyond the bedchamber door.

Those same guards and servants send the Nameless Lover pitying smiles. Edgorn's anger radiates like a quake in the ground.

Edgorn shrugs off his red coat with a pointedness that preludes a storm. His brows are drawn, his mouth curved into a scowl beneath his dark mustache. The Nameless Lover sits on the edge of their canopy bed, shoves his bejeweled wrists under his thighs, and waits for the storm to blow through.

Edgorn lays the red coat neatly on the bed and begins unbuttoning the gold shirt beneath before speaking. Surprisingly, his first words aren't roared in anger, though a fire blazes bright in his brown eyes.

His words come low with danger instead, an unyielding calm. Edgorn's control never lasts long. It will snap like a fine thread if tugged on too hard. "What was that behavior at dinner tonight?"

The Nameless Lover sighs heavily, considering his choices. Considering duty.

The Nameless Lover doesn't feign ignorance, unlike other instances where he's played the dumb and doting arm candy. "My conversation with Lady Zahara was nothing out of the ordinary." The Nameless Lover isn't attracted to ladies, despite his past affair with the queen of Coromoda. Edgorn truly has nothing to worry about. Not that he knows that.

Not that he knows anything about the Nameless Lover.

"She was mooning over you, and you were making eyes at her," Edgorn snaps. The buttons of his cuffs come undone next, all with a punctuated sharpness even as his fingers shake. Too much wine. His face flushes red with it. "People flirt with you all the time. Understandable, looking as you do, but normally you're oblivious. I don't know what made you open your eyes tonight, but remember this: you are mine. No one else shall have you."

He comes round to the other side of the bed, looming over the Nameless Lover. "Are we clear?"

So many times before, the Nameless Lover has averted his eyes and accepted Edgorn's incontestable declarations without complaint. Without so much as a word. Edgorn is king, and the Nameless Lover has always been happy to let him think he holds the power.

"Yes," the Nameless Lover says.

"Good." Edgorn continues unbuttoning his shirt, pulling it free of the trousers it was tucked into. "Get undressed and get on the bed."

That's a command the Nameless Lover has heard all too many times, not just from Edgorn. He's always grinned and bore it, duty and all that, but something in him hesitates tonight. He did choose to acknowledge and cautiously return Lady Zahara's flirtations instead of tactfully ignoring them. He's still not sure why he did it, because even as he did, standing under red lights and red ceilings, he knew it would elicit this reaction from Edgorn.

Maybe it's because he wanted to see how Edgorn would react, find out if he could get away with it. The Nameless Lover has strived to evoke Edgorn's anger deliberately in the past, but never without reason. The Lover always works with purpose—never more, never less. He is surgical in his methods, his plans, and his executions, and he never strays from them. He is emotionless. He can mold to whatever shape his current role needs.

He is perfect, untouchable. However, sometimes an outcry of disdain ignites in his heart, and he struggles to put it out. Struggles to banish the desire to walk away from people like Edgorn, Cadhan, Isabella, and live a life of his own. Herra is the only thing he has left that's real. But Herra is far, far from here. The Lover is alone.

"Cardamom," Edgorn says, the fourth name. "Get undressed."

The Nameless Lover takes a deep breath and raises his head. He looks Edgorn square in the eye, swallows, and says, "No."

Edgorn's eyes darken, and his hands leave his clothes. The Nameless Lover can only brace.

He stands and smoothly ducks the blow that Edgorn tries to deck him. He has dealt with an incensed king before, an incensed queen once too, but never with as much fiery anger as King Edgorn's.

"Bastard!" Edgorn roars, his face flushed the same color of his country's crest.

As the Nameless Lover dodges blows within the bedchamber he has shared with this man for the past six months, the sweetness of relief floods through him. He's longed for this moment since the day they met. Normally, his targets—his lovers—dictate when things end, and the Nameless Lover doesn't encourage them to end things a moment sooner. They'll think the affair ended on their own terms, and the Nameless Lover will rejoice in his victory while they're none the wiser. They'll think it's his loss, when it's truly theirs.

He must never be the one to break things off. He broke that rule tonight, and Herra will be incensed. He fears that storm far more than Edgorn's.

She never said he had to beg to stay, though, with any of them.

Edgorn spits curses and insults at him, stumbling over himself and the bedposts. Edgorn's size and inebriation and pure rage inhibit him. He's not refined, and he's never been able to turn his rage into power, not with the Nameless Lover. Edgorn has wisdom when his head is clear, so much so that it scares the Lover sometimes. But right now, this king is nothing more than a scorned lover just like any other. The Lover can handle that.

The Lover backs himself up against the south wall. Edgorn stalks up to him with triumph burning in his eyes, thinking he's won. His hands reach out for Cardamom, but they clutch at air. Edgorn looks around, bewildered, but doesn't notice the ajar window in front of him.

The Nameless Lover climbs down the windowpanes on the outside of the palace into the night, the moon at his back. Edgorn bellows, yelling for his guards and a search, and the Lover can only pray he's not seen.

Despite the storm of guards he'll have to evade in the city, the bounties on his head, all the Lover can feel is mind numbing relief.

His time with Edgorn is over, and it's his own fault.

PART ONE

THE FIFTH NAME

CHAPTER ONE

The first words out of Herra's mouth are, "Were you seen?"

"Hello to you, too." The Nameless Lover runs the water in the cracked marble sink. He combs his fingers through his hair, dyed white and cut close to his head. A bottle of brown dye—the closest match he could find to his natural color—rests next to the bronze faucet.

He hasn't seen his natural color, only a shade darker than his skin, in years. His hair changes each time he switches targets, one step in the process of discretion. Wouldn't do for his old lovers to recognize him on the off chance they'd run into each other.

"No, I wasn't seen," he says, glancing at Herra in the dirty mirror. She hasn't changed since their last meeting six months ago. Her black hair rests in a loose and messy braid over her shoulder, thick bangs and loose strands sitting next to her light brown skin. Her arms are folded over her blue jacket, dark eyes glinting in the low candlelight.

"Not to my knowledge," he adds.

He squeezes a bit of dye onto his gloved hands, listening to Herra rustle in the doorway. Though they're not visible, he knows she's covered in knives, and her sword clangs in its sheath when she moves. She is never without a blade, not even here on her home turf. "So, what did he do?" she asks.

The Lover begins running the dye through his hair. He would hate to do this when the strands are long, though this time he means to grow it out. His roots will do the rest. "What do you mean?"

She shoots him a withering look in the mirror. "Edgorn. What terrible crime did you commit to drive him away? Or did he simply declare that he was done with you?"

The Lover's hands fall still. Breaking up with Edgorn so suddenly and violently was a risk he was well aware of, and he's spent the entire journey back considering what he'd tell her. He wishes he could lie, but Herra would see right through.

Therefore, the truth. He tells her everything that happened from the moment he left to become the lover of the king of Ele to the night he climbed out of Edgorn's window. He's aware of the glaring hole about why he left so suddenly, when he's done this twice before without a hitch. When he knows his duty. They both know their duty. Why, why? It's a question he's been asking himself just as much.

As predicted, Herra is ruthless. "You're a fucking idiot and a coward, but at least Edgorn was never going to be an emperor."

The Nameless Lover grumbles, "You're a heartless bastard. If you don't like my methods, go find someone else to do your hunting and spying. At least Isabella was nice when she dismissed me. Let me go gently, didn't make a fuss when I slipped out in the night. She never said I couldn't stay in her court." She probably knew his interest in her was fake on principle. She's smarter than Cadhan and Edgorn combined.

Herra says, "I would make a fuss."

"You'd make a cruel emperor."

"Good thing my duty is not emperorship, then," Herra retorts, "only picking one."

The Nameless Lover sighs and goes back to dyeing his hair. "I suppose you have someone new and shiny picked out for me?"

Herra thankfully drops the issue of Edgorn and gets back to business. Each time he departs, she prepares someone new, knowing it's only a matter of time before he comes back. She chooses his targets carefully. He is spying on her account, after all. "Yes. King Ricarda Donati the Fifth."

He pauses. "Our own king?"

"Yeah. Got a problem with that?"

"No. It's just—really? Him?"

"Him? What do you mean? He's closer to you in age than any of your previous targets. You should be on your knees thanking me. What do you want me to say?" She shrugs. "They say he's attractive enough. Nice."

"They say that about all of them."

She scoffs. "No one has ever said Edgorn is nice. Anyway, forget him, as you seem so eager to do. Don't know what ticked you off about him. I could deal with a temper, it's something like Cadhan's vanity that would drive me up the wall. With Ricarda, you'll be happy."

You say that about all of them. The Lover swallows his remarks, knowing they'd get him nowhere. His fate is sealed, and he shouldn't draw her suspicion by fighting her. She'd ask what makes this time so different, and to that there is no good answer.

He resigns himself to his fresh fate with a sigh, running the brown dye through his hair with another pass, leaning against the dirty sink. This little dilapidated washroom has stood here in the heart of Mitzi as long as he's been hanging around it. It's always his first stop after a job.

"When do I leave?" he asks.

"Whenever you're ready," she says, the same open-ended answer as always.

The Lover could stay in Mitzi for months without her raising a fuss...but the implication is always there. He must go back.

"I'll leave in the morning." He'll need to buy some hair extensions to disguise himself until his hair actually grows that long. And some clothes befitting the Mariosan court instead of the Elen one, and forged documents, some new boots—

Maybe two mornings.

The Lover returns to the dyeing process, expecting her shadow to disappear from the mirror the next time he looks up. But she doesn't leave until he's worked all the dye through his hair, until he turns around to wait for it to set.

She grips his arm. Up close, he gets a glimpse of her dark eyes. Deep and daunting. She always swears she's not his friend, only his employer, but the eyes can't lie. She is concerned.

"Be careful," she says, and he grips her wrist in return.

He can't help but grin. "Nice to know you care about me."

That closes her eyes to any kindness in an instant. She releases his arm with a harsh jerk. "No," she says patiently, as she has three times before. "It would just be—"

"A pain to replace someone of my talent, yes, I know," he repeats, waving her off. "I've survived three courts, including a king with a raving temper. I'll survive the court of the pretty king. Don't you worry your hot little head about me."

Herra sighs. The Lover turns back to the sink, and when he looks up again, she's gone.

BLACK AND WHITE BANNERS are the first thing the Lover sees when he steps out of his carriage.

They're everywhere in the capital, Allicé. Strung from lampposts, hung from balconies and fences, even hung from the merchants' carts lining the cobblestone streets.

Mariosa's symbol of death, a black background with a white rose painted in the center. Despite the proclamation of death, the Mariosans here don't appear especially sad. The Lover smiles, in fact, when the merchants call excitedly to a new face. Timeless and charming as always, the greed of city folk.

The city is sunlit and golden, marble buildings and oil paint decorating it into a dream. Mariosa is the golden country, and Allic é the golden city. In all his time living in Mariosa, the Lover has never been here.

He follows the cobblestone roads toward the palace, a thing of beauty resting on a slight incline over the rest of the city. It's white with golden roofs, shimmering in the sunlight. Everything here smells of roses, though he can't see any growing.

The hustle and bustle of a crowd slowly moving toward the palace can only mean there's a ball on tonight. Though he prepared for that possibility, the Lover pauses in his tracks. He's forever conflicted about arriving at new courts on the nights of parties. The commotion helps him blend in, yes, and if something goes catastrophically wrong then there will be other matters for the crowd to focus on.

On the other hand, the balls make him blend in, and the monarch in question might not have time for him. The first impression must stick in their mind. He almost lost Cadhan's attention that way, by never gaining it in the first place. That was a fault of the Lover's own arrogance: thinking that he could draw Cadhan's heart to him with just a look, a few well chosen words. Oh, how naïve he was.

The Lover waits for the crowd to flock indoors before approaching the palace himself. He walks up the flight of marble steps alone, the red glow of the sunset casting onto his back and warming his skin as a familiar chill settles into his bones. His soul will be locked away until he climbs through another window or gets thrown unceremoniously out the very front doors he now approaches.

The heavy wooden doors are wide open, and the sound of laughter and revelry spills out. The soft warmth of candles, the glow of music—the Lover is well familiar with these sounds and sights. But none of the previous three courts have felt as welcoming as this palace.

Pace yourself, man. You're not even in the damn door yet.

The doors are flanked by guards in shining gold armor. "Name and business?" the one on the left asks from behind their helm of gold, feathers fanning out on the top.

The Lover smiles, shaking out the longer ends of his new brown wig. He's still getting used to it after six months of close cropped hair. "Marquis Leonidas Sartini of Belimati." He presents his generic invitation to the ball, a suitably tailored fake that he's always in the habit of carrying.

The guards let him in after a perfunctory glance over, thinking him nothing more than the rest of the riff raff in flowing skirts and shining buttons. Leonidas accepts that perception readily.

He steps into the ballroom and breathes in the sweet scent of roses and the sharp spice of something cooking. The golden, dim candlelight is just what he expected, as is the glittering chandelier hanging by golden chains. He can see his reflection in the marble tiles below his boots.

A soft piano melody floats around the room, mingling with the conversation. A thousand sparkling jewels flutter past his vision, as well as dozens of flowing ballgown trains and delicate hands adorned with rings. It all leaves him breathless for a moment, standing in awe of the finery. Part of him will always be the little boy who grew up in a cabin with his mother who whored for a living.

Pull yourself together. This is not the first court you've seen. Act like it and stop gaping.

Leonidas adjusts the lapels of his gold brocade coat, scanning the room for his target. There is no throne here. Perhaps it's in a different room.

No, he thinks, observing the layout. An enormous multipurpose floor, the ceiling that attempts to touch the heavens, the long tables lining the walls. This room is the hub of activity, even if it's currently done up for a ball. There's a reason it's the first thing you encounter upon entering the palace. There doesn't need to be a throne for power to be implied.

After minutes of scanning, his eyes land on the king—because that is what he unquestionably is—sitting at the high table, overlooking the room. Beyond the embroidered white tablecloth and the tapestry behind the table is the king, with an aura entirely different from Edgorn's.

From the shimmering gold half cloak on his left shoulder to the long green tunic he wears under an overcoat, the handsome sword strapped to his side, every inch of him says royal, regal, divine. Rich blooded and young and beautiful. Everything Leonidas has used as a means to an end, swearing to hate while pretending to love. Just tools. Just for Herra's sake, never his own. But there is something distinctly different here. It sticks out to Leonidas within seconds of looking.

His previous targets have all been beautiful. Edgorn—well, perhaps ruggedly handsome is the term that would suit better. Queen Isabella's beauty is sung from east to west, black skin and dark endless braids, but Leonidas' heart and loins have never favored women. Cadhan was attractive, fair haired and a challenge head to toe, but he was too proud and vain for things to have ever been real.

But the king of Mariosa—oh, something is very different about him.

Looking past all that finery, he is gorgeous. Tight brown curls fall over his forehead and his ears, flopping forward no matter how many times he shakes them back. A hint of a mustache rests above his fine, wide lips, curling into smiles and laughter at everything said around him. Piercing green eyes, dark and bright and vibrant, rest under long feathery eyelashes.

Suntanned white skin is decorated with scars. The king is famously an adept soldier and swordsman, and his dynastic sword rests in a golden scabbard at his belt, adorned with gleaming inset jewels of green and blue and purple. No jewelry on him other than a heavy gold ring strung around his neck—his signet ring, carved with the symbol of Mariosa's double lions intertwined with green vines.

A glint of white teeth shows when Ricarda Donati V smiles. He is perfect, beautiful like something out of a painting, something unreal and otherworldly. Someone who only exists in stories and dreams. Someone who sits before Leonidas in the flesh, someone whose eyes darken when they land on Leonidas and stick there. Leonidas stands tall in the face of that intense gaze, hardened by his long years of experience, but it's a near thing he doesn't look away.

Leonidas is gravitating toward him before he knows what he's doing, like his feet are not his own. As he pushes through the crowd, parting the sea to get to the king, Ricarda's eyes never stray from him. A woman sits beside him, talking in his ear. He doesn't seem to hear her, and she doesn't mind that he's not responding.

Leonidas hasn't worked with a target who already has a lover. A jolt of panic flashes through him, soothed with a breath. He'll find a way around it. He always does.

He supposes he could achieve his goal without getting into Ricarda's bed. That won't be the place he determines if Ricarda is

Herra's perfect emperor. It's just easier. People are so susceptible to the yearnings of their loins, and Leonidas is an expert in that field. Anyone can be manipulated into answering any question in those circumstances. People tell on themselves without even realizing.

Leonidas has never worked with someone who didn't feel those yearnings, another possibility he must consider. Again, Leonidas will figure it out as he works. For now, not getting thrown out of the Mariosan court is a good first step.

The golden guards give him suspicious looks as he climbs the steps to the high table, but Ricarda doesn't stop him, so neither do they. Ricarda is still staring as Leonidas approaches.

"My king," Leonidas says, smiling pleasantly, throwing just the right glint into his brown eyes. The brilliantly dressed woman at the king's side glances up. Leonidas weathers scandalized looks at his bold move, just walking up like this without invitation.

Leonidas extends his hand. "Marquis Leonidas Sartini of Belimati. Pleasure to make this introduction."

To the west, in Ele, they would say *honor to be in your presence*—Edgorn always was a self-centered bastard. King Ricarda's smile here is warm and genuine, his eyes dancing with interest. Such a dark shade of green, pulling you in.

"The pleasure is mine," he says, never breaking eye contact. Instead of shaking Leonidas' hand, he leans down to lay a firm kiss on the back of it. His fingers are firm and callused, rough from a lifetime of swordplay, but still gentle. He looks up at Leonidas through his eyelashes with a playful grin.

Not a more noble man exists on this earth, Leonidas has heard of the Mariosan king. He watched Edgorn smile in public only to sneer in private too many times; he won't relate one gentle touch of Ricarda's to nobility. However, Leonidas keeps that door open, and shivers as Ricarda releases his hand.

The woman at the king's side finally butts in and extends her own hand to Leonidas, saying, "I am here, too, Ric."

"Apologies." The king raises his hands defensively. "My lord, this is my sister—"

"Honored and divine and sister."

He rolls his eyes. "Stuck up and bratty little sister, owner of my entire heart, Antonia Bevelia Donati. A threat against her is a threat against me, and I would lay down my life for hers in an instant, though she needs no one to defend her."

Leonidas smiles, looking back and forth between them. He knew the king was young, and Herra said as much, but he's still surprised at the glinting innocence in Ricarda's tone. He and Leonidas must be the same age.

"My lady," Leonidas says, accepting her pale hand into his dark one to press a kiss there. Her nails are painted a fine rose gold, matching her brilliant strapless ballgown. The more he looks at her, the more detail he finds, from the pink roses embroidered onto her skirts, to the large and flashy ring decorating the middle finger of her left hand.

The oval gemstone of pale pink is comically huge against the gold band. It looks heavy. Leonidas expects a princess to wear resplendent rings, but the only other jewelry on her person is a thin golden locket, worn with age. "My pleasure to make this introduction."

She smiles with the same warmth that her brother carries. Her hair is the same rich brown as her brother's, but hers hangs over her shoulders in curls loose enough to be called waves. Like her brother, her skin is pale. Every bit of both of them shines. Royals. "My pleasure to make yours, Marquis. I haven't seen you around here before."

"There is a good reason for that, my lady. I've never been to court before." The beginning and end of the truth he can give to these people. He's used to the dull ache that comes with lying, especially to someone as pleasant as them. Maybe they'll both turn out like Edgorn, monsters behind closed doors. That would make Leonidas' feint of indifference easier. "I came into my title recently, after the death of my distant relative who held it previously."

"I'm sorry to hear about the passing of Lady Filipa," Ricarda says solemnly. "I wasn't aware she was unwell. That must have been difficult, to come into your power so suddenly."

Leonidas took precautions to ensure he would not be caught in a lie, though he's always found the use of assassins distasteful. Lady Filipa is safe and alive, living out her elderly days in a little villa far away from her proper estate. Leonidas has merely taken steps to keep her there.

"It was," Leonidas says, drawing sorrow into his voice, "but I like it at Belimati. There's a beautiful lake nearby, quite refreshing in this heat." He flashes a smile, and Ricarda returns it.

The king pulls out the chair next to him. "Where are my manners? Please, sit. Be our dining companion for tonight."

Leonidas nearly raises an eyebrow. This is exceptionally easy, but he won't inspect a gift such as this for flaws. He obediently sits, happy to rest in one of the familiarly soft royal cushions. There are certainly worse jobs he could have.

Another man comes running up to the table in a dark blue jacket that complements his golden hair, sitting in a loose ponytail over his shoulder and tied with a ribbon in a bow. His eyes shine the same dark blue. Leonidas braces for the guards to apprehend him, but Ricarda lets him come up without a word, without a second glance.

The man, out of breath, says, "Ricarda, what are you doing sitting here like a sad overlord, you should—" and then trails off when he notices Leonidas sitting beside them both. His brow furrows. "Who's that?"

"I am Marquis Leonidas Sartini of Belimati," Leonidas says, getting used to the words in his mouth, knowing he'll have to make the introduction hundreds of times over the coming months. At least no one here will call him Cardamom, so he won't be tempted to answer to it. He'd be surprised to hear the word at all, since cardamom itself isn't common here. "Pleasure to make this introduction."

The man looks at Ricarda and Antonia and back to Leonidas. Finding approval on the royals' faces, he breaks into a grin. "Alessandro de Rege, heir to the Grimitata estate," he says, scrambling to the other side of the table and shaking Leonidas' hand vigorously. "Lovely to meet you. Call me Aless."

"This is the other sorry soul I'm stuck with," the king says, but he's smiling. "The greatest friend I could ever have."

"Those two have been making trouble together since childhood," Antonia says to Leonidas with a sigh.

Ricarda adds, "The lovely piano was Aless' performance. He has a touch for music unlike any I have ever heard."

"That's one way of putting it," Antonia chuckles.

Alessandro climbs around to the other side of the table and drops into a seat beside Antonia. "Oh, please, don't stroke my ego." He delicately tucks back one of his loose hair strands and bats his eyelashes. "Antonia, how lovely you look tonight." He raises her ringed finger to his lips for a kiss, glancing up at her from beneath the eyelashes.

She rolls her eyes. "You've already told me that. Three times."

"Always bears repeating."

Leonidas looks between them.

"You can ask," the king says.

Leonidas says, "Are you two—"

Antonia waves her middle finger, the one with the ring. Alessandro says, starry eyed, "The first day I saw her, I fell into the depths of love, and I have not crawled back out. I proposed six months ago, and she has yet to accept or deny it, as you can see. I live for the day I will see a second ring on her finger. She feigns indifference, but I know in the depths of her own heart, she harbors a love just as fierce."

Leonidas racks his brain on Mariosan proposal customs. He's not Mariosan, strictly speaking, despite having been born within their borders. He's not anything, really, or anyone. He just becomes a costume for a time before taking it off and replacing it with another.

He also knows the look of someone uncomfortably trapped by the unwanted affections of another, unable to find the words to deny them. He's seen it in the mirror countless times.

Leonidas feared for a moment that this was the situation with Alessandro and the princess, but from what he can tell, Antonia is not the trapped victim Leonidas has been before. He's always been good at reading people. He's had to be.

The custom of presenting your beloved with a ring as a question and waiting for them to buy themself a second ring in answer slowly comes back to him. "Ah," he says. So, they're in the *it's complicated* phase, though anyone with eyes could see the affection in Antonia's.

"You were eleven when you first saw me, Less," Antonia says fondly, patting his hand.

"You can't expect me to change my narrative this late," Alessandro says. "Bad continuity."

Leonidas finds himself stifling a smile, something rare and slightly concerning. The last thing he needs is to start developing a fondness for these people.

Ricarda smiles and jerks his thumb upwards, looking at Leonidas again. "You haven't said anything about the fresco. Everyone says something about the fresco their first time here."

"What f—" Leonidas looks obligingly skywards and cuts himself off with a gasp. The fresco in question lines most of the high circular ceiling, a beautiful background of red filled in with Mariosan royalty. Colors of all varieties intermingle and streak together in a myriad of beauty, limbs of all shades reaching for one another, a sea of people blended in color. It's ancient, it's beautiful, and it takes Leonidas's breath away.

Alessandro smiles with a glint of mischief in his eye. "New here, are you? Can't believe you didn't notice it more quickly."

"Less," Antonia scolds, "the way to win my heart is most certainly not by insulting our new companion."

Leonidas has gone from stranger to companion in just a few minutes. That is a feat, even for him. He's not sure how he feels about it. Edgorn didn't have friends—it wasn't in his nature to be a decent, respectable person capable of caring for others on the same level he cared for himself. Isabella isolated herself willingly, and Cadhan made himself a bore and a joke to be around.

Edgorn had subordinates, Leonidas included. He made pawns out of the nobles filling his court. He had armies of people who were scared of him. He had people who only existed in his world to serve his purpose. He had no friends. Leonidas is sure he didn't know the meaning, and he's sure Edgorn will be buried alone, in an empty and opulent graveyard.

"I meant no insult," Alessandro says, raising his hands.

"I took no insult," Leonidas says. "Pay it no mind, my lord. And in answer to your question—my eye was drawn to other features." He looks at the king when he says it. Years ago, he would have worried about forwardness, but now he knows not to waste any time. The monarchs generally like it better if they get what they want sooner. Leonidas shares that sentiment.

The king grins. "Are you suggesting I'm nothing more than a piece of pretty artwork in this ballroom of fools, something to be ogled like the fresco?"

"Never, Majesty," Leonidas says. "Your beauty could charm royals and bend nations to your will, but what I've heard of your mind's brilliance far outshines it."

Ricarda tips his head back and laughs. Such pretty compliments never worked on the toughened Edgorn. He always scoffed at such things. He was a challenge, and not the fun kind. Leonidas is pleased, as he takes in the long column of Ricarda's throat, to find that the Mariosan king is susceptible to such words. "Oh, I like you. A flatterer."

"At least I have the decency to encourage people not to stroke my ego," Alessandro says, chin in his hand, looking utterly delighted.

"It can't be an uncommon sentiment," Leonidas says.

"Maybe not," Ricarda says. His eyes twinkle in the lights. "But rarely from beauties such as you."

Alessandro groans. "No. I dreaded the day I would see my own sickness mirrored in Ric's eyes. My lord Marquis, get out while you still can."

Ricarda scowls at his friend. Leonidas smiles. "Forgive me my ignorance, Your Majesty," he says. "I have a question." Sometimes acting demure and inquisitive, without a thought in his head, can get monarchs talking. This is the experimental stage—finding out what type of demeanor Ricarda likes.

"About Mariosa? Ask me anything." Ricarda spreads his hands, his green painted nails catching chandelier light, and smiles. "I will never pass up a chance to share my knowledge. You can stroke my ego further."

"Please, for the love of the gods, don't encourage him anymore," Alessandro urges. "Spare us all a bit of pain." Antonia nods, but

Leonidas is ruled by Ricarda's devious grin. He is why Leonidas is here, after all. Nothing matters except worming his way into Ricarda's trust.

He makes a mental note of Ricarda's reaction—he likes sharing knowledge but doesn't get off on proving his superiority to others. He wants to have a normal and mutual conversation above all else, it seems.

Leonidas asks, "What unfortunate soul passed to warrant that many banners in the city?"

The jovial air falls from the table, replaced by a deep silence. Leonidas tunes in the sound of someone else playing piano, the clinking of glasses, the murmuring of voices, but all he truly focuses on is the silence.

"Today is the sixth anniversary of my father's murder," the king says softly, deep and laced with sorrow. His eyes point to the table, long eyelashes hiding them. He twiddles his fingers. "Remembrance Day. Tonight's ball is to commemorate him."

A pit opens in Leonidas' chest, and he can't speak fast enough. "Forgive my callousness, Majesty," he says, nearly tripping over his words in his haste to get them out. For the most part, they're genuine.

A hundred apologies couldn't atone for this guilt. He had no warm and fuzzy family of his own, but he's always carried sympathy for those who have. And for one's own father to be murdered, mother dead from disease—gods. He can't imagine. "May your father rest in peace."

"It's no worry," Ricarda says. Leonidas winces at the lingering sorrow in his voice. "I'm just so surprised you didn't know."

Leonidas scrambles for an excuse. "I have been out of the country for most of my life, Majesty. I haven't kept up on Mariosa's news." That's not a lie, either. "Of course, the murder of your father can never be forgotten, but the date sometimes evades my mind."

Ricarda nods in understanding, and Leonidas sighs in relief. "Please, call me Ricarda. All my friends do."

So quickly elevated to—to friend? After one dinner and one horrible flub? He'll take it, but by gods, an emperor shouldn't be so gullible. Leonidas finds himself disappointed.

The sooner you find Herra an emperor, the sooner you get to be free. It's natural to be disappointed when his new target is less than perfect—but, granted, they got off to a much better start than any of the others. Perhaps being gullible is just a sign of trust. Edgorn certainly didn't have trust in abundance. Leonidas can't decide if trust is a good or bad quality in a potential emperor. It's not his place to decide, it's his place to observe and report back to Herra.

Commotion from across the ballroom draws his eye. A group of guards in gold are lugging an enormous parcel across the floor, parting the crowd to do so. Everyone but Leonidas seems to know what it is, and the partygoers start to jeer and shout at the object they carry.

A cage, Leonidas realizes, with someone inside it. The metal bars are molded to the shape of a person but barely big enough to fit one. Yet fit one it does.

The figure inside is small and dejected, pale as snow with hair that's flame orange. Their eyes find the ground, and they have no reaction to the rotten fruit the partygoers throw at them. Their clothes are threadbare, ragged, and hang off a frail and thin body. Without the cage to hold them up, Leonidas suspects they'd fall to the ground. Their thin fingers clutch at the bars, helpless. The look of someone who has utterly given up on life.

Ricarda's voice darkens. "My father's murderer. I wanted him to burn in this life and in whatever afterlife awaits him, but I was persuaded that this would be a better fate. For the eternal suffering he has brought Antonia, myself, and the entire empire, he is condemned to the prison beneath these floors. He will know only a life of darkness and solitude. Once a year, on this day, he is brought up to face the public for what he's done."

Leonidas looks between his dining companions, the prisoner in the cage, and the jeering crowd. A part of him is horrified, another simply fascinated, another trying to contextualize this and weave it into a scenario where it's acceptable to leave a prisoner in the dark underground for six years with only annual days of sunlight.

Far worse things have been done to far more people. A year of Edgorn's terror aboveground would amount to the same suffering as this. This man killed the emperor, the father of this kind king. He is the reason you're here in the first place. This should not upset you.

But Leonidas has never given a shit about the emperors.

"What's his name?" he asks, trying to keep his voice level.

"Jona," Ricarda growls. "He's Ilyakan, but we've never been able to glean more than that despite our extensive...interrogations. We don't know where he came from or who hired him or why my father had to die."

Leonidas shivers, but tries hard to put himself in Ricarda's place, if that were his father. His nonexistent memories of any father and his less than perfect memories of his mother make that difficult, but he tries. He always tries.

The high table doesn't throw rotten fruit at the assassin Jona—apparently they're above that—but the glare in the princess's eye speaks of a yearning for knives. The sad, sorry prisoner is shouted at, cursed, and dirtied all the more until the guards slowly push the crowd back.

Ricarda stands up, and his voice carries across the room with all the might of a king. "That's enough." The crowd slowly calms down, and attendants come swooping in to clean the floor of fruit while Ricarda speaks. "Prisoner, every year I offer you the same deal. A lesser sentence, the release of death, or perhaps even freedom in return for information about the crime you committed."

Leonidas, looking up at the imposing figure the king makes with his broad shoulders and half cloak and jutted chin, knows Ricarda will never grant this prisoner freedom. But the young man's eyes—gods, he can't be any older than them either—dart up a little, perhaps in hope. They're clearwater blue, bright and almost childlike if not for his grim condition. He says nothing.

Ricarda continues, "You have never given an inch on our deal, always choosing loyalty to your accomplices. I suppose I must admire you for that." A pause. "Do you change your mind this Remembrance Day, my prisoner? Have you any names to give up? Even just an apology for taking my father from me?" He reaches for Antonia's hand and holds it on the table for Jona to see. Siblings united in revenge.

The man raises his head inside the cage, defiant somehow despite his circumstances. When he speaks, his voice is thin but still strong, and his thick accent carries across the room. "Never. You may keep me here a hundred years, but I will never tell you anything more."

Ricarda laughs and spreads his arms. "Don't you see? Your companions have never come for you. Never come to plead for your release, never sent a messenger, not even a threat—not a word. Some friends they must be to cut their losses and abandon you like this. Whoever they are, I hope they're worth it."

A silence spreads over the room, and all eyes turn back to the caged prisoner to hear his retort. "They are. You know nothing," Jona growls, clutching the bars with a strength that's surprising for someone in his position, flicking bits of tomato out of his hair, "and you will hear nothing further of it from me."

Ricarda shrugs. "Fine by me." He signals to the guards, and they drag the caged prisoner away. Jona makes no sound of protest.

Instead of shrinking back into the depths of the cage, he keeps his hands on the bars and his dirty head raised high. Clear blue eyes hold Ricarda's gaze and flick to Leonidas for a moment as he's taken downstairs.

"Welcome to court," Leonidas mutters to himself as Ricarda raises the call for dinner to be served.

CHAPTER TWO

C aptain Arthur di Mars watches two horses circle each other, directed by their masters a few feet away.

The crowd around him stares breathlessly at the scene. Which horse will triumph? Arthur's horse is one of the two; a brown beauty plated in gold and teal armor. The silver blanket strung across his back shines in the sunlight.

The opponent is a small dapple gray, adorned in red and brown. The masters with their potions and swords shout encouragement into the pen, but all the horses do is stare each other down. They're evenly matched, hesitant to fight despite the might backing each of them up. The other defeated horses hang back with their masters, watching silently.

"Ah, gods damn it. This is never going to end if we just sit here and keep throwing shit at the wall. Fine, you fucker, you win."

General Lasilas Catiana throws down his losing dapple gray horse card, anger crossing his face for the first time today. It's gone in moments, replaced by mirth in the depths of his blue eyes.

Arthur's brown horse card sits face up on the table, the winning master card beside it. Lasilas tosses the figurine trophy to Arthur, signaling the official end of the game.

Arthur eagerly collects the coins piled in the center of the green table, adding to his already substantial stack. The other captains groan—most of them bet on Lasilas—and mutter lighthearted curses.

"It was obvious who would win," grumbles Dainthi. "Arthur's horse was so much bigger and stronger."

"I resent that. The statistics stated that we were evenly matched," Arthur protests.

"Not necessarily stronger," Lasilas says. "Don't forget who you're talking to. You don't have to be big to have the advantage. Often, it's a disadvantage."

Callum, Arthur's loyal champion, weakly adds, "His horse master had the best kits."

"Yeah, because he snatched everything good up at the beginning of the round," Dainthi mutters.

Lasilas says, "That's three rounds now that I've lost! Zagas is rigged, I tell you," and throws back the rest of his drink.

"Were we supposed to let you win, sir?" asks Nyer, another of Arthur's fellow captains seated at the round table with them. Nyer rises and busies themself relighting the lanterns in the tent, nearly burnt out because of how long they've been playing. Dawn is cresting, and a wave of exhaustion spreads over Arthur with a yawn.

They played because they were too wound up after their real battle to sleep, and the game seems to have done its job mellowing them out.

Lasilas pulls back in mock offense, shaking blond hair out of his face. "Absolutely not." He gets up to refill his glass at the pitcher on the table across the tent—he refuses to let his captains serve him in any way. He is unique like that, all about fairness and honor, yet he teases Arthur about his old fashioned notions of chivalry and respect for one's superiors.

"You've already had one victory today, sir," Arthur points out, squinting at the sunlight outside. "Well—yesterday, if we're being technical. Leave some for the rest of us."

"Again, nonsense. That battle was won by us all. One person, no matter how many medals or titles they might have, cannot win a battle on their own."

"It's not late enough for you to say things like that," Dainthi says, throwing her cards down.

"It's too late for any of us to be awake any longer," Lasilas points out. "All of you, go find your beds. We'll stay here until our wounded are healed enough to transport. No rush to move until I get further orders."

A chorus of *yessirs* echoes through the captains' recreational tent. Despite Arthur's exhaustion, Lasilas puts a little spark of life back into him.

Lasilas is all that keeps them going in times of loss, but now, in times of victory, he expands their joy tenfold. He is a beacon, a mirror, an amplifier, and they are all drawn to him like heaven's light.

Just as Arthur is standing up and popping stiff joints, the tent flap opens and a young corporal sticks her head through. "Sir?"

"Present," Lasilas says.

Arthur notices her eyes bugging out of her head. The sight is almost enough to bring him back from the brink of exhaustion. "There's a visitor, sir, with a message from the city of Elenne. They said they didn't want to be announced."

"Let them in," Lasilas says, leaning back in his chair and putting his feet on the table, the picture of power and ease. Arthur envies that.

The tent flap blows open and in comes their visitor. As they all see who it is, Arthur watches Lasilas choke on his drink and set it down hastily. "Your Majesty," Lasilas says, scrambling to his feet just to duck into a bow that ends in a kneel. Arthur and the other captains hurriedly follow suit.

Lasilas says, "I'm pleased to report that the skirmish went exactly as we planned, and it was a total victory. Lady Seiren won't be troubling you anymore, sir. She has firm ideas now of where the borders lie. I have stationed guards here in case your niece redirects her forces to take this city back, but we don't anticipate her."

"Rise," King Edgorn commands, hands clasped behind his back. "I am not here to talk about the battle, though you would have heard from me if it had not gone well. I expect nothing less than perfection."

Lasilas bows his head, rising slowly. "Yes, sir. How may we serve you, then?"

"Do we have privacy in this room?"

"Yes," Lasilas says. The drink and the sleepless night show on his face, and Arthur winces, knowing how harshly Edgorn judges his servants—because even fighting for him, that's all they are to him—and how much Lasilas hates to be judged. All Arthur knows is how much he hates Edgorn.

Edgorn gestures at the captains as if stating some obvious point. "Then get them out of here."

"I trust my captains with my life, sir," Lasilas says, meeting Edgorn's eyes with a raised chin. Arthur keeps his eyes firmly trained on Lasilas' profile, going nowhere near the king. "They will be informed of whatever you tell me anyway. Might as well save me some breath."

Edgorn means to spare Lasilas no annoyance, however small, but he doesn't raise protest further than a grumble. Arthur lets his eyes stray to the king for the first time, taking in the long red train on Edgorn's robes, the embroidered long sleeves and the gold thread carried throughout. His sword is a thing of beauty, nasty and heavy with red detail etched throughout to make it look like it's always covered in blood.

Lasilas is a prince and a general, but he hates to flaunt it. He's rarely out of his armor in Arthur's sight. Arthur's never seen royalty dressed like royalty is supposed to be, and it's intimidating as all hell. His eyes drift back to Lasilas' profile.

"Your efforts to enforce my borders are being replaced by another of my armies," Edgorn says bluntly. "Your new duty is to take your army and march east, to the Mariosan city Alizima. Do you know it?"

Arthur watches five emotions cross Lasilas' face in the span of a second. "Yes, Your Majesty," he says. "What need have you in Alizima, sir?"

Edgorn slowly strolls around the tent, dragging his train with him, glancing at their messy card table. He can't judge them for that, can he? Edgorn was a soldier in his youth. He won Ele by conquest. He must know the habits of off duty soldiers, even generals.

Then again, Arthur doesn't think he's ever seen a genuine smile cross Edgorn's face the handful of times he's seen him. There's always a tinge of disapproval, disappointment, judgment. Arthur is just lucky he's never had that look directed at him.

"I am going to make my bid for emperorship," Edgorn says, dark eyes sparkling with danger, "and you, Lasilas, are going to lead that charge."

Shocked silence settles in the tent for a few moments, and then, "Are you sure that's wise, Majesty? Going to war on such an"—a nervous pause—"ambitious campaign in the middle of a civil war?"

"You are not the one to question my decisions," Edgorn snaps. "You just carry them out. I have enough headache-inducing advisors to last me a lifetime. Fucking gods, you even sound like them. Making it sound like I've never heard the meaning of wisdom."

"My apologies, Your Majesty," Lasilas mumbles, stepping back and bowing his head. This is what Arthur hates. No one can make Lasilas look as small as Edgorn does. "We will make our way around to Alizima, using the secret roads and back ways I am aware of. It will be quiet, and with the shortcuts I know, hopefully fast."

"I do not want quiet," Edgorn says, picking up the little gold trophy figurine on the table that won Arthur the game. Zagas, or horses, is an Ilyakan game, one Edgorn should have no knowledge of. Indeed, he seems to inspect the pieces and the Ilyakan writing on them with vague curiosity—but always from over that stiff nose, like it's something beneath him.

"I want the whole continent to know I'm coming. I will remain here for a short while, dealing with the troublesome matter of my niece's rebellion, but I will be following behind you with my own force at my heels. You are the heralds. Whoever gets in your way, you fight. The Coromodans, the Delainians, the Mariosans, the Ilyakans, the Minyans. Fight them all.

"Take your time. Let the others gather their armies against me if they wish. Give them time to prepare so that when I come to crush them, the sweetness will be all the greater. Take the message of Emperor Edgorn with you across the continent." His eyes still shine. "Stand at the forefront of the new era with me, General. An era where one does not need an Ancient to become emperor, only might and strength. It will be beautiful."

He's finally lost it, Arthur thinks with awe. *Without that lover of his to keep him in check, he's finally cracked. He's going for emperor without an Ancient's approval. Does he know how he sounds?*

Most pressing of all, *How can Lasilas keep a straight face?* Arthur exchanges startled looks with Dainthi.

"Yes, Your Majesty," Lasilas mutters demurely. "Gladly will I be your herald. What would you have us do once we reach Alizima?"

"Assert yourself and take the city. I will not be far behind, but do not strike without me. I will have the glory of the first war call."

Arthur nearly scoffs, but he values his neck attached to his body.

"Of course," Lasilas says. "Shall we leave immediately, Your Majesty?"

"Yes. I want to see you in Alizima by the time the first snowflakes are falling. Send me weekly reports as always." Hands still clasped, red train still trailing behind him, Edgorn sweeps out of the tent with as much force as he entered with.

Once he's gone, Lasilas looks back at his captains. "This news stays with us until we've all had our naps," Lasilas says slowly. All of them nod, relieved that they don't have to pack up camp and march on no sleep. It is settled, and Arthur falls onto his cot with the matter all but forgotten.

"YOU'RE BEING SERIOUS?"

Arthur didn't think for a moment that Lasilas was considering accepting Edgorn's order. Arthur thought that *wait until after we nap* meant *wait to laugh at Edgorn's ludicrous demands and hideously enlarged notions of himself.* Not *let's sit in the captains' tent around a map, deciding our route of attack.*

Lasilas pauses, his hand on the little soldier figurines stationed across the map of the continent.

"He's seeking to break centuries of tradition," Arthur says, incensed. "How could we possibly enable that? How could you be considering fighting our own countrymen?"

The other captains are staring at him with warning in their eyes, but Arthur's respect for Lasilas hasn't gone out the window. Rather, his respect for Lasilas is the very reason why he's so angry. Angry that Lasilas lets Edgorn walk all over him like this. Such a brilliant general deserves better.

"This route will bring us nowhere near Ilyaka," Lasilas argues, stabbing a finger at the fucking map again. Arthur doesn't care about the fucking map, and he barely manages to bite his tongue on those words.

"He wants to be emperor," Arthur says slowly, drawing himself up to his full height. He rarely makes a show of his height, but when he does, they can all see how much taller and broader than Lasilas he is. Even across the table. "He will make us campaign in Ilyaka eventually, because that's what emperors do. You know this. We do not fight for Ele, dammit."

Lasilas smiles sadly. "What language do we speak?"

Arthur furrows a brow for a moment before realizing what Lasilas means. They're speaking Elen, not Ilyakan. Lasilas has served Edgorn with his army since before Arthur joined him.

Lasilas ducks his head, sighing with one pale hand on the bridge of his nose. "If anyone wants to leave," he says slowly, "they are free to do so now. Edgorn won't care who's with me—I doubt he'll remember any of your faces. I'm the only face he needs to see at Alizima. I will find replacements for your positions, and there will be no questions asked. You are free."

A wall of silent but fierce protectiveness rises throughout the room. "We would never," Arthur says, speaking for them all. "I—we are loyal to you, General, not King Edgorn. That is the crux of the problem."

These words, slightly safer, give Dainthi the courage to say, "Yes. We would follow you anywhere, Lasilas, even into ruin, as long as you felt it was right. It is your orders we follow."

Lasilas shakes his head, and the weight of his burdens becomes apparent. "Don't ever let Edgorn hear you say that." When he raises his head, the mirth has returned to his blue eyes. The sight of his smile is enough to let Arthur breathe.

CHAPTER THREE

"For gods' sake, Ric, no one is going to care what your collar looks like!"

"I am the king," says an affronted Ricarda V, fiddling with his red velvet collar and the loose gold thread on the embroidery. "Of course people are going to be looking."

"You're not that pretty," Antonia retorts.

"You've had a lifetime of being too close to me to make that judgment. Besides, you're my sister. You're never going to pay me any compliments." Ricarda turns to Leonidas. "Leonidas, please. Be a dear and settle the matter?"

Leonidas has been watching them bicker over the thread in Ricarda's collar for fifteen minutes. Neither of them has the strength to yank it free. He smiles, staring at the thread in the dim light of this theater box.

"If people are going to be looking at you," Leonidas says, "it won't be the thread their eyes will linger on."

Ricarda grins, full blown and wild, as Antonia groans beside him.

It took precious little effort for Leonidas to win his way into their company again after that Remembrance Day dinner. Ricarda himself sent a fancy invitation to the palace suite Leonidas is staying in, requesting his presence at today's concert. Well—Leonidas assumes it was him. Could've been written by one of his many scribes or secretaries, now that he thinks about it. At least the sentiment came from the king.

They've gone from calling him Marquis to Leonidas, and Ricarda interacts with him as easily as he does Antonia and Alessandro. After that disturbing display with the prisoner Jona, Ricarda has been all laughter and smiles, not a hint of the darkness that consumed him as he leered at the cage. Leonidas hasn't been able to get it out of his head despite Ricarda's pleasantries, fearing a hidden tyrant that frees itself behind closed doors. Fearing, in essence, a second Edgorn.

The flirting helps Ricarda loosen up, and he doesn't move when Leonidas reaches for his collar to firmly grip the thread. Holding one end of the stiff collar gently, he gives a great yank, and the thread snaps off.

"Thank you, my handsome knight," Ricarda says loftily, smiling at him. "You have done me a great service."

"Both of you, shut up. The show's starting," Antonia says as the lights dim to a simple spotlight on the center of the stage. Leonidas has little experience with opera or theater of any kind and doesn't know what to expect. The Donatis haven't given him many impressions.

Cadhan liked to waste time watching performers. Often, he would squirrel them away to sleep with before or after Leonidas. They always came to him in the palace. The king of Delain couldn't be bothered to drag a retinue of guards out into the city where his unpopularity could hit him in the face.

Leonidas remembers many boring evenings sitting at a lower table in the throne room—of course he wasn't to sit beside Cadhan on his throne, lowly concubine that he was—just waiting for the singers or dancers to be dismissed.

Cadhan never smiled at them, rarely thanked them, and often threw them out if they told the stories or played the songs in a way that displeased him. Leonidas had never cursed Herra more than in those days, but he didn't know what lay in store in the future.

The terror of Edgorn. The unfortunate competence of Edgorn that forced the Lover to stay and observe if Edgorn could be a good emperor despite his rotten soul. At least with Cadhan, the Lover knew quickly that the cause was lost. The man couldn't be trusted to cut an apple by himself.

His mind lingers on Jona again, and he sits wondering, wondering, almost hoping.

For what?

"This is my favorite part," Ricarda says, drawing Leonidas out of the past. He sits up straighter in his chair to watch.

Ricarda was affronted when he learned Leonidas was unfamiliar with theater, but he swore that would change. He called it a lucky thing that Alessandro is performing in this concert.

Applause ripples through the theater as the curtains open, so Leonidas follows their example. His yellow coat with puffy sleeves and gold embroidery is a rather fitting accompaniment to Ricarda's red frock coat, though it's a sad reminder of Edgorn. Mariosans have wonderful taste in clothing, he'll give them that.

He chose yellow because it goes well with his skin, but mostly since it made Ricarda's eyes widen when he saw it. Perhaps that was because the shade was so bright. Leonidas is not sure.

Herra is always telling him to stop underestimating his own beauty and to believe in his own seductive wiles. "Everyone in those gods' forsaken courts does," she would say. "May as well fit in."

It's been easier to blend in here than anywhere else. Leonidas has found it a little too easy to return Ricarda's flirtations, laugh along with his sister, and this is only their second meeting. Hopefully he won't do anything to fuck it up. He can't afford to squander this perfect opportunity he's set up for himself.

The parted curtain reveals a singular piano under the spotlight, gleaming black. A blond figure walks onto the stage in a long black coat, greeted by a new flurry of applause. Leonidas grins as Alessandro sits down on the piano bench.

There will be murmurs, jealous whispers that say Alessandro only sits in that seat because he's the best friend of the king. But Ricarda has assured Leonidas time and time again that Alessandro fought to be here just as hard as the other competitors. He was the most surprised out of everyone when he actually made the part.

"He doesn't believe in his own talent. He thinks of what he does as an idle hobby, but nothing remarkable," Ricarda told Leonidas during the ride here. Alessandro took a separate carriage, with Antonia's ballgown skirt taking up half the king's carriage easily.

From his observations this week, Leonidas has determined that Antonia favors rose gold, gold, bronze, and other shades of pink in her ballgowns. The lighter colors, easier on the eye, with ample embroidery and beading. She also almost never wears her hair up, rare for Mariosans but bold and elegant. Glamorous head to toe.

She's not his target, but she's close enough to the king that Leonidas takes silent notes on her anyway. The more he can learn, the deeper he can get into these people's heads, the better his chances.

Every eye in the theater sticks to Alessandro with breathless anticipation. Leonidas leans forward in the long moment between watching Alessandro take his seat and the moment his fingers press down on the keys. Eager silence settles over the theater.

Alessandro's playing is pure poetry. The piano he played at the Remembrance Day Ball escaped Leonidas' notice, as Aless meant nothing to him then, so he couldn't truly appreciate it. But now—

"By gods, he's good," he breathes. Ricarda chuckles.

In the middle of the performance, the spell is broken when one of Ricarda's guards leans between them to tap his shoulder. Antonia doesn't notice him at first, still too enraptured with Alessandro's performance. The glitter in her eyes speaks to the hidden fondness that Alessandro hopes for. Leonidas catalogs this with a private smile.

"Your Majesty," the guard says, quiet enough not to disrupt things too much, "I'm sorry to interrupt, but you're needed at the palace."

"What is it, Maurice?" Ricarda asks, not taking his eyes off the stage. "Can a king not go to one outing without being recalled? I thought the point of being a king with a council that makes all the decisions for him is that he just gets to go out, sprawl out, and look pretty."

"It is that very council who demands your presence now, Your Majesty," Maurice answers with a patience that Leonidas wagers is a product of practice. "There is a carriage waiting outside."

"Of course there is," Ricarda sighs, finally drawing Antonia's attention. He pats her hand, fingers lingering knowingly on her ring. "You stay here, sister, enjoy the performance."

She frowns at him. "I'd be happy to go with you. We can watch Less play anytime and he made it clear he didn't care if we were here or not."

Ricarda smiles. "You know that's not true, and you know that you're the only face he really cares to see staring down at him. Stay. I'll be back in a few minutes, I'm sure it's nothing serious. They need me to break a tie over who looks prettiest, or something." With a glance at Leonidas, Ricarda raises an eyebrow as he stands. His half cloak fans over his left side, falling like a waterfall of silk. "Coming or staying?"

Like the Lover's going to pass up a chance to glean some gossip, even if it is just the councilors arguing over looks. Always something to be learned, something put to use. "Coming, if I'm allowed."

"I wouldn't ask if you weren't." Ricarda pulls out his chair, and they're escorted outside with a quiet rustle and minimal fanfare. Alessandro's piano in the midst of the concert's symphony follows Leonidas outside, fading slowly, distracting the patrons so that no one notices their king's departure.

The guard Maurice sits with them in the carriage now that Antonia's ballgown isn't in their faces. Because of that, Leonidas stays quiet the whole ride, and a tense silence fills the air. His mind races, wondering what it could be that has them thundering back up the cobblestone streets to the palace.

The guards shuffle them out and escort them through a back entrance. Leonidas has been to enough royal courts to know that royals only take the front doors if they're seeking attention and flashiness. Attention right now would just be a hindrance, and Leonidas is glad of its absence.

They wind their way up marble floors and ceilings, gold railings lining the stairways, low burning lamps that illuminate the red carpet under their feet. Leonidas wishes he had more time to take it all in.

"Alright, what's going on?" Ricarda asks loudly once the doors of the royal council chamber open. He blows in with a lifelong confidence. "Whose stockings are in a twist over the color of someone else's?"

"Ric," one of the councilors says with relief, stepping forward. Leonidas raises a brow as he stays back with the guards. Rather bold, even for a councilor, to call the king by such a casual nickname. Almost like family.

"Matteo," Ricarda says patiently. Memories of rumors tug at Leonidas' brain—whispered words of how close Councilor Matteo and Ricarda have always been, that they're like father and son, that Matteo and Ricarda' father were especially close in life. Now, Matteo rests a dark hand on Ricarda's shoulder and looks him in the eye.

"Ric, I need you to be serious for a moment. Can you do that?"

"Yeah." Ricarda straightens up and shakes his unruly curls out of his eyes. "What's wrong?"

Matteo glances at Leonidas, chewing his lip. Leonidas tries not to flinch under the weight of those dark eyes—not unkind, but not trusting, either. "You need to leave."

"It's okay," Ricarda says quickly. "He's a friend. You can trust him."

By gods, thank all that is holy that Ricarda does not have absolute sovereignty over Mariosa.

"I don't care, this meeting must be secret. There are things I will say that will knock even you to your knees, Ric," Matteo snaps. "He must go."

Leonidas steps toward the door—he'd just listen in anyway—but the king beats him to it. "He stays." Ricarda's tone of voice darkens, and though Leonidas suspects he's just insisting to prove a point, that doesn't make him sound any less serious. "I am king. Right?"

Matteo sighs but bows and steps away. "Yes, Your Majesty." He grabs the back of a chair, glancing again at Leonidas, who's too busy examining the other councilors to care. Eight in total, Ricarda to break the tie. Tiebreaking is often his only involvement with governing his own country, Leonidas would wager.

Leonidas hears a muttered, "He must be good in bed," from across the room. It's murmured in a loathing but resigned tone he's heard all too many times before. Ricarda doesn't seem to notice, or at least he has the grace not to say anything.

"Ric, sit down." Once he has, Matteo sighs again. "There has been an attack on a small Coromodan town."

Ricarda folds his hands on the table. "And?"

"And, the invaders flew the flag of King Edgorn of Ele, loudly proclaiming their allegiance to him. They shouted the purpose of their attack. He means to move across the continent, attacking anyone who stands in their way. No one is safe." Matteo bites his lip, and when he hangs his head his long coil of braids falls around his face, the barest hints of gray in each one. "They made that clear."

Leonidas breathes sharply in, resisting the urge to bolt.

"No," Ricarda says, chuckling, confused. "Wh—that makes no sense. Why would King Edgorn do that?"

"Why? Because he wants to become emperor, of course," Matteo says. "He's always been ambitious—a conqueror. Your father and I watched him rise to power when you were a baby, before Antonia was even born. He doesn't care about the tradition of being selected by an Ancient. He means to return to the barbaric days of rule. I've always feared this would happen. We all have." Another heavy sigh.

Leonidas can't stop himself from interjecting. "Is Edgorn at the front of the line?"

Everyone in the council chamber looks at him like he's grown a second head. He realizes belatedly that he called the king of Ele by name, a flub he can't take back and one he can only hope to salvage.

Gods, why couldn't he just keep his mouth shut, blend in with the artwork on the walls? He's made a career out of extracting people's secrets without them ever realizing they gave anything away. What's changed? Are his talents finally crumbling?

"I've heard that he likes to be at the frontlines," Leonidas quickly adds, "stealing the glory from those who work hardest."

Matteo huffs. "You don't mince your words, I see." He unrolls a map and lays it out across the long ovular table that takes up most of the room, around which the other councilors are seated. Leonidas strolls over to a window to recover from his catastrophe, wondering how it happened and worrying over how easily it did. Mariosa is doing something to him, and he's only been here a week.

"Edgorn was not seen at the frontlines," Matteo says. "His trusted and prized general Lasilas Catiana was at the front of the attack."

"Isn't that the runaway Ilyakan?" Ricarda asks, scratching his head.

"The banished Ilyakan prince, who probably considers himself lucky to be in Edgorn's employ. Banished Ilyakans carry that shame on their shoulders for the rest of their lives. Something in their culture."

No one, no matter how desperate, would consider themself lucky to be in Edgorn's employ, Leonidas thinks.

Gods damn it. If he hadn't simply bailed on Edgorn, if he would've stuck it out, then they wouldn't be here. Leonidas had the unsavory but necessary job of soothing Edgorn back from his mighty bouts of anger, so much so that his staff often relied on Leonidas when Edgorn got into a tirade. It was one of the reasons he stayed so long. He was worried about what would happen if he wasn't there, leaving Edgorn unchecked. His fears were based in truth. Look at what's happened now.

A wave of guilt swallows him, stealing his breath. The one time he chooses selfishness, his choice burns other people.

"So, what do you want me to do?" Ricarda asks just a touch too impatiently.

"Gods, Ric," Matteo says, "don't sound too eager to do your job."

"We all know it's my job only in name. You all are the cogs behind the clockface. It's not like the war is in Mariosa."

One of the other councilors starts to interrupt, but Matteo silences her with a look. Leonidas imagines the conversation before Ricarda was sent for: *I can reach him, I am best suited to handle him, so let me handle him and don't get in my way. Don't make this any more aggravating than it needs to be.*

"What we want you to do, Majesty," Matteo says patiently, "is simply be ready. Be prepared to fight back and enter war if need be."

Leonidas inhales. Ricarda laughs nervously. "There hasn't been a war in Mariosa in years. That's not something my father ever had to worry about."

"Well, your father is dead," Matteo says bluntly enough that even Leonidas winces, "and you are king. This is now. He was then. Nothing else matters. Speaking as councilor to king."

His voice softens. "Speaking to you as the son you have always been to me, I'm sorry, and I wish things were different. We will stay on the defensive for now, watch our borders, hope that Edgorn's niece Iliath succeeds in her rebellion and finishes him off. She doesn't have any ambitions to conquer the continent, from what I've heard. All we can do is stay vigilant and prepare for all possibilities. Just know that I will be right by your side through it all."

Ricarda smiles wearily. "Thank you. Is that all?"

"Yes. Try not to offend any Elens while out in the city. How is Alessandro doing with the piano, by the way?"

As if they're alone, Ricarda stands up, finally grinning again. "Better than ever. He would've liked to see your face in the crowd at his performance."

Matteo scoffs, tossing one black braid out of his face. "One pseudo royal is quite enough for one theater, thank you. Now go." He shoos them both out, giving Leonidas a reassuring smile he didn't know he needed.

As soon as they're outside, Ricarda grabs Leonidas' wrist and says, "Come with me." Leonidas hardly has a choice as he's tugged through back hallways done up in gold and white. Leonidas breathes freely, happy to let himself be pulled to Ric's will. Whatever he can do to leave Edgorn behind.

They end up in front of a pair of dark wood double doors, which Ricarda opens with a flourish. Leonidas supposes they're giving up on going back to Antonia and Alessandro, if Ricarda was ever planning on going back at all. Ah, the clever bastard. Leonidas sees it now, from the words Ricarda used to the way he's doing everything to encourage that union.

He smiles privately to himself. At least he's finally getting a moment alone with Ricarda, what he has been wanting all week. A moment to do his duty, what he's best at.

"Welcome to my sanctuary," Ricarda says, gesturing with a sweep of his cloak to the grand room before them.

On the back wall, from floor to very tall ceiling, is a mural displaying the entire Donati line. The names are written in gold, faces cut from paintings with just a hint of shoulder and clothing resting within frame. Leonidas sees where the maker cleverly hid the seams under more gold leaf borders.

Aside from that, tall bookshelves of dark oak and green velvet line the walls, accented with gold. Old books with broken spines and faded gold letters are packed onto the shelves. In the center of the room sits a table with a green lamp, a chair on each side, and a chaotic mess of notebooks and ink stains all cluttered about. A few books lie open on the table.

Leonidas spins around a few times, taking it all in. He's seen some beautiful monuments and historical buildings on his travels, but nothing as homely and warm as this. Even without the gold, this room would be beautiful beyond comparison. "What is this place? It's beautiful."

Ricarda preens. "It's my asylum, otherwise known as the palace library. No one ever comes in here but me and my friends, however, so it's public in only the loosest of terms. I don't think it's unreasonable of me to lock the doors while I'm in here. All of this is technically mine. I come here when I'm stressed or overwhelmed and need a moment to bury myself in the past."

It sounds terribly similar to running away. Leonidas would look down on him for it if he didn't have the same problem. Why else would he be working willingly for Herra, sending himself to cesspit court after cesspit court over the years? Nothing so pitiful as a man without direction. He and Ricarda just seem to have wildly different ways of dealing with it.

Ricarda smiles and gestures to the table. "Please, sit."

Leonidas does, admiring the stained glass window at the back of the room. He can't keep his eyes long from the wall, admiring the Donati lineage. One painting in particular captures his attention; Ricarda I and his consort Francesco standing side by side.

They're both smiling, but there's something playful and familiar about them that the other paintings lack. Their portrait is the biggest. There's something different about them. They're not the first Mariosan kings, but they're the first of the Donati dynasty, and one of Mariosa's most famous ruling pairs.

Leonidas says, "I suppose Ricarda the First put this up, and all his successors have added to it in their reigns?"

Ricarda stares up at it with a contemplative frown. "Oh, no. I made this myself. I may have defaced many of the paintings of my ancestors to do so. Not the best ones, though, only the ones hidden away in storage rooms collecting dust. Still, my mother was furious when she found out."

Leonidas' jaw falls, examining the wall anew. "You made this yourself?"

"Yes." Ricarda's gaze burns on his profile. Though the urge to look into those innocent green eyes is tempting, Leonidas can't tear his eyes from the homemade family tree.

"How old were you when you made this? What help did you have?"

"No help. I was, oh, fourteen, fifteen?" Ricarda shrugs. "This place has always been my sanctuary. A hideaway from my tutors, my parents, the noise of the court. At first, my customizations were accidental. I started slowly making this place into my home—my true home. The palace is beautiful and grand, and I wouldn't trade it for the world. I've seen the looks you give me, Leo. I know my privilege."

Leonidas' chest tightens, ashamed of being caught out. Ashamed he let that happen so fast. This role is spiraling out of his control. He refuses to drop his gaze, looking back unflinchingly.

"However, there's something about my own little corner of this maze." Ricarda purses his lips, shakes his head. "I don't know how I'd survive without it."

Leonidas doesn't point out the obvious, that his councilors do all the hard work. He's sure Ricarda has heard such sentiments a thousand times. Doesn't mean his stress is any less real. Leonidas reminds himself to go easy on him.

"I consider myself a bit of a historian." Ricarda laughs with a tinge of insecurity that Leonidas picks out all too well. "Easy, I admit, when the subjects of my study are famous and already well documented here in this very room. I have little work to do. Is it possible for a king to be a historian?" He frowns.

"A king can be anything he desires, Majesty," Leonidas says tactfully.

"Call me Ricarda, please. No titles while we're in here, if there must be titles at all."

Leonidas looks at him and sees a man who has lived his whole life getting what he wants. Edgorn was the same way, but there is something fundamentally different about the two of them. On a base level, there shouldn't be, but Leonidas couldn't look at either king and see traces of the other. Why is that?

"Who are the subjects of your study, then, M—Ricarda?"

Ricarda grins. "Oh, you have awakened a monster, and Aless will surely hate you for it, but I am not going to discourage you from asking. Thank you, my dear Leonidas, for giving me the chance to tell this tale to someone who hasn't threatened to rip my head clean off my shoulders if I ever told it again."

Leonidas sits back in his chair and dares to put his feet up on the table. Ricarda doesn't chastise him. His eyes turn dark with danger and excitement. Gods, everything about him is so very different from Edgorn in all the similar ways. How many times has Edgorn looked at an opponent like that? Again, what is it about Ricarda that makes him so different?

"My predecessor and namesake, Ricarda Donati the First," Ricarda says, standing up and perusing the shelves before selecting a few well worn volumes, "kept diaries. One for every year from the start of his reign to the end of his life. I discovered them when I was thirteen and have been making notes on them ever since."

"Diaries of Ricarda the First are not as well documented a phenomenon as you proclaimed, Ricarda," Leonidas says, watching with awe as Ricarda dumps these very diaries on the table in front of him.

Ricarda sighs good naturedly. "You sound just like Aless the first time I told him. Anyway, one and only one of the diaries is missing. The one missing is from the year his beloved consort Francesco died in battle."

They both look at the painting cutout of the couple in question. It's the only full body painting on the wall, and rightly so. Ricarda I resembles Ricarda V quite closely, with the green eyes and dark brown hair hanging in shaggy curls around his ears. Francesco couldn't look more different. Also pale skinned, he had hair of flaming red that reminds Leonidas of Jona in that cage. He shivers with the memory and tries to banish it.

The two hold hands, adorned in the richest of clothes, the picture of serenity and control. Ricarda I wears the seal ring currently sitting on a chain around Ricarda V's neck, and Francesco wears two brilliant rings on his middle finger—wedding rings. Gaudy and showy, they are everything Leonidas imagines a royal wedding ring would be in Mariosa.

"I have never been able to find Francesco's second ring, his wedding ring." Ricarda V sighs dreamily. "I've always wanted to propose to my lover with that ring. Or be proposed to. I don't much care which. Isn't it beautiful?"

"Yes," Leonidas says, trying for nonchalance as panic roils through him. "Do you have a lover, if you don't mind my asking?"

Ricarda bursts out laughing. "Do I? I don't see them. Aless is convinced you and I are meant for each other, but Aless is a fool, you know that. Ignore him and all his meddlesome comments. Probably just payback for everything I've said about him and my sister. Once that damn fool I have for a sibling sees what is right in front of her face, perhaps we'll all know peace."

Leonidas nods numbly as a knife rips right down the center of him. What is he supposed to do with this? Edgorn called him ugly names, proclaimed hatred, and often threatened violence, but he would always kiss Leonidas straight after. Not as an apology, but a different type of proclamation. *You are mine and you're not going anywhere, but don't you think for a second that I actually care about more than your body.*

Leonidas knew what to do with that—nothing, mostly. He kept his silence and his peace. But what does he do with this? Does he keep flirting? Does he risk getting thrown out of Ricarda's inner circle as quickly as he entered, or does he proceed?

"Is something the matter?" Ricarda asks.

"No," Leonidas coughs. "Carry on, Majesty. Francesco?"

"Yes, yes. I have admittedly fallen in love with the love between Francesco and Ricarda the First, and my expectations for a future spouse have somewhat risen as a result of reading Ricarda's diaries." Ricarda puts his chin in his hand, his green eyes dancing. "The man knew poetry like no other. It's truly beautiful."

Leonidas smiles nervously, squirming under the intensity of Ricarda's stare. "Is it not a little strange to admire your own ancestor like that?"

Ricarda laughs. "They lived three hundred years ago. The only connection I have to them is a name and a duty, and the only evidence I have of them that's not some grossly overstated account is this painting and these diaries. Have you never smiled watching your parents dance together, smile at each other, revolve in their own little world? Have you never wanted something like that for yourself after listening to how they got to that point?"

Keeping a lover isn't that easy, Leonidas thinks while looking Ricarda dead in the eye, a lifetime of practice keeping his own emotions from slipping out.

He never had parents happily in love who he could watch. The Marquis of Belimati would, however, so he cannot say that. "Sometimes," he says instead, playing with the ribbon bookmark sticking out of one of Ricarda I's diaries. "What happened to that missing ring and the missing diary?"

"No one has any idea," Ricarda says. "Well—fools with theories that don't go past one sentence. Aless tells me I should put out a challenge to Mariosa, that I will marry the one who brings Francesco's wedding ring for my finger."

The possibility makes Leonidas' heart skip a beat. His other targets either made themselves difficult to be with or turned down each fool who came to win their hand. They never had an abundance of suitors for Leonidas to compete with. Advisors and council members were the more meddlesome influence on the mind he was trying to infiltrate.

Isabella, for example, is a wonderful queen with a golden heart hidden behind her calculated silence. If Leonidas were actually attracted to her, he might've wanted to stay in Coromoda a while longer. He knows she would've cracked under the pressure of empresshood, discerned from all their nights alone with not another suitor in sight. She had many, but she turned them all down. Leonidas was lucky to become her friend and then her lover. She deserved better than to be used by him.

That is not the case with Ricarda. The man has a court full of people who would jump at the chance to wed him. Leonidas can imagine it now, thousands of fake Francesco rings cupped in the nervous hands of courtiers.

Ricarda is young, handsome, and kind. It's no wonder that he should accept the affections of anyone who captures his eye. Leonidas wonders how many people approached the king just before Leonidas arrived at court. How many have been in his bed, perhaps in his heart.

Leonidas has to take his chance before another does.

CHAPTER FOUR

Arthur knocks hesitantly on the doorframe of the small house that's serving as Lasilas' office for now. The Coromodans in the city Ta Kama welcomed them, close to Ele and under Edgorn's influence as they are. They were more than willing to carve out some space in their village for the army. The first stop on their long, intensive trip east, up around the Mariosan Mountains that prevent them from just marching straight to Alizima from the west side.

Lasilas has his head down, penning a letter. Arthur is sure to scuff his feet. "May I come in, sir?"

"By all means." Lasilas smiles briefly, returning to the letter. "I'm just writing my weekly report to Edgorn."

Arthur doesn't want to talk about Edgorn. He doesn't even want to remember that Edgorn exists.

"Can I do something for you?" Lasilas asks. Arthur is momentarily distracted by him, the only light thing in this dark room, the candles burned down to the base. Lasilas has been here in this excuse for an office all night, busy working after a long day of traveling. It will be another long day tomorrow, and after that, and after that. Arthur won't know peace or ease for some time.

He wonders when he started thinking of Edgorn's border skirmishes with his rebellious niece as easy. He recalls the glint in Edgorn's eye when he ordered them to attack everyone who got in their way, no matter the cost, and shudders.

He will not fight Ilyaka.

"Arthur?"

Arthur draws himself to attention, subconsciously obeying the order of his commanding officer. Lasilas is smiling at him, chewing on the tip of his pen.

Arthur came here on an impulse, a wild desire he couldn't explain. Certainly nothing he can give to Lasilas as an excuse. Soldiers can be restless, worried, but it's not something they can go to their commanders to fix. Commanders have much bigger problems. The weight of foolishness drops onto Arthur's shoulders. "Um—I'm sorry, General, I'll just—"

"No, Arthur," Lasilas laughs. "Stay and sit. Please. I would love the company, even if you have nothing to say." He gestures to the chair on the other side of the dark oak desk. "Just sit, please."

Arthur chooses to take it as an order and sits stiffly, his armor clanging and his gauntlets resting heavily on his knees. He polished everything only this morning, but the shining red and gold has already turned dull with the dust of travel. At least no blood mars it today. He wonders how long it will stay that way.

Lasilas, on the other hand, is out of his armor. He's always favored long uniforms of varying shades of blue, usually a pale greenish blue like today. It matches his eyes, shining in the dark light of the room.

"Do you like the camp?" Lasilas asks, trying for small talk, still writing away. Arthur screws his eyes shut, clenches his fists within the gauntlets. He doesn't want to be reminded of Edgorn, like a stain of blood himself, in this town of all places.

This town.

"This is my hometown," he blurts out. There it is, that source of restlessness inside him. The ghosts that shadowed him as he walked through the outskirts, memories of a childhood spent wandering the hills. They all come fading back to him.

Lasilas looks up from his papers. "Really?" A long pause. He puts the damn pen down, at least. "Is that...good? Or bad?"

Arthur shakes his head. He can't decide. Within his chest is a pocket of wind and laughter and childish excitement that he can't recall no matter how hard he tries. He pictures, above all, his mother's face, their skin the same dark as the night sky. Her smile was as warm as the sun. "I haven't been here in years. Since I went out to look for you and join your army."

"Ah." Lasilas leans back. His long fingers tap on the table. He's so thin and lanky and pretty, Arthur wonders not for the first time how he ended up a general of Edgorn's army. He was a prince before, after all, in Ilyaka.

The Ilyakans don't choose their roles, as Arthur's mother instilled into him. The priests do not read the body, they read the soul. Anyone from anywhere of any look can hold any position. Not because of any skill they were born with, but because it is the will of the gods, the sacred flowers.

Lasilas is a prince and a general where Arthur is not because the gods decree it, despite the looks of doubt that Edgorn casts them. The looks that make Arthur want to tear the man's head off for ever doubting his commander.

"I still remember the first day we met," Lasilas says casually. All Arthur can remember of that day is the brightness of Lasilas' eyes, sparkling blue under pitch black sky, and the smile that could charm nations. Genuine and warm. Lasilas is always as honest as he can be with his soldiers.

"I admit I thought you a bit of a bumbling idiot at first," Lasilas says. "You said something about an honor to meet me, blah blah, I hardly remember. But I saw your potential, and your earnest desire to fight. That is all I ever want in my men. Desire." He looks straight at Arthur with those clearwater eyes.

Arthur ducks his head, feeling his face heat.

"You were a fine addition, and you caught on quickly," Lasilas says. "You're one of my greatest captains. You're also one of the only ones who sought me out voluntarily because of my reputation instead of letting me bully you into joining."

You couldn't bully anyone if you tried. Arthur smiles tiredly.

"Do you have any family still here?" Lasilas asks.

"Yes, my mother."

"Your mother is here and you're wasting time talking to me?" Lasilas grins. "Go, go. See her." His smile drops. "Unless there's some reason you haven't already, and that's what you came to me about. I don't mean to be insensitive."

"I wasn't sure I was allowed to just leave the camp," Arthur says. "I am one of your captains. We are entering a war. We aren't at home. For those reasons and more, I hesitated."

"Oh, Arthur," Lasilas sighs. "When I said all of you were free to leave with no questions asked, I meant it. I mean this affectionately, but you can be dense sometimes. Must be all that bulk taking up your focus. Go, go." He waves at the door encouragingly, his blond locks catching the light as they settle around his chin.

Arthur goes, wondering how he stumbled into Lasilas' office not knowing what his problems were and having them sorted by the time he stumbled out.

His feet know the way. Up the hill that still makes his calves burn, between the twin trees that have towered above him since he was a child. Arthur pauses a moment to take it all in, noting the slight changes in the surrounding landscape. He and his mother moved here when Arthur was but two years old. It's all he's known.

Arthur wonders fleetingly if the house will still be there. It's been a long three years since he left, with only letters exchanged between them. She could've moved, though she would've told him something like that, wouldn't she? His heart is a hammer in his chest. He doesn't know what he'll do if he doesn't find her here.

Arthur does wish he had the sense to bring a lantern, because he smacks into dark trees on the way. He wasn't this tall and wide when traveling these forests as a kid.

Through the trees, across the dirt road, Arthur finally spots the little log cabin where he spent the majority of his life. A grin breaks out. Home.

Arthur hesitates with his fist raised above the door, thinking of his appearance. He may not be physically different by much—he was training to fight long before joining Lasilas' army, so his bulk is nothing new to her—but he's wearing Lasilas' armor, and he has a new scabbard on his belt from when he became a captain. It's embroidered with the white and light blue of House Catiana in Ilyaka. Lasilas may be an exile, but he finds ways to reconnect to the life he left behind here and there.

At least Arthur's not bloody head to toe, fresh out of battle.

Giving in, he knocks and waits a long breathless moment. His mother always liked to be home in the evenings, preferring to work on her woodworking before going to bed instead of going out to the taverns with her friends. That could've changed. She often stayed home for Arthur's sake, after all, no matter his insistence that she should be free to go where she will.

After running circles in his own mind for a few moments, the door opens, letting a ray of orange light spill out. It's just as warm as he remembers. He holds his breath, rendered speechless by the mere sight of the figure standing in the doorway.

Arthur and his mother stare at each other, taking the other in. She hasn't changed beyond growing her hair out, which now hangs in long locs. There are a few more wrinkles on her face than he remembers. But just as he remembers, she carries the sweet scent of red roses, her patron flower of grief and loss.

Finally, she unfreezes and shrieks, pulling him down so she can wrap her arms around his shoulders. Arthur wraps armored arms around her in return, marveling at how small she feels in them. He is the one who has changed.

She's sobbing out a symphony of relief, interspersed with his name and thanks to her patron god. "I'm so happy to see you again," she cries. Arthur can't find the words, doesn't want to talk over her, but his heart squeezes just the same.

"Mother." He finally pulls back and gets a look at her, watching her wipe her eyes with colorful nails. "I'm sorry I haven't been here to visit sooner. I found General Lasilas, and he's—"

"I know," she cuts in. "I've heard of your place at Lasilas' side."

"You have? I—what?"

She smiles, and it's as brilliant as he remembers. The corners of her eyes crinkle, much like Lasilas. Arthur's heart seizes again. She says, "He's not the only one with a reputation. His army is just as famous as it was when you left to find them. When I heard there was an army in town, I couldn't have been more overjoyed to see General Lasilas' banner hanging from the poles. Oh, gods, I'm so happy you're here."

She pulls him in again. Arthur soaks it up, the comfort he can still feel from childhood. He knows he can't stay in this blissful peace forever. That's only confirmed when she asks, "What in the gods' name are you lot doing here in Coromoda? Little Ta Kama, of all places. No place for an army as great as his. Isn't your place near King Edgorn, putting down Princess Iliath's rebellion?"

Arthur doesn't ask how she knows that—she's always enjoyed gossip, and news like that is common enough anywhere. "Mother, I—" How to say this? That he might not come back? No, that's the easy part. She already knows that. They both knew that when he left with her full blessing to find Lasilas three years ago. The possibility of his death is imminent every time he heads into battle, and he doesn't need to reopen that wound of hers.

"Edgorn is making a bid for emperor in the Mariosan city of Alizima," Arthur says. "He's ordered Lasilas to head it for him. Our journey took me here for the first time since I left, and I knew I needed to see you again. I'm sorry if it's painful for you."

She releases his shoulders and bows her head, nodding. "Sight of you could never be painful, my boy." She presses a hand to the embroidered rose crest on the breast of her shirt, absently as if just remembering it's there. "Come inside, come inside. Into your own home. I have something for you."

Arthur follows her, marveling at how little has changed. The living room is still an utterly chaotic mess. That mess always seemed to put itself back no matter how hard they tried to clean it. Piles of books and scraps of wood litter the benches and tables, sawdust covering every surface, dull tools hanging on the walls. It's a mess, but it's theirs.

Maybe he has grown a bit since he's been away, since he needs to duck his head even more than he remembers to fit in the doorway. He smiles fondly as his mother bustles around, taking the moment to admire her new wooden creations. They range from carvings and sculptures to a new dining table to a rocking chair in the corner.

She goes into her bedchamber, and Arthur watches from the doorway as she pulls a key from around her neck—the very bronze key she's had his whole life—and fits it into the lock of a wooden chest. It's as long as his arm and wide as his torso, carved with designs of every Ilyakan god flower. The chest has sat in the corner of her room his whole life, and he's never been allowed to know what's in it. But now, she hasn't told him to go away, and childish curiosity within him leaps for joy. Arthur stays.

Her back is toward him, so Arthur can't see what she takes out of the chest. Arthur hears the unmistakable sound of metal clanging together, a sound he's used to hearing in camp, whether it's from swords or armor or any other adornment befitting a soldier. It's become a routine noise, a noise of comfort that just fades to the background.

It's not one he ever expected to hear in his mother's cabin.

She rises to her feet and hands him a pile of armor. "Take it," she insists, making him wrap his arms around it. He studies it with a frown. "Take this. Wear it to your first battle."

The armor is beautifully made, there's no denying that. It's the purest, brightest silver he's ever seen, embossed with designs of the sun and god flowers and a blunt hammer. In his arms, it sings, and its weight doesn't feel as heavy as it should. In the depths of his chest, a rightness clicks into place, a weight lifted from his shoulders. The sensation steals his breath for a moment.

Words slowly come back to him. "I've already had my first battle, Mother, you know that—"

She shoves the armor more firmly into his chest. "Take it. It was your father's."

That at last makes Arthur hesitate. His mother has rarely shown bitterness, always harboring a hope for the world that he tries to echo. She has rarely mentioned his father. He suspects that it causes her too much pain to do so. But now, she smiles.

"He promised this to you. He wanted you to have it no matter what or where we ended up. Before he died, he made me swear to give it to you. Even when you went off to look for Prince Lasilas, I didn't want to give it to you. I was too selfish. It was the last piece of him I had left."

She takes a shaky breath and presses a hand to the rose crest again, a manifestation of her grief. "But it should not be collecting dust in a box any longer. It should be with you, gathering glory and getting polished every day. As your father intended."

Arthur's heart skips a beat. "He is—is he—" He has so few memories of his father, all intertwined with his mother's stories until he's unsure what's his own memory and what's hers. Arthur was so young when he and his mother left Ilyaka, his father's homeland, to come back to Coromoda, his mother's.

The only memory Arthur has of Ilyaka is his father's face. A warm smile behind a brown beard and browner eyes, the serene green field where they sat. His mother wasn't there that day, but she claims it could've been any of hundreds of days when Arthur's father took him to the Ilyakan springs. Where the flowers grew brightest. Where the blessings of the gods spilled over into the real world.

They prayed together, ate lunch together, played in the lush green under the cover of thick leaves, bathed in the cool respite of the river. Arthur misses it like a limb, though the memory is fuzzy and only enforced by the paintings and sketches his mother has of his father's face. Arthur had to inherit his artistic calling from someone—he sees some of her newest work on the walls of her room.

He can't get the rest of the words out. His mother says, "Darling, I wouldn't lie to you about something like that, especially not for this long. I told the truth when I said that illness took him while we were in Ilyaka. For all the talk of family and loyalty in your father's culture, I knew that the pair of us would find no place there. He knew that too. So you and I packed up and left after seeing your father back to the earth, just as I said." She dabs at her eyes, and hands her handkerchief to Arthur to do the same.

"The armor was one of the only things we took with us. I can't count how many times I looked in the saddlebag to see if it was still there." She chuckles, strained, and Arthur clutches her to his chest. His love for her threatens to choke him, boiling over.

"You have his build," she says quietly, smushed into his chest. They both remember when he outgrew her—it was a hilarity as much as it was a shock for both of them. Now, he's a head and a half taller than her and nearly twice as broad. "His eyes."

Arthur smiles. "You both had brown eyes, Mother."

She reaches up to caress his cheek and says stubbornly, "You have his eyes. Take his armor, wear it, and feel him. He is always with you." She touches the daisy crest on his breast over the armor he wears right now. Arthur shifts his father's armor and presses his palm to the rose crest on her own left breast, returning the intimate gesture.

He tries to feel the weight of his father in his arms in place of the armor. He tries to believe that his father is there, as his mother believes.

"And take these," she adds, pulling away to rummage in another chest. This time, she shoves pots of paint and brushes into his chest.

Arthur rolls his eyes, inwardly sighing when she presents him with a canvas. "Mother, I didn't have room for them when I left, and I don't have any room now—"

"*Take them.* You never know where inspiration will strike. You could make your fortune selling your paintings in those vain Mariosan courts, if you're lucky, but you can't do that if you don't have any paintings to start with."

Arthur smiles.

CHAPTER FIVE

"**O**h, you bastard!"

Ricarda V, esteemed and beautiful king of Mariosa as well as a child in a twenty three year old's body, shrieks when Leonidas splashes him with water.

Leonidas wonders if Ricarda would be interested to know that he is actually a bastard—and if he would even count as a bastard when he's the son of a whore and her nameless one night lover. People generally don't give a fuck about bastards unless they're the children of someone important.

Among the cheap society where Leonidas wandered the streets as a child, bastards ran rampant and no one cared. His mother's people had no honor, but no shame either. Leonidas never saw his mother despair over her profession, the profession he wound up in inevitably after her death. It wasn't a question of if she would die and if he would fend for himself in those same whorehouses, but when.

Leonidas draws himself from those thoughts, returning to the pool with Ricarda V. Above them, Alessandro laughs from his perch on the palace balcony overlooking the wide pool in the center of the courtyard. Mariosans take advantage of their sunlight with outdoor lounge areas. Alessandro teases, "Ric, you're so cowardly. It's just water. You're a king. Act like it."

"You act like it!" Ricarda retorts with the tone of a sad, drenched kitten. He shakes his hair and spits water out. Leonidas chokes down a laugh.

Ricarda tries to toss some water up at Aless in spite—he's far too high for it to work—and Aless shoots down a devious grin, tossing his hair. It's loose around his shoulders, a sunhat shading the drink in his hand. His legs dangle over the side of the balcony, casting a shadow over the shallow pool.

Leonidas has never spent a summer in Mariosa that wasn't by the seaside in Mitzi, where the breeze did its job of cooling things down. The only thing to ease his suffering in this heat is the thought of Herra suffering beside him.

"What's so funny?" Ricarda asks, wringing out his hair and stalking over. Water drips from his generous muscles. Leonidas is momentarily distracted, slowly dissecting Ricarda's words.

"Oh, I was just thinking of a—a friend. She would be miserable in this heat."

Ricarda chuckles, walking up to him and throwing an arm around his shoulders. "I would love to meet the soul who wouldn't be miserable in this heat."

"A friend, hm?" Aless leans over the balcony further, pillowing his chin in hand. If he fell, it would be safely into the pool, but Leonidas prays he doesn't. Alessandro and Ricarda are both incessant whiners. "Tell us about her."

"Aless," Ricarda chides, "don't pry. Leonidas' business is his own."

"Ah, no need." Leonidas smoothly slips out from under Ricarda's arm. "My desires are not pulled towards the womanly wiles."

"Well, Ric, you really have a chance then."

The memory of Ricarda's utter dismissal of that possibility threatens to ruin this perfect outing. Leonidas recovers with a small breath, laughs and shakes his head. "Sorry to disappoint your judgment of my taste, Aless."

Predictably, Aless makes a wounded noise. "How could anyone—except her brother, Ricarda, I know what you're going to say before you say it—not spend an hour in the wonderful Antonia's company and not fall in love?"

Aless doesn't see Antonia herself come up behind him, wearing a thin shift with shorts fit for the pool. "I don't know," she says, and Aless gasps and whirls around. Ricarda grumbles and closes a hand around Leonidas' arm, pulling him away from those two. Aless is already spouting his freshest poetry while Antonia endures them with laughter.

"For gods' sake," Ricarda groans. "Ann, please, just go buy yourself a second ring! End our suffering. I'll give you the money myself. Anything but more of this."

"You really think this will stop once we're married?" Antonia calls down, her hand resting on Aless' shoulder. His hand hesitantly covers it, and he treats it like a gift from the gods, struggling to move into a kneeling position without spilling his drink or taking a tumble down into the pool. Leonidas wants to sit back and watch the endless stream of entertainment, but Ricarda has no such patience.

"Come on. Let's leave those fools alone." He drags Leonidas from this pool into another one. The happy couple on the balcony don't notice.

"It's always been like that?" Leonidas asks, sighing in relief as he sinks into the coolness of the water. *Think of Herra, think of Herra...*

"Since Aless knew what love was. I'm surprised it took him this long to propose. I know she loves him too. I wish the two of them would just get it over with."

Leonidas studies him. "Have you ever been in love, Ricarda?"

The king smiles. "No. No one has caught my fancy longer than a few days, despite what those two will tell you. I've had affairs, as many of us are bound to do, but..." He shakes his head. "I can only hope and yearn for a love like that of my predecessors. The year I start courting the one for me, I will keep a diary series of my own. I'll wax poetic for my own successors to swoon over." He sighs. "I am a historian, but I am also a romantic."

Leonidas' heart is thumping like a war drum. "I myself know a bit about romance, my king," he says softly, sliding closer to Ricarda. He watches Ricarda's eyes dart down to his lips.

That awful realization in the library is overshadowed by the way Ricarda laughs every time Leonidas remarks on his beauty or his mind, the ease with which he fires compliments back. That has to mean something.

Ricarda never takes his eyes off Leonidas' lips, parting his own as they move ever closer. *Let Aless make all the comments he wants*, Leonidas thinks with what measure of thought he has left. *Let Antonia, too. Just let me have this.*

Ricarda is close enough for his curls to brush Leonidas' temple, warm breath against his cheek. A loud groan from the balcony startles them apart, closely followed by a cold and shocking splash.

Leonidas gasps, looking in betrayal at Antonia, who's grinning from behind rose tinted glasses meant to block the sunlight. She sinks and reclines into the pool. "My love, she has left me," Aless is moaning, one hand cast dramatically over his forehead. "All the light has left my world."

Ricarda scowls, evidently just as vexed about being interrupted as Leonidas feels. He halfheartedly splashes his sister, but she scampers back to the first pool. Ricarda calls, "Aless, cut it out. We're here because the sunlight is so abundant and hot that Allice became insufferably stifling."

"No. My love has left me."

Ricarda sighs. Leonidas glimpses the devious genius of a king in power, a man with a plan. "Come on," he whispers, leaning close enough for their foreheads to touch before Ricarda has hold of his wrist.

Leonidas is sure the wig he's been wearing in Mariosa will fly off at the speed Ricarda runs. Leonidas is laughing, maybe shrieking a little when Antonia tosses water at him from the other pool. He's lighter on his feet than he's been in years.

Ricarda and Leonidas race up the stairs of the palace, shifting to holding hands somewhere along the way, until they reach the floor leading to Aless' balcony. Ricarda bursts in and tackles Aless. "I'm going to get you, you little bastard!" Ricarda yells as Aless fights back, wrestling just as hard and shrieking just as loud.

The two of them fight with Antonia calling encouragement, until something slips and Aless does indeed fall over the side, screaming.

Leonidas approaches the edge, concerned at most, only for a mighty splash to reach his face. Aless fights back to the surface, sputtering, and attempts to recover by lying on his back in a seductive position for Antonia. She's leaning back against the side, looking at him through her glasses, amused.

"If I would've died there," Aless calls, out of breath, "I would've found a way back to haunt you for embarrassing me in front of my love."

Ricarda sighs over his fruitless endeavor.

ARTHUR IS COVERED IN blood.

At a break in the carnage and the flow of Coromodans, he looks down at himself. His new armor, his beautiful armor is streaked in trails of red, his sword bathed similarly. His mother more or less told him to break in the armor with a bath of red, but Arthur still fights a sting of guilt.

This was his father's. His mother kept it in a homemade chest for twenty years because she couldn't bear to let go of it. Of him. And now Arthur is here dirtying it up just like any other set of armor.

But it's not like any other armor. That became clear quickly.

It's not just Arthur who is bathed in red—all of his brave soldiers who fight with their captain are even worse off than him. Lasilas has always taught them to fight in a circle around their captains, just like his captains form a circle around him if they must.

No soldier is more valuable than another; Lasilas' governing principle is that he will never ask his folks to do something he would not do himself. They fight this way so that someone may give orders, keep the chaos under control, boost morale and keep the spirit alive. By fighting in a circle formation, no enemy may sneak up on them. However, this has always meant that those on the outskirts get the most bloodied up, and Arthur has always felt guilty about that.

The circle system works, and most of the time even if they have to fall back, they can regroup and form new circles, new leadership, new orders. It's a system that prevents everyone from scattering and getting picked off one by one.

Arthur remembers the sayings more than the training upon after joining Lasilas' army: *if you get separated or cornered, just run. Find a circle to join. Find a circle. Stay with your fellows, get back to a captain, even if they're not yours. Follow the leading voice.*

"Left flank!" Arthur calls out, watching Rina dart out from the circle to surgically slash through the Coromodan.

He says a quiet prayer for the Coromodan's peace as they pass the body. These are just innocent Coromodans trying to defend their town and their honor. Arthur and Lasilas are the invaders, the bastards whose names deserve to be cursed. All for the cruel glory of a cruel man.

He doesn't know what kind of magical properties of myth are embedded in this armor, but it's been giving his circle good luck this whole battle. They've barely sustained any injuries, no casualties, and the blood that covers them all is Coromodan. Arthur doesn't know if that's worse.

Before battle, everyone was asking about his new armor—where he got it, why it's so decorated, why it's so new. "It's a family heirloom, my mother gave it to me," became Arthur's default response as nerves ate him alive for the first time in years. He's been scared before battles, and on a few rare occasions elated, but not since his first battle in Lasilas' army has he been nervous like this.

Arthur tries to quiet his mind and focus on callouts. He sees the town in the distance, thankfully not in flames. *We don't want to hurt you*, Arthur wants to shout out to these Coromodans. *Our commander just doesn't know how to cut off his loyalty.*

Arthur can't pass all the blame to Lasilas, though. Lasilas gave each and every one of them a chance to leave, and they didn't.

Perhaps he should've. At least then Arthur's hands would be clean. At least he wouldn't be getting his father's armor bloody with the life of innocents.

The night becomes a long, painful blur. No one in Arthur's squad receives so much as a scratch, and the Coromodans don't see them coming until it's too late. They scrape past the town they never wanted to fight and make camp a safe distance away.

Arthur stations new guards in case of a midnight attack, then orders his folks to find some food and their beds. He takes off his new helmet and luxuriates in the cold night air on his sweaty face, drawing precious breath. Warm breath that the Coromodans don't have.

His other captains give him curious glances as he walks through the firelit camp, hanging his head with exhaustion. He wants to ask why they stare, but he doesn't want to rub raw nerves at this hour, after the battle that wrung them all dry.

He stumbles to the mess tent, where a pair of wearily smiling cooks serve the tired army. Arthur takes his seat, still wearing his bloody armor—most of them are—only to receive more dirty looks. Dainthi sits beside him at the communal tables, her black hair pulled tightly up into a bun, daring anyone to challenge Arthur with her dark glare. Arthur tries to eat and ignore it.

Those stares follow him all the way back through camp. Despite his exhaustion, if he tries to sleep now, he'll only end up tossing and turning, agitated and grumpy.

So, Arthur sighs and turns around again, still clutching his father's helm under his arm. His feet lead the way, and he ignores all the looks and the whispers, following his heart to the only peace he knows he'll find.

General Lasilas' voice reaches well beyond his tent, soft and lulling yet firm. Arthur peels back the tent flap, and hesitantly asks, "Sir?" Just like the night he went to see his mother, he feels a fool for not knowing why he's here. Maybe he could ask to just stand in the corner quietly while Lasilas meets with his officers to discuss the battle. Arthur could find his rest here.

No, that would be even more foolish. Captains have duties, and he should be doing them instead of just loitering in his commander's tent like a nervous young private.

"Ah, Arthur. I was hoping you'd show up." Lasilas looks up from his reports, flashing a bright smile. Arthur suffers a moment of breathlessness as Lasilas dismisses the latest messenger.

"You—you were?" Maybe his worries were for naught.

"Yes. I was just about to go to the clifftop. Inside this stuffy tent is nowhere to celebrate a victory. In the clear night air is where I belong—where we belong, wouldn't you agree?"

Arthur can't find words as Lasilas walks around the desk to greet him, smiling still. His eyes flick to Arthur's armor, and Arthur braces for questions, but none come yet.

"Come with me," Lasilas says quietly, so of course Arthur does. Outside in Lasilas' company, no one dares give him dirty looks. Not in front of Lasilas, at least. Behind his back, once they've exchanged friendly smiles with the general, nearly everyone casts Arthur that same look of doubt and suspicion. Tell me why, Arthur nearly begs, but he just scuttles after his commander like a good little soldier.

Lasilas walks through the camp like he knows this place as well as he knows his home. Arthur is in awe of his sheer confidence, how he doesn't care what anyone thinks of him, how he can walk with his hands clasped behind his back and whistle without a care in the world.

They reach the clifftop over their camp and sit on the edge of it, looking down at the firelight. Arthur turns his face to the moon and prays for peace.

"Something is troubling you," Lasilas states. Arthur winces. The words are on the tip of his tongue: *nothing you need to worry about* or *I'm fine, you have bigger problems than me, don't let me waste your time.* But those would be the words of a stronger man than he. The truth comes spilling out instead.

"Everyone has been giving me strange looks. Dirty looks. I don't know what I did wrong." Arthur hangs his head, keeping his fists clenched at his sides as the moonlight rains down upon them. The piercing focus of Lasilas' gaze reaches Arthur even with his eyes closed.

"Is it because of your new armor?"

Arthur huffs out a laugh. "Must be." After a pause, "Are you going to ask where I got it? Shouldn't you be offended that I'm not wearing the armor you gave us?"

Lasilas smiles till the corners of his eyes crinkle, brighter than any sunshine. "You should know I don't care. I gave you armor because you had none of your own when you joined me. If anyone joins me with their own armor, I let them keep it. Where you got it is your business, not mine. You don't owe me anything."

Arthur has to chuckle at that. Sometimes he wonders if Lasilas knows truly how much his soldiers would give for him, how much they adore him. How easy he is to follow. For gods' sake, the man traveled from country to country in the wake of his exile from Ilyaka, gathering wayward folks who were just as lost as him. He gave them a new home. He built his own legend, made a reputation that every restless young soul like Arthur longed to be a part of.

Arthur says, "The armor was a gift from my mother—well, my father, really. When she and I left Ilyaka, she took my late father's armor and swore to give it to me someday. She's kept it with her until now because... Well. Her patron is the red rose."

Lasilas nods. He pats the red rose on his own breast. "I heard of your squadron's success. No casualties, no injuries. The most kills out of any of the squads tonight."

"I'm sorry, sir, I should've reported sooner."

Lasilas shakes his head. "I would've happily waited until morning. If there was a problem, I know you would've told me immediately. I trust you, Arthur."

Arthur swallows. "General, with all due respect, having the most kills is not something to be proud of. What we have done is—" He can't even find the words. They slaughtered an innocent town in the name of Edgorn. Of Edgorn. Can there be anything worse than that?

"Despicable? Diabolical? Disgusting? I agree." Silence hangs between them for a few moments.

"Why do you fight for such a despicable man?" Arthur asks. "We could be fighting against him. We could stop him and his insane plans. We could turn in an instant, and we would cripple him. Why are you still loyal to him?"

Lasilas' smile drops, and Arthur worries he's gone too far. "Because he threatens me," Lasilas says, "because we met on a lonely road early in my journey after exile, and we dueled, and when I lost, he made me pledge my allegiance to him. He was thrilled, naturally, to have an Ilyakan battalion in his arsenal." He raises his eyes, captivating. "I am not the only one he threatens to ensure my loyalty."

Arthur can't imagine Lasilas losing to anyone.

"We could fight anyone he throws at us," Arthur protests. "You shouldn't let those threats get to you. We are better than him."

Lasilas cracks another smile, but it's not pretty. "Hubris is man's greatest flaw," he says softly, bitterly. "You haven't been in his presence alone, on your back while he stands over you with his sword above your stomach until you say the words he demands. That is a fear—being pinned under him again—that I have never banished. I would do anything to never be in that position again."

Lasilas shifts. "About the staring—they probably think that you cheated somehow. That new armor gave you good luck, and we all know it. They suspect some dark trick, some evil begotten boon. They're not just jealous of your success. They're worried about you, Arthur. They want to make sure you didn't acquire that armor through some deal to sell your soul. I meant it when I said you were one of my best captains. They don't want to lose you either."

Arthur considers this.

"Should I stop wearing it?" he wonders, putting his head in his hands.

Lasilas' hand lands heavily on Arthur's shoulder and stays there. "No. Judgment from other people should never have an effect on your behavior. Not in a bad way, at least." He smiles and winks. "I'll talk to them about reserving judgment. No deaths or injuries is a good thing, no matter their stares."

Arthur wants to protest, wants to handle his own problems without Lasilas being forced to intervene like a parent saving their cowardly child from bullies. But he can't deny it's damn nice to have that support, to know he has his general at his back. The reminder helps him breathe out and nod, raising his head to find Lasilas looking right back at him. His gaze is sharp and intense. When is it not?

"Thank you, General," Arthur says. "That means more than you know."

"Of course. Take care of yourself, Arthur," Lasilas returns, clapping his shoulder one more time before standing up. He clasps their wrists together, though Arthur suspects it's an excuse to look at the embossing on his gauntlets. Arthur needs to give his armor a thorough washing and polishing, but Lasilas looks upon it now like it's the finest shining silver he's ever seen. His eyes dart up again. "I need you in top shape. My captain." His lips quirk into a playful smile.

Arthur squeezes his wrist and says, "My prince," hoping to return some of the fire that Lasilas lights within him.

"Not a prince anymore, Arthur," Lasilas sighs. "Only in your dreams. I'm only a general now."

"You could never be *only* anything, Lasilas," Arthur says as he's walking away, back down the cliff, back toward camp. "Never forget that."

CHAPTER SIX

There is more to this Jona business—to the Ricarda IV assassination—than any of us thought. My begrudgingly cooperative but endlessly infuriating companion has told me to ask you to ask around about an Ilyakan named Zera Musiek, Jona's sister. That soul Jona is innocent.

Don't miss you at all, endlessly happy you're anywhere but here, all that usual shit. Have you gotten into his bed yet? It almost seems like you're dragging this out on purpose. Don't tell me he's actually caught your eye. Don't, or you will quite certainly never hear the end of it.

With all the hate due from an employer,

Herra

Leonidas smiles and lets his eyes linger over the letter a moment longer before bringing it to the ready flame. He wonders what sort of sorry soul tamed Herra enough to let them stay with her while still remaining in the infuriating companion category. Leonidas' mind wanders as it often does to love, quietly laughing at the thought of Herra under such a spell. That is his field. The image of her like that is downright silly. He would like to meet this companion, whoever they are.

Luckily, Ricarda hasn't had an abundance of time lately to barge into Leonidas' suite and see him lighting a candle in the heart of summer. He's been occupied with council meetings at all hours, tracking battles that have been sprouting up among the Coromodans.

Thankfully the Elen army will have to curve around the Mariosan Mountains, since crossing an army through has proven impossible time and time again. One person could cross the mountains without issue, but not a whole army eating each other's dust.

Every day, Leonidas battles the guilt of leaving Edgorn behind. He prays for Iliath, Edgorn's niece and leader of the rebellion against him, to succeed in taking him down before he becomes a real problem.

Between Ricarda's council meetings and Aless taking Antonia alone on a vacation to his parents' villa in south Mariosa, Leonidas has been mostly alone the past few weeks. He worried that he lost his privileges among Ricarda's companions, but for the first time in his career he was relieved to learn his king was busy preparing for war.

He's kept himself entertained with Herra's letters and a thorough exploration of the city, encouraged by an apologetic Ricarda. He gave Leo free rein of the library to make up for the lack of Ricarda's, "Truly incomparable presence." He and Aless rub off on each other.

Leo has made full use of that library, searching for ways he could seduce Ricarda much faster, but it's not a typical research library. It's more an archive of Mariosan history and a catalog of the monarchs from Ricarda I onwards, when the Donati dynasty was founded and the capital was moved to Allice.

Beyond citing some of Franceso's poetry, Leonidas is relatively clueless about how best to win Ricarda.

He will gladly have you if you just let him, he's told himself too many times, too many sleepless nights in his bed of gold silk sheets. He doesn't know why he doesn't just pull Ricarda to him in a hallway of the palace somewhere and initiate true affection between them. Denying it and dragging it out opposes his goal.

But he likes this game, this back and forth, the heated glances Ricarda sends his way. Leonidas has rarely felt this flutter in his belly when he's flirting with someone, this giddy grin he struggles to tamp down.

He can put up with Alessandro's insufferable whining and Antonia's knowing smiles—in fact, Leonidas rather likes them. Other than Herra and a few of her folks, his ex Tasian among them, he's never had friends. Certainly not ones as carefree as this, ones who don't meet every attempt for a hug with a threat at sword point. Ricarda's sword is as much a vanity figurehead as the rest of him.

As if beckoned by thought, a familiar knock comes to Leonidas' door. He allows himself a grin as he runs to answer it.

Ricarda is there with his bright smile and enchanting eyes. "Done with your meetings?" Leonidas asks.

"Yes, finally. The entire continent can destroy itself in war for all I care, if it means I get to opt out of these stupid meetings." Ricarda sighs and flops dramatically onto the golden couch near the windows. The views in this place are breathtaking. Floor to ceiling windows line every room on the south side, overlooking the entire city.

"How goes the war?"

"Oh, no, I don't want to talk about the war. I never thought being king of Mariosa would mean, you know"—Ricarda gestures at the wall—"actually being king. I don't know how my father did it—being both king and emperor. It's taught me a few things about proper responsibility, this war. I'm going to step up. I'm a bit ashamed that I haven't before."

Leonidas settles onto the couch a safe distance away. Not too far to seem cold or rude, and close enough for Ricarda to wrap an arm around his shoulders if he so pleases. Leonidas secretly hopes that he will, that Ricarda will initiate things between them and finally end this torrid back and forth, the uncertainty roiling in Leonidas' heart.

Herra's perfect emperor needs to have a firm grasp on responsibility, a willingness to fight for their kingdom and an understanding of what lies at stake if they don't. Leonidas is nothing but a master of his craft, and he will perform some subtle manipulation to turn this man into the emperor Leo knows he can be. He will if it kills him. He doesn't want to give up on Ricarda.

"I'm sorry we've all been so absent, leaving you alone," Ricarda says, lolling his head over and staring at Leonidas with those bright eyes. "I've missed you. We didn't forget about you, I promise. Seeing you has been the best part of my day."

"But I'm just a courtier, Ricarda. Why should you miss me?" A deflection, but also a test. Does Ricarda actually care about him? Did he mean what he said that day in the library about the idea of a romance between them being silly?

Ricarda sits up straighter, draping an arm around the back of the couch and looking Leo squarely in the eyes. Stupid, stupid man, with his stupid eyes. No one has eyes that green. No one except heroes and knights of fairytales.

In a hurt voice so soft it threatens to break Leonidas' heart, Ricarda asks, "Is that really all you think of me as? You, just a courtier, obeying the whims of your whimsical king?"

"No," Leonidas says before he can stop himself, forgetting his plans and going with his gut instinct of keeping Ricarda in his graces. "I enjoy spending time with all of you. Genuinely."

Ricarda grins, and Leo's breathing calms. The thought of Ricarda being mad at him is more vexing and concerning than he thought it'd be. Interesting. Inconvenient.

"Good, because you're going to be spending a lot of it with us tonight."

"Us? Aless and Antonia are back?"

"They wouldn't miss tonight's ball for the world."

Right. The ball. "What is this ball for? Remind me."

"I'm not sure." Ricarda shakes his curls out of his eyes. "Some councilor's birthday, some anniversary I don't care about. My heavenly staff will inform me when I need to know. Do we need to know when it's just an excuse to dress up and make a toast?" He sits up. "Please tell me you have something picked out to wear."

"Why? Don't want to be embarrassed by my unholy fashion choices?"

"No. I fear for your sanity and mine if Antonia gets her hands on you near a closet."

Leonidas frowns. "She has wonderful fashion sense." He wanders over the wardrobe stocked with clothes, bought from the funds Herra gives him for each target, and Ricarda follows easily.

"Oh, I never said she didn't. In fact, I will gladly fight anyone who dissents. But not only will she make us all late trying to choose, she takes such care deciding that she makes me want to rip my own hair out. I can't be in the same room as her when she's getting dressed or dressing someone else. She banned me for killing the mood."

He surrounds the words with air quotations, sitting on the edge of Leonidas' bed with his legs folded in a convoluted position under him. He tucks his chin in hand and somehow manages to keep his balance. "Poor Aless doesn't know when to leave well enough alone," Ricarda continues, "and he's not careful what he wishes for."

"I'm sure being trapped in a room under Antonia's scrutiny is not the worst thing in the world for him."

"Mm. Choose quickly, or we'll be late."

Where are your guards? Leonidas thinks, marveled and amused. *How did you get in here with so little fuss? Do your guards really take you for such an idiot that they don't bother having you lug them around?* In all their private outings, only at the theater did Leonidas notice any guards. He wouldn't put it past Ricarda to simply slip them off like bracelets when he feels like it. He's like the wind, beholden to no one.

Leonidas dresses silently, without the courage or the desire to ask Ricarda to step out. He slips on each layer while Ricarda rambles on about his day behind him.

Brilliantly dressed as always, tonight Ricarda is wearing a dark green coat that goes well with his eyes and offsets his hair. Whoever decided that Ricarda should have complementary green eyes and dark hair is cruel, so cruel. His gold half cloak is draped over his shoulder, the Mariosan crest embroidered in green on the shoulder. It's not just a preference, but a symbol of the Mariosan king.

The door to Antonia's dressing room is shut when they arrive there. Voices drift out, but Ricarda's greeting draws no notice. Leo has never been in here before. He busies himself admiring the impressive array of sewing garments when he notices a set of strange silver tools mounted on her pink walls.

"What are those for, if I might ask?"

Ricarda grins. "Has it never come up that she dreams of being a surgeon? Making dresses, while joyful for her, is not her true calling. She trains vigorously with her apprenticeship master, the fine palace surgeon. Always more studious with her lessons than I ever was."

His voice turns soft, his arms crossed, looking at all the instruments on her walls and the papers strewn about. "She decided long ago that since she would never be queen, she would occupy her life with something else fulfilling. Always a joy seeker, that Antonia."

"How impressive," Leo remarks. "Did she ever say that she wanted to be queen?"

Ricarda shrugs. "She'd leap at the opportunity if it came. However, since she will only be queen in the event of my untimely death, I'm not eager to see her ascend the throne." He steps toward her dressing room door, raising his fist to knock but finding the door already ajar.

The two of them push open the door to find Aless and Antonia wrapped up in conversation, too animated to notice them. Aless' hair hangs loose around his shoulders, a flush resting high on his cheeks. His eyes follow Antonia's every movement, jittery and nervous.

Antonia stands in a simple shift and shorts with her hair loose, holding some sort of measuring device to Aless' shoulder. That shoulder is draped in the soft silks she favors, the silk that flows down and widens into the skirt of a ballgown.

Aless is wearing a ballgown.

It's a dark navy blue with a skirt as wide as any of Antonia's, and a black jacket with wide shoulder pads on the top. Antonia is saying something like, "Mine are too bulky, aren't they," and Aless replies quickly with, "No, no, love, it's perfect. Utterly perfect." Watching her face over Aless' shoulder, Leonidas watches her smile with the radiance of the sun.

Her eyes catch on Ricarda and Leonidas standing just outside. She offers a smile.

Following her gaze, Aless' eyes widen with horror. He yelps and attempts instinctively to hide himself, but the ballgown is far too large for him to cover anything. His cheeks bloom brightly in red. "Nothing. You saw nothing."

Ricarda raises his hands defensively. Leonidas turns his gaze obediently to the floor, wondering about what words he could say to assure Aless that he has nothing to be ashamed of. Ballgowns aren't to the Lover's taste, but they are exquisite, and they offer power no matter who wears them. He's worn them a few times at the insistence of Cadhan, and other than Cadhan's greedy stare, Leonidas didn't hate the experience.

Alessandro has nothing to be ashamed of. However, Leonidas knows those words would fall on deaf ears, so he stays silent.

"Just give us a minute. These things don't come off quickly, you know." Antonia pushes past Aless' skirts to slam the door shut, right in the face of a disgruntled Ricarda.

"It's almost like they were having a tryst," Leonidas murmurs. Behind the door, Aless sputters through threats and denials while Ricarda groans. Leonidas smiles.

AT LAST, ANTONIA RELINQUISHES a blushing Aless to the arms of Ricarda and Leo, dressed in a normal jacket of dark gold with his hair braided and black trousers back on. He's still blushing, and Ricarda is smiling, but no one says anything.

After ten proclamations of, "We're going to be late, why does she take so fucking long," the door creaks open again. Leonidas looks up to the sound of a low gasp.

The gown is not that different to what Antonia wears day to day, except this one leans more into the pink and less the gold. Her skirt shimmers and sparkles with the light, devastating shades of rose gold with thousands of tiny beads sewn onto the skirt. On the bodice, a flat neckline is decorated with light pink embroidery in designs of flowers and crowns.

The skirt of the ballgown flares out around her, the click of her heels the only sound as she floats out of the room with all the grace befitting her title. As usual, the dress has no straps, and at her throat hangs the gold chain locket. She revealed to Leonidas a few days ago that it contained a small portrait of her mother.

Her hair hangs round her shoulders in loose, dark waves, her eyes like shining emeralds. The golden bracelets about her wrists glitter, and the jewelry on her fingers consists of Aless' ring and some others with gems inset. Her nails tap on the doorframe.

"Well, boys." Antonia smiles with the devilishness of someone who knows exactly what she's doing. "How do I look?"

Alessandro is staring at her wide eyed and openmouthed, like words will never return to him.

"Like a star itself," Leo praises, walking up to kiss her cheek. She smiles warmly at him, tilting her head so that her rose gold tiara sparkles in the chandelier light.

"You don't look so bad yourself," she says, running a hand up the sleeve of his golden brocaded coat.

Leo glances at Ricarda to gauge his reaction, but he's busy reaching under Aless' hanging jaw to snap it shut. She winks and smiles at him, accepting his hand as she floats across the room. He nearly trips over his feet in his rush to follow her.

Leo smothers a smile and stands up to follow his friends to the ballroom.

"Say, have you ever heard of a woman named Zera? An Ilyakan?" he asks Ricarda under his breath as they walk.

Ricarda frowns thoughtfully. "Zera? No, can't say I have. Why?"

Leonidas shrugs as they enter the light and applause of the ballroom, those elusive guards announcing the royals. Ricarda is already losing himself to it, and Leonidas works to keep the stars out of his eyes. "Nothing. Just heard it somewhere in the court circles."

Herra and her theories can wait.

CHAPTER SEVEN

Arthur tears through Coromodan after Coromodan, the circle broken and his team scattered. The luck of the armor seems to have worn off on that front, which he's equally confused and relieved about. Lasilas' talk with the others about spreading rumors and misplaced distrust can only go so far until Arthur can prove that he should be trusted.

These Coromodans are actually fighting back. They're the ones who started the fight, so Arthur releases his hold on the thing inside him that kills all too easily.

The armor is strong, sturdy, and never feels too heavy on his skin—like it was made for him. Was his father a smith? His mother never said.

The armor ensures he never gets injured, so tightly and intricately are the pieces all locked together. He's never had armor that covers his whole arm before instead of just gauntlets. Wearing this ensures that every part of him is protected. In the lulls between kills, between the beats of battle, he looks down at himself, making sure he's not dreaming as a result of hidden blood loss.

The armor is bloody again, and inside he's dripping with sweat, but everything is holding together. Some armor gets bent if people throw knives at it or attack with blunt weapons. Not this. Truly marvelous.

Arthur has no more room for thinking as Rina calls to him, gesturing him back over to the circle. Arthur hurries inside, calling for his soldiers to watch the rain of arrows from behind. He takes his mind off the logistics of the armor for a moment. The only thing that matters is that it works, and by gods it does, better than any he's ever even seen before.

The Coromodans are aggressive, but the battle is shorter than their first one, with a derisive Lasilas victory. They make camp, flying Edgorn's flag from the poles, and Arthur starts to turn sick again.

He always liked the strategy of battle best, the ability to get cornered and come back from it with his enemy's back to the ground and Arthur's sword to their throat. He loved training with Lasilas, with the other captains, with the soldiers he was assigned to. He liked it when the danger ended there, when he was never going to be taking lives.

He's never liked killing, though he can, and he does it well. Maybe that's what Lasilas means when he says Arthur is one of his best captains.

Lasilas. After a perfunctory check of his armor, thanking it for sustaining him through battle, Arthur meets the smiles of everyone in camp and tries to ignore their heavy stares on his back once it's turned. Again, Lasilas' words can only do so much.

What do they want from him? To let them have some of the glory? Arthur thinks it shouldn't matter how they win as long as they do, and he doesn't understand how they can disagree. Lasilas' army has always been above the lust for battle, the baseless fury, or so Arthur thought.

"Arthur!" comes a jovial, pleased shout from the center of camp. Arthur brightens. At least someone is happy to see him.

"General," he returns, clasping his wrist. Lasilas is seated on a pile of empty supply crates, grinning like an errand boy. "Good battle, hm?"

"Good battle," Lasilas agrees. "You did marvelously. That armor is truly special."

"Yes." Arthur sighs. He doesn't want to talk about the armor. He just wants things to go back to normal. The armor feels less and less like his father is with him and more like he's wearing an unwanted burden on his skin. Gods, the weight of those stares. Most of the captains have remained on his side, but others have joined forces and decided Arthur deserves scorn. He tries not to let it get to him, following Lasilas' advice, but it's easier said than done.

"Walk with me, Arthur," Lasilas says, standing up. Like Arthur isn't going to oblige that.

They stroll through the camp and go beyond it, away from prying eyes and ears. The dark of night has never scared Arthur, but his heart thumps loud in his ears now.

"Arthur," Lasilas says slowly, "have you ever heard of the legends in Ilyaka? The Silver Hammer and the Golden Chisel?"

Arthur smiles. Lasilas doesn't make assumptions. Besides the no questions asked policy, he never judges. Most Ilyakans, full blooded and not, would discount Arthur for not knowing the stories of his culture. But Lasillas doesn't. Lasilas doesn't care.

By gods, Arthur will follow this man into battle and die there for him.

"No," he says, proud that he has no shame to swallow. Lasilas' eyes have never looked more earnest, more open. "No, my mother never told me those, and she's been my only source of my true homeland."

"Is Coromoda any less of your homeland? Just because Ilyakans are strict about family and loyalty doesn't mean your mother's heritage and the life you had growing up here is any less important." Lasilas smiles again, reassuring, while Arthur tries to catch his breath.

Go take your smile to someone else, he wants to say. *I am too weak an individual to bear it.* Yet, if he ever spotted Lasilas smiling at another the way he does at Arthur, a shard of him might crumble inside.

"The Silver Hammer and the Golden Chisel are protective knights in Ilyakan folklore, put simply," Lasilas says. "They have been nothing but legend as long as we've been around. They're siblings, folks in arms, meant to exist at once, as one, to protect Ilyaka together. Their bravery and strength are unmatched. They each have a trusty steed, a special weapon. A special set of armor."

"They sound lovely," Arthur says. "What houses are they from? Are they god sent?"

"They have no house, and they pay tribute to no particular god. They serve all nine. They are independent in every way except their loyalty to Ilyaka. That is eternal, and that never fades. It is their entire purpose."

Lasilas pats the spot of ground at the edge of the forest bracketing their camp. He's bloodstained up to the neck, but he's never looked any less beautiful than with blood in his white blond hair, hanging in locks down to his chin. His blue eyes still shine when they look up at Arthur towering over him, all muscle and bulk in his magical armor. But they make no mistake which of them is the leader.

Arthur sits gingerly. "General, truly, I couldn't be more honored to hear stories of our culture from you, but I wonder what the purpose is. If it is just for the sake of the story, I would like to know. I am going mad trying to glean a deeper meaning."

Lasilas' gaze is tinted at the edges with darkness, with sorrow. With hope. "It is just the two of us in this darkness, Arthur. Would it not hurt for you to call me friend instead of commander? Unless you do not think of me as a friend."

"I do," Arthur can't say quickly enough. "I do. Trust me."

Silence hangs between them with nothing more than the song of crickets to fill the air. The sky is clear again tonight, and Arthur marvels at the stars, the sheer beauty of night. Everything seems so much simpler, looking at life this way.

"You didn't answer my question, Lasilas."

"That's because I wasn't done. The most defining feature of the Silver Hammer and the Golden Chisel in every piece of art and every archive, is their armor. Silver and gold respectively, each of the finest and purest material you could imagine. Strong enough to resist all manner of attack, protect the wearer, and—" Lasilas runs his fingers up Arthur's arm, uncaring of the blood. Even through the metal, Arthur shivers, watching the path of his fingers.

"Both armor sets are embossed just like this. A sample of all the world encapsulated on one hero's body."

Arthur stares, dumbfounded, at his arm. Lasilas' long fingers grip tightly. This must be a joke. This cannot be real.

"Lasilas, I—I have none of those things. Exceptional bravery or strength. I haven't set foot in Ilyaka since I was two. My connection to it is not as strong as any other citizen's."

Lasilas smiles. "Don't be so sure, Arthur. Someone's loyalty to a place is not determined by how much or little they've actually been in that place. Lovers who have only loved through the letters they exchange across the world, for example, would swear that their devotion is no less than lovers who spend every second of every day together."

"I'm not the Silver Hammer," Arthur says. "I just learned about it."

Lasilas' hand rests on Arthur's knee. "I can't imagine how hard this must be, but it is undeniable to me. In case you're wondering if you need a hammer to be the Silver Hammer, you don't. It's only a name. An instrument to be put to use for Ilyaka, like the Chisel. But besides the armor, your grace and skill in battle has always been well above average. You were brilliant before the armor, but now, you are even more of a force to be reckoned with. I don't think you realize your own power."

"Like I told you, the kind of killing we're doing isn't something to be proud of," Arthur says stubbornly. Gods, if Edgorn found out he could have a famous Ilyakan warrior of legend on his side as well as an exiled prince general? Arthur shudders at the thought.

"Imagine fighting for a just cause, then. For Ilyaka. Using your legendary armor and your bulk and your skill to defend instead of attack. Receiving thanks and honor and gifts everywhere you go. Being revered."

Arthur raises his head, knowing there must be stars in his eyes. Lasilas smiles, perhaps reflecting on the time he was revered as a prince before his exile. Exiled from his homeland for the massacre of the House Catiana prince council, a crime that needed a punishment beyond prison time.

Arthur doesn't know the details, the context, and neither did his mother, since it happened long after she left. Lasilas is the only one who would answer his questions honestly, but like hell Arthur is going to ask him that.

Lasilas adds, "I think the stares and rumors would die down if you told people who you are. They would learn to believe in you and cheer for you if only you'd let them. However, of course it's your decision. I am here for you, my Hammer, whatever you need."

Arthur sighs, tired from much more than the battle. He wonders if his mother knew what the armor meant. If his father did. He should be asking Lasilas these questions, and he will, but right now he doesn't have the strength to do more than lay his head on Lasilas' shoulder. Lasilas' fingers run through Arthur's short hair, not caring that they both need a wash.

He is the Silver Hammer, whatever that might entail. He is someone important, with a purpose further than a captain in Lasilas' army.

"What's going to change because of this? What will I have to do?" A pause. "I don't have a steed. I don't have a special weapon."

"Not yet," Lasilas says. "Did you think the moment I told you who you were, a horse perfect for you would appear from the ether and everything would fall into place? Nothing is ever that easy."

"I just wish one thing could be. One thing."

Lasilas hums in sympathy. "We'll get through it together, whatever happens. I need my captain by my side. My hammer. Promise me you'll stay, Arthur. Promise me."

"Only if you promise the same," the Silver Hammer says.

Lasilas presses a kiss to hair and murmurs, "I promise."

CHAPTER EIGHT

Ricarda has his head in his hands. This is nothing new.

"I insist that we should be readying our defenses much more aggressively," Councilor Astan is saying, slapping the side of their palm against the table. Their voice, so dry yet so grating, could put Leonidas to sleep. "Gathering our armies, running through drills in the palace, tightening our defenses and stationing more guards along the borders. I don't think that's an unreasonable request."

"The Elen army has shown no interest in Mariosa thus far," Councilor Piera argues. "We need not expend resources and waste money and cause a panic just yet. We should wait and simply keep an eye on the army. We'll see what it does before revealing our cards."

"It's not even an Elen army. It's an Ilyakan army, headed by that ex-prince. Lalisas, or something."

"They work for Ele, it's the same thing, I should think! They're an army going on a rampage throughout the continent. If Edgorn is going for emperor, as we are theorizing, then he might end up in Alizima. That's where the emperors are appointed. That's all I care about."

Leonidas joins Ricarda by resting his head in his hands. He's not even seated at the table; he's leaning against the wall where he will blend in and go unnoticed. The guards on either side of him aren't quite good enough at hiding their boredom.

"Enough," Councilor Matteo cuts in over a fresh round of bickering. He's the one in charge, even if there is no head councilor. "King Ricarda, what do you think should be done? You've heard the reports. Six battles now, all won by this army working for King Edgorn.

"Queen Isabella of Coromoda has taken no action in vengeance for the Coromodans killed. The Elens are nearly at the border of Delain now. We will have to see how King Cadhan reacts there."

Leonidas expects Ricarda to freeze up, mumble a weak answer and default to Matteo for guidance, but he does none of these things. The threat of the looming war seems to have finally gotten through to him, and he's rising to the occasion with more maturity than Leonidas expected.

"I think we should stay on the defensive side for now," he says, looking at Councilor Piera, "but it wouldn't hurt to put a bit more effort behind readying our troops, as Councilor Astan wisely suggests."

Leonidas knows Councilor Astan is going to be riding the high of Ricarda's compliment for the rest of their days at this council table.

"We will keep watch," Ricarda says, "and I want additional sentries and archers posted at our major fortresses along the eastern border, particularly towards Minya. We know they will have to come that way, not through the mountains, so we have time to prepare. I want to hear the moment they are spotted near our border. Who knows, maybe we will get lucky and find out they are going for Ilyaka instead."

The councilors chuckle, diffusing the air. "Very well," Matteo says with unmistakable pride in his voice. "Anything else to add, King Ricarda?"

"Not for now," Ricarda says, thumping the table and standing up. "Meeting dismissed."

The councilors shuffle out. Matteo gives Ricarda a hearty shake and a proud smile, and then Ricarda and Leonidas are alone with the guards.

Ricarda leans in close to Leonidas and whispers, "Come with me." It's not the first time he's asked. *The world's weight is too much for me to think about right now, I need to hide away, and I want you to be with me.* Beyond it being Leonidas' job, he's truly honored to be trusted like that.

His other targets, with the rare exception of Isabella, would banish him and all others when they were stressed and needed to be alone. Not surprising, completely understandable, but still flattering when Ricarda chooses to embrace company instead. Especially considering he rarely lets Antonia or Aless join him in the library.

Ricarda grabs Leo's hand and runs off with him, not giving pause for his guards. Leonidas has observed them and learned that they follow at a distance to stand in front of the library, where they know Ricarda will be safe.

Once the library doors slam shut behind them, Ricarda leans against them and gives Leo the smile of a conqueror, of a king. They are alone.

"No one is interrupting us this time," Ricarda declares, and for a heartstopping moment Leonidas thinks he's talking about all the times they've nearly kissed and been intercepted. Either by Antonia and Aless, or by a messenger reporting another battle in Coromoda.

But he quickly realizes Ricarda is talking about their studies of the diaries. Ricarda has been forcing Leonidas to look with his fresh perspective. He claims that fresh eyes on the text might yield some new results about where the missing diary and ring might be.

So far, they've had no success, but Leonidas has appreciated the private time with him. Ricarda is funny and endlessly charming, and his face is a wonder to stare at. Leonidas struggles to keep his eyes on the diaries most of the time.

Ricarda pulls out their chairs, offers some snacks, and just like that the stress of the meeting and the impending war dissipates. Leonidas doesn't have to worry about war, he just has to worry about seducing Ricarda. He can do that. It's all too easy not to think about Edgorn and his insatiable guilt when he's with Ricarda. Things are easy with Ricarda.

Through poring over Ricarda I's diaries, Leonidas has started gaining an appreciation of his own for the beautiful metaphors and poetry. In Cadhan's court, the Lover took the role of a struggling but talented poet, using poetry from Tasian—his lover at the time—to prove his case.

He always thought Tasian's poetry was good, better than good, and Cadhan was impressed. But with all credit due to Tasian, they have nothing on Ricarda I.

Ricarda V has taken a liking to reading Leonidas his favorite passages, mostly because Leonidas hasn't heard them a thousand times before like Antonia and Aless have.

One of such is, "My love Francesco finished construction of his beloved fountain today. He might be a warrior and me his simple conquest, but he has a soft touch and a softer heart, and I am honored and pleasured to be in his company where I can observe his genius from afar. I am even luckier to be the one he rambles to at the end of his long days, admiring his genius from the comfort of our bed." Ricarda leans back and sighs dreamily, tipping his head back.

He gives Leonidas the full force of his attention with an intensity that nearly makes him look away. Leonidas, the master of espionage and seduction, undone by the gaze of his current target just because his eyes are a little bright. Leonidas tries to pull himself together, and then Ricarda speaks.

"As I'm sure you know from reading all this, it was said that Ricarda the First loved his Francesco's green eyes. Bright like the food which fuels us and decorates our pleasure gardens. Natural beauty like our mother earth provides."

Leonidas smiles, standing up and leaning over Ricarda, one hand bracing his weight on the table. Two can play this game. "Wasn't it said that Francesco loved Ricarda's smile? That it could solve his every woe just to look upon it, like a thousand sun's rays?"

Ricarda smirks, but Leo hears his breath hitch. "Mm. It was also said that Ricarda the First would lose his breath with every second he stared at Francesco, bright and brilliant as he was. Any dolt with a brain could see Francesco's beauty, but few had the talent to understand and appreciate it like Ricarda."

Ricarda scoots closer and reaches a hand up to Leonidas' hair, which is finally long enough for him to wear without a wig. Ricarda commented on the slight difference in hairstyle, but nothing otherwise. "He said he loved Francesco's hair, a shade of brown that reminded him of the peace he experienced in the wilderness, among the trees of the same color."

Leonidas smiles. "Francesco had red hair."

Ricarda smiles back, warm eyes tinged with glowing gold. "I know what I said." His hand drifts to Leo's hair and grips, bringing his head closer. "Ricarda kept his diaries," he whispers, their faces close enough for their breath to mingle, "that he shared only with Francesco himself. Just as I now share mine with you."

Leo takes his cue to look around. "I see no diary."

Ricarda looks up at him, curls falling into place effortlessly with one shake. Leo is in awe of his beauty, built like a marble statue, with the sharp jaw and endless eyes of his predecessors. No wonder Francesco fell in love.

"I am a man of words," Ricarda murmurs, glancing at Leo's lips, darting up and back, "written, spoken, and read, but I think enough words have floated around tonight."

Leo shifts from leaning over Ricarda to finally crawling into his lap, Ricarda's hand still planted firmly in his hair. Ricarda is so warm. He's never been anything but. "What would you suggest instead, Your Most Esteemed Majesty?"

"There are other ways of dancing the dance of language. Call me Ricarda, and let me show you," Ricarda says, and his voice is honey dipped in candlelight and the scent of old paper that surrounds them, bathed in warmth that wraps Leonidas up and prods at his heart. Ricarda's smile is a flash of the sun. Ricarda, surrounded by all his favorite things.

"Aless said we were meant for each other," Leonidas says, airing long festered wounds, "and you said to ignore him, that he was a fool."

Ricarda's smile falls. "I did not mean it like that," he says, nearly choking on the words. "I didn't want to pressure you or scare you away. I only meant to relieve you if you thought Aless was too intense. But my dear, I have wanted you since the first glimpse I got of you that day in the ballroom. Even through the crowd my eyes picked you out. The most enchanting one in the room."

"Tell me you locked the door," Leo says, not letting Ricarda close that final distance between them just yet. Ricarda's eyes are green fire, burning and waiting to plunder. Leo smiles at the look on his face, the hunger.

"Of course I did," Ricarda whispers. "Nothing but your own denial and rejection will keep me from you any longer." He waits, giving Leo a final out.

"Kiss me before I do it myself," Leo murmurs, practically into his mouth. He doesn't know where to look. Ricarda's eyelashes are so long and delicate, hiding a gaze that tries to be innocent.

"You say that like it would be a bad thing for me." He leans up slightly out of his seat and kisses Leonidas, finally. Leo's eyelids flutter shut. Ricarda is all encompassing, so warm under and all around him, one hand on Leo's thigh and the other in his hair like he's afraid he's going to run away, even more afraid of what he'll do if Ricarda dares move his hands anywhere else.

Leo meets him and does his best to relieve those worries, hand on his chin and eyes open to admire his eyelashes. The air is still, the lights blooming, the world nonexistent but for this room with the diaries on the table beside them.

"Leonidas," Ric murmurs, husky. He says the name like it's a sacred breath, something to be treasured and said with care—*Leo-ni-das*. Each syllable is carefully handled. The Lover has never heard anyone say any of his names as delicately, as lovingly, as Ricarda does.

It's perfect, Ricarda is perfect, and Leo feels like he could die like this, resting in Ricarda's lap with their lips together and touching everywhere. Leonidas is falling hard, harder than he's ever fallen for any of his targets before. This is real, this is true, and there's nothing he can do to escape it, for all he's tried.

Victory has never felt more like an utter loss.

PART TWO

THE ANCIENT

CHAPTER ONE

"**M**adam, we have a prisoner."

Herra of the Ancients, leader of the Blue Feathers, divinely chosen appointer of emperors, turns and raises an eyebrow. "Oh?"

She wonders if Leonidas has managed to get himself captured or arrested somehow already. He's always bragging that he's above that, but getting captured one day after his departure would be a record she'd be all too happy to tease him about. She almost hopes it is him for that reason.

"It's not my arrogant ex," Tasian, Herra's right hand, mutters with rolled eyes. They toss back a braid of black hair that threatens to come loose from their coil of braids. "He's smarter than that. It's an Ilyakan. A member of House Grimash."

Herra's eyebrows shoot up, and her hand goes to the sword at her side. "Oh? What in the gods' name are they doing here? Where did you find them?"

"She was loitering around Alma's territory. We found her when we were doing patrols. The Ruby Rings weren't very happy to see her, so we made a deal and took her off their hands. She came kicking and screaming, but we have her in the dungeon." Tasian smirks.

Herra marches toward the hallway, clapping their shoulder. "Excellent work, Tasian. I'll interrogate her immediately."

Tasian catches her arm. "It might be wise to keep her alive for a time," they advise. "Try to control yourself."

Herra smirks. "Have you ever known me to be anything but steadfast and unbreakable? I am the model of control. Don't worry. She's not getting out of life that easily when she has me to answer to."

She brushes past Tasian to the maze of hallways that the Blue Feathers call home. Their townhouse takes up a whole block, and it could be a palace in its own right, as real and deadly as any that Leonidas spends time in.

Those are the courts of vipers, the ones Herra would rather die than immerse herself in, just as Leonidas would rather die than spend a long amount of time in the gang streets of Mitzi. Understandable. However, no one could ever govern Herra's territory in south Mitzi as well as she does.

Murmurs of, "Madam," or, "Boss," or sometimes, "Herra," follow her as she stomps through the narrow hallway at the back of the building, passing a line of loitering Feathers. Each of their backs straighten up in tune with Herra's stiff posture and firm steps, a leader from head to toe. It is all she has fought to be in the six years since her life was upended, her family stolen. Stolen by House Grimash.

A meeting with one of their members, bound and hopeless and waiting to answer every question that has been burning within her all these years...Herra can't fathom it. Revenge has been her fantasy for six years, and today, her fantasy will come true.

The dungeon, as Tasian called it, is not a true dungeon. Mariosan homes are rarely designed with basements, unlike the ones where Herra grew up. Mariosans have ample storage space above ground. So, the dungeon here is really just their dirtiest, darkest room, the one they had no use for and the one they've never bothered to clean. Its only light is from a tiny window high up on the wall, overlooking the seafront. At least their prisoners have a decent view.

Florence and Dea, the two guarding the cell, nod to Herra and swiftly unlock the door for her. Once Herra realized she'd need a room for keeping prisoners, she had hefty locks installed on this door.

Inside, Herra blinks to give her eyes a moment to adjust to the darkness. Mariosa is so golden compared to the green homeland she was used to. She's become spoiled with gold sunsets and sunrises, daylight till late in the night. She hardly ever has to worry about darkness like this.

She takes her time, hardly glancing at the prisoner on her knees with her hands bound. Herra unbuckles her sword belt and props it against the corner, slipping out a small knife from her boot sleeve instead. The prisoner's backlit head darts up at that, and Herra smiles, tapping the blade against her palm as she slowly approaches. There's nothing else in the room, nothing to get in her way.

"I did nothing wrong," the prisoner hisses when Herra gets close. Her accent is thick, as some Ilyakans' tend to be. She speaks Mariosan, if haltingly. "I was just minding my own business, and your goons grabbed me. Why did you arrest me?"

Herra laughs. "Arrest you? Is that what you think this is?" She lunges forward and grabs the prisoner's collar. "Darling, I'm no law abiding citizen. No one in Mitzi is. That was your first mistake, believing that." She shuffles her hand, easily dodging the way the prisoner tries to buck her off. "Your second mistake—wearing this in broad daylight."

She grips onto the crest she knows by heart, even without sunlight directly on it. The crest of House Grimash, a white pansy, one Herra has long studied in her quest to understand why.

"Because my name is Herra of the Ancients, the last of my line, and I run things here. If you were anyone else, I would give you some leeway, being as new in Mitzi as you are. But you're House Grimash, so I'm not feeling particularly sympathetic to any of your plights. I'm only inclined to worsen them."

Herra pulls back and cracks her across the face, the first of many. She doesn't get a cry, no more reaction than a swift jerk of the prisoner's head, but she can feel a glare burning on her face. She smiles.

All she can see of the prisoner is her long, tumbling hair, running in greasy clumps over her shoulders and back. Her frame is thin. Too thin. "I'm not scared of you, Ancient," she growls.

Herra smiles, angling her head so that the sunlight streams across her face. "You should be. Soon, you will be." She lets the knife glint in the sunlight, watching the prisoner's eyes track the movement. "Now, we can do this the easy way, or the fun way."

She pushes the prisoner to the ground and straddles her. The knife follows as they go down, tracing lightly along the prisoner's sternum. She says nothing, eyes darting up to Herra's face.

Herra says, "First question. You're a long, long way from home. What's a pretty little Grimash doing in a place like this?"

The girl glares daggers up at her, silent. She will be hard to crack, this one. Herra looks forward to it.

"Let's go with an easier question." Herra drags the knife along her cheek this time, applying the slightest bit of pressure. "What's your name?"

The prisoner still glares up at her with hatred in her eyes. She should know that will only fuel Herra, not discourage her. "Augusta Tanner," she growls, her hair falling into her eyes.

Herra leans back, giving her a foot or so of leeway to lean up. "Tanner," she muses, turning the knife over and over in hand. "That's a common name. A worthless, commoner name. What's a commoner doing in the House of Grimash?"

"Call me Augusta Grimash," the prisoner spits, "if it will make you feel better about dealing with the likes of me." She raises her head, defiant and bloody. "I would love to see the sweet horror on your face every time you remember exactly what House Grimash has done to you."

Herra smiles, feeling it tug at the scar on her cheek, the scar put there by House Grimash. "You shouldn't have told me your name was Tanner." She slaps Augusta harshly across both cheeks, then follows up with a nick across the collar from the knife. "We're going to have a lot of fun, sweetheart."

She's just raising her arm to strike Augusta Tanner again when the door to the cell creaks open and Gwyn comes in. "Herra. A moment?"

Herra sighs, rising to her feet. "It's your lucky day, Grimash," she growls, slapping the knife blade against her palm again. She watches Augusta's eyes follow the movement with every breath. She follows Gwyn outside, the door sitting ajar behind them.

"Gwyn," Herra says, trying for patience, "I am in the middle of interrogating a woman from the House who murdered my family. Whatever it is, can't it wait?"

"I know, I know," Gwyn says apologetically, grabbing Herra's arms to steady her. All of Herra's girls know how prone to sudden outbursts of violence she is, and many have taken measures to avoid that. "It can't really wait. It's Alma."

Herra throws her head back, blowing her bangs out of her face. "Causing trouble?"

Gwyn cracks a smile. "Seems like she's causing trouble more often than not these days, hm?" She gestures to the cell.

Herra smiles back, relishing the thought of getting back in there. Blood—Grimash blood—stains her palm from the knife tip. It's a rush. "Make no mistake, that prisoner will be anything but trouble, just you wait."

"I'm sure you'll have us all thanking the gods she landed in our care," Gwyn says patiently, "but first, we need to deal with Alma and a group of her Rings infringing on our borders."

"Which one?"

"East."

Herra sighs and looks back into the cell. "We just took this one off her hands. She should be thanking us."

"The world does not revolve around you, Ancient, whatever your overinflated notions might be telling you. I can help."

Herra and Gwyn both whirl around to face Augusta in the cell, surprised for one that she could hear them, and two that she understood that much rapid Mariosan.

"This Alma, she is Ilyakan, yes?" At their startled looks, the prisoner shrugs. Her face is still hidden in shadow. "I have been here a while. It is not my first day in this fucking filthy city."

Herra hastens inside and shuts the door in case Augusta gets any ideas, not that she's made an attempt so far. Ignoring Gwyn's protest outside, Herra says, "What do you mean, you can help?"

"I can speak to her. The language of Ilyakans—it transcends all else. She will see me as a sister, and she will understand. She will leave you and your borders alone. You, on the other hand—" Augusta grins. "You will be in my debt."

Herra grabs her collar and yanks her close, though the grin stays. "Understand this," she growls. "I will never be in your debt. You are in my debt right now because I'm letting you breathe a few more seconds of precious air instead of sending you to your death to face my family. They eagerly await you."

That's a bluff, not that Augusta will know or care. Herra's family would never approve of her methods here, the choices she's made since they've been gone. They would counsel mercy, finding vengeance in the act of setting this woman free to live with her crimes instead. If Augusta Tanner is still this arrogant and proud of what she's done after six years, Herra doesn't see why she can't have a bit of fun.

The other bluff is that Herra would never let her go that easily.

Augusta shrugs, jingling her chains. "All I have heard in all that you've told me is that I have nothing to lose. Whether I'm with her, with you—I will turn out the same. Dead. I would like to pick the path."

Herra chuckles. "Don't you start thinking that you have ownership over any part of your life right now, sweetheart." She stands and turns away, crossing her arms to think. There's no way she's even considering this. Not only would it not work, she'd be a fool for ever thinking it would.

Augusta speaks, her heavy accent thick with some hidden emotion. On the surface, it comes off almost lazy. "Right now, you're thinking you couldn't possibly trust me. She and I are both Ilyakan, so when we speak our language, you will know not a word of it. You think she and I have been working together behind your back for some time, and I will simply give her the order to attack you.

"You think that I will break free in the chaos of the fight, and you will lose your precious Grimash prisoner, your borders, and your pride. And yet you're considering it anyway because you want to test me, see what I can do, and because you are out of options."

Herra looks sharply at her. Augusta raises her head, bringing her face to the strip of dying sunlight, and smiles. Herra sees that her skin is white, her eyes the purest, brightest crystal blue she's ever seen. Freckles dot every inch of her face.

Herra lunges across the room and grabs Augusta by the collar again, only for a sharp sting to cut across her arm, tearing her fine blue jacket.

"Ah! Fuck." Herra pulls back, leering at her new cut. It's not bleeding much, not deep enough to turn into a scar, thankfully.

She glares, seeing now that Augusta's hands are free. That's the disadvantage of being in a dark cell.

Not bothering to retie them, she cuts deliberately across the meat of Augusta's shoulder with the same knife that Augusta hid somewhere on her body. Fuck, Herra's girls have got to do a better job of frisking.

That finally earns her a cry, Augusta's head still bowed and hidden by her curtain of hair.

"Relax. It's the thick part of your shoulder," Herra says. "You should be grateful."

Augusta glares up at her in that strip of sunlight. Herra returns the look in equal measure, pleased when Augusta finally drops her eyes.

"Evidently, you have a gift for anticipating thoughts," Herra says. "Perhaps it is how you knew where my family each sat when you came to slaughter them."

"I did not work alone, you know. You cannot lay all the blame on me."

"When I have other members of House Grimash on their knees in my cell," Herra says, "I will start spreading blame around like a dish at a communal dinner. If you even know what those are, you selfish, dirty Ilyakan scum."

She punctuates her words with another cut, digging harshly into Augusta's thigh—though Herra is careful to avoid the veins that if opened, would kill her. "Your assessment was missing one vital piece, however."

"Oh? And that is?" Even dripping blood and her cheeks red from Herra's slaps, Augusta has the nerve and the ability to look smug. To sound in control. Herra aims to let that tone fade to nothing but begging whimpers.

Herra smiles nastily, letting it pull at her scar. "You and Alma aren't the only Ilyakans in this city. I have a half Ilyakan on my team. She will understand everything you say."

Surprise flashes in those blue eyes, and Herra laughs.

"So, prisoner," she says, dragging the knife tip along Augusta's chin and relishing the way she flinches away, "would you still like to help us?"

Augusta looks her in the eyes, her mouth pulled tight. "Yes," she growls from the depths of her chest. "But do not think for a moment that I serve you. I serve only myself."

"Ooh, I wonder what your House would think if they knew how disloyal you were being. Maybe they don't love you either. Maybe they cast you out and you were left to fend for yourself just like you and your people did to me."

"That's not—you don't get it," Augusta protests, sounding genuinely distressed. "We didn't kill you because of something personal you did. It was because of what you were, your duty—"

"I wouldn't care if the reason was a dare or a bet," Herra says. "The point is that you did it, my family is dead, and nothing can ever bring them back. And nothing you can ever do will make up for that. So, I think you'd best keep your mouth shut if you want to see tomorrow, Grimash."

Augusta is obediently silent, but Herra still feels the burn of her smirk when she hauls her to her feet. "Not a word," she reminds her, growling. She binds Augusta's wrists in chains this time.

"I didn't say a word, Ancient."

The door opens, exposing them both to the bright sunlight of the Mariosan seaside. Herra gets a good look at Augusta for the first time—long orange-red hair that holds a golden sheen in the light. Her skin is covered in filth.

She's young, probably Herra's age. What sort of rituals do they practice in Ilyaka to induce the young into the business of murder?

The murder of innocent foreigners, no less, peacekeepers who've never hurt anyone in their lives.

Herra's life was upended at fourteen, her family taken from her cruelly and unfairly. Herra was the only survivor of the massacre, and the crescent scar on her cheek is one of the only things she has left of them.

"Somebody go fetch Liss," Herra snaps to her girls, watching Gwyn scurry off with a murmured word. "We're having a liaison with Alma to tell her to fuck off or face the consequences. The prisoner is coming with us. I want extra weapons on everyone."

"Liss?" Augusta asks, tilting her head toward Herra. They lock eyes in the light for the first time. Curiosity furrows Augusta's brow, not fear. Herra resolves to change that, wondering how many more cuts she has to make to see those blue eyes turn cold and pleading.

"Not a word," Herra whispers, "or I might be forced to cut out your tongue."

"Fine, fine." And yet Augusta, squirming to get comfortable in her chains and Herra's tight hold, still speaks. "I do have one condition for my generous aid, however. These off." She rattles her chains. Herra scoffs.

"Grimash, you're not in the position to make demands, and you're crazy if you think I'm going to let you go so easily. You'll just slit my throat once you're free, anyway. Finish the job. Probably take over my gang and Alma's to boot."

A pause. "I wouldn't do that."

Bitterly, Herra says, "Sure you wouldn't. You had no problem doing it six years ago, you wouldn't have any problem doing it now. Clearly you have no remorse. I dread to think of what you would've learned over the years."

Augusta mumbles, "At least just consider it."

Herra is saved the indignity of having to reply once Tasian and Liss and Gwyn arrive. Florence and Dea abandon their posts in front of the empty prison cell to flank Herra.

Tasian pulls her aside, as Herra knew they would. After handing Augusta to Gwyn and marveling at the fact that Augusta is actually staying quiet, Herra lets herself be pulled.

"What the hell are you doing, boss?" Tasian hisses. "The prisoner is just going to walk right into their arms!"

"That's why we have Liss, to ensure that doesn't happen. Don't think I'm not prepared to slap my hand over Augusta's mouth and cut her throat. We can bring a gag if it'd make you feel better."

Tasian raises an eyebrow. "Damn, boss, you got her name out of her already? It's been ten minutes."

Herra smirks. "Did you doubt me, Tas?"

"I never have, but boss, think about what you're doing. Use your head instead of your fists for a moment. There are other ways of taking Alma down. Quieter ways, ways that are less risky. You shouldn't take the first route that comes to mind. Have patience. You're wise that way, Herra."

Tasian has been with her since she got here almost five years ago. They were her first recruit, the first to believe in her vision, the first to support her as a leader. That support was direly needed, and Herra and her gang would not be here without them. Their advice will always be the one Herra most treasures. Their trust and approval of the Lover is the reason Herra ever decided to keep him around.

For this and this alone, she hesitates. "What would you have me do?" she asks. "You don't have to point out that it is a foolhardy, headstrong, arrogant plan that factors in my own false notions of invincibility. I already have the Lover chattering about it in my head. I don't need that from you as well."

Tasian smiles. "I don't know, boss, just—give it some time. A few hours, at least. I highly doubt Alma would be stupid enough to invade right now."

"Never underestimate the desperate."

"Madam," Gwyn quietly interrupts, stepping between them, "Dea just spotted the Red Rings on our border buildings through her glass. What's the plan?"

Herra looks apologetically at Tasian. Where she would snap others' heads off for even suggesting orders, she does hate to disappoint Tasian. They nod. The Blue Feathers don't have the luxury of time to plan out a thorough retaliation. Now is the time for foolhardy plans of action.

"We move out," she replies to Gwyn. "Gather everyone who's not with me and have them guard the block. We confront her like the strongarms we are, not like the cowards we're not."

A roar goes up through the ranks of the Blue Feathers.

Herra takes a bandage and a cloth from Gwyn, wet and wrapped in poultice—always on hand because of how frequently the Feathers get injured. She pulls Augusta's tattered cloak aside to tend her bleeding shoulder. Herra leaves the thigh alone for now, knowing her cut was shallow enough not to be a danger.

Augusta looks down in surprise. "I wasn't expecting this sort of treatment."

"Infected, you're useless to me," Herra says, pulling the bandage tighter than strictly necessary just to hear her grunt. She'll bind her own aching wound on the way. "Don't get any ideas of your worth."

"Wouldn't dream of it," Augusta murmurs.

CHAPTER TWO

A lma, gang leader of the Ruby Rings and Herra's longtime rival, is smiling.

Augusta is hidden behind Herra, held tightly in Tasian and Gwyn's arms, flanked by a whole troop of Blue Feathers. The gangs stand on their respective border lines, ready at any moment to burst into action. Herra is just holding her breath, waiting and praying.

Alma stands tall with her arms crossed, red coat and redder hair, leaning to the side to peer over Herra's shoulder. Her smile is wicked, ruby lips and blue eyes giving a false sense of sweetness. She laughs and speaks in Mariosan. "By gods—of all the places in the world, this was not where I expected to find you, Augusta. Pleasant all the same. So wonderful to see you again. Been a long time."

Herra looks between the two of them, trying to pick apart their relationship from the cues. Distrust tugs at the edge of her senses, scanning for cues that they're working together against her. They know each other somehow.

All at once, epiphany dawns on Augusta's face. She growls and yells with fury, shouting in rapid Ilyakan while Alma's smile never breaks. Herra glances at Liss, who just shakes her head and murmurs, "Insults. Obscenities. Nothing notable."

Augusta is fuming, straining against Gwyn and Tasian's hold with all her might, to no avail. Alma remains calm and composed, smiling with the cockiness of someone who has never believed she's been wrong in her life.

"How do you two know each other?" Herra demands, shaking Augusta by the shoulders and slapping her to get her to focus. She stops writhing at last, out of breath and furious. Her cheeks are flushed. Herra gets no answer. "Alma, answer me, at least."

"Her name," Augusta growls, "is not Alma. It's Zera. Zera Musiek."

Herra glances at Alma-Zera, who makes no dispute, just keeps smiling like she's certain the world will burn in her favor. "Who is she?" Herra asks.

Augusta laughs, though it's a hacking sound—an ugly one. She raises her head, reborn in the image of grief and revenge. Looking Herra in the eye, she says, "She is the reason I am here."

Herra shakes her head. "We're not here to discuss your pasts, both of you," she says boldly, though they all know she'll be slamming Augusta into a wall and questioning her later. That she knows Alma is concerning, far worse than the simple connection of the two of them speaking Ilyakan. "We're here to treat." She shoves Augusta forward, growling in her ear, "You do your duty."

"Do the chains come off?" Augusta whispers back.

Before Herra can scrounge up an answer, Alma says, "Why, Herra, I'm disappointed. You need to keep your ambassadors chained and held prisoner to do your bidding? I would hate to think of what you do to those who don't wear chains."

Alma's fellows smile and jeer. Herra burns, fighting the childish instinct to defend her honor. That goodness belongs to the Herra of the past, the one who would've never set foot outside the Appointers' Court if not for the massacre. "I wonder the same of you," she says, smiling to tug at her scar. Better people fear her than love her as a hero. Love is where people get hurt.

Alma laughs. "Is that the best you can do? I suppose we can't all be masters of the tongue."

"Enough!" Herra shoves at Augusta again.

Augusta still glares at her. "I will not treat with this woman. Not now, not ever. She is dead to me."

"What if the chains come off?" Herra is nervously eyeing Alma and her forces, their restlessness, the restlessness building on her own side. She doesn't want a brawl to break out. She thinks of what Augusta accused her of being afraid of, how real the possibility of Augusta's escape is. She gives the chains a firm rattle just to check their security. Let Augusta think whatever she will.

Augusta gives her a long look, searching. "Look me in the eyes, Ancient," Augusta growls, so Herra does, trying not to let her indecision show.

Make up your mind, she thinks, noticing with increasing desperation the way the Ruby Rings are approaching.

"Let me at her," Augusta says after a long moment, apparently satisfied with whatever she finds in Herra's gaze. "Torture me if I go to her side—you're just going to do it anyway."

"Stop that," Herra commands. "Stop talking like you're innocent."

Augusta shoots her a grim smile from behind her curtain of greasy hair. It was probably once fine, once bright. "What's the matter, Ancient? Don't want to be reminded of your own cruelty?" She puffs her lip out and widens her eyes. "Please, Madam, don't hurt me anymore. I'll do anything."

Herra's hands tighten on her bound wrists, ignoring Gwyn and Tasian's feeble attempts to keep control. Herra and Augusta might as well be alone. As angry as Augusta is making her, this is not the place to have this conversation. Herra won't let Augusta get to her, lest she explode right here in public.

"You do not have the right to speak of cruelty," she whispers before shoving Augusta, still chained, to the forefront of their party.

Augusta's mouth curves into a wicked smirk. Herra shifts her weight. She should've just listened to Tasian. This can only end in disaster.

But Augusta's words in Ilyakan are quiet and softspoken despite the smirk. That doesn't mean they're nice, but a glance at Liss doesn't spell impending doom. Neither does a glance at Alma.

Herra resolves to learn Ilyakan after this if only so she can save herself this agony in the future. Alma says something quietly back, arms still folded, red hair resting around her shoulders, calm and composed. Augusta's face tightens and her fists clench. They exchange words again.

"Liss?" Herra asks softly, not wanting to break Augusta free of this trance or let Alma remember where she is. Zera. Whatever her name might be.

"They're speaking about someone named Lasilas," Liss says quietly, right at Herra's shoulder. "There's regret involved in both their parts. And anger that they're both trying to stow." She looks between them. "I get the impression that they were once close, but things ended badly. Something related to Lasilas."

Herra raises an eyebrow. "Anything about Alma's infringement upon our territory?"

"Nothing at all. I don't think asking Augusta to talk about that would yield any results. At least she's keeping Zera occupied and nonviolent for the moment, yeah?"

"Alma."

Liss smiles apologetically. "Zera is answering to that name. It seems real."

The Ilyakans converse for minutes more. Herra stands perfectly still until at last, Zera-Alma smiles and says, "Well, Herra, we've reached a satisfactory conclusion, I think. If you could invite me over for tea, we could discuss the terms of a treaty that would benefit us both." She winks. "If you can achieve that level of civility."

Her people chuckle, lowering their weapons and smoothing out their menacing expressions. Herra is too busy staring at Augusta with what must be a comedically dumbfounded expression to care. Augusta sneers, shaking her wrists behind her back.

"In a moment," Herra whispers, attempting to unscramble her thoughts. "Fine, Alma. Don't think I trust you for a moment, even if I end up signing something that says we'll tie our glorious profits together and swear to die by each other's side with smiles on our faces."

Alma just laughs, tossing her mane of flaming hair. "Like you think I've ever trusted anyone in my life."

Augusta starts chomping at the bit again, shouting and growling and straining. Liss quietly translates her ugly curses as they drag Augusta away, making Herra smile. Herra is just happy that Alma—Zera, fuck—didn't ask for Augusta as part of her terms.

Only once they're behind their own borders again, safe within the walls of the townhouse, does Herra let the others release Augusta. She won't worry about Alma breaking her word for now. Tasian is watching from the walls with a handful of others.

Augusta is on her in an instant, shouting in her face and pushing her against the wall as best she can. Herra calmly lets Augusta go at her while Gwyn undoes Augusta's shackles, shaking her head at Herra over Augusta's shoulder. "I hope you know what you're doing," she mutters.

Herra dismisses them all with a wave. "Your hands are free."

With dumbfounded expressions and prayers for Herra's life, the Feathers quietly slip out of the room. Augusta raises her freed hands to her face.

Their eyes touch for a long moment. Woman to woman, human to human. Herra waits to see what she'll do.

Augusta dives for the window on the far side of the room.

Herra smiles and lunges for her wrist with both hands, her fingers easily circling it. Augusta squirms and struggles to get free. "You're not going anywhere, sweetheart."

Augusta glares, but she's done it so many times it's quickly losing its heat. "Hey! You said—"

"I never said you'd be free. Only that the chains would come off." Herra lets go of her wrist and stands in front of the window, holding a knife to her chin. "You're going to sit here and tell me how exactly you know Al—Zera, and what bad blood there is between you two."

Augusta's face tightens, and Herra predicts about ten more arguments waiting their turn. Augusta sighs, apparently growing wise to the fact that Herra has a refutation for each and every one. She shrugs in simple defeat.

"I saved her life once. Kept her from slipping into a river," Augusta says, starting out in halting words, though she's made it clear her ability with Mariosan is not the problem. Herra is interested to know where she learned to speak it so well, but that will come later. She doesn't want to push Augusta hard enough to make her clam up again.

The only reason she let Augusta out of her cuffs is the hope that she'll be more pliable if she thinks she has some measure of influence over Herra. That Herra would ever grant requests as absurd as that so easily. Also, it will help if she thinks she has some semblance of freedom. It doesn't always pay to be violent, to show one's true colors.

"That was where it started," Augusta says, leaning back into a chair like it's her gods given right to be here in this house, as comfortable as a cat. "She was beautiful and kind and that smile..."

She smiles and says something in Ilyakan. Herra wonders if she's already forgotten she's not alone, like an elder telling stories.

But then her eyes, crystal blue, lock onto Herra's again. Herra remembers her sharpness, the crest of House Grimash on her tattered cloak. That means something. "I have thought upon her as much as you have thought upon me and my house," Augusta says. "That smile hid a serpent lurking in the shadows. That smile was never real at all. She's never cared for me. Never trusted me."

"Get to the point," Herra snaps.

Augusta shrugs. "You're the one who wanted to hear it. The point? The point is that she slaughtered the princes of House Catiana all except for my brother and one other, got my brother blamed and exiled for it, and fucked off the next morning. I was..." She shakes her head. "I was someone important, but I left out of shame and fear sometime after. I knew something would befall me if I stayed longer, and there was nothing for me there anymore."

"What's House Catiana? And—what about House Grimash? Why wouldn't they be on your side? Don't your people take family seriously?"

Augusta smiles, her greasy clumps of hair hanging in her face. "Who do you think spread the rumors of my treachery?"

"What do you mean, your treachery? What are you leaving out?"

Again, with faux innocence, "I thought you wanted the point."

Herra lifts her eyes to the sky. "You are the most infuriating fucking Ilyakan I have ever met."

Augusta's grin is wide. She jerks her head toward the window. "Even more than the one out there?"

"Especially that one. Easily. She's just a pretty face with a few hidden knives."

Augusta casts her a demure look. "What makes you think I'm any different?"

The knife in the cell that she cut Herra's arm with flashes to mind. Herra curses herself for a fool for not checking a second time, her arm aching anew with the reminder. She lunges for Augusta to pat her down.

Augusta laughs, bearing it willingly while Herra checks the empty sleeves of her boots and every place that Herra would hide a knife on her own body. "I'm just fucking with you."

Herra releases her breath and stands up again. Augusta has bled through her bandages by now, but Herra doesn't care. "Fill it in. The story."

"What more is there to say? I have no idea why she did it. It was one of the things I asked her today." A pause. "She betrayed me at the basest of levels. We had been lovers for months when she asked if she could come with me to visit my brother Lasilas at House Catiana—the house of nine princes that rule our country. I didn't see any harm in having her come just to visit. Nothing could go wrong!" She laughs hollowly. "Gods, I was such a fool. And I never got a reason why."

Neither did I. Herra and her family, the longstanding appointers of the continent's emperors, never did anything to harm the Ilyakans or House Grimash. They lived in Gina, an independent city in the Minyan mountains. They kept themselves and a life of pacifism, retiring to a quiet cabin beside the mountain hot springs after fulfilling their duty and naming a successor. They never did anything to anyone and look what they got for it. A centuries old line ended just like that.

Now Herra is the last, having barely escaped with her life. The only piece of her past that she still has is the appointer's seal ring strung on a chain around her neck, safe under her clothes, waiting for the day she gets to crown someone new. Her ancestral duty.

"Righteous things come to those who slaughter entire houses," Herra says.

"Then let me help you take her down," Augusta pleads. "We'll both get what we want. I'll be your good little servant, never raising an argument. Just let me get my hands around her neck.

"You wanted to know what House Grimash was doing in Mitzi. Well, here is the first of your answers. We're not infringing on your territory, and we're not coming for you. It's not a *we* matter at all. It's just me, coming alone, in my own self-interest. I've been away from the House ever since my brother was exiled."

Herra pays no mind to the hints of bitterness in her voice. She smiles bitterly. "Her death is not what I want. I don't care about Ilyakan matters of state. I care only about myself. And I'm not interested in removing Zera from these streets—we need her here to disrupt our monopoly so that no one else tries to take us down. Competition is good, even if she's infuriating. We need her."

Augusta bares her teeth. "Do you want to know why House Grimash slaughtered your family?"

Herra whips toward her before she's even finished speaking. Augusta grins. "You don't know what to do with me," she says. "You can't let me go, and you can't let me roam free in your territory, but you're reluctant to lock me away again, for whatever reason. So, let's do something you know what to do with. Make a deal."

Augusta leans forward in her chair. "I'll tell you everything you want to know if you let me stay here, your honored guest, and agree to look the other way when I get my hands around that bastard's neck. You don't even have to help me. You can try to stop me if you'd like, make a show of it. Just let me have a head start."

"I could keep you here and just torture those answers out of you," Herra suggests.

Augusta puts her hands out in front of her, offering them for captivity, raising an eyebrow. "Why don't you?"

Herra looks between her unbound hands and her face, waiting for Augusta to comment on her cowardice, her weakness. She doesn't.

Herra hesitantly clasps her wrist, pulling Augusta to her feet. "Alright," she says quietly, unable to believe herself. "But we are not friends."

Augusta smirks lazily, shrugging off Herra's grip and rising to her feet. She slips smoothly past. "I never said we were, *sweetheart*. I suppose it would be too much to ask for a bath? I smell worse than an Ilyakan stable."

Herra's instinct is of course no, but she hesitates, thinking of Augusta sleeping in her house tonight. "Fine," she grumbles. "You look as bad as a stable, too."

"Ha! I do? I bet you haven't seen a mirror since you were born."

CHAPTER THREE

"**N**o, Arthur, I really don't think—"

"I know what you really don't think. You've told me five times already."

"Remind me which of us is the commander again?"

Arthur sighs, at least grateful that Lasilas is smiling and not angry. "If I am the Silver Hammer, then let me prove it to everyone and see what that reputation is really worth. It should earn me some respect."

"Yes," Lasilas says patiently. "You. Not me."

"We'll be together!"

Lasilas grins. "Aren't we always?"

Arthur sighs again. Indeed, sometimes he wonders which of them is supposed to be the responsible commander and which one is the subordinate taking the piss.

They're speaking of the meeting of the Ilyakan princes. Lasilas has told him before that the nine princes of House Catiana, Ilyaka's joint rulers, hold their quarterly meetings in random locations throughout the continent. They attempt to familiarize themselves with the outside world that many of them consider mythical, preventing Ilyaka from isolating itself entirely.

The princes are having their next meeting in Ta Laia, a town just inside the border of Delain, not too far from Lasilas' camp. Lasilas made the mistake of mentioning this to Arthur. Arthur, who has been trying for the past half hour to convince him to force his way in and reclaim what is rightfully his.

"You were wrongfully exiled," he tries. "Everyone thinks that. You deserve that place at that table. It is rightfully yours. You were the crown jewel of Ilyaka, the favorite prince—"

"None of you know what really happened with my exile. Either way, the princes won't care," Lasilas snaps. "They'll hate me. They'll barely even look at me, let alone let me into their meeting. They'll think I obtained its location through—I don't know, torturing another Ilyakan in a fit of jealous rage—"

Arthur grabs Lasilas by the shoulders. "If they're going by that logic," he says slowly, "then they should be thanking you. After all, in their eyes, you gave them the positions they have now." By killing their predecessors, as they all believe Lasilas did. Arthur's never known if it was true. The truth wouldn't change the admiration he has for Lasilas, either way.

Lasilas throws his head back and laughs. "We're not that crass, Arthur dear, and rarely that frank." His frame is stiff with tension, but he doesn't remove Arthur's hands and he does muster up a smile. Arthur is grateful for that. Grateful that he tries.

"Please," Arthur says. "For me? Just give it a try. We already know the worst that can happen, so things can only go better than we think, right?"

"Than you think, maybe," Lasilas sighs.

Arthur is almost at his wit's end. "There's got to be a reason they've kept a slot open on the prince council."

"Yes, and it's because they don't have enough qualified people."

"I highly doubt anyone they have there now is as good as you were."

"Your bias, because that is unquestionably what it is, is appreciated and overly flattering," Lasilas says with a tender smile, gently removing Arthur's hands from his narrow shoulders.

Arthur wonders if Lasilas knows the boundless limits of his army's devotion. That they would walk into fire and swim out to him in the deepest sea. That they would let the wind carry them up through the clouds just to find the one where Lasilas was being kept.

They would fight any battle, answer any call at just his word, as long as he believes it's right. It's not just bias. It's because Lasilas is the kindest, fairest, and bravest person Arthur has ever had the pleasure of serving under, and he wouldn't change a thing.

Arthur stares. "Well?"

Lasilas sighs, long suffering. "Fine, fine," he says, muttering about pretty captains and their prettier brown eyes, drawing heat to Arthur's cheeks. "I'll go. Because the Silver Hammer, my cultural legend, commands it of me, I'll go."

"Thank you."

"Be warned," Lasilas says, "they will not take you seriously. They will think I've just dressed up my most gullible private in the first silver armor set I could find and sent him on to give legitimacy to my presence."

"Will they say this aloud?"

Another ducked head, another hidden smile. "I don't know. I haven't had the pleasure of meeting the new princes."

"Another thing we're going to change," Arthur declares. "Las—you do want this, right? I won't force you to go if—if you genuinely don't want to. I only will if you're being a stubborn, self-demeaning ass about it."

Lasilas smiles wearily. "I can assure you it's only the latter. I never thought, never considered for a moment since the day I was exiled that I would ever get back to where I was. That has not changed, and I doubt it ever will. I thank you for being bolder about it than I could ever be. I just don't have your unfounded hope."

Arthur fights the urge to lay a gentle palm to Lasilas' face and cup it, protect it from the world. Captains do not do that with their commanders.

"You're the one who taught me how to hope in the dark times," Arthur says as his heart pounds, as if he's riding a horse that's just leapt over a chasm in the earth. Danger with a split chance of survival on the other side, but a momentary high that he wouldn't trade for anything. "If anyone should know about hope, especially unfounded, it's you. Not just for me, but for all of us."

Lasilas doesn't reply. Arthur stifles a sigh, ducking out of Lasilas' tent to mentally prepare for the meeting tomorrow.

"Hey, Arthur," Dainthi says casually, leaning against a nearby tent pole. "Haven't seen you much lately."

"Sorry," he murmurs on default, thinking of what exactly he's going to do and say in that meeting to get the princes to take them seriously.

"You've been spending a lot of time with General Lasilas."

"Mm." Will his armor really be enough to win the princes' respect for them both? It has to. He'll test their loyalty to this supposed legend. And yet he can't help but feel like a fraud, using a myth he just learned about to bully his way into an audience.

It's his birthright, and just because he doesn't feel like the Silver Hammer doesn't mean it isn't true. He just has to get them to see that. He has to act like it.

He'll do it. Anything for Lasilas.

Dainthi nudges his arm and breaks him free of his spell. "What's going on with you and the general?"

Arthur furrows a brow. "What do you mean?"

She grins. "Come on. You're a little dumb, but you're not that dumb. I haven't seen any flowers in either of your hair yet, but that doesn't necessarily mean anything."

Arthur blinks. "What in the name of the gods are you talking about, Dainthi?"

"That you two might be lovers!" she says, looking exasperated that she has to say it. "I thought I was your friend, Arthur, a friend that you would share these things with."

She doesn't sound bitter—if anything, she seems amused at his embarrassment. "I am the general's friend," he says haughtily, drawing himself up. "As we all are. I live to serve him, as you do. Nothing more."

"Then why did I hear you arguing with him about gods know what in his tent? Alone?"

"Sometimes he needs help getting his head out of his ass."

Dainthi's grin doesn't wane in the slightest.

"Stop looking at me like that!"

"Lovers," she says, still grinning as she walks away. "Someday soon, you're going to thank me for opening your eyes."

"Fuck off. You have captainly duties to attend to instead of bullying your fellow captains. Go do them."

LASILAS MIGHT HAVE been right.

Arthur was expecting...well, he's not sure precisely what he was expecting from the prince council. That they might be willing to see past the past, grant Arthur and Lasilas an immediate audience on the principle that they're all Ilyakans. But at the door to the meeting room—a small cabin in the middle of the midnight field—Arthur and Lasilas are greeted by guards at sword point.

Teeth grit, Arthur says, "I am the Silver Hammer, protector of Ilyaka. I demand that you give this rightful prince, Lasilas Catiana, an audience. Give us an audience. Convey this message to Their Highnesses."

The Ilyakan guards, each with their god crest embossed on the outside of their armor, grit their teeth and duck inside to do so. Arthur tries to ignore Lasilas shaking like a leaf beside him. His heart aches, wondering what he could be doing to make this better.

The guards return a minute later with a begrudging bow to usher them in. It's Lasilas they're taking issue with, not Arthur, but the insult rolls over his shoulders all the same. They walk into the house with the horses outside in the stables, under the heavy eyes of guards.

"Lasilas," says one of the princes inside, a man sitting at the back of the round table in the center of the room. A light hangs overhead, but other than that the room is bare. "Been a long time."

Lasilas smiles thinly. "Long time, yes, Heires." Heires, the only other survivor of the massacre. The one who exiled Lasilas.

Arthur takes stock of all the princes around the table. Of the nine, only one or two bother hiding their glares and their scorn. That one at the back, Heires, holds himself with more authority and confidence than any of the others. Arthur knows none of their names. He should've asked Lasilas before coming here, but if the princes won't bother giving Lasilas the respect due, then Arthur won't give it to them.

"Silver Hammer," Heires says, looking Arthur up and down. His dark eyes shine with interest. "It's an honor and a pleasure to meet you in the flesh. What is your name, and to what do we owe this honor?"

Arthur holds his head high. "I am Arthur di Mars, and I demand that you let this rightful prince take his rightful seat at this table and participate." He ignores the pressure of Lasilas' gaze on his profile.

Prince Heires looks Arthur in the eye and says with utmost innocence, "My lord Hammer, this is no prince we recognize. This is a lowly exile who brings shame upon the house he used to belong to."

Arthur grits his teeth and fights the urge to simply force his way through this. Lasilas told him to expect this, but Lasilas has already accepted defeat. Arthur will not allow this to deter him.

"If you will not treat with him as a peer," Arthur says, "then treat with him as an ally. We are committed to protecting Ilyaka from all who would attack it."

He can practically feel Lasilas wince. Soon enough, a prince who introduced herself as Lydia cries out, "You say this as a representative of the army who has been flying the conqueror King Edgorn's banner after raiding and ravaging the continent? We all know it's only a matter of time before he comes to take Ilyaka. What do they all call it? The empire's crown jewel. The ultimate prize."

Arthur looks her straight in the eye and says, "Do you think an army with the Silver Hammer in it would harm Ilyaka?"

She returns his gaze evenly. "I have no way of knowing."

She's bold, so openly questioning her culture's protective mythical figure. The air chills in the room.

"Then let me give you my vow," Arthur says, laying his palm face up on the table, "if not as the Hammer, then as an honorable soldier and a worshipping Ilyakan. I would not lie as long as I wear my goddess' crest upon my breast."

He puffs his chest out, hoping to draw the eye to the embossed green daisy on his chest plate breast. "I vow that I will never knowingly harm the Ilyakans. I will protect my—our people—till my dying breath."

Lydia studies him. "Leaving yourself some room, I see. Never knowingly."

Arthur smiles back. "Not all of us can be perfect."

Lydia runs her cold gaze up and down his body like she longs to see past the armor, see the man beneath. Arthur doesn't blame her, but damn if it isn't unnerving. "Thank you, Arthur di Mars, but we are not eager to trust you just yet. We had the Golden Chisel, and she was just as much of a traitor and a loathsome rat as her brother."

Arthur glances at Lasilas, wondering why he hasn't heard this from him before. Maybe Lasilas hasn't heard—it'd make sense, given how long he's been away. "You had her? Who is she?"

Heires leans forward this time, a smirk forming on his lips. "Why, has he not told you? The Golden Chisel was his sister, Augusta Tanner, who walked out and hid her precious armor somewhere none of us have been able to find."

Lasilas stares at them; Arthur stares at Lasilas. He looks like he's just taken a punch to the gut, eyes wide and breath hardly coming. Arthur wonders which part he didn't know: that the sister Arthur didn't know he had was the Golden Chisel, or that she deserted Ilyaka.

"Oh, you didn't know?" Heires says pityingly, placing his chin in his hand and batting his lashes at Lasilas. "You didn't know that your darling sister was just as much of a useless fucking traitor as you are, abandoning our values and our gods and kneeling at the altar of selfishness?"

"Heires," says a prince named Magna gently, placing a hand on the back of Heires' chair. "Let's be civil, now. We are not animals."

Arthur doesn't realize how tightly he's gripping the tabletop until it starts to come off the legs. He quickly lets it go, trying to rein in his seething anger. Lasilas is bearing it silently, without rebuttal, head ducked. Like how he behaves with Edgorn.

One day, Arthur thinks as he blinks and smiles pleasantly. *One day you all will feel the Silver Hammer's wrath at the way you forsake one of your own.*

A voice that sounds suspiciously like Lasilas' inside his head whispers, *you don't know the circumstances. You don't know if his exile was in fact justified or not. You don't know anything.*

Arthur only knows this isn't the place to ask Lasilas about that, and quite possibly anyplace would be better. He resolves to finally ask Lasilas once they get out of this nightmare. The nightmare that is entirely Arthur's fault.

Gods, what has he done?

LASILAS IS ALLOWED to sit in on the meeting, and Arthur stands at the door to listen. The princes discuss the war, Edgorn, internal things to Ilyaka that Arthur has little knowledge of. Lasilas sits at that table with them, silent the whole time, but him being there is what counts.

When the meeting finally ends, Lasilas slips out the door like there's an assassin on his tail. Arthur, as always, is close behind him.

Lasilas finds cover and peace under the starry night sky, knees pulled up to his chest where he sits on the crest of the hill. Arthur hangs back and observes him for a moment, though he has no doubt Lasilas knows he's there. Lasilas looks so small and frail with his chin resting on his knees. Arthur will dedicate his life to building Lasilas up again, if that's what it takes.

Arthur sits down next to him, armor clinking, and lets the warm sounds of night envelope them before speaking. Lasilas has a blank stare. Arthur's heart seizes, wondering if his words will even reach through to wherever Lasilas has retreated.

"Lasilas, I'm sorry. I didn't know all of that was going to happen, though you warned me, and I should've expected it. I didn't protect you like I promised I would. I will resolve to do better by you in the future."

No response.

Arthur tries, "Lasilas, what happened with your exile? With your supposed murder of the House? I understand if it's too painful for you to talk about, especially if that's the way you're treated every time you do." He gestures to the cabin behind them. "However, you should know that there'll be no one more willing to listen than I, if you did ever want to share. There is nothing you could tell me about yourself that would make me flinch away. Even if you did slaughter House Catiana with your bare hands."

Lasilas doesn't speak for a long while. Arthur doesn't force him to talk. He's not entitled to any of Lasilas' story, no matter how thin Lasilas' resolve might have grown.

Finally, Lasilas turns his head, shaking out his messy blond curls, and says, "Even if I confessed to murder, Arthur? You mean that? You would still follow me then?"

"Always," Arthur whispers. "Las, we commit murder every day when we slaughter these innocent Coromodans and Elens and Delainians."

Lasilas ducks his head to smile. "No one but my sister has ever called me Las. I have a sister, by the way."

The abrupt reminder gives Arthur pause.

"I'm sorry I never told you," Lasilas murmurs, clutching Arthur's knee. "Any of you. I never saw a fitting way for it to come up in conversation, and I suppose I thought none of you would care."

"I know all of your soldiers would go groveling for scraps of information about you and your past life," Arthur assures him. "We all care. Not just about what you do, but what you are. You're worth more than that to us."

Arthur gathers his courage, then asks, "Did you—did you know she was the Chisel? Or that she left? Did you know any of that?" Lasilas' silence is its own answer. "Heires could be lying,"

Arthur quickly adds. "All he seemed to care about was twisting his knife. I doubt any of the others could be arsed to correct him."

"He's not lying, dearest Arthur," Lasilas says kindly. "I know he's not. I've been examining all the signs since we got out of there. I mean, all the stories say that the Hammer and the Chisel must exist in the same generation, but I never thought—"

Arthur understands. He couldn't imagine if that were someone like his own mother. He couldn't imagine being in Lasilas' position.

"My exile, my exile." Lasilas sighs and tips his head back, looking at the stars. "It all relates back to my sister. She had a lover of six months who she was infatuated with—hair red as a sunrise, eyes like the sky, a smile that could melt frozen hearts. She was kind and charming, and she treated my sister well. I rarely saw them, because we were in such different houses and mine traveled around so much, but when I did see them, I had the time of my life.

"One day, her lover wanted to come visit us at House Catiana. None but diplomats and the family of the princes may know the true location of the House, but Augusta begged and begged me to let her lover come with her. I was the world's greatest fool and allowed it. Anything for my sister."

Arthur takes a chance and wraps his arm around Lasilas' shoulders, pulling him close to his broad armored chest. Hopefully the armor has been made warm with his body heat. Cold or warm, Lasilas takes a shuddering breath of thankful relief and leans his head into the hollow of Arthur's neck.

"I was giving her—Zera, that was her name—a tour of the house while Augusta hitched the horses outside. I had thought the house would be empty that day. It's one of the only reasons I agreed to bring Zera along, but I had gotten dates mixed up, because when I brought her to the main council room, I found it full. There were a few seconds of mutual horror while I wondered how I was going to explain this to the other princes. And then she stepped in."

He closes his eyes. "I still see it all. The blood, the bodies, the unnaturally fast way she did it. She was trained, no doubt. I've never known how or by whom. It was over before I could even draw my sword. All of them dead but Heires and I, and he was only spared because he wasn't in the room.

"Zera snuck out the window and went back to Augusta while Heires walked in and found me there with the bodies. Never mind that my sword wasn't bloody and neither was I—he always hated me, and here was his excuse to get rid of me once and for all. Who would believe my version of events, after all? At the very least, I'd be barred and disgraced for allowing a foreigner into our House.

"As the only prince left, he banished me under penalty of death if I dared return to Ilyaka. He turned the public against me. No one could defend me, no one could raise a bad word against him. There was no proof either way. Zera slipped out the next morning. I'm assuming she was never seen in Ilyaka again."

"Why?" Arthur asks, anguished. "Why would he do such a thing?" He fights every urge to march right back into that cabin and take Heires captive, make him answer for his crimes.

Lasilas takes his head out of Arthur's neck to smile, of all things. "Because I was too popular, and he was jealous. I didn't mean to, but I dictated many of the prince council's decisions. Everywhere we rode, people waved to me first. After I was gone, he remade the council with the list of princes that he liked best. The ones we just met. The ones who worship him now, and the ones that make sure the citizens wave to him first when they ride through."

Arthur shakes his head. "Do you think your sister thinks you did it?"

"I sincerely hope not. I never did get to say goodbye to her." He smiles wryly. "I am innocent. I have always believed this, trust me. It was not that kept me from telling you. I tried to defend myself, tell everyone that Heires was just a dirty liar. I wore my voice hoarse with all the screaming and arguing I did the day of my trial. But I learned quickly that saying anything otherwise would only result in a headache for me, so I just went along with it all."

"That's horrible."

Lasilas shrugs. "It's to be expected. Like I said, there was no proof either way. My word against his. I saw the doubt in Augusta's eyes, though she defended me till the last moment I was within Ilyakan borders. I imagine her guilt concerning Zera was eating her alive. I'm sure we've both wondered if Zera ever loved her at all, or if the whole affair was just a ploy to get to the House."

What a horrible concept. Arthur's stomach twists. "Would they have been forced to drop the charges if Augusta had been the Golden Chisel then and pled for you?"

Lasilas sighs again. "I'm glad I didn't know that about her until today. I would've driven myself mad with possibilities otherwise."

"I'm sorry I brought it to mind, then."

"No, no. Don't be sorry for anything." Lasilas sits up and strokes Arthur's chin, smiling through the tears beading in his eyes. Arthur whispers for him to let them out. *I won't let anything happen to you ever again.*

"You are the first and only I've trusted this with. I've never told anyone before. The burning anger and the sting of betrayal have kept my mouth shut thus far, but you—I have a sense that I can tell you anything and emerge unscathed. I've never known someone as magical as you before."

Arthur smiles. "Let's attribute it to the armor."

Lasilas returns the smile as the first tears begin running down his cheeks. Strangely, the sight of his tears makes Arthur heave a breath of relief. To have Lasilas finally fall apart in his arms under the warmth and safety of the stars with that hell house behind them—it's not a duty Arthur would entrust to anyone else, a selfish thought it may be. Silver Hammer or not, there isn't a world where he wouldn't want to protect Lasilas.

Looking up at Arthur like he is a star, Lasilas says, "It's not just the armor."

CHAPTER FOUR

Herra of the Ancients, last remaining appointer of emperors, leader of the Blue Feathers, knife wielding menace of an archer, wakes up tied to her bed.

"T'hell?" Herra mutters, weakly yanking at the rope tying her left hand to the bedpost. She looks around, finding herself alone in the room, thankfully alone in bed. Sunlight streams through her open curtains and window, mocking her for how late she's starting the day.

She looks at her wrist again, dumbfounded. It's a good knot, one she can't simply slip off or untie one handed. The rope is soft instead of coarse.

She wonders how this affair came about. From her clear memory of last night, she spent a terse dinner in the tavern across the street where she and Tasian met. Where the Blue Feathers were founded, where they gather in times of ease.

Last night, Augusta was never two paces from her side, and Herra tried her hardest to ignore the looks she received from her fellows after introducing Augusta. Augusta gave her the most infuriating look of all.

Herra's proclamation that, "She's going to be here with us for an indefinite amount of time, and I would ask that anyone here consult me before hurting her," seemed to seal the deal. She received glares, scoffs, and lot of devious smirks.

Herra tugs on the rope again with a grimace. She doesn't even want to know the rumors this will start if this gets out. Gods forbid anyone finds out Augusta tied the leader of the Blue Feathers to her bed; she'll never hear the end of it.

With begrudging acceptance, Herra shuffled around the furniture to make a spot in her room for Augusta. What she told her Feathers, she had to accept herself. Augusta isn't going anywhere. Herra is going to have an ex member of House Grimash staying in her house. She didn't trust Augusta to stay in anyone else's room, and like hell she was letting Augusta stay in a room of her own, free to slip out the second the door closed. Augusta was surprisingly pliant about the arrangements. Now Herra sees why.

Herra curses herself for letting her guard down so easily. For fuck's sake, did she sleep through Augusta tying her up? Did Augusta drug her drink?

Of everything that happened last night, she doesn't remember any rope involved with anyone, no faceless bedfellow that Herra might've dragged back here to have some fun with. Herra forgot she keeps rope in here—or does she? Everything's fuzzy, as it usually is in the mornings, not just the drunken ones.

After several minutes of fumbling and maneuvering, she successfully slices the ropes with one of the many knives she keeps with her. She hopes Augusta doesn't doubt her intelligence enough to assume that this will be anything more than a short inconvenience. The window is open, teasing and tantalizing. Augusta is taunting her. She might as well have left a note or a lipstick stain on the window.

Herra stumbles out of bed and into new clothes, arming herself with daggers and her sword belt. She reaches for her mother's bow in its mount on the wall, thinking she'll teach Augusta a lesson and perhaps show off a bit, only to find it gone. Hanging on the hook instead is a note that reads, "Find me if you dare, Ancient," in the shittiest handwriting Herra has ever seen.

Bastard.

She throws open the door, going from annoyed to incensed. "Did anyone see which way that bastard went?" she asks of the first person she sees—Bella, standing guard outside her door. Bella jumps at Herra's sudden exit, but recovers quickly, smiling with mirth Herra is firmly not in the mood for.

"No one left your room. If the Ilyakan escaped, she escaped through your room, Madam. I think that's a problem you have to solve on your own."

Herra glares out at the sunny hallway of devious smiles. She grumbles before slamming the door shut in their faces. She'll have some privacy while she shimmies out of her own window like a shame faced whore, thank you very much.

Dropping into the thankfully empty streets, Herra looks around and wonders where she would go if she were Augusta, a stranger in this foreign town. At least as much of a stranger as she can be. Augusta knew of Alma's reputation, and she said she'd been here more than a day. Would she be foolish and headstrong enough to go for Zera's neck straight away?

Herra snags the arm of the first person she passes. Someone just out for a morning walk looks up at the fearsome leader of the Blue Feathers with a raised eyebrow. "Has a little red headed bastard come down this way?" she demands. When they hesitate, she tries, "Someone scurrying away in a hooded cloak, perhaps? A bow in hand? Head cast down in shame?"

Their face brightens. "Oh, yes. They didn't have their head down in shame, though. They seemed quite proud of themself. They tossed me a coin and went that way." They point. "I watched them go into that tavern over there."

Herra presses a gold coin into their hand, walking away in the wake of their sputtering surprise.

Once inside the tavern, it's not hard to find Augusta. It's the morning, after all, and only the comatose souls from last night remain in the building. There's a lone figure at the bar, crouching over the counter on a barstool. She's wearing one of Herra's cloaks, her favorite periwinkle one with a white flower embroidered as the clasp.

Herra marches up to the bar, sword drawn. Her mother's bow rests on the countertop, and she quickly snatches it back.

Augusta casts her an unconcerned look. She has a mug of coffee in front of her, the barmaid nowhere to be seen. Herra checks—there's no body behind the bar. That would be terribly inconvenient, since this bar is in her territory and the barmaid is her friend. It'd be an embarrassment. This little stunt will provide enough humiliation for a year.

Augusta says, "I didn't think it would take you that long to get free."

Herra bristles. "Of course I'm free. It was only one hand, and besides, what did you expect me to do when I woke up tied to my own bed, just stay there and luxuriate? How did you get out so quietly, anyway? Did you drug me?"

The ghost of a smile passes Augusta's face. "No. Maybe you're just a heavy sleeper."

"Bullshit. Were you trained to be able to sneak away like that?"

Augusta arches an eyebrow. "Did you hit your head trying to climb out of bed, Ancient? Do you forget where I come from?"

Herra straightens her back. *Yes.* "Of course not. I was just trying to extract some information from you...about your childhood in House Grimash?"

Augusta throws her head back and laughs, her freshly washed hair falling like a red curtain around her face. She had her much needed bath last night, and Herra has to admit she's much easier on the eye now. Her wounds are freshly tended, just as Herra's are. They both reek of poultice. "Sure, sure," she says, smiling at Herra. "Ilyakans wouldn't share anything about our inner culture with a foreigner that easily. You'd have to pull every tooth and hair from my head."

"Don't give me ideas."

Augusta rolls her eyes. "I suppose you're here to drag me back to polite society?"

"Yes."

"Mm, that's unfortunate for you. I'm not going anywhere." Augusta takes a long swig of her coffee before turning to look Herra in the eye. Somewhere outside, a woebegone lute player sings their heart out to solemn lyrics. Probably still drunken, by the sound of it.

Augusta gestures grandly at the bar, the streets outside, the sunshine streaming in. "So this is it for you, hm? This is your little kingdom?"

Herra is not having this conversation. "We're going back to the house right now."

"Come now," Augusta says, shrugging off Herra's grip around her arm. "Do you really want a fight at nine in the blessed sunshine? I told you my life story. You should tell me some things about yourself. Would it be too much to ask to know my captor?"

"You did not tell—" Herra sighs and takes a few steadying breaths. Augusta's right, she doesn't want a fight right now. She just wants things to go quietly. To have taken Augusta in was clearly a curse. A foolish decision. Tasian was right.

She is your prisoner, not your guest, and you are certainly not her prisoner. You don't have to accommodate her, only follow the path of least resistance.

Tell that to Augusta.

"What do you want to know?" she grits out, keeping her eyes closed so she doesn't have to see Augusta's smug smile.

"Tell me why the last remaining Ancient from the appointers' court is fucking around leading a gang on the Mariosan coast instead of fulfilling her divine duty. Before you can say it, yes, I know it's my fault you're the last of your line. You don't have to give me that speech every time, you know. It's getting tiring."

Another deep breath. Herra counts to five. "I'll tire you out as many times as I want, Grimash."

Augusta raises an eyebrow. "Is that a threat or a promise, Ancient?"

Herra wants to punch something.

"I would ask you to fight me, Ancient," Augusta says, "but I want to spare you the loss of your dignity. Don't you laugh, I'm being honest—you haven't had my training. The appointers' court doesn't teach swordplay, last I recall."

"And when was the last time you bothered to recall?" Herra clutches her mother's bow tighter in her fingers. The finely polished wood is the same brown as her and her mother's skin. "This was my mother's, and it wasn't just a novelty item. For your information, I *am* fulfilling my divine duty of appointing an emperor."

Augusta raises an eyebrow.

"It's not a fast process." She bites her lip, hesitating. Augusta will never be out of her sight long enough to do damage with what she learns at Herra's side, this morning's escape excluded. "I have a man working for me. He infiltrates the royal courts of the continent and the minds of its monarchs, trying to determine which one will serve best. I want to choose an emperor who will serve every citizen well. I will not be callous in my choice. It has been six years, after all. I take my time. It is a large decision."

"And? What is his verdict?" Another swig of coffee. Augusta slumps over the bar top.

"He's on his fourth target now."

Augusta snorts. "Yeah, they'll all be like that."

"All like what?"

Augusta sighs. "You wouldn't understand."

"Try me."

"It's just—" She gestures incomprehensibly. "Ilyaka has been burned by the emperors over and over in the past. We don't exactly have high opinions of them."

"You're not the only ones." Herra still remembers that terrible day six years ago when Ricarda IV, King of Mariosa and Emperor of the Continent, was assassinated in his study. Her grandmother was in the midst of selecting his replacement when House Grimash came, the worst day of her life.

The barkeep, Ryn, clicks into the main room in their usual heeled boots. Herra had an affair with them once—dark hair, dangerous smile, deadly wink. Leonidas once accused her of wanting to fuck herself.

Herra raises a hand to them. "Ryn, hey. Sorry that this bastard stumbled in here and ruined your morning for you." Herra slides a coin across the counter. "For your trouble."

Ryn smirks, polishing the glass in their hand. "Oh, it was no trouble at all. She paid well."

Herra stares between them. Augusta is grinning, and it dawns. "You helped yourself to my money as well?"

Augusta winks and stands, bowing with a flourish. "Drag me back to polite society, oh great leader. I am yours to do with as you will."

Ryn laughs. "I like your new lover, Herra. She's got spirit. Come back anytime, sweetheart, you hear me?"

"Aye," Augusta says. "Finally, a Mariosan I get along with."

"She is not my lover," Herra snaps, glaring at Ryn and dragging Augusta roughly by the arm out the door.

Three mornings pass in a similar fashion: Herra wakes tied to her bed, even after clearing all of the ropes out of her room and locking them in a storage closet. Augusta finds them somewhere, somehow, and each time steals something of Herra's to motivate her to come to Ryn's tavern. Ryn and Augusta are endlessly amused. And, Herra suspects, so are the members of the Blue Feathers when her back is turned.

The third night, Herra sleeps in Tasian's room, in the bed without a headboard and with her weapons to her chest. The door is locked and Augusta is locked in Herra's own room. Still, come morning Augusta ties her to the bedside lamp, which comes crashing down and shattering after her initial confused yank.

"Augusta Tanner Grimash," Herra roars, walking into Ryn's tavern the final morning. She has her bow in hand, since her sword was stolen from under her arm. It's now sitting beside Augusta at the counter, taunting her as smugly as ever. "You are going to come back with me this moment."

"No," Augusta says in a sickeningly sweet tone.

Herra balls up her fists. "Why are you doing this?"

Ryn disappears into the back to give them some privacy.

"Because, sweetheart," Augusta says with her usual grin, hair braided over one shoulder today, "you don't know how funny it is to watch you growl and swipe at me to no avail."

"What do I have to do to make you stop?" Herra grounds out.

Augusta raises her hands. "What's the big deal? You said it yourself—it's just a little rope, nothing you can't handle. I make it easy for you by waiting for you in the same place. That barmaid is very charming."

The problem is the humiliation, though she'll never say that to Augusta's face. The problem is the idea she's giving the Feathers that she can't wrangle one woman day after day. Gods forbid Zera hears about this. The small remaining shred of Herra's dignity will be shattered.

Herra has a sneaking, sinking dread she already has.

"I want you to stop," she tries. "Please?"

"I think we're well past the era of pleasantries."

Herra does the only thing that will get Augusta to come back in the short term; sitting beside her at the counter and reclaiming her sword. "Tell me more about what you said the first day," she says, listening to that same sorrowful bard belt out his song in the streets. "About the Ilyakans getting burned by emperors in the past." She has a theory, and she wants to test it.

Augusta shakes her head, downing today's coffee. Ryn's tip sits on the bar top. Herra has little need for money thanks to the gang's work, but Augusta's theft of her pocket change needs to stop for reputation's sake. She doesn't want real pickpockets getting any ideas.

"You know of the pass," Augusta begins haltingly. "The Amarinthine Pass in Ilyaka that connects to the rest of the world."

Of course she does. Herra would like to meet anyone who hasn't heard of its importance.

"It's the reason emperors want us," Augusta says quietly, with a thinly stifled and bitter hatred. "The perfect crown jewel to stack on top of their gleaming, glorious empire. We are small and beautiful, and they won't leave us the fuck alone. That pass is ours, and the fee they pay us to use it is pitiful. Laughable. For centuries, we've had to deal with their greedy fucking fingers in our pie."

Herra stays silent.

"The emperors want what we have to offer," Augusta says, "but they don't want to include us in any of the conversations they have with the rest of the continent. They never consider Ilyaka in their decisions. They just like to forget about us after we're conveniently folded into the mix. They send our folks to die in their wars, and what do we get for it? Fuck all. No emperor has ever done anything for us that wasn't contractual, that didn't also benefit them."

She drinks to that. "May the emperor stay long dead. We've been happier as a people than we have in centuries, these past six years."

"This war that's been brewing in Coromoda," Herra says. "King Edgorn's force."

Augusta nods, expression tight. "Led by my brother."

Herra hesitates. She keeps forgetting Augusta is the sister of a prince. Anywhere else, that would make her a princess, and Herra is tempted to call her that just to get a rise out of her. She remembers that Ilyaka works differently. They might be siblings in blood, but what matters are the houses they were assigned to at the age of six. Augusta went to House Grimash, house of necessary protection, and Lasilas went to, what—the royal house—Catiana, is it?

Herra asks, "Would Ilyakans fight against Edgorn? Would they fight for the emperor that I choose?"

Augusta looks her up and down with blue eyes dark and daunting, freckles caught by the light. "I don't have to tell you anything. I've already told you too much."

"I thought the deal was that you tell me anything I want to know and I look the other way when you go after Zera."

"Yes," Augusta says. "Zera's head still stands on her shoulders."

"We can start working on that today. Excuse me for being a bit reluctant to help you, as I keep waking tied to a bedpost."

"You're still welcome to lock me in that room and torture your answers out of me," Augusta says casually, the way one might say *we're getting a new shipment of coffee today.*

Herra attempts to shake it off. "Answer my question. Would the Ilyakans fight for my emperor against Edgorn?"

Augusta cuffs her. Herra lets out a rather undignified yelp. "Did you hear anything I just said? Of course not. You don't even know who it'll be yet. The Ilyakans will never fight for an emperor, but they will fight an invasion of our homeland to defend ourselves. Nothing more, nothing less. We would all be happier if you just stayed out of our affairs."

"For what price can I get them to fight Edgorn?"

Augusta takes her time finishing her drink, smacking her lips before looking at Herra. "Independence from the empire. No emperors, no overlords, and absolutely no ownership over the Amarinthine Pass. They'll have to pay out the ass to transport their goods through it. And no invasions to try and take it back. No loopholes. Just our own land in our own hands. That is all we desire. All we have ever desired."

Herra inhales. "That will never happen. The Amaranthine Pass is too valuable to lose."

Augusta abruptly stands. "The damn pass. That's all you foreigners ever think about! The political advantages or disadvantages of dealing with Ilyaka. You never think about the people within, those who slip through the cracks! Gods forbid we have a culture, a desire, a future of our own, and gods forbid it has nothing at all to do with you."

Augusta heaves a breath. "You're proving that. That's all we are to you—a mountain pass through which to bring goods. As much value as a garden tool. We just exist as a funnel and when you're done, we're done too. Your fucking people are the ones who seal our fate for us. You, Ancient. Maybe you can understand a bit better why you were supposed to die with your family, and why the very sight of you makes me want to burn down your entire enterprise."

When she falls silent, Herra is grateful the tavern is empty. Augusta shakes her head in disgust and runs out, cloak hood pulled hastily up. "Augusta, wait. Come back." She races up out of her seat, cursing herself for letting Augusta get out of her hands so easily. The girl is a weasel.

She's not far. She never is. Her head is hidden in her cloak hood—Herra's cloak, dammit—and she's as still as the wind in the mountains.

Herra lays a tentative hand on her shoulder, concerned about her getting away. "Augusta—"

Augusta slaps her hand away, but she doesn't run. Her anger toward Herra appears to ground her. "Tell me a single fact about Ilyaka other than the damn pass."

Herra pauses. Augusta grunts in grim triumph, but Herra says, "I know that you're not ruled by any one king, but by a council of princes that come together to rule in joint. I know that your children are separated at six years old into groups based on the tasks and roles chosen for them by your priests. Siblings, twins—it doesn't matter. No one is spared, and training for those roles begins immediately. The kids grow up in one of nine different houses based on their chosen tasks."

She pauses. "I know that we all do what we think is best for our people. No one can fault you for that, or for your anger about the pass."

Something softens in Augusta's eyes like a ripple in a river. The cloud is gone when Herra blinks. Augusta looks her over, up and down, and nods in something like approval. "Better than I gave you credit for. You're not going to lock me up for telling you that you should've died with your family?"

"No."

"You think I didn't mean it?"

"Oh, I know you meant it. I also know that you're right. I was never supposed to survive. I've known that since the moment it happened." She points at her cheek scar.

Augusta snorts, leaning against the wall and turning her pretty face to the skies. "Never thought I'd be having a civil conversation with one of you bastards."

Herra exhales. When she lays a hand on Augusta's shoulder, this time she doesn't slap it away. "Are you going to come with me peacefully?"

It might be the sun in her eyes, but Herra swears Augusta smiles. She says, "You drive a hard bargain." Augusta lets Herra drag her back to the townhouse anyway. "I still want to burn down your entire enterprise."

"I know. It seems I can never afford to sleep again." Herra keeps a looser grip on Augusta's arm today. The next day, Augusta doesn't tie her to the bed.

CHAPTER FIVE

H erra hates the theater.

She just *knows* that Leonidas, living in Allicé with his charming king, is laughing at her. Laughing his heart out over the misery and misfortune she's going to describe in her next letter. Perhaps he'll read it while he gets ready to go to the theater himself. Maybe he'll make up some alias for her just for the pleasure of spreading the tale to his new king and his new friends.

It doesn't change the fact that right now Herra's head is tipped back while she heaves a loud sigh, utterly dying of boredom in this uncomfortable chair in this theater full of Mitzi's most pompous. If she sees one more frilly scarf or bejeweled collar she's going to throw something, preferably a knife.

"Get it together," Augusta whispers beside her, lightly slapping her hand. "It's like you want to draw attention."

"Everyone in this city knows who I am," Herra whispers back, not bothering to be as quiet. "I don't give a fuck if I'm interrupting someone's midweek luncheon date."

Augusta rolls her eyes. Herra sighs again, trying to tune out the poor attempt at poetic waxing made by the actor on stage.

At least in Allicé, the plays are probably decent.

She keeps checking the timepiece on the far wall, trying to ignore the gaudy white wallpaper with the golden swans. Beneath her own ridiculous frilly cape, she wears a long jacket that she dug out of her drawers for fancy occasions such as this. The theater is stifling, and Herra is counting down the minutes. To make matters worse, Augusta actually seems to be enjoying this production. Herra's not unconvinced she's just doing it to spite her.

Herra reluctantly dressed up to blend in, yellow and gold and orange silks that haven't seen the light of day in years. She has to admit that Augusta looks good in the blue silk coat she stole from Herra—there's never been any denying her beauty, and she can see why Zera went for her—but of all things, honestly. The theater?

She'll have to show Augusta the art of archery sometime. Introduce her to a proper art instead of this.

"Hey, you were the one who dragged us here," Tasian whispers from their seat behind Herra. "You set this deal up. You don't get to complain."

"I'm the gang leader, I get to complain all I want," Herra snaps, and practically hears them roll their eyes. "But it was Zera who set this up, not me. She chose the fucking theater, of all places."

"Oh, excuse me, Your Royal Highness," Tasian whispers.

"Are you two going to shut up?" Augusta asks, and Herra's hackles rise at how easily Augusta has gained control over the Blue Feathers in the recent weeks. She can order them around freely to her will. Herra will swear to her dying breath that she is different, resistant to Augusta's mindless orders, and anyone who succumbs is a weak minded rat who should be ashamed of themself.

However, as Herra falls silent, she can feel Tasian's knowing smirk on the back of her neck.

Herra's hair being loose is hard enough to deal with. It's worn that way because Augusta announced that she'd only come to the theater if Herra dressed like an upstanding citizen. Unfortunately, Zera insisted on Augusta coming along, and Herra had no choice.

The way the Feathers grinned when Herra walked out of her room like a grumpy cat, dressed in these frills and silks—little in the world could be worse.

Bored out of her mind and with nothing else to do, she stares at Augusta, tracking her line of sight toward the stage. They've moved from simple acting to elaborate singing numbers. Augusta is wide eyed and breathless with awe, staring at the lead singer on the stage, a woman with dark skin and a voice that reaches the heavens.

She's singing about being heartbroken, as many do, and flings her arms out on either side of her. Ensconced in drama and sighing with heartache. She's glamorous from head to toe, dressed in stunning blue, vain as a bird.

Herra even catches Augusta's lips moving silently along. She wants to ask how she knows this song, this gods awful play, but fears the unsavory results of Augusta's wrath. No wonder she makes such a fuss when Herra talks over the play.

So she keeps her mind occupied with the way Augusta admires the stage with equal parts awe and jealousy. She stares at the singers, the lights, and the clothing. Herra notes it all.

Finally, intermission hits, and Herra is saved from this loathsome prison. Scanning the room, it doesn't take long to find a waterfall of red hair done up in a high braid down Zera's back, accenting her green gown. She locks eyes with Herra across the room and smiles, beckoning her over.

"Let's go," Herra says, rising to her feet.

Zera is gone when next Herra glances over, the view blocked by the sea of people rising from their seats and excitedly chattering about the production.

Herra grabs Tasian and Augusta by the arms, wishing to hell Zera would've let her bring more than two companions, and steers them toward her. They find Zera by one of the back exits, her companions nowhere to be seen.

"Thank you for meeting me," Zera says, flashing a smile from behind ruby lips. She aptly named her gang. "Let us go in here, where it's more private." She peels back the curtain leading to a hidden business parlor, furnished with plush chairs and a wide table.

"Wait," Herra says as Augusta starts to duck inside, pulling her back by a tug on her arm. Augusta made a snide comment earlier today that she should get a tattoo of Herra's fingerprints around her wrist, for how often she rests them there. "You fool. Has she taught you nothing?"

Augusta flushes but steps back. Herra enters cautiously, knife in hand.

"My, my, Augusta," Zera says. "So quiet. That's new. In Ilyaka, you would never let anyone so much as look at you wrongly without retribution. Something has clearly changed. It appears that a master with a better dog collar has trained you."

"Tasian," Herra warns, but she doesn't need to say it. They have their strong fighter's hands around Augusta's arms before she can get to Zera, though it's a near thing. She's kicking and squirming like the first day they met, but thankfully she has the wisdom not to yell.

Zera's smug smile makes Herra's fists curl. "Haven't learned how to control your anger after all this time, I see. Maybe not as well trained as I thought. There appear to be some cracks in the Golden Chisel."

"Do not put that name in your mouth," Augusta hisses, devolving into some Ilyakan. Gods damn it, she should've said fuck Zera's little quota and brought Liss along too.

"What does she mean, Augusta?" Herra asks, calling her name until she breaks free of her rage. Even then, she doesn't spare Herra a glance, finally settling in Tasian's grip.

"None of your business."

Herra doesn't contest it, though a blind woman could see that Zera hit a sore spot. Herra fights the longing to simply put a knife through her neck and call this done—or better yet, let Augusta do it. Maybe after Augusta has gotten what she wants, she'll be easier to deal with.

There's no reason she'd stay with you in anything but chains if Zera is dead.

Herra sighs and waves everyone inside, finding the room clear of Zera's bullshit. "Let's get this over with."

"Please," Tasian murmurs, and carefully lets Augusta free.

They find their places in respective overstuffed chairs. Herra takes the half couch, noticing that only three chairs are posed around the table. With no other place to go except the indignity of sitting on the floor like a dog, Augusta takes the other half of the couch. Her posture is stiff and straight with her hands folded in front of her. She looks ready to pounce at any moment, her gaze locked on Zera. Herra's attack dog.

"So, uh—" Herra gestures at the grandeur of this theater, the fresco painted on the ceiling that they can glimpse through the gap in the curtain. Leonidas has raved about the fresco in the Allicé palace in his letters. Herra bets he would scoff at this one, connoisseur of Mariosan art that he now is. "Zera. Why the theater?"

Zera sighs and smiles, running a hand up the wall like she would a lover. "Theaters have always brought me joy," she says, tapping sharp red nails against the doorframe. She is made of knives. "And peace. A place to think. I grew up in an acting troupe. My mother was a singer of House Liele, the house of artists in Ilyaka. Listening to productions like these still remind me of her."

"You never told me where you grew up," Augusta growls.

Zera laughs, a sound like tainted sunlight, artificial, the kind that burns. "I never told you a lot of things," she says, and Herra squeezes Augusta's wrist. She would've liked to cuff her, but that would be too unseemly here, and it would swiftly dispose of the little of Augusta's trust she has earned. At least she's sitting beside Herra where she can be controlled.

"This is the treaty I have drawn up for us. All you need to do is sign." Zera reaches beneath the folds of her dress and pulls out a stack of papers, a jar of ink, and a quill.

Herra almost laughs as she takes the papers. She quickly realizes the first flaw. "It's in Ilyakan."

Zera shrugs. "A girl can write in whatever language she likes. Come on, Herra, were you really expecting us all to conform to what's comfortable for you? Officials from different nations sign treaties that are not often in their native language. They obtain copies."

"They have translators," Herra says through gritted teeth.

Zera shrugs again. "Then you should've brought your translator." Her eyes dart to Tasian, who gives her a mean smirk in return.

Augusta raises a tentative hand. "Um, hello, full blooded Ilyakan here. Translator."

Yes, but I don't trust you, Herra nearly says, but Augusta has no reason to lie in Zera's favor. With a sigh, she hands them over.

"On the twentieth day of Tibren, this treaty between the Blue Feathers and the Ruby Rings is put into effect under the sanctity of King Ricarda the Fifth's law, yeah, yeah, all that bullshit...I, Zera Musiek, hereby swear under the penalty of law to"—Augusta's eyes widen—"serve Herra of the Ancients under any circumstances that she sees fit.

"Herra of the Ancients will serve me, Zera Musiek, by committing no acts of violence against me or any member of the Ruby Rings. If any of her people or Herra herself commit acts of violence against the stated parties, this treaty is forfeit and any violence on either side will run uncontested." A pause. "That's it."

Herra stares at Zera, trying to find the flaw, the crack that Zera will slip through to fuck her over. Still, Zera maintains that pretty smile, hiding knives behind ruby lips.

"I work for you, and you leave me be," Zera says. "Deal?"

"Hold on," Herra says. "Any circumstances I see fit?"

"Yes."

"Anything at all?"

Zera smiles. "Yes."

Herra and Augusta exchange glances.

"What does this mean, no acts of violence?" Herra asks. "You and I have been enemies—"

"Rivals."

"Enemies for years, Zera. Alma. Ever since you showed up in Mitzi, you've never seemed to want peace. What aren't you telling me? What lofty demand must I meet? Do you want me to give her to you?"

Augusta stiffens beside her.

"If I wanted you to give me Augusta," Zera says, "I would've put that in the treaty, wouldn't I?"

"This is not a treaty," Augusta says. "This is a contract."

Zera shrugs. "Same thing." She leans forward, still smiling, while Herra tries to discern the emotion behind her eyes. "So, do we have a deal?"

Herra holds out a hand, though the signature is the real seal. Zera's fingers are cold, her nails wickedly sharp. "Deal."

Augusta doesn't say a word as Herra signs the papers. "I don't suppose you brought spare paper so she can copy this into Mariosan?" Herra asks.

Zera produces a piece of parchment, and Herra sets a furious Augusta to work.

"Right." Herra stands up, copy in hand. "Let's get out of here before the second act starts."

Zera stands gracefully, the folds of her gown settling around her. "I am going to stay and enjoy the play." She waves those razor nails. "Nice seeing you again, Augusta."

As expected, Augusta is seething with a rage barely contained. The walk back to the Blue Feathers house is tense and silent, and Tasian slips away the moment the door shuts behind them. Augusta keeps herself contained until they get up to Herra's office, a room bathed in the glow of the sunset and a soft Minyan rug that reminds her of home.

When Herra takes the risk of turning her back to Augusta to lock the door, Augusta speaks.

"You broke our deal, Ancient. That bastard still walks free. In your pocket, no less."

"Too bad for you," Herra retorts. "I told you I didn't want her dead. I need her in order to keep the peace between my gang and all the ones that would take my crown from my head. That treaty may be too good to be true, but until I find the loophole, I'm going to milk it."

"Then the deal is off. I'm leaving." Augusta makes for the window, but Herra's fingers close around her arm like they have so many times before. Augusta's glare has lost its potency by now.

"Would you like to be chained up again?" That gives her pause, and Herra slowly releases her arm. "You don't have a lot of options, Grimash, so you'd better pick the best one. You're never getting free until I say so, which means you can have the freedoms I've granted you or none at all."

Augusta's lips curl into a sneer, but she doesn't argue further. She shrugs Herra's hand off instead of trying to fight her again. How many times have they danced this dance already?

That damn tattoo comment, Herra thinks.

"Think about this," Herra presses. "Zera agreed to anything I want, anything at all. We can force her to tell you why she betrayed you. We can force her to sit there while you hurl all the insults at her you've ever dreamed. As long as no blood is drawn, we'll own her entirely."

Augusta's eyes light up, but only for a moment. Something bigger is obviously eating at her. "What's wrong?" Herra asks.

"Is that how you think of me?" Augusta asks. "As a dog? Too dumb and too violent and too unpredictable to be left alone without someone close by to slap something around my wrists?"

"Maybe if you controlled yourself better, we wouldn't have to slap something around your wrists," Herra snaps back, tired and annoyed and done with playing nice with House Grimash. She makes an effort to lower her voice, though Augusta might accuse her of being patronizing. There's no pleasing her. "What do you want?"

"Zera's head on a pike, her blood dripping down my wrists."

Herra rolls her eyes. "I know that. I mean—what would make you cooperate with me? How could I get you to work with me a little more? This would be an easier arrangement if we weren't at each other's necks every turn."

Augusta doesn't dismiss the question outright, which is something. She collapses into Herra's chair and stares out the window for a while, stroking her chin.

Herra chose this room as her office for a reason, back when she and Tasian found this building empty and decided it would make a perfect headquarters. The view from Herra's office window shows the greenest part of Mitzi, hills in the distance dotted with colorful flowers.

The view is the closest thing Herra has to a view of home.

"It's not entirely my fault," Augusta says finally. "You have a temper too."

"I know. I should work on that." Gods. A self-improvement session with Augusta Grimash. If she weren't so wired, Herra would laugh.

"Just—" Augusta gestures inarticulately. "I don't know. Don't treat me like a dog you can't trust. I can handle myself. I got here from Ilyaka on my own. I had no experience with the outside world and no other language on my tongue, and yet I'm still standing. Not to mention I was in House Grimash in the first place, and that's no easy place to grow up. Treat me with respect. That will endear you to me a little bit."

Herra smiles. "That's it?"

"It does wonders," Augusta says, looking up at her. "And it wouldn't hurt if you could give me a weapon. I've never gone this long in my adult life without one. I feel naked without it."

Herra hesitates.

"Imagine if you were without that precious bow and sword of yours," Augusta points out. "You'd feel naked, too, wouldn't you?"

"Thanks to you, I have been without them." Herra sighs and sits down across from her at her own desk. "I'm going to take you on patrols with me for a week," she says, already regretting the words, "and if you can keep your temper that whole time without us having to intervene, then you can have a weapon."

Augusta grins.

"A small knife," Herra clarifies.

She still grins. "And you? What can I do for you?"

"What do you mean?"

"How can I treat you differently, you ninny," Augusta says slowly, like she's explaining something to a child, "so that you're not tempted to treat me like a dog in the first place?" She shrugs at Herra's disbelief. "It's only fair."

Herra can hardly believe she's asking. She, who is the prisoner. "Stop trying to deliberately provoke me, I suppose," she mumbles. "Let's work together."

The words ring out as foreign in the room. "Together," Augusta says slowly, her lips twitching up into a smile. "Are you going to ask about—about the Golden Chisel?"

Herra forgot about that till now, with the contract burning a hole in her jacket pocket. "Not yet," she says. "I don't want to push my luck today. You'll tell me when you're ready."

"Or when you shove me into a wall and drag it out of me. If you do, I'll tie you up and steal your sword again."

"Yes, ma'am."

"Look at you finally using your brain." Augusta is still smiling. "Together," she says in wonder, playing with one of Herra's quills on the desk.

"I still hate you, you know," Herra adds. "You're my greatest enemy. The one who killed my family."

"Oh, believe me, sweetheart," Augusta says, the word that's always sounded the strangest in her thick accent, like she can't quite wrap her tongue around it, "the feeling is mutual. But, and this is purely out of hate—you look good with your hair down like that. Makes you look less like a ruffian and more like a sophisticated member of society."

As a child, Herra's hair was always a bad thing. Too long, too thick, too fuzzy, too wild. Her mother would help her twine it into a braid after a wash, always muttering fondly, *quickly, before it dries and grows into an untamable dragon.*

Herra rarely saw anyone but her own blood family, as is the way of the Ancients. However, the few times they would be invited to a royal court or a local government gathering, she would wear her hair down because that's what all the other courtiers did. Instead of the awed comments and swooning smiles the others got, she received frowns and stares and pointed fingers.

She forgot until today just how wild it becomes when it's not hanging in a braid over her shoulder. It's always been easier to just braid it up and forget about it. She's never had anyone except her family tell her that her hair looks good down before. She hasn't been reminded for a long time that she thinks so too. The reminders rarely come, and who would've thought they'd come from as unlikely a source as Augusta Grimash?

"Oh, gods," Herra says, though her cheeks have grown warm. "All the more reason for me to put it back in the braid, then."

They both smile.

CHAPTER SIX

One, two, three, the arrows land. Herra leaps onto a new perch, loosing another arrow into the targets below. She doesn't stop to check if it hits or not, just keeps moving, improving her speed and sacrificing a bit of her accuracy. If she fires a dozen arrows in one minute, one of them will hit, even if her mother would chide her for the waste.

She pulls the last arrow from her quiver and flips into a daring jump, firing from midair before landing in a roll on the ground. It's been years since she's done that. She stands up and halts to catch her breath, admiring the arrows that rest in each of the painted targets. Not all of them rest in the center, but like she thought, quantity does come over quality sometimes.

A slow clapping brings Herra out of her reverie, drawing her eye to the figure walking onto the training patio behind the Blue Feathers' townhouse. "Even I could never shoot like that," Augusta says, coming to stand beside her.

Today she's wearing a yellow jacket with puffy shoulder pads, gold buttons running down the front, orange hair settling over her shoulders. Herra scoffed when Augusta picked out the color of the jacket, thinking it'd clash with her hair, but surprisingly it works.

Herra realized quickly after their declaration of peace that Augusta couldn't keep wearing her clothes or filching from the other rooms as she saw fit. She had a meeting with Herra's personal tailor a week ago to build her a wardrobe, further instilling the fact that Augusta is going to be staying here a while. Herra is trying to make peace with it—rather, make peace with the speed at which she made peace.

Augusta insisted on having an embroidered crest of a white pansy sewn onto the left breast of every jacket. An Ilyakan religious custom.

For the first time, Herra rose from bed before her and tiptoed out of the room without waking the bundled ball of violence on her pallet. Most times when Herra gets up alone, Augusta can be found in Ryn's tavern or downstairs in the Feathers house, talking with Tasian over a cup of coffee and making snide comments about Herra's sleeping habits. Herra's greatest friend and her greatest enemy banding together against her. Wonderful.

It's not that Herra's a late riser—at least, not by that much—it's just that Tasian and Augusta are two freaks of the world that feel a need to beat the sunrise. One of these days Herra will drag herself out of bed and watch it with them, find out what's so goddamn beautiful about it.

Early rising, not out of necessity but out of preference. Perhaps due to training. A taste for coffee instead of tea. A fondness for padded shoulders. Herra is learning these things about Augusta—seeing her as a person instead of a dog. It's working. They haven't had a screaming fight since the theater.

These days, Herra wraps her fingers around Augusta's wrist not to keep her from tearing someone's head off, but to grab her attention. It's more effective and faster than speech, and it works every time.

Ironically, like a dog, Augusta has developed a response to it. The simple touch of Herra's fingers on her wrist makes her pause, which is all the time Herra needs to get her point across. Often, she needs something translated. Herra finds herself reaching more for Augusta and less for Liss to translate these days.

Presently, Herra scoffs, picking up her arrows from around the courtyard. "I didn't think you knew anything about the bow. Did they teach every type of weaponry in House Grimash?"

"No, smartass. We didn't learn the eastern *kanna*, used by the forest's *reshwii* guard."

"The what?"

Augusta smiles. She's been doing that a lot more, too. "Fighting styles beyond your comprehension. You said this was your mother's?" she says, running a finger along the smoothly polished bow. Herra jerks it out of reach. Augusta has laid her sticky fingers on it too many times already.

"Yeah."

Augusta raises her hands defensively. She now carries a short sword, short enough to be considered a long knife, ever since she passed the patrol test. During that week of patrols, she was the picture of pleasantry, flashing smiles when needed, keeping her mouth shut more often than not.

She came up with clever responses in the face of insults that made even Herra grind her teeth. Herra suspects Augusta has done that sort of diplomatic touring before. House Grimash must've served as guards to House Catiana, Ilyaka's royal house, before.

"She was everything to me," Herra says, letting herself get lost in memories for a moment. The brightness of her mother's rare smile, the scent of her perfume—a thick woodsy aroma. "My biggest inspiration, influence—she taught me everything about the world, about the bow, about my duty.

"My father was my emotional support, my hug when the world got too hard. He was everything to me, too, but my mother had an effect on me no one else did." She closes her eyes as a wave of grief washes over her. Even after six years, it's just as strong.

"Can I ask you something?" Augusta asks.

Herra can't tear her eyes from her in the morning light, the bright sun and the cool breeze drifting up from the seaside. Augusta has never seen the sea before, and Herra is still yet to change that. She gets an idea. "Only if I get to ask you something in return, and if you take a walk with me."

The motions of her mother's guiding hand through it all—the fletching of arrows, the positioning, adjusting to the tension of the bow, the shooting, the repetitive motion of collecting the arrows—it all comes back to her in that moment, almost as if her mother is there in a whisper of breath over the back of Herra's hand.

Augusta heaves a sigh. "As always, I receive the lesser end of the bargain. In that case, I get to make a second demand."

That startles a laugh out of Herra, waving Augusta over to her. "And what would that be? I would hardly call a question and a walk demands."

"Trust me, they are. My demand is that you wear something other than dark blue one of these days. Really, it's astounding how much of the same thing a person can have in their wardrobe." They fall into step together. "I've met that darling seamstress of yours. I have half a mind to take her to bed."

"Please don't."

"You know a seamstress," Augusta stresses. "She can make you clothes. You have the money for them. I don't see what the problem is."

"There is nothing wrong with my dark blue!" Herra says, wondering what the Blue Feathers might think of the two of them arguing about clothes on a sunny morning walk by the docks. "It's just—nothing else looks good with my features. Blue compliments brown, right? Problem solved."

Augusta stares—no, gawks. "Oh, you poor soul. Did they keep you in uniforms up in the appointers' court?"

They did, but those uniforms were priestly white robes, not the tacky uniforms of guards or schoolchildren. Theirs held a purpose.

Augusta interprets her silence. "Good gods, I'm going to have to bring you out of the darkness and into the fashionable light. If you think yellow doesn't look good with brown you've never seen the two together before."

Herra rolls her eyes. She's seen Leonidas in yellow and gold many a time, and she just wore yellow to the theater. "I wasn't aware you were a clothing expert."

"I'm not, I just know about color theory. Bitch." Augusta shoves her. "At least wear a purple, or something! It's close enough to blue, and it'll do the same job. Looks good with your hair. Anyway, ask your question."

Herra almost hesitates, not wanting to ruin the moment, but she's never backed down from a challenge before.

"Who is the Golden Chisel?"

Augusta smiles. "Ah. That question. Good on you for resisting this long."

A supply hiccup in Mitzi has kept Herra's attention off any chisels, golden or otherwise, for the past few weeks. The damn war of the north has been interfering with Herra's business, but let Augusta think what she will.

"I am the Golden Chisel," Augusta says. "You should be asking *what* it is. It's—" She fumbles and gestures, as she sometimes does when struggling with Mariosan. Her fluency is not absolute. "A protector, a warrior."

She tells Herra the full story, the Silver Hammer as the counterpart, their respective armor, the guards and servants and legends of Ilyaka. "I found the armor in a long forgotten chest in House Grimash where it had been collecting dust for gods know how long. I tried it on and knew it was meant for me. Nothing had ever fit me as well as that." A pause.

"I accomplished great feats as the Golden Chisel, everything the stories said I would. Protecting innocent families. Furthering the growth and prosperity of Ilyaka. Honoring our gods. Having the towns bow to me and adore me. It was lovely for a while. Lonely.

"It gave me a purpose. Something to do after my life had been totally upended. I'm lucky I wasn't expelled from House Grimash out of association to Lasilas. No one ever believed that Zera came to House Catiana that day. No one but the two she hurt most.

"I always hoped to find my counterpart, but I had no such luck. I wished—I wished above all else that Lasilas could know. He worshipped those stories when we were young, though some of our less faithful dismissed them as children's fairytales. I know he'd have been so proud." She smiles.

Herra never had a sibling, but she couldn't imagine being in Augusta's place. "Were you two close as children?"

"Oh, we couldn't have been closer. We were best friends, though he always tried to protect me despite me being the one in House Grimash." Augusta chuckles, tossing her sun touched hair. "The guilt ate me from the inside out when he was banished. If I hadn't been so foolhardy, so starry eyed and charmed by Zera...gods, I was such a fool."

Herra purses her lips. "Where is your armor now, then?"

"I buried it when I left," she says faintly, and it sounds like truth. "Somewhere no one will ever find it."

"Why did you leave, if you had that purpose in life?"

"I've told you. I was ostracized. People thought I might be Lasilas' accomplice, but after I grew into my destiny as the Golden Chisel things only got worse. People smiled to my face, but I heard the whispers. People thought I crafted the armor myself or stole it or paid someone to amplify my tale. Not that the Tanner sister could possibly be the legitimate Golden Chisel." Another pause.

"I think they were expecting Hammer and Chisel to be princes from House Catiana. Lasilas would've been the classic choice before his banishment. Not me. Just because I said my prayers as a member of House Grimash didn't mean I could be the mythical Golden Chisel." Her voice turns cold and biting. Herra senses an old, unhealed wound.

She says, "So, Ilyaka isn't perfect after all."

Augusta rolls her eyes. "I never said it was. The White Goddess does not heal all, despite what the priests told me."

"Oh. Is that what that's for?" Herra gestures to the crest sewn onto her breast.

Augusta smiles down at it. "The white pansy is my—House Grimash's—patron goddess. She represents revenge, and justice, and the necessary corruption of good beings after trauma."

"Perfect for you, then."

"I am what I have been made," Augusta says simply. "Do you think I was violent and harsh from the time the priestess read me at my birth? Well, I suppose I must've been, for her to assign me into House Grimash."

Herra finds herself sympathizing with Augusta's plight more than she ever has before. She quickly catches herself. *This is the woman who murdered your family. You hate every last bit of her, remember?*

Herra firmly does not sympathize. And yet, as they walk along the seaside and Augusta gasps at the first sight of water, Herra catches Augusta's eyes lingering in a shop window. At the front, a brilliant doublet of light blue sits on a mannequin. It has shimmering blue beads decorating the shoulders, which predictably puff out like risen bread. Herra pictures it on Augusta. If yellow would complement her as well as dark blue does, then Augusta would stun in that.

Herra says, "I'll buy it for you if you sing for us."

Augusta looks at her like she would a stranger. A smiling, not altogether opposed stranger. "Whatever gave you the impression that I could sing?"

"You were staring at the singers in the theater," Herra replies. "Mouthing along."

"Better than mouthing off, isn't it?" She draws herself up. Herra knows the look of someone too embarrassed to know what to do with themself after being caught out. "I could just be a fan of the musical arts."

"Yes," Herra says patiently, "or you could own up and just admit you like singing. No shame in it."

Augusta snorts. "With you, there's always the threat of shame. Fine, I have been known to annoy my housemates with singing on occasion. I'm not a member of House Liele, though. Now what's this about buying me that coat?"

Herra ducks her head to smile. "Sing for us at a dinner, and I'll consider it."

"Ha! Over your corpse." Augusta stops to sigh and soak in the sea air, the mesmerizing way the waves slosh back and forth. She asks, "So how did you end up down here, an Ancient so far from home?"

Herra shrugs. "Same as you did, I suspect. There was nothing left for me at the appointers' court. No one. Even if I had an ample food supply up there, the ghosts would've haunted me night and day. I knew I couldn't stay. So I went south, wandering and stumbling through country and city and farmland.

"I stopped when I couldn't go south any further, because the ocean was in the way. I met Tasian, and the Lover, and settled here. We started the gang. I sent the Lover on his first mission. Alma waltzed in shortly after and took charge of the rival gang. All in all, it's peaceful."

"Did you..." Augusta pauses, and Herra follows her gaze to the Ancient seal ring, resting against her chest. She forgot to tuck it beneath her clothes today. She fingers it self-consciously.

"Every day of my travels, I thought of my duty," she confirms. "But I had no place to start. I remembered my grandmother's rigorous selection process. I knew I would do nothing less."

She pauses, wondering if Augusta deserves this cruelty, then wonders when she started thinking of it as cruelty instead of justice. "My grandmother was in the midst of choosing Ricarda the Fourth's replacement when she died."

Augusta nods.

"Funny that all three of us from that corner of the world ended up in the same place so far away," Herra says, wondering what drove Zera here.

"Mm. I had only been in Mitzi for a month or so when you caught me. I was perfecting my grasp of the language, memorizing the city, learning the dynamics. I never saw Zera's face, obviously, but I heard of her, and of you. I was stupid enough to go and get myself captured."

Herra knows better than to make a snide remark about how prettily Augusta is sitting right now. "What were you doing around our territory that day?"

"Wandering aimlessly. Either asking for charity or directions, depending on which one failed."

They both laugh.

CHAPTER SEVEN

Arthur's mother taught him the great theories and rules of art, the complementary colors and the proper techniques for brushes and paints, the way elements blend to craft masterpieces. As a child, he listened with rapt attention at every lesson. She never meant for them to be lessons, only the casual sharing of knowledge while she stood at the easel. Arthur soaked them up all the same.

Looking at his painting now, he's convinced that everything she taught him is bullshit.

He steps away from it with a sigh and wipes the battle sweat off his forehead, wondering if he should just seek a bath and food like most soldiers do after battle. He should just give up. His heart only stopped pounding with exertion and adrenaline ten minutes ago—that's hardly the mindset for a painter to do his best work. His mother would say he needs rest, but something keeps him in the abandoned shed he's using as a studio.

The worst problem is that Arthur can't identify the problem. He thought that coming back to this after battle would jumpstart the inspiration he needed, but so far nothing has improved. The lines, the swirls, the face that's trying to emerge from the blob of red he painted at midnight—something is just off to him.

A knock draws Arthur out of his reverie. A softly murmured, "Arthur?" makes him draw a steadying breath. Lasilas never made him nervous before. He's not sure what's changed to make it so. "By gods, the rumors are true. My best captain really did run off to the shed after battle instead of seeking food or bath."

Arthur smiles and stretches his muscles, stiff from being over a canvas for so long. He leans back to inspect his work, making a face. "Lasilas, hello. Can I do something for you?"

"My captain, I'm insulted," Lasilas says with no heat at all. "I thought we'd moved past the point of only seeing each other when we need something."

He approaches Arthur's canvas, hands folded demurely behind his back. When he gasps softly, Arthur begins to stutter through pointless apologies about how he knows the painting is horrible, he's not sure what went wrong. And then with the breath of heaven, Lasilas murmurs, "I didn't know you painted."

Arthur exhales. "Well, I, uh—I do." He sets his painting brush down in its cup of water before he drops it. "It calms me down, usually. Before and after battle. I started this panting at midnight because I couldn't sleep, and—" He cuts himself off before he can ramble himself into further idiocy. "Anyway. It's not going very well. I think it's too soon after battle. Anyway, what can I do for you?"

"It's beautiful," Lasilas says, turning his head to inspect it every which way. Arthur prickles with self-consciousness. Lasilas ignores the question. "You know, in Ilyaka, there's a whole house for artists."

Arthur perks up at that. "Really? My mother never told me about that."

"House Liele," Lasilas confirms. "House for painters, sculptors, poets, actors, writers, singers, all that. And you know. Prostitutes." He smiles. "We're broad in our definition of art. I bet you would fit right in there, with talent like this."

Arthur smiles, shifting on his feet. "I learned from my mother."

"Well, I would love to see some of her creations, if they're anything close to rivaling yours. Did you know there are some art shows in Ilyaka a few times a year?"

"No," Arthur says, smiling in earnest now. He always assumed if he ever belonged to an Ilyakan house, he would be a guard serving House Catiana, possibly under the crest of the blue carnation, the protector. Not an art house. No matter the house, the sense of belonging makes warmth gather in his chest.

Lasilas nods firmly. "House Liele artists of all kinds go around entertaining the other houses, diplomats who come to Ilyaka, and often the princes. I remember looking forward to their visits as a child. They were a break from my studies and my training. Houses Grimash and Catiana are not the only useful and valued ones.

"Now, there is a reason I came in here other than to distract you and waste your time," Lasilas admits. "I would be most pleased if you could come by my tent tonight after we've had a bath and a nap. A quiet evening, a quiet meal, just the two of us." Lasilas smiles widely. "There's something I want to give you."

Arthur wonders what Lasilas can't give him right here, right now. Does one of them have duty soon? Arthur racks his brain about the roster...not that their roster follows a routine pattern these days.

"Yeah," Arthur says. "Sure. I look forward to it."

Lasilas smiles again, wide and giddy and childlike. The fact that Arthur could put that look there is enough to make him smile in return.

He finishes his painting ten minutes later, the mess miraculously untangling itself, practically tripping over itself to make sense to him. He dedicates it to Lasilas, signing his own name on the back in Coromodan so that if Lasilas somehow gets a hold of it, he won't be able to read the embarrassing little declaration.

NYER AND CALLUM, TWO of Arthur's fellow captains, stand guard on either side of Lasilas' tent when Arthur approaches. Rested and bathed, he's out of his armor and dressed in the nicest clothes he has; a lace up shirt of greenish blue with green daisies embroidered on the collar in place of a crest.

The trousers are plain black, but at least they're not bloody or dust stained. He's clean. He tried his hardest to scrub the dirt from his boots.

Lasilas isn't going to care what he looks like just to pick up a gift.

Arthur agonized over this for far too long, and Callum was definitely giving him strange looks before he went on duty.

Arthur spent more time agonizing over why Lasilas called him here before finally dragging himself to the commander's tent. The only indication that it's any different from the others is the stripe of dark blue on each side of the entrance.

The tent is not any bigger or more opulent than the others, as it must be in Edgorn's camp. And those stripes, Lasilas says, are just so people can find him easily. Not to claim any sense of superiority.

Arthur keeps circling back to the possibility that he did something wrong and this is Lasilas' kind way of having a word with him, saving him the public humiliation the way so many generals like Edgorn would relish.

Arthur naturally tried to determine what his fault could be. Being in camp around his fellow soldiers has been much more bearable since he's revealed his identity and the purpose of that strange armor. Today, Arthur's squadron didn't even break their circle! The battle went smoothly and was over quickly, which is as much as he can hope for.

What did he do?

"Good evening, Arthur," Nyer greets with a sly grin on their face.

"Good evening," Arthur replies stiffly. "Am I permitted entry?" He sees light streaming from under the tent and wants nothing more than to blow past his idiotic friends, but he'll go through the decorum he drills into all his soldiers. He has long been mocked as the rule follower and chivalrous enforcer, and he will not ignore that when it's convenient for him.

"I don't know," Callum says. "You'll have to tell us your purpose with Commander Lasilas first."

Arthur casts him a long look. "He asked me to join him for dinner."

"Ooh," Nyer says. "Should we be padding the tent to help mitigate the sound?"

Arthur feels his face heat. "It's not that kind of dinner," he snaps. "That—that would be inappropriate; we are focused on our duties. Besides, he is my commander. I would never—not like that. No."

"The strangest denial of feelings I have ever heard, but it's you, so I believe you," Callum says, pulling aside the tent flap with a flourish. "Have fun."

Arthur quietly curses him as he enters, praying that Lasilas heard none of that.

"Arthur," Lasilas says with the usual bright tint. It helps Arthur relax after dealing with the fools outside. Lasilas is standing by a table at the back of the room, on which rest a few bottles of liquor and two empty glasses.

"Hello, Lasilas. Good evening." Arthur has never been in Lasilas' personal tent before. He's been in his official tent countless times, sure, but never the one where he sleeps and rests. Of all the times Arthur stood guard mindlessly in front of it, he never thought he'd get a chance to go in like this.

Gods, thinking like that reminds him of Callum and Nyer's sly little comments. He turns away from those thoughts with a new flush. Instead, he looks around the room. The inner walls of the tent are the same dark blue as the stripes, contrary to the plain tan of the outside.

A collection of burning lanterns hanging from the ceiling lights up the tent, with a bed of furs curtained off in the back corner and a fold out writing desk beside it. Arthur has lived three years now in wartime tents, and their accommodations have become just as homely and comforting as his mother's cabin. In Lasilas' tent, Arthur's shoulders soften of tension.

"My one little indulgence," Lasilas confesses when he notices Arthur admiring the blue walls. "Please, sit, be at ease. Call me anything but Lasilas and I'll send you out."

It would help if he didn't say that in such an imperious tone. Arthur smiles. "Yes, Lasilas."

"Drink?" Lasilas pours a fine brandy, by the looks of it. Arthur wonders where he got that stuff out in the field. Alcohol can be found almost anywhere in the world, but nothing of that quality. Lasilas is a general.

"Yes, thank you, but I must ask. Have I done something wrong?"

"What?" Lasilas' face falls. "No. Whatever gave you that impression, Arthur?"

"Oh." Relief spills through his chest like a flood. "I don't know. I suppose I wondered why else you would call me here if not for a talking to."

Lasilas' face falls further, if possible, as he stands. "Let me make this very clear," he says slowly. "I want you here because I want your company. Nothing less."

Arthur nods dumbly, hardly believing his ears. It's a better alternative to what his mind conjured up for him, at least.

"Now," Lasilas says, a smile breaking through, "will you sit and have a drink?"

Arthur sits. He has a drink.

"How is your painting coming along?" Lasilas asks, seating himself and ringing a bell to get one of the privates to come through the back flaps with food. Arthur's face burns hot at the scene it makes. It's like they're eating at the finest inn in a city, with bells to summon servants, drinking the finest, smoothest brandy Arthur has ever had, making pleasant conversation.

The only thing that would better complete the picture would be a bard or a minstrel or something to crow to them as they eat. It's a pompous affair, all of it, and through his blush Arthur starts to accept it. He's never had this treatment before, and he's certainly never going to have it again.

"It's done, thank you," Arthur says, pausing until the 'servers' have finished setting down steaming dishes before speaking again. Knowing Lasilas, he gave those privates a handsome bonus and some extra shifts off duty for dressing up in neat clothes and doing this. They were probably tripping over themselves to volunteer. "Your visit seemed to give me the missing piece I needed to finish."

Lasilas winks and sips his brandy. "I'm happy to be your inspiration, my captain."

Arthur wants to melt into the floor as heat swallows his face.

Knowing what gossip the privates are going to spread, knowing what the captains and the soldiers who saw Arthur come in are thinking, and now hearing that—

It's almost too much. He breathes and keeps his composure, knowing he might just cry if he dared ruin this perfect night for himself.

"As tempted as I am to stare at your lovely face all night," Lasilas says, "forgive me if this food commands my attention. Not all of my attention, though. Not when you're in my sights."

Just dig Arthur a grave.

He's offered a moment of respite when they both dig in. Arthur is almost too busy trying to remember the courtly manners his mother taught him to enjoy the food. But once he clears his brain, has another sip of brandy—it's damn good—he properly tastes the food and nearly makes an indecent sound. Lasilas, however, has no such qualms, and tips his head back at the first taste of their steak. Arthur's eyes follow the movement of Lasilas' throat as he swallows before quickly busying himself with his plate again.

"So," Arthur says, belatedly remembering not to talk with his mouth full, "how is King Edgorn? Any news of him and Iliath back in Ele?"

Arthur certainly isn't complaining that Edgorn hasn't joined them yet. These days of peaceful travel with Lasilas, coming into his role as the Silver Hammer, the easy companionship with his squadron and fellow captains are almost enough to make Arthur forget that Edgorn exists. Minus the battles, these days are better than the ones before Edgorn walked into that tent and ordered them to make him emperor.

Lasilas laughs and talks with his mouth full. "Oh, gods, let us not discuss such matters on a night as fine as this. Save those headaches for the morrow. Tell me more about your art. Frankly, I'm ashamed that I've had you in my army for three years, two of those as a captain, but I didn't know this about you."

"There's not much to tell," Arthur laughs nervously, shoveling a forkful of spiced rice with herbs into his mouth. It's hot, banishing any cold he might feel from the northern night, and warms him to his core in more ways than one. The brandy is certainly helping with that.

"I would rather hear about you, if I'm honest. We know so little about you." He hesitates, but decides that if Lasilas is going to be

such a blatant flirt, then the least Arthur can do is show that he
cares. He's just afraid of showing that he cares too much.

Arthur adds, "I know so little about you. I'm honored that
you told me how you ended up here, but I want to hear the jovial
stories. The funny ones. The ones that make you blush, from before
or after your exile. Can you do that?"

Lasilas doesn't smile, but he doesn't dismiss Arthur outright
either. He's studying him, head tilted, like he's curious. "Alright."

Lasilas has stories to tell. Stories of his sister when they were
children, his fuzzy memories of the six years before they were
separated. The eyes they got from their mother, a fierce woman
from House Catiana who always knew her children were destined
for the warrior's path, even before their readings.

Their other parent was a person of true kindness who could
thaw the most frozen soul and turn them kind with a look. Augusta
and Lasilas received schooling from them before they were
separated and went off to train with their respective houses.

Arthur soaks up every bit of the Ilyakan upbringing he missed
out on, though he knows he would've hated being separated from
his mother. He laughs along with Lasilas at a story of his childhood
mischief, and Arthur puts his chin in his hand when Lasilas speaks
of the day he and Augusta chose their patron gods. It's rare for
Ilyakans to take a patron god that's not the crest of their House, but
it happens. Arthur probably wouldn't have conformed. He'd have
been bedazzled by choice.

Lasilas smiles and loses himself in his memories. His eyes dance
and glitter. He's never looked more beautiful, his armor forgotten
and hung on the wall, his fine green clothes almost enough to make
Arthur forget they're in wartime.

Simply put, it's the best evening Arthur has ever had in his life.

When Lasilas finally runs out of words and long after they've
run out of food, Arthur leans back in his chair, sated and content

and much more relaxed thanks to it all—not just the brandy. "You said you had something you wanted to give me?"

Lasilas smiles. "Oh, yes." He gets up and rifles through a drawer in his writing desk, returning with something hidden in his hand. His eyes are sparkling gems when he sits back down, and Arthur is simply caught in his light.

Lasilas leans forward, close enough for their breath to touch, and tucks a yellow tulip as bright as the sun behind Arthur's ear. His fingers are warm when they brush his skin, and Arthur has a feeling that if he had hair longer than a dusting Lasilas' fingers would linger in it.

Arthur's eyes dart to the small mirror Lasilas has hanging from a hook across the tent, and softly gasps at the sight of the flower against his dark skin. "Oh, Lasilas, it's beautiful. Thank you."

Lasilas grins like a schoolboy.

A knock comes at the tent frame, followed by Callum's voice. "General? There's a messenger here for you."

Lasilas sighs. "Yes. Let them in. What is it?"

The messenger struts in and leans down to whisper the message in his ear, but Lasilas waves that off. "My companion will just be hearing it anyway. Might as well save us the breath."

A sigh. "King Edgorn demands your army's presence a few towns further up the river, sir." The messenger pauses. "I got the impression that he was not happy with your slow progress."

Lasilas sighs heavily. "He wants me there to start another battle?"

"Yes, sir. He says he will be held up with Her Highness Iliath only a few days longer. He has almost put down her rebellion in its entirety—in his words, sir, 'only a matter of fucking time.'"

"Thank you." Lasilas presses a coin into the messenger's hand. "Tell him that I'll be on my way at first light. Find food and a bed somewhere, be in no rush to hurry back."

"Thank you, sir," the messenger says with a grin. "I've half a mind to work for you, with that kindness."

"I'd be happy to have you. Might be the kick in the ass old Edgorn needs."

Arthur chokes on laughter.

"Hell," Lasilas says, still firing on, "does he repay you as he does me?"

"Um," the messenger says, "my wages are fine, sir, I really don't know—"

"Oh, I wasn't talking about wages," Lasilas says, and slaps the messenger's arm. "Be on your way."

Arthur ducks his head to hide a wild grin. With displays like that, it's a mystery how Lasilas doesn't know he draws loyalty everywhere he goes.

"One night," Lasilas mutters. "Can I not have one night to myself for some rest without thinking of gods damned—" He cuts off with a bitter sigh, a weary smile. "I'm sorry, Arthur, truly. Duty calls."

"Of course," Arthur says. "Please let me know if I can help with anything."

Something softens and swirls in Lasilas' eye like fresh paint, like a thousand colors mixing together under Arthur's brush. "You are a god in a sea of foolish men," he says, squeezing Arthur's hand and lingering over it before departing.

Arthur leaves the tent and is hit with the force of stares immediately. He walks hesitantly out, weathering loud whispers of *he's got a flower,* and *is that yellow? The rumors are true, I see,* and, *I'm jealous, but I'm not sure of who,* as he walks.

It's just a flower, Arthur wants to say to them all. *Why is that a big deal?*

But everywhere he goes, the eyes follow him. It's a sensation he never thought he'd have to get used to. These stares feel more innocent than the stares he got for his armor, or even after revealing his identity as the Silver Hammer.

Finally, Arthur gives in and stops next to Dainthi, who's sitting beside a fire. He raises his arms. "For the love of the gods, what is it, Dainthi? Why is everyone staring at me like I've grown a second head?"

She shakes her head, smiling. "Nothing, dear friend, nothing at all. Ah. Just—ah. Carry on. Forget any of us did anything?"

"Right," he says, unconvinced and more confused than ever. At least he looks pretty.

CHAPTER EIGHT

Of all the places Herra might've expected to find Augusta, singing on a balcony in the Blue Feathers house was not one.

Guessing Augusta had a hidden desire to sing had been mostly a shot in the dark. Until this moment, Herra wasn't sure that shot was worth the humiliation and scrutiny of Augusta's gaze. Now she can say unequivocally, it was.

Herra hangs back in the doorway, watching with her arms folded as Augusta's wavy hair flutters in the breeze, loose around her shoulders and curling at the ends. It catches the midday sunlight, varying shades of red and gold and bronze in different lights. Herra blinks, and Augusta is a thousand people all at once.

Her jacket is red today, the boldest and finest one from her new collection, puffed sleeves embroidered in shimmering gold beads. She turns halfway toward Herra, and yes, there is the white pansy crest, so stark and out of place. Augusta touches a palm to it.

And her voice—her voice is as soft and light as the summer breeze that carries her hair, breaking on certain notes. She thinks she's totally alone.

She's singing in Ilyakan, a song with tones of distinct sorrow and longing which Herra feels all too keenly in her bones. The yearning for home. Though they think of two different homes, images of the appointers' court in a small mountaintop village worm their way into Herra's thoughts.

Tears sting her eyes as she remembers her last glimpse of it. The blood, the bodies she tried desperately to avoid seeing, the way she never found her father's. She remembers all too clearly watching a white cloaked Grimash throw him over a cliff while she stood still in shock. Her cheek bled and bled after one of the attackers hit her with a rock.

She wonders if it looks the same as she left it, or if earth has reclaimed their buildings and temples and gardens like the appointers were never there at all.

Herra is tempted to leave Augusta in peace, but she came here for a reason. She'll give Augusta just another minute to finish her song.

Funny—Herra can't remember ever being patient for anyone like this. Patience does not run in her bones, not since the slaughter. She gets things on her terms, her time, period. Apparently Augusta is an exception.

Finally, Augusta finishes the mourning song and ducks her head. She appears to be praying.

Herra walks out and slowly claps, just as Augusta did for her that day she was shooting. "You're very good," she says. "Never heard anyone sing like that. Certainly not the theater bastards."

Augusta's freckled cheeks turn red. She nods faintly, lost in her own grief.

"Come on," Herra says, more gently than she intended. She almost reaches for Augusta's silken sleeve to yank her over, but stops at the last second. Augusta is not a dog. Augusta can control herself. Herra will not force her to follow. "There's something I want to show you. Let's take a walk."

"Always going somewhere, doing something," Augusta mumbles, wiping her eyes. Ah. Herra wonders how she didn't see. "Do you know the meaning of rest—" Augusta's fingers fall, and her eyes widen. "You're wearing purple."

Fuck. Herra forgot that in her usual sleepy state of waking, she stumbled to her wardrobe and remembered Augusta's words from the seaside walk. Her half-awake mind is far different from her fully waking mind.

"Yes," she says, puffing out her chest. Might as well own it. The jacket is the same style as her blue uniforms, as Augusta has dubbed them. This is a birthday gift from Tasian she never got around to wearing, with sleeves slightly more detailed and shorter in length. The color is a bright, dark purple, and she has to admit it looks good against her brown skin.

Augusta grins, and Herra does not like that look. "You're wearing purple."

Herra scowls, shaking her bangs out of her eyes. "Yes. Got a problem with that?"

Augusta's fingers run over the beading on Herra's collar. Their gazes lock. "None at all."

Herra finds she can breathe normally again only when Augusta puts some space between them. "Now, where is it you're taking me?"

Right. Yes. "Follow," Herra says, folding her hands behind her back and walking inside.

"I am not a dog!"

Herra smiles despite herself.

She purposefully takes the less used hallways in the house, not wanting to endure the sly looks her folks give her. Thankfully she doesn't need to think much about the route. She and Tasian refurbished this rundown house from the ground up, so she knows its layout better than her own mind. "Maybe tonight you could make yourself useful and entertain our dinner guests by singing."

"First of all, no, I am not your show dog. Second of all, since when do you have dinner guests? Makes you sound distinguished and pompous."

Herra rolls her eyes. Augusta knows how much she hates being compared to foppish nobility and has exploited that more times than Herra can count.

"We're inviting members of the Blue Feathers who don't live in this house, people we contract, people like Ryn and my seamstress—"

"Ooh, I'll be having fun tonight, then."

"As well as members of the Ruby Rings," Herra swiftly finishes. "I'm attempting to be civil under Zera's contract." The contract she hasn't yet taken advantage of.

Augusta barks a laugh. "And I thought she was doing you the favor! I say it's interesting that you haven't exploited her end of the bargain utterly and ruthlessly to the ends of hell. Just think of the possibilities—you could make her crawl at your feet and lick your floors after your boots have touched them. You could make her lick the floor after *my* boots have touched them. You could make her call you the queen of the world, above all others. You could—"

"Yes, yes," Herra says. "I get it."

"She really offered herself on a platter for our revenge, and I'm ashamed of both of us for not taking advantage yet." Augusta's voice grows higher and more excited with each word. "I believe you promised me some fantasies of torture?"

"Psychological torture. No blood drawn."

"Ah, damn. Still good though." Augusta seems to have abandoned her plan of taking Zera's head from her shoulders for now.

Herra leads her down the set of back stairs she uses when she's not in the mood to be hounded by questions and vying looks. They lead into the streets, where Herra takes several winding turns around sharp corners. Across alleyways worn with grime, up short flights of steps.

Augusta groans, "Good gods, Ancient, where are we going?"

"I'm not trying to get you lost or make you disoriented, I promise. The route is honestly this complicated."

"I'm sure you could've hopped rooftops and it would've been faster than this," Augusta grumbles, but keeps following all the same. Finally, after an age of climbing spiral steps in a dark stairwell, Herra emerges into sunlight again. She and Augusta stand at the top of a building, an old clocktower where the clock no longer works and no one ever bothered to fix it. Herra likes it better that way.

She leans on the railing, glad of the overhead shade provided by a suspended roof. She peers out over the city. "This is the highest point in Mitzi," she says. "I came here often when I was new in this city, still building my reputation, exploring anything and everything. This place helped me think."

Augusta comes up beside her, mirroring her position. "Is that why you brought me here and utterly wore out my calves? To think?"

Herra shrugs. "If that's what you'd like this to be, then yeah. Fine. Come here any time, I won't stop you. Humor me today."

For once, Augusta keeps her snide comments to herself and obeys.

"Do you see that group of fishing folk, over there? Down by the docks?" She points before Augusta can say something like *there's dozens of fishing folk*. "The woman in the middle is new to the group, and the others don't take her seriously. They give her the menial labor—carrying gear and the like—and laugh when she complains of fatigue and pain.

"However, the leader is on my payroll to give me a cut of his profits in exchange for a monopoly on this section of the harbor. I send someone to go remind him of his place every once in a while. I'm going to send Florence tomorrow, and then we'll see how he treats that woman."

She points next to two figures dancing in the streets, drawing the attention of a crowd. "You see those grimaces on their faces? That's because they're two of the nastiest, meanest fighters on my side of Mitzi. See their muscles, those scars? They were causing a ruckus in my territory, fighting each other every day, threatening any who got in their way or tried to get them to stop.

"I issued them an order: work together or get thrown out of the city. Or get killed by my poison darts from this very rooftop the next time I saw them fighting."

"Why were they fighting?" Augusta asks.

Herra shrugs. "It was one of those cases where it'd been so long since the fighting began, neither of them could really remember why it started. I gave them some suggestions over how they could begin to trust each other, and dancing was one. A good collaborative activity, you know? They looked at me like I was crazy, but of all my offers, that one seems to be the most palatable, and look where we are."

She lets silence ring in the air as they watch those two stumble through a few twirls, argue over who should be dipped. "Whenever they have the urge to fight each other, they dance. When they have the urge to fight together, they come to me, and there's always someone I need to teach a lesson. They do it for me.

"And that pair of women over there." She gestures again. "They've been lovers since before I was born. They have been working together all that time. They're in my pocket, too, but they won't fight anyone they don't believe deserves it. They've always worked for hire, but they've always reserved the right to turn away any job they don't want, and any employer. They're loyal to none but justice itself.

"They help me defend my borders and intimidate terrorizers. My own personal mercenaries. When I was building up my empire, they were instrumental to helping me keep anything I won. I paid them well when I started getting successful, and now we're thick as thieves. They'll be at the dinner tonight."

She looks at Augusta. "I could point out to you a thousand other people like this, but the message will be the same. Just think. If there are this many problems and conflicts and little relationships in Mitzi—*Mitzi*, not even the biggest city in Mariosa—imagine how many there are across the entire continent. Unfathomable, right?"

Augusta says nothing.

"I've been thinking about what you said that day at Ryn's tavern," Herra says. "I didn't have a good answer for you then, but I do now. It's been right in front of us." She gestures out at the city. Her kingdom.

"This is why the continent needs emperors. Sometimes, all that people need to gather together is a force to rally behind. One person, or a council of people. In this case, me. Without me to look in on people and make sure they're behaving and keeping the peace, the city would turn to anarchy. In the continent's case, the emperor has that job. Someone to bring everyone together."

Augusta smiles. "The continent has done pretty well for itself in the last six years without an emperor."

"In some ways," Herra admits. "Not this war, though. Edgorn is vying for the emperorship the old way, through conquest. No one wants that, and now look at what's happening. His army is charging through Delain now that they've stormed and conquered Coromoda."

"Look at those people," Augusta says, pointing to a group of members from a smaller Mitzi gang known as the Black Chains. They're Herra's allies in the sense that they like her better than Zera and they run their stolen liquor through the same port. The friendliness ends there. "Don't they fear getting swallowed up by the larger gangs and lost in the mix?"

"Sometimes. But I have given them my blessing to do as they will as long as they stay away from my business. They pledged the same. And even if we did have a disagreement that demanded bloodshed, they defend themselves and defend themselves well. They never have to worry."

"Not everyone is as generous or forgiving as you." Augusta meets Herra's eyes unflinchingly. "Emperors have done nothing but fuck Ilyakans over for centuries. Ricarda the Second let his folks kill any Ilyakans who so much as breathed at them wrong. Empress Marcella Anton put us at the frontlines of her wars to die first, to preserve Mariosan blood.

"Alexandra of Dimas conquered us and then forgot about us, as most of them do. We had none of our own rights. Our princes and our gods were overlooked, our temples destroyed. We were just pawns in their eyes. That's all we have ever been—pawns with a pass they want for trading. You. Your emperors, the ones your family appoints."

"That's why House Grimash was asked to murder my family? Because we appoint the emperors that fuck you over, ruin your lives, and scrape your armies into ruin. Without us, there'd be no more emperors, no more trouble, nothing more to fear. Is that right?"

Augusta is silent.

Herra frowns. "Be honest. Are you here to kill me? Wipe away the line of the Ancients once and for all?"

Augusta's face contorts into anger so quickly it might be humorous in any other circumstance. "You think that after all of this, all of my honesty, I would lie? About this?" Her voice is scraped raw, and the depths of her eyes speak of nothing but pain. Herra remembers the song Augusta was singing, its haunting notes of sadness.

"Grimash," Herra says, grabbing her wrist when she goes to step away. "I didn't believe it. I didn't want to believe it. I never thought you lied, honest. I just had to check every box."

"Why does every box seem to end up with me as the villain?" Augusta yells, and it takes them both by such sudden shock that the words ring out uncontested, hanging in the breeze with the sound of birds chirping.

"If you are the villain, then so am I," Herra whispers, slowly letting her wrist go. "For what it's worth, I'm sorry for all that Ilyakans have suffered at our hands."

"That apology is not yours to give," Augusta says, "but I appreciate the intent." She sighs and lets the wind blow her hair. Herra is mesmerized.

"There's something I need to tell you," Augusta says quickly. "My hands are clean of blood. I never killed any of your family. I was the only one in my squad who refused to raise her weapon." She grows the strength to look Herra in the eye. "I am innocent."

She whispers the words, but they're thunder on the breeze.

After several flabbergasted moments, Herra asks, "Why didn't you tell me?"

Augusta shrugs. "Didn't think you'd believe me. Didn't want to start a fight. Didn't want to disrupt—I don't know, whatever this is." She gestures between them.

"Why did you think that would disrupt things instead of strengthening them?"

"I don't know," Augusta snaps. "You had this fixed idea of me and my crimes in your head. So do I. I tried to put myself in your place, and figured that perspective wouldn't be easy to change if I was you. Apparently I'm wrong."

She looks up with a thin sliver of hope.

"You're wrong." Herra hardly knows what to say. "Augusta, I'm sorry."

"You have nothing to apologize for. We both belong to institutions we didn't invent, and we hurt each other because of it. I say that we have to try and be better instead. You apologizing to me about this is like if you told me that Zera wasn't the reason Las was banished, so I shouldn't feel guilty about letting the fox into the henhouse."

Augusta musters up a smile. "I understand. And, also, I understand what you mean about the emperors. The rest of the continent is a plate of fools who need someone to govern them. I just wish Ilyaka didn't have to be a part of it."

"I will make sure the emperor I choose has Ilyakan sympathies, then."

Augusta shakes her head. "No, that's not good enough. We want our freedom from the matters of all emperors for the rest of time. Nothing more, nothing less."

Herra doesn't know how she's going to manage that, but she'll try. "Noted. We can...we can go back down now."

Augusta chuckles. "You should be glad I'm not afraid of heights. Can I go back to practicing my stunning vocals for my performance tonight?"

"No, I'm not done with you."

"Ooh, Mistress, grant mercy."

Herra tugs Augusta down the spiral steps with a grip on her wrist that gradually turns into a grip of her hand, both of them laughing and shrieking at how close they come to tumbling over the railings. This is definitely dangerous, and Herra's never felt more alive.

"What windy balcony are you taking me to now?" Augusta laughs, bumping into every passerby.

"One you're quite familiar with."

They end up back at the house eventually, though Herra admits to getting lost because she's too busy listening to Augusta's carefree laugh.

Augusta's grin finally fades when they stop in front of the dark cell where they met. "Ancient," she says warningly.

"Relax, Grimash. I'm not putting you back in shackles. I have someone else occupying them today."

CHAPTER NINE

Herra pushes open the door, nodding to the guards on either side as it shuts behind them both. She goes through much the same routine she did with Augusta. Take off the sword, prop it up, unsheathe a knife. Except this time, she watches Augusta do the same.

"Zera," Augusta greets, glancing at Herra with hungry eyes. "I see I spoke too soon about the treaty."

Herra smiles. She had this arranged while they went to the clocktower, a nice surprise for Augusta to come back to.

"Augusta," comes Zera's voice from the darkness. "Thought I'd be seeing you sooner than this."

"Soon you'll be wishing you'd never seen me at all. I'm going to make you regret ever introducing yourself to me." Augusta's face turns a shade paler behind the freckles. "Is Zera even your real name, you lying bastard?"

Zera smirks. "Find out for yourself. Touch me if you dare."

Herra touches Augusta's wrist with a warning look. The last thing they need is Augusta breaking the contract in the heat of the moment. If there's ever a place it would happen, it would be here, with Zera entirely at her mercy.

She is not a dog.

Herra circles the chained Zera, who's staring up at them with all the dignity she has. Herra touches the tip of her knife to the underside of Zera's chin, drawing those blue eyes up. So different

191

from Augusta's in every way, cold where Augusta's are hot and fiery with passion, calculated and quiet while Augusta is explosive and loud.

"You're going to tell us why you slaughtered House Catiana and then fucked off. Why you even bothered to bewitch Augusta when you could've just slipped in and killed them in the night. You're going to tell us everything, and you're going to give her"—she nods to Augusta—"an explanation for all her years of anguish."

Zera laughs. "That is something I will not even tell you under torture, which is strictly forbidden."

"No, bloodshed is forbidden. There's a difference. Your mind is narrowed by the possibilities of violence to break people. For example—" Herra runs her finger instead of her knife down Zera's shoulder line, through her hair, tilting her head this way and that. She's beautiful. "We could leave you here to rot. We could make sure you never see sunlight again beyond this little window in this little cell. You said you would serve me under any circumstances I see fit." Herra smiles nastily. "I see these as fit."

"That was on the condition of no harm toward me and mine. Keeping me in a dark cell for all of eternity will raise some questions."

"You said no violence," Augusta cuts in, stepping forward to let Zera get a good look at her. It's terribly fitting that she's wearing red today. Herra wishes she could say it was planned. "You should plan your contracts better, Zera. Seems that you used up all of your brains in Ilyaka. If you are even Ilyakan."

Zera's face becomes something ugly, showing her true colors. She spits out a series of foreign words. Augusta's breath hitches in response.

"What is it? What did she say?" Herra asks.

"An Ilyakan proverb," Augusta says, "twisted to say that I'm a—well. Surely you can glean the meaning." She looks at Herra with ghostly eyes. "It's her way of proving that she is Ilyakan, I think."

"You don't know that. She could've studied your culture somewhere. Don't let her manipulate you."

Zera laughs. "All this time, Gus, and you're still not over me?"

"Don't call me that," Augusta growls.

Zera still grins. "What? You don't like hearing the name your brother used for you? I still remember how he looked at you—like you were his world. Your poor, sweet, sad, pathetic brother, the filthy rat who never should've been in House Catiana in the first place—"

Augusta lunges. Herra sees it coming and quickly grabs her wrists. "Don't. She's just trying to provoke you into breaking the contract."

"I know." Augusta struggles on instinct before wrenching free. "Doesn't make me want to break her face any less."

"I know," Herra says patiently. "But there are other ways to get what we want, ways that will reverse our roles. Please."

Augusta is silent, and Herra takes her cue.

"Why did you kill the members of House Catiana?"

Zera shrugs. "Because I felt like it."

Herra sighs. "Okay. I was going to save this for later on, but I'm not in the mood to do you any favors." She steps outside for a moment to take a small bucket of water from Gwyn. "Augusta, hold her down?"

Augusta's eyes light up. "I'd rather be the one to hold the bucket, if you don't mind."

"Not at all."

Not quite fear—something more like apprehension—flashes through Zera's eyes for the first time as Herra goes behind her and pulls her to the ground, holding tightly to her bound arms just in case. After patting her down for hidden weapons, she gives the go ahead to Augusta.

"The first of many revenges," Augusta vows before pouring it all onto her face. Herra watches Zera jerk up, try to jerk out of the way, but Herra holds her firm. Zera wheezes and coughs, chokes, and a little smirk makes its way onto Augusta's face that charges every nerve in Herra's body. She feels like she can't breathe herself, but it's the good kind of danger. They lock eyes once, and Herra smirks in turn.

When every last drop of water has been emptied onto Zera's face, Herra says, "No blood drawn, see? No violence. Everything is just fine."

Zera looks at them both with burning hatred. "My Rings will be hearing of this. This will not go unpunished."

"Maybe, but then they'll also be hearing about how their leader contracted herself to the every whim of their greatest rival."

Zera has no answer for that.

"Tell us," Augusta says. "You owe me this, if you will give nothing else. Tell me why you did it. Did me or my brother or House Catiana commit some offense against you?"

Zera's fate seems to dawn on her in cold hard truth for the first time. She doesn't look up as she speaks. "This was never about you, Augusta. You were just a means to an end. It was Lasilas I needed."

Augusta goes perfectly still, and Herra braces in case she needs to intervene again. But Augusta keeps her temper just as Herra asked. "What did you need of Lasilas, then?" she asks too lightly, too casually to be genuine.

"My employer needed him driven out of Ilyaka, lost and desolate and vulnerable," Zera says. "I had the freedom to pick the method."

"Who was your employer?" Herra asks, pouncing on the slip.

Zera laughs. "That is a name I will sooner die than give you, for to give it would be death anyway."

"Well, you're going to end up dead either way," Herra says. "Your choice about which way."

"That would be breaking the contract."

"I don't give a fuck if your death starts ten wars," Augusta growls. "I want to know more about why you apparently needed my brother desolate and vulnerable and alone." Horror dawns on her face. "You wanted to get him exiled that whole time. There was no purpose to the deaths of the princes."

"Finally, you use your mind." Herra is pleased that Zera's voice is so destitute itself, quiet with defeat. Herra wonders if she's ever been defeated in her life.

Herra is almost too slow to place herself between Augusta and Zera when Augusta lunges for her that time. This isn't because of provocation, this is calculated. Herra can hardly blame her, but she ends up bearing the blow Augusta meant for Zera.

"Shit," Augusta says, and winces as Herra wipes her cheek. Her fingers come back bloody. "Sorry. I meant what I said, dammit. I don't care if it starts ten wars, I want this bastard to get what she deserves."

Herra whispers, "She's never getting out of this cell alive, don't you worry about that. She won't be alive to let anyone know about the contract or any breaches of it. But let's try to get some more information out of her first before I let you beat her up, okay?"

Herra needs Zera pliant. As long as she still has hope that no violence will be done, she'll open up to them.

Augusta grumbles, "You're no fun," but shakes out her fists and complies. Herra steps out to ask for more water.

Herra's suspicions are confirmed as Augusta pours the water the second time: Zera has probably never suffered a day in her life, never had to own up to the consequences of anything she's ever done. "Who is your boss?" Augusta roars, her face something feral, something furious. Herra's heart rate spikes again at thought of what she might be like in battle, in full Golden Chisel regalia with a true weapon in her hand.

"Edgorn," Zera sobs. "Edgorn, Edgorn, dammit!"

Augusta and Herra exchange glances. "Explain," Herra says when the water runs out.

Zera sputters and coughs, but Herra holds her all the tighter. "He paid me to drive Lasilas out of Ilyaka in a way no one would think was abnormal."

"Why?"

"He needed him for this war. He needed an Ilyakan on his side. Someone who knew how to get in and navigate the terrain. Someone who would know where House Catiana was, so that Edgorn could go and conquer it."

All this time, Edgorn's been planning this bid for the emperorship. "How did he get Lasilas to work for him?" Augusta asks, desperate for the answer Herra knows has been bugging her most. Why would her honorable brother work for such an odious emperor?

"I don't know," Zera sobs. "Edgorn only told me what I needed to know, and I don't know what happened to Lasilas after I was done."

"Of course you don't," Augusta growls, and this time Herra doesn't stop it as she cracks into Zera's face.

As Zera tries to recover, covered in water and blood and still held tightly down, Augusta says, "You know, it's sad. Whether you die at our hands or we send you to die at Edgorn's, no one will miss you. There's not one person in this world who loves you. I pity you."

Herra thinks it's just one of Augusta's methods of revenge before she feels Zera freeze up, plain as day.

"You do have someone," Augusta laughs. "Silly me. You had to be birthed from someone. You had to learn all the moves you used on me with someone. Tell me about her. Is she pretty? Is she missing you? Does she know the truth?"

Zera says nothing, and nothing shows on her face.

"I hope she was wise enough to move on from you in the time you've been away, assuming she's from the north like all of us." Augusta tilts her head, musing, and her hair catches the sunlight coming in from the small window. "Or maybe it's not a lover, but a sibling. A sister? A brother?"

After each word, they both watch Zera's face, and only after the word brother does she have any reaction. She tenses again, just slightly, relaxing too quickly to try and recover.

"My, you're a genius, Augusta," Herra says. "Smarter than I gave you credit for."

Augusta grins. "So, confess." She taps Zera's cheeks with the sword she keeps at her side. "Who is this brother of yours?"

Zera's eyes are icy and closed off. Hatred is the only thing to burn through. No, that's not quite right—hatred with a hint of sorrow, of longing.

"Did you get him killed in your typical carelessness? Your failure to care about anyone and anything but yourself?" Augusta props Herra's sword over her shoulder and stands tall, shaking out her hair. Seeing her slightly sweating, slightly bloody, Herra starts sweating too.

"Fine, fuck it," Zera yells, straining with all her might against Herra's hold. "You're never going to let me out of here? Fine. Any circumstance." She smiles nastily at Herra. "His name is Jona, and he's spending life in prison for my crime."

All three of them go quiet, then Augusta laughs. "Damn, you've been fucking up people's lives for a long time, haven't you? What was the crime?"

Zera glares with hate, and with purpose. "You can douse me in water, cut me a thousand times, but I will never give you more of that than what I already have."

"Sweetheart, you gave me your brother's name. Nothing noteworthy."

"Mm. And don't be so quick to say you won't break," Herra adds. "Have you ever been burned in your life before, Zera?"

No answer.

"Like hell I'm going to pass up an opportunity to douse you again," Augusta says with a shrug, stepping out for more water. Herra doesn't know when she started trusting Augusta to roam on her own, but she tries to think of the last time she shadowed Augusta through every step of the house's halls. She is confined to Herra's territory through the honors system and the watchful eyes of the Feathers, but she hasn't attempted to violate that rule since the start of their acquaintance.

"I am going to give you a chance," Herra whispers to Zera softly. "You can tell me all that you know right now, and I'll talk her into giving you a quick death. It's far more than you deserve." She doesn't add that she aims to keep Zera here a while, leaching information out of her when she needs it. Herra's new pet prisoner. Especially now that she knows Zera is mixed up with Edgorn, and that this war has been planned years in advance.

She'll have much to write Leonidas about, especially considering he mentioned a Jona in his first letters. A prisoner being kept in a cage. He described how it disturbed him, the one flaw he could find in Ricarda V. Poor boy doesn't even know he's in love yet.

What was it that Jona was locked up for? Herra racks her brain, wishing she had time to go fetch the letter from her desk.

Before Augusta comes back—gods know why she's taking so long, maybe she's chatting up a guard and boasting about the torture—it dawns. Herra grins.

"Jona...this wouldn't happen to be the same Jona that's locked up in the Mariosan royal court for killing the emperor, would it?"

The way Zera goes still is her answer. Herra laughs. "Sweetheart, you really need to work on your reactions. For someone in your field, I'm surprised you haven't learned more self-control. Grimash, get in here!"

"I know, I know," Augusta sighs as she comes back in, lugging another pail of water. "I was in the middle of a dilemma about which of your lovely associates I am going to spend the night with after the party—or all three. I wasn't expecting you to be so eager. I thought I was the one thirsty for revenge." She grins and holds up the water bucket.

Herra sighs. "Augusta, this Jona, Zera's brother—he's imprisoned in Allicé for the crime of killing Emperor Ricarda the Fourth. That's Zera's crime, unless there's another mix up in this tangled mess."

Augusta's grin is slow and appreciative. "Killing an emperor, Zera? Admirable for an Ilyakan, but a shame if you made your brother take the blame and spend life in prison. It sounds like something you would do, though."

Zera thrashes in Herra's arms. "I did not make him do anything!" she growls. "He took the fall voluntarily. He never ratted me out."

Augusta shakes her head. "Six years, and you haven't broken him out. If you could pull off what you did with Lasilas, I know you could free your brother if you put your mind to it. Which means you don't want to put your mind to it."

Zera turns her head, sets her jaw. She still retains some pride, even after all this, even with her wet hair stuck to her neck. "It's better this way. This way, no one suspects me, and Jona doesn't have to suffer my company."

Augusta guffaws. "Selfish and using the oddest justifications to the end."

"Why did you do it?" Herra asks, her head spinning. In her arms is a woman the entirety of Mariosa and much of the continent would die to get their hands on. For six years, they've been blaming the wrong person.

"The same reason House Grimash killed your family," Zera growls. "Because emperors and Ilyaka do not mix, and they never should have."

Herra smirks, glad that she and Augusta went to the clocktower before this. Zera looks surprised that Herra isn't angry, that they're both so calm.

"Any other questions in this little interrogation?" she asks, tossing her hair.

"Are you that eager to die?" Herra asks, hoping the bluff won't be called. "Of course we have more questions. I'm sure Augusta has many of a personal nature, but I have not even begun questioning you about Ricarda the Fourth's murder, and your methods in the House Catiana murder. These kinds of secrets—as well as a confession from your lips before your head goes on a pike—can earn me thousands." And they would undoubtedly give Leonidas an edge at court, a bargaining chip with which to twist Ricarda around his finger.

She and Augusta exchange glances, wondering if it might be a better fate for Zera to spend the rest of her life in a prison cell in Jona's place. It would be the suffering she deserves.

"No, let me ask her a question," Zera says. "Augusta, darling, you know I only did what I had to. I never wanted to hurt you or Lasilas, but coin was coin. I never thought you'd hold a grudge this long. You're far from the first." She shrugs. "No hard feelings?"

Augusta's face contorts in grief and anguish, and finally she releases the words she's had in her mouth for years. Herra braces for the storm as it hits.

"No hard feelings? No hard feelings? I loved you!" she cries, explosive, shrill, and crazed. Her utter self. Her true self. "You were my world. I would've done anything for you. I gave you my trust, my heart, my body, the whole of myself, and what did you give me in return?

"A plate of lies I swallowed like poison. A wound I can never close. Exile for myself and the person dearest to me in the world. I left behind my home, my destined purpose, everything I have ever known, because of you. I lost everything because of you. You ripped out my heart. I have never been the same. No, you never meant to hurt me, because you never cared about me one way or the other. You heartless, greedy little bastard."

She pauses, probably wondering if Zera has anything to say for herself. In a hoarse voice, the broken Zera whispers, "I gave you freedom."

Augusta pulls back. Herra is at her side before she can overthink it, wrapping an arm around her shoulders so that her gaze is taken from Zera. She doesn't know why. It just feels right.

"Let's go," Herra whispers into her ear, holding Augusta close. "She's not going anywhere. We have all the time in the world to question her."

Augusta takes a long, shuddering breath, before nodding into Herra's chest. Herra's other hand starts stroking her back. "I will never forgive you, no matter how long you sit and rot," Augusta spits out, giving Zera one last long look before letting Herra lead her out of the room, the fresh bucket of water forgotten. Let Zera drink it if she likes—it won't do her any long term good. If she's smart, she'll suspect it of being poisoned.

None of the Blue Feathers say a word as the two pass, quiet and desolate. Herra's arm is still wrapped around Augusta's shoulders. They walk with oddly heavy footsteps to Herra's chambers, with the only sound the chirping of birds and the breeze through distant leaves.

Herra closes the door softly with a snick. Questions fill her head. Not just why Zera killed Ricarda IV, because her excuse is too flimsy for Herra to believe. Zera isn't as purehearted in her motives as Augusta.

There's also the question of why Zera gave herself over to Herra like game on a platter. She made it far, far too easy. Perhaps she only gave up those answers because she's not used to torture. By the sound of it, she's used to having others take her fall while she slips away free with money to boot, leaving broken hearts in her wake. Bastard.

Augusta collapses into the nearest chair to stare out the window.

Desperate not to let her spiral, Herra says, "I have something to show you. Something I'd like you to wear at the dinner tonight." They both have to change, covered in water and blood as they are. Herra's purple jacket is ruined. Her cheek still burns where Augusta punched her.

"How can anyone think of dinners at a time like this?" Augusta mumbles. Herra has seen her helpless, feral, furious, and agonized, but never deflated. And that is what she is now: deflated and exhausted in every way, from her limp sprawl across the chair to the dead look in her eyes. Herra guesses she's reliving old memories and comparing them against the new ones Zera put in her head.

"You're right," Herra says carefully. The last thing she wants right now is for Augusta to get mad and kick her out, though she'd have every right. Herra thought she was offering Augusta a prize on a plate with Zera captured, but she should've foreseen this side of it. "You don't have to come if you don't want to. There will be plenty more dinners for you to sing at, plenty more chances for you to bully me. You can make a mockery of everyone before spending the night in someone's bed."

When that gets not a word, Herra says, "I understand if it's hard."

"No," Augusta says, turning her head. Her eyes have some life at last, like a flowing waterfall in the sun. "You don't understand. You only understand a different kind of hardship, your own kind. Not mine. Just as I do not understand yours, and I will never be able to atone for what my people took from you. But we can help each other."

Herra nods. "Wear it, never wear it, go, don't go, I don't care. I just want you to see what I got for you. Come here."

Augusta's footsteps, a sound Herra has grown accustomed to hearing behind her the last few months, follow her further into the room. Herra pulls back the sheet that's been hiding the item on a hanger, the blue doublet from the shop that day by the seaside.

Augusta gasps, approaching the shirt like it's a dangerous weapon requiring mindfulness. Her finger traces paths through the embroidery on the breasts and the beading. They fall still when they land on the white pansy flower crest, sitting on the left breast pocket like all of Augusta's custom-made clothes. Her eyes land back on Herra. "You—you were serious?"

"About getting it? Yeah, of course. But you don't have to go, and you don't have to sing."

Augusta looks at her like she's the most mystifying, astonishing sight in the world. It's unnerving. She sticks out her arm, palm up. Herra, more than a little confused, meets her offer and lays her wrist on top.

Augusta's eyes shine with tears.

Herra smiles. "This over a shirt. You Ilyakans must be the most boring people—"

Augusta throws her arms around Herra's shoulders, drawing her close. Herra is shocked into silence for a few flabbergasted moments before wrapping her arms tentatively around Augusta's waist, breathing in the scent of her hair. Wildflowers. The soap they keep in the house. She's warm and soft, so close like this.

"Thank you," Augusta says, pulling back. "I, uh—sorry for that."

"No, don't worry. I keep my word." Herra watches the way Augusta runs her hands over the shirt again, the utter joy and awe on her face. She tries to contend with the warmth in her own chest. She got Augusta to look like that again.

"You will have to drag me out of it," Augusta vows, turning it over and gasping softly at the matching detail on the back of the neck, the lapels that could fold up into a collar when it's cold. "I will wear it every time I am seen in public."

Herra grins, taking a seat in one of the chairs, setting down a tray with a pair of drinks for them both. "You did well with Zera," she says. "Come here, have a drink. Let's celebrate. I have a bit of time before Tasian comes hunting my ass for sport for leaving them with all the work for tonight."

Augusta snorts, though she sits and accepts the offered glass. Fine whiskey, some of Herra's best, a gift from a merchant smuggling it through the harbor. She's been looking for an occasion to drink it. "How can you say that? I broke down crying like a green new soldier."

Herra wants to say, *you're tougher than anyone has any right to be in a situation like that. You have nothing to be sorry for. She's the only one in the wrong.*

What she says is, "At least you didn't go berserk and slit her throat. I count that a win, Augusta."

Augusta goes quiet. "That's the first time you've ever used my name."

"Is it?" Herra truly hasn't noticed.

"Yes. It's always Grimash, if you call me by anything at all."

Herra thinks it over and realizes she's right.

"Well, Augusta," she says slowly, with purpose, "will you go to the dinner?"

Augusta's smile is sunlight, and Herra's breath floats away on the breeze. "Only if you wear something other than blue."

"I'll let you pick it out myself," Herra says, already regretting it, "if you sing."

Augusta throws her head back and laughs. "Get enough of these in me and I might." She throws back the whiskey and demands a refill.

Herra gives it. "Good job, Grimash."

Augusta rolls her eyes, though a smile breaks out on her face. "Fuck you, Ancient."

Herra smiles.

PART THREE

THE RING

CHAPTER ONE

Leonidas is regretting becoming Ricarda's lover—for Ricarda's sake.

Alessandro de Rege hasn't stopped yammering for the past five minutes, bouncing off the walls of the dressing room while they all wait for Antonia to get dressed. He's gone from waxing poetic about her to complaining about Ricarda's fondness for Leonidas after they booed him for the incessant chatter. This is little better.

"Ric never shuts up about you when you're gone. It's all, oh, Leo did this, and oh, Leo looked like that. By the sweet gods, I can't catch a break. My ear will fall off from boredom *and* disgust at this rate." Aless imitates retching.

Ric pulls Aless' hair, but Leonidas will not be distracted. His mouth curves into a slow smirk. Maybe this is better after all, if the look of sheer panic on Ricarda's face is any indication. "Oh? What does he say about me?"

Ricarda attempts to slap a palm over Aless' mouth, sitting behind him on a settee. Aless squirms out of his grip with a glare. "Why are you fighting me, you dimwitted man? You're just going to make him think you say vile things when he's gone!" He stands, ignoring the crash as Ricarda falls to the floor, having reached for Aless and counted on his weight being there to balance him.

Leonidas lets the groaning king of Mariosa pick himself up while Alessandro says in a poor imitation of Ric's voice, "Oh, Aless, you would never know my woes. His hair—soft as the grass beside a mountain stream, I tell you. His lips, like the sweetest drink I have ever sipped from, and his eyes, the most beautiful shade of brown, like mud in a pasture."

"I did not say that!"

Aless continues, "It's all mine, and I fear I will not survive the onslaught!" He flops back onto the long settee, brocaded gold covered in wine stains. He spreads his limbs, boneless as if exhausted, and heaves a great sigh. It's not hard for his eyes to take on the starry eyed affection Leonidas is all too familiar with in Ricarda. He takes comfort in the thought that Aless is thinking of someone else to conjure such a look. "And his hands, by gods, capable of—"

Ricarda tackles him, cutting off his words with a shouted curse that has no real heat. "Unhand me at once, you foul beast!" Aless shrieks.

"Only if you promise to shut up!"

"You should be an actor," Leo says, watching with amusement as they roll around on the settee that's definitely not meant for two, arguing incomprehensibly, "instead of a pianist."

"Bold and rather rude of you to assume I can't be both." Aless wriggles out of Ricarda's grip again, scrambling to his feet and attempting to salvage his hairdo. Leonidas is abruptly reminded that they're supposed to be getting ready for a ball instead of messing around like children.

Leonidas shoves him back into the vanity chair with a sigh, taking over the job of fixing his hair. "And a poet, too," Alessandro adds, gesturing again. He's never been able to sit still for more than a moment, and Leonidas gains sudden extraordinary sympathy for everyone who has had to attend him in his fidgety lifetime. "With skills aplenty as mine, it's a true wonder and a sin that my Antonia will not look my way!"

"Oh, now we've done it," Ricarda groans.

Ignoring him, Leo says, "What do you mean, a poet? You were quoting him, weren't you?"

Aless sniffs in offense, tilting his head just as Leo gets a lock of blond wrapped around his finger. "Why, good sir, you accuse me of plagiarizing? A good writer uses only the genius formed in his own mind, at the very least a paraphrase!"

Ricarda breaks in, "Can you plagiarize spoken—" but is cut off by Aless' loud gasp. Leo and Ric turn in tandem to see what Aless is seeing in the mirror, and both fall still at the sight.

Antonia stands at the foot of the stairs, smiling and clutching the skirts of her gown, hair done in braids more immaculate than any of the three of them could ever hope to do. As always, words evade Alessandro at sight of her despite his proclamation of skillful poetry.

Leo waits for Alessandro's obligatory flow of words, attempting to convince the smiling and twinkly eyed Antonia that she would know no greater joy than by his side. Instead, his mouth hangs open and his eyes shine, starry eyed and childlike. Leo stifles a laugh. He and Ricarda aren't *that* bad.

"Why was I fighting, indeed," Ricarda murmurs, and fakes retching himself.

Quiet enough that she won't hear, Aless shoots back, "You shut the fuck up."

"Are we ready?" Antonia asks.

"We still have a few more minutes," Ricarda says. "Gods, Ann, do you remember the waits during Father's reign?"

"He'd keep us cooped up in this room while he made his grand toasts and speeches. Didn't want us to steal his light." She folds her arms, making her look like a petulant child instead of the princess who could whip them all into shape, the woman who spends her days elbow deep in bloodied bodies learning with her master.

A knock comes at their dressing room door. "Come in," Ricarda says, pulling on a pair of golden evening gloves to match his half cloak. Underneath, he wears a white jacket with gold beads and pearls to contend with the cooling air.

It hangs loosely from his shoulders, and the dip it makes in the center of his chest, showing a hint of gold skin, draws Leonidas' eye. Unlike Aless with Antonia, he has the wisdom to keep his eyes on where he's walking lest he bump into a doorframe. He doesn't want to know how many injuries Aless has sustained while looking at Antonia.

In comes a messenger with a letter clutched in hand. "There's a letter for you, Lord Marquis," they say, bowing low over the letter. Leonidas plasters on a smile and a thanks. He's never received a letter from Herra in the presence of the others before, so he's never really had to formulate an excuse. He's always received her letters in his room. And this one is off schedule, too. Why?

"Who's that from?" Alessandro asks, predictably.

"Less," Antonia chides. "Leave him to his privacy."

Leo knows that if he doesn't answer, that will be even more suspicious, so he swallows a sigh and says, "Just a letter from an old friend down south. Nothing significant." It's the truth, anyway. He tucks it into his pocket and hopes they'll forget about it. He'll gladly endure more whining from Aless if that's what it takes.

"You don't mention friends often," Ricarda says casually enough that it proves he's not thinking seriously about it. Leo has no real cause to be worried. "You don't mention much of anything at all from your life down south. Am I not a charming enough conversationalist?"

"Your charm knows no bounds, my love," Leonidas says easily, raising protest from Aless and restoring the levity to the room. The boys go back to bickering, Ricarda whining about the banquet they're minutes from attending, but Antonia catches Leonidas' eye and holds it. She's always been ten times sharper than those two, and Leo has to watch out for her.

For now, he flashes her a friendly smile and takes her arm as they prepare to walk out. The boys take each other's.

For weeks, Ricarda has been bemoaning the diplomatic gatherings in Allicé for the biannual summit, but you would never know it as he steps out. He's greeted with cheers and waves, and offers the crowd a stunning smile in return. The perfect, golden king, fair and kind and young and handsome. Perfect on the outside. Leonidas is still trying to determine if he's as perfect on the inside.

When the noise dies down, Leonidas tears his wandering eyes from the fresco to listen as Ricarda says, "Welcome one, welcome all, to the golden court of Mariosa. It is my honor to host this summit, and I hope everyone here will have a fruitful and enjoyable visit that they can take back to their homes."

Leonidas looks out in the crowd and finds Coromodans, Delainians, Minyans, even the Ilyakan princes seated at a round table. He looks for Elens, but finds none. He wonders whose choice that was. If only Iliath could've shown up here to speak on behalf of her country, but she's busy fighting the war with her uncle. The greatest people are wanted in more than one place at once.

Ricarda waits while the translators convey his message to their employers. Leonidas is fighting the urge to pull out Herra's letter and read it right here. Why is she writing out of turn? Once every two weeks, they exchange updates. That was the deal. That's always been the deal. It's only been one week since her last letter.

Maybe she'll finally get around to telling him who companion precisely is. At least long distance, he can give her romantic advice without the immediate threat of her biting his head off.

He'll have to be extra patient, since the evenings when he used to pore over her letters are no longer a period of solitude. Being Ricarda's lover has upended his life, but he's used to the lack of privacy and free time when he's a royal's lover.

"I would rather be in the middle of the ocean than here, hosting them," Ricarda whispers to him once he's given his blessing for everyone to start eating. Negotiations and meetings and the like start officially tomorrow, so perhaps while Ricarda is locked in long meetings all day Leonidas will be able to put his attention on Herra.

Those meetings ensure that Ricarda will be insatiably needy in the evenings, unhappy till he gets Leonidas' hands on him, whether it's just for a hug after his long day or something more. Leonidas is rather fond of the clinginess, if he's honest, and fond of Ricarda's bed the size of this palace.

"It's only two weeks," Leo whispers back. "Then you'll get back your court of fools and vipers."

"I would hug a viper to trade for this."

"Focus, you two," Antonia hisses under her breath. "All kinds of eyes are on us that we're not used to. Ricarda, yes, we get it, you don't like being king, you wish you were anything else. Stow it."

Ricarda's expression sobers. "I never said I didn't like being king," he says.

"You have. Multiple times."

He waves it off. "I don't like *this*. All the foppish bullshit. I like leading. I like fighting when my name is called. I like helping people. I like having an impact. I like imagining my name on the library wall." He smiles. "A legacy as good as my father's. What I don't like is having to placate fools."

Emperor, Leonidas thinks, and smiles like a good little lover when the glowering Ilyakans look at the high table.

Dinner and conversation pass uneventfully. Before the dancing can start, Leonidas excuses himself and departs with a soft kiss that sets his heart fluttering. Feigning fatigue, he exits the ballroom early. Ricarda has more than enough to keep him occupied, and Leo frankly can't wait another moment to read Herra's letter.

Settling in his easy chair in his room, he unfolds the letter. There's no blood on it, no stain of tears. Why the urgency?

Fingers shaking, he starts reading, fearing the worst still.

Leonidas,

I urge you to find information about the death of Ricarda IV, particularly related to who I mentioned before—Zera Musiek. Leonidas, she's the sister of that prisoner you mentioned. Zera admitted under torture to me and my companion that she's the murderer of Ricarda IV, not her brother. He took the fall and the blame. It was her choice not to go back for him.

Why did she do it? Because emperors have screwed over Ilyaka in the past, apparently, and she wanted revenge. I'm not sure I believe her motives, but it'll have to do for now.

I don't know how much you know about the slaughter of House Catiana in Ilyaka years ago, but Zera is responsible for that, too. My companion and I have known this for weeks, but Zera told us the why at last.

Edgorn—yes, that Edgorn—asked her to do it so that Prince Lasilas would wind up with Edgorn. Edgorn wanted an Ilyakan on his side once he started his war against the continent. Convoluted, I know. But it's the truth. All of this has been in the making far longer than we suspected. Keep your wits about you. Try to uncover the truth from your end.

Best of luck,

Herra

Leonidas sets the letter down and puts his head in his hands. Since when has Herra cared about the intricacies of Ilyakan politics—hell, about Mariosan politics, or about Edgorn's past beyond whether he's fit for emperor or not? Since when has she expected him to get involved like this?

They never do more than their jobs require. Keep their heads down, do their work, and get out. Nothing like this. She appoints the emperors after he judges them, they don't dictate what the emperors may and may not do.

He wonders how he's ever going to breach that topic to Ricarda V. The true murderer is a woman none of them have ever heard of, and the man they've kept under the floor for six years is an innocent one. At the very least, Ricarda would deny it, say Leonidas has addled his own brains. Doesn't help that Leonidas can't reveal where he gets his intel.

The only thing that would satisfy Ricarda would be Zera in chains at his feet, confessing to the murder while professing Jona's innocence. She'd have to have proof that only the murderer would have, and even then, Ricarda might not believe it. The Donatis want the matter to be cut and dry, with Jona a symbol to be brought out from the dungeons once a year. It's called Remembrance Day for a reason.

Thanks, Herra, Leo thinks with a sigh. Damn her, he knows he'll snoop in the library later for mentions of Jona and Zera. The mystery will eat at him otherwise.

Thankfully Ricarda will be occupied. Thankfully he gave Leonidas a key.

It eases his heart a little to know that Edgorn has been planning this war for years, that it wasn't the Lover's departure that kickstarted his tyranny. Edgorn is explosive, and he was bound to go off sometime with or without Leonidas. Still, a weight he didn't realize he was carrying lifts from his shoulders as he scans her loopy script again.

RICARDA HAS NEVER LOOKED more like a king than he does sitting upright in his chair, tapping the reports and itineraries spread out before him on the council table. He's dressed in traditional Mariosan gold today, glimmering head to toe. Leonidas stares as Ricarda tosses his curls out of his eyes.

His fingers, long and elegant, dance across the papers. The flurry of people in the room settle in with their coffee and find their places. This is the first of many meetings, but today he's hosting the Ilyakans for the summit.

Ricarda could've picked an easier delegation to begin with. Though the Mariosans haven't spoken a word, the princes are already glowering like they're dealing with the scum of the world. Hopefully Ricarda's kind smile will be enough to crack them, and the treaty updated generously in their favor will do the rest.

Ricarda gestures vaguely in Leonidas' direction, still not looking up from his reports. "This is Marquis Leonidas Sartini. Pay him no mind."

"If he is not instrumental to this meeting, why have him here?" one of the princes asks in questionable Mariosan.

"Our servants are not instrumental," Ricarda says. "The guards, translators, advisors on both sides are not instrumental. I feel that much more could be accomplished if we could leave it all behind and face each other folk to folk, without any of the bullshit in the way, but I understand why we cannot. Therefore, he stays."

Leonidas closes his eyes. He's always wondered if Ricarda is a genius or a fool by using such direct words, cutting like knives. The answer has never been more unclear.

Either way, no one raises further objection to Leo's presence.

"Let's get started, shall we?" Ricarda says brightly. This is going to be a long meeting.

Councilor Matteo says, "Right, so Prince Heires, if you would, I would like to discuss an amendment to our withstanding treaty on the matter of—"

"I want to speak about the war here in the west," Prince Heires interrupts, a man of dark skin and dark eyes and dangerous demeanor. None of the princes are the smiling type, but he especially carries a malice that makes Leo shiver.

The councilors exchange glances. Ricarda keeps his cool demeanor, his emotionless expression.

"Certainly," Matteo says. "It would be marvelous if you could lend some aid. It is only a matter of time before Edgorn's army reaches Alizima, and we will need every ally—"

Heires thunders on. "So it is as I expected. You expect Ilyaka to fight the man who would be emperor."

Matteo looks confused, but Ricarda steps in. "Yes. An arrangement that would benefit all."

Heires laughs—it's a hacking, harsh, bitter sound. "You are no different from all the filthy vermin of the west. You believe that when we help you, all will be satisfied."

Ricarda doesn't break. "Edgorn means to invade Ilyaka too. You must know that."

Heires smiles. None of his fellows move to halt him. "Yes, he means to fold us into his empire as so many have before. But when peacetime comes and we are all conquered, you all will clamor for your rights. You'll demand your representatives in his court, your governors, and your little freedoms. He will grant them to you. He might even apologize. He would treat you as an equal.

"But Ilyaka would be forgotten except when he needs to brag of his accomplishments, when he needs someone to terrorize, or when he needs to let his soldiers take out their frustrations."

"Yes," Ricarda says, confused. "So help us fight him."

"Do I see any delegation in this palace from the mountainous east?" Heires spreads his hands and makes a show of looking around. "The eastern queen keeps herself separate from worldly matters, and none bother her. When the emperors come to sweep across the continent, flying their banners, they leave her blissfully forgotten and ignored. Why? Because she is not the one with the Amarinthine Pass, the channel to the rest of the world."

"Edgorn wants you for more than just your pass," Ricarda insists. "He wants all of us."

"Then why do you not let us turn down your invitations to these pointless, pompous summits?" Heires stands. "Why do you threaten us? Why do you not leave us alone when we tell you how utterly little we want to do with any of you, as the eastern queen has? You do not let us hide behind our trees, among our gods in their garden temples. You do not set us free." He grips the back of his chair so hard it rattles against the floor. The whole room is still.

"Set us free from those constraints," Heires murmurs, "swear to let us follow the path of the eastern queen, with our independence from you and your wars and your empires, and we might fight with you. For our own personal freedom—not yours. Say it, and things will be different here."

All eyes turn to Ricarda. Leonidas is holding his breath.

"I cannot agree to that as only one man," Ricarda says, hands folded on the table. "And I will not make such a lofty promise when I do not know that it can be kept. The eastern queen did not receive her independence as easily as a few spoken words. If you'd like, I can call the Delainians and Coromodans and Minyans in here and we can discuss it further. I desire for all parties to leave this convention satisfied."

Heires sits down and leans back leisurely in his chair, his courtly jacket gleaming red. "That will not be necessary," he says with the air of a man who's never been more confident, nor more disgusted, in his life. "I ask only that you keep it in mind. No further questions. Go on with what you were saying about the new treaty."

CHAPTER TWO

With nothing more than a whisper of breath, a faint stirring in the air, the Silver Hammer quietly drives his sword through the heart of the Delainian guard.

She falls with a gurgling cry Arthur does his best to muffle with his palm. His heart twists as she grips at his arm with her final bit of strength. He says a quiet prayer for her as her body hits the ground, hoping that the gods will forgive him for this. He asks them to deliver her to a safer, better world in the clouds.

Of everyone involved in this war, including Edgorn himself, the one Arthur hates most is himself. He fights revulsion as he creeps through the ground floor of the villa that Lasilas asked him to clear. Crouched down, slowly advancing, Arthur pushes open a new door without a squeak, surveying the two guards in the room with their backs toward him. The candles flutter with Arthur's sigh.

What kind of sick, twisted Ilyakan stabs people in the back like this? People who have done nothing wrong, people doing just their own jobs under their own commanders? Why has Arthur not found the strength to leave, to resist the sympathetic eyes Lasilas casts him when he needs Arthur to do something like this?

A better, stronger soldier than Arthur would give this all up and leave it behind, no matter his loyalty to Lasilas. He would scoff at anyone else in his situation. *You followed the murderers because you were loyal to them? Oh, oh good for you. Tell that to the dozens you slaughtered.*

If not for his own morals, he should at least desert for the Silver Hammer's sake. The Silver Hammer should never be used for such treacheries as this. He knows Lasilas wouldn't track him down, wouldn't beg him to stay. Though it would hurt like hell when they met on opposite sides of the same battlefield, Lasilas would probably be proud of him. He would smile so gently, so sadly as he does.

Arthur will not tell him this.

With quiet precision, Arthur clears the rest of the ground floor and then the second and third. The third is the smallest, but it's the most packed. He gets into a brawl, trapped in a small corner in near darkness at the top. He wishes he could've done this all without raising the alarm. At least here he will regain some honor by fighting face to face.

The house cleared, his pristine armor covered in blood, Arthur opens the window at the top and raises a candle as a signal. Dainthi raises another in answer.

Slowly climbing back down, Arthur is met with slaps on the back and murmurs of congratulations. The army moves into the house.

Tell me that Lasilas was watching, Arthur thinks. It's foolish to hope that Lasilas watched his shadow move against the curtains as he painted a show of the bloodshed. However, Arthur is desperate for anything to redeem this. That some good can come from it.

If only this whole campaign could be a lonely bad memory. If only he could go back to the campaigns from before Edgorn stormed into the captains' tent. Better yet, if only Arthur could be free to be the Silver Hammer in Ilyaka, protecting it as he was meant to. He closes his eyes as the privates drag the bodies out of the house, with blood trails to commemorate them.

This would all be so much worse if Edgorn were here in person with them, so Arthur is at least grateful for that. Capture a small village, raise the Elen flag bearing Edgorn's personal crest, leave a few bodies and some blood to soak the ground, loudly spread Edgorn's message—that's usually enough for Edgorn to be satisfied. Helps if Lasilas glamorizes the battle in his weekly report—what war commander hasn't—although this is for far different reasons than usual.

Arthur finds a log to rest on and puts his head in his hands, seeing blood behind his eyelids. The weight of what he's just done settles onto his shoulders like a mantle.

The quiet murmur of voices and the soft patter of footsteps swim at the edges of his awareness. He lifts his head only when he feels the heavy weight of a gaze. Dainthi stands before him, her arms crossed and a concerned frown twisting her lips.

She says, "Our scouts found an abandoned Ilyakan temple nearby. No one knows why or how, but it's there, and it's functional. You can visit it in the morning if you want." She shrugs, looking him up and down with a sigh. "Go get some sleep, Arthur. You did your part—more than. You've done enough. You need do no more tonight."

"I'm fine," he says weakly, but it seems to land on deaf ears. She smiles sadly, squeezing his arm before walking away to tend her own duties. Arthur was sent in to clear the house all by himself because he's skilled, he's the Silver Hammer, and they wanted it done quietly. He realizes now why Lasilas was so reluctant to ask it of him.

Almost all of Arthur's wounds could be assuaged if Lasilas came to him right now and agreed that what he just did was a monstrous act. That truth would be a better balm than any false smile or sympathetic frown.

With heavy limbs, Arthur finds his bed. He struggles out of his armor before he's asleep like the sun disappearing behind the horizon.

THE TEMPLE TO THE ILYAKAN gods is easy to find and impossible to mistake, even though Arthur has never seen one in person. His mother's paintings and Lasilas' starry eyed descriptions are enough. The itch to sketch the sight tears at Arthur's skin, making him clench his fists and desperately wish for paper and pencil.

What were once walls of clear glass meant to give the worshippers an uninhibited view now lay in broken ruin. Probably sacked by the Delainians—Ilyakans will rarely find kindness for their own gods outside their lands.

The only parts of the temple still standing in the open green field are the three main walls. The glass is dust covered, though it was once fine. They're smashed in pieces. None of the standing walls come past Arthur's shoulders.

Arthur glimpses an altar inside, reminding him of ceremonies his mother took him to as a child. Despite his lack of memories in Ilyaka, his mother made their home in Coromoda feel like it. Unfortunately, there were no Ilyakan temples in Ta Kama.

Thick green vines climb the standing walls, and the temple is lined on all sides by colorful flowers. They're the brightest thing around for miles, thriving with a spark that goes beyond life. The vines would be here even if the temple were intact—the temple attendants don't cut back any of nature's holy reclamation, and they remove as little as possible to build the temples in the first place.

The floor under the marble benches is tall grass, still thriving under the sunlight filtering in from the triangular glass roof. Nine flowers grow in clusters, representing each god.

Arthur kneels amongst the overgrown weeds outside, minding the broken glass near his knees. He left his armor in his tent. It can't protect him here.

You never wear armor or blade to a temple. You come as yourself, as much as you're able to.

Arthur's chest tightens with longing to see the true Ilyakan temples, grand and overgrown. One of his prayers, head ducked, is that he lives long enough to see Ilyaka once again.

"I wonder if there's a flower that would grant forgiveness," comes a voice from behind. Arthur whirls around and smiles when he sees it's just Lasilas standing over him, staring at his patron red rose. Arthur sometimes forgets that Lasilas' crest is different from his house. He chose the red rose, for grief.

"Do you mind if I join you?" Lasilas asks.

"Of course not. The temples are for all."

Lasilas chuckles and kneels beside him. "This is not much of a temple, and I'm not much of an Ilyakan anymore. Not sure how much this counts."

"Would you call me less of an Ilyakan because I haven't been there since I was two? Would you say I don't deserve to wear a crest and kneel by the flowers?"

Lasilas shakes his head, his smile sad. His face is drawn, haggard. It's the first time Arthur has seen him since he ordered him to slaughter the house of Delainians. "Ah, Arthur. Smarter than me as always."

Arthur wonders what Lasilas could possibly need forgiveness for, but it's not his place to ask. If anyone needs forgiveness, it's him for the lives he took last night, never mind that he's a champion of Ilyaka. None should be exempt from the stain of blood.

Arthur can only bow his head and pay his respects to the flower embroidered on his breast, the green daisy. Some call her purity, others innocence.

When his mother guided him through the flowers he could pledge himself to, impressing onto him that he could change whenever he liked, he was drawn to the green. Even before he knew what it meant, Arthur felt the call of the peace it offered. There was hope in that shade, like grass in the heart of summer. Like the grass in this temple.

When he told her that he sought peace, she thought he would like the black lily, representing serenity and a peaceful calm, usually worn in the wake of a tragedy. But that was not what Arthur meant. In the green daisy, he saw a smile. He saw the childlike innocence that he found in the mirror, in the colors of the world around him.

Even that young, he knew from his mother's honest teachings and his own observations that the world was anything but a green daisy. But his mother said that as long as he had a flower sewn to the breast of his clothes, he would keep its charm with him always. So Arthur chose the green daisy and never looked back.

"Red wasn't always my patron flower, you know," Lasilas says casually when he's done praying. Arthur looks at him in surprise.

Lasilas smiles. "Always so polite. You're allowed to ask, you know."

Arthur swallows. "Who—who was it before?"

Lasilas tilts his head. "I thought you'd ask why I changed." Arthur shakes his head. Lasilas' business is his business. "The blue carnation, as I'm sure you've guessed. The crest of House Catiana."

Arthur looks down, remembering that he stands in the presence of a prince, one ninth of their country's rulers. No matter what Heires says, Lasilas is the prince of Arthur's heart.

Lasilas is not a prince like Heires, not like the silent bastards who mocked and abused them both at that meeting. No, Lasilas is a true noble prince, one Arthur would follow to the ends of the earth. Someone deserving of the blue carnation, crest of honorable soldiers.

He almost wishes Lasilas weren't royalty. A commander is someone Arthur can handle, but not a prince. He wants so desperately to act normally around the man who has made everything better even when that seemed impossible, but manners put a blockade in the way. Never mind the magical evening they spent in Lasilas' tent, laughing like they could ever work as companions. Decorum comes first always in Arthur's mind.

Arthur tries for a nonchalant tone of voice, praying it doesn't crack. "I would've thought that'd be the crest of House Grimash." His voice thankfully does not break. "The warriors. Defenders."

Lasilas laughs, and it's the sound of sunlight, of the bright color before them. His blue eyes dance. "I think they might take offense to the suggestion that they have honor. I'm also surprised you don't have the crests memorized."

Arthur's cheeks burn. He does, but the truth is that Lasilas befuddled his memory for the moment. "I'm sorry, Las—"

Lasilas' hand finds his shoulder and shoves, squeezes. "I'm just teasing, Arthur. The only Ilyakans who have the house crests memorized are schoolchildren and diplomats. I forget them often."

Arthur stares in mild horror. "But you're a prince."

Lasilas smiles like he's talking to a naïve child. "My fellow princes get their scholars and servants to brush them up on the names and crests of their own Houses just before every meeting. I am guilty of the same. But no, House Grimash wears the crest of the white pansy. House Grimash might seem like the noble defenders of Ilyaka's freedom, but they're more brutal. We use them sparingly, and only when we wish to intimidate. They are nothing like the gentle, merciful guard I have built up."

Yes, because they don't have a beacon of sunlight like you at their helm.

"My sister was House Grimash," Lasilas says with deep sorrow, staring at the white pansy. Arthur understands better why he wears the red rose, for grief and loss. What in this man's life hasn't he lost, had cause to grieve? His position, his house, his sister, his friends, his country. He has to carry them all in his heart instead. "Are you going to ask why I changed my crest to this?"

Arthur shakes his head. "No, Lasilas. It's personal. I would never pry."

"Again, so polite."

Arthur wonders how Lasilas can keep up a conversation when he's struggling to remember all his manners and maintain his professional decorum, when he has Lasilas' smile to stare at. Why did Lasilas have to remind him of his status now?

"Besides," Arthur says, "I already know, I think."

Lasilas looks at him in surprise, one pale eyebrow arched. He's so beautiful like this, the wind blowing in his hair, his eyes dark and deep. Sorrowful though he might be, Arthur remembers when Lasilas let himself cry in Arthur's arms after that horrible meeting. The princes are in Mariosa now, far from where they can hurt him, but the wound Heires dealt Lasilas will never heal.

Arthur would kill him for Lasilas in a second, not that he thinks that would fix the problem. But he'd do it anyway.

"Thank you, Arthur," Lasilas says, reaching for his hand over the flowers. "Sometimes I feel like you're the only one I have left who understands me. I don't know what I would do without you."

Arthur thinks of the blood, the bodies last night, the weight of a thousand stones added to his chest with each kill. He looks at Lasilas and decides, cautiously, that for him it's worth it. For him, every atrocity is worth it. "I care about you too, Lasilas. More than you know."

Lasilas smiles with wet eyes. Arthur scoots closer to him to wrap an arm around his shoulders and pull him close, giving into instincts and saying fuck decorum for now. Hearts full of grief, guilt, and a sliver of hope, Lasilas wraps his arms around Arthur's shoulders and holds on for dear life under the sun.

It's enough.

CHAPTER THREE

The next two weeks are long, with few sightings of Ricarda. Leonidas spends his days in the library conducting a thorough exploration of anything related to Zera and Jona Musiek, but finds nothing. After he's exhausted the books there and written Herra about it, nagging for further hints about her companion, he continues Ricarda's pet project: searching for the locations of his ancestor's missing diary and Francesco's ring. Leo has no luck there, either.

The days are spent with a tired Alessandro, who's been busy comforting a tired Antonia after all the work she's had to do to help with the meetings. Her medical apprenticeship had to be put on hold for her princess duties, and Aless says she's never been more miserable.

The nights are spent with a Ricarda who's tired in mind and body, one who always comes to Leo's chambers instead of the other way around because, "I want to forget that I have duties for a little while. Staying away from my desk piled high helps with that."

He's too tired for lovemaking most nights, something Leonidas has grown to miss in these two weeks. Normally during these jobs, he takes every moment of respite he can get and hoards it greedily.

Aless remarks that with all the work Ricarda has been doing, he'd make a fine fit for emperor. Leo wouldn't know; he stopped going to the meetings after the one with the Ilyakans made it clear he was neither needed nor wanted.

The truth of Zera being the murderer weighs heavily on Leonidas' heart, as heavily as that letter weighs in his bedside drawer. He wishes it had a lock. He wishes he had the courage to burn it like he has all of Herra's other letters. Yet he hasn't, partly because he'll need it as evidence whenever he tells Ricarda, and partly because it's the last scrap of something genuine that he has.

He misses Herra, misses Mitzi, like a limb. This fake golden paradise with Ricarda cannot last forever. Sooner or later, he will have to ruin it like he did with Edgorn—though that was never a paradise.

When Ricarda comes to his chambers, he manages to stay awake on the balcony half an hour before falling asleep in Leo's bed. He's low, absentminded, distant. And then the meetings with the Ilyakans finish, and the calm Coromodans take up the council's time instead. The world breathes, and Ricarda comes to the chambers much earlier one afternoon, while the sun is barely yet descending.

"Hello," Ricarda says in his soft evening voice, and hugs Leo around the waist from behind. He sighs in contentment, leaning his weight on Leo's back, and hooks his chin over his shoulder. They rest there for a moment, swaying softly side to side, Leo wrapping his arms over Ricarda's at his stomach. They're the same height, but Ricarda gives the illusion of being taller with his weight bearing down like that.

He's warm and big and soft, his curls tickling Leo's neck. Ricarda pulls Leo's hair free of its tie. Usually on jobs Leonidas takes care to keep his hairstyle the same lest his targets decide they don't like a change. Something stopped him this time.

He's been growing into this role, and it's come ten times easier than the other three. He likes it here, likes the changes, and he's been letting his hair grow longer than he ever intended. Ricarda says he loves his hair the longer it gets.

"Should I be undressing us?" Leonidas asks, ready to change mindsets. He's used to that, constantly pleasing his targets in whatever form that might take. With Ricarda, he's actually excited to do it.

"No," Ricarda says, surprisingly. "Not tonight. Let's just stay like this for now." He squeezes tighter, nuzzles into Leonidas' neck. If there's one thing that he's learned from being Ricarda's lover, it's that Ricarda likes physical affection, closeness for the sake of closeness. He likes it often.

Leonidas feels no pressure to move, only a pure contentment to remain where he is. He sighs and leans back into Ricarda's embrace, taken by utter surprise when the closeness brings tears to his eyes. Try as he might, he can't think up an explanation for that.

At last, Ricarda pulls back, and Leo wonders why he's almost mourning the loss. But Ricarda doesn't go far, only far enough to grab his hand and tug him toward the bed. Leonidas readies his mind again, but still Ricarda doesn't seem to have intimacy on his mind.

Instead, he pulls Leonidas down on top of him, simply laying there on Ricarda's chest, nothing more. He presses a soft kiss to Leonidas' cheek when he turns his head, and the sunlight streaming through the windows warms them from head to toe.

"How were the meetings today?" Leonidas murmurs.

"Nonexistent. They never happened. I don't want to think about stubborn Ilyakans or King Edgorn's war any longer. Not when I have you here." Ricarda rolls them over so that Leo winds up on his back, looking up at a grinning Ricarda. He looks so joyful, so boyish with his curls falling into his eyes.

"Do you want to move to your room?" Leonidas asks, twining his arms around Ricarda's neck. "Get something to eat? Go out on the—"

"No, no." Ricarda flops down and breathes in his neck again—his new cologne, Leo realizes belatedly. Again, trying change. "I don't want to move, or do anything, or change anything. I very keenly want to do nothing after the way my days seem to blur around me. I truly can't wait for our diplomats to be out of here."

Leo smiles up at him. "No speaking about diplomats while you have your lips on my neck." He turns his head into a kiss, sighing as Ricarda melts into the bed. The gentle touch of Leo's hand over his cheek makes him shudder and sigh, leaning into him all the more. Leo's heart flips up and down like a stone across a lake before settling in his chest.

"Your beauty is an art that can never be captured," Ricarda recites softly, quoting from the diary of his ancestor. Seventh diary, Leo faintly remembers, as his own Ricarda sweeps him up in a haze. "Your soul a sun that I long to touch. I would bury myself in you and curl up beside your warmth like the only fire on winter's most biting night."

"I have always been in awe of those completely unaware of their own beauty," Leonidas recites in turn, still running his thumb over Ricarda's cheekbone just to watch it turn pink. A smattering of freckles has gathered there thanks to the summer sun, only visible this close. "It makes the beauty all the more precious."

When Ricarda smiles, it's not just a turn of his mouth. It's his eyes, a spark of life that won't die unless Leonidas puts it out. It's nothing like the smiles he gives the diplomats, strained and forced. This, he does with his whole soul. Leonidas has been the reason for a monarch's smile before, but there's something different about making Ricarda V smile. "You make me so happy."

Leonidas smiles in turn.

"I changed my mind. Let's go somewhere," Ricarda blurts out, sitting up again. "Let's just go wandering in the city and ditch my guards."

"That's highly unwise."

Ric rolls his eyes. "I don't need a second Matteo to talk me out of it, I need a lover with whom to recklessly risk my life. If we could go anywhere in the city—no, fuck that, I'm king, we can go wherever we want—anywhere in the *continent*, where would you want to go? What would you want to see? Under which streetlight glow would you like to kiss me?" He grins with teeth, propping his chin in his hand.

"I don't know," Leonidas mumbles. "Whatever you'd want, my love. I'd be happy seeing you happy."

Isabella would give him knowing looks whenever he said things like that, but Cadhan and Edgorn would puff out their chests and describe their ideal days down to the style of their hair if even slightly prompted.

Instead, Ricarda sighs, disappointed. "That's what you always say."

"Is that not what you want to hear?" Leonidas asks, confused that there could be a king not in love with his own ego.

"No! I appreciate that you care about my opinions—well, you say you do. Everyone says they do."

Leonidas says nothing as Ricarda stands up.

"When I come here, it's because I want to spend time with you. I want you, Leo, my lover. I don't want a yes man. I want to forget my duties for a little. Just—" Ricarda sighs and gestures. "Why can't you be more like Aless, bossing me around without fear of consequence?"

His face falls the moment the words leave his mouth, and he falls back to the bed, stricken. "I'm sorry, Leo, fuck. I didn't mean it like that. I want you just the way you are." He kisses the back of Leonidas' hand in apology. "I don't want you to change. I just want you to feel the freedom to express yourself like the rest of us oversharing bastards, okay?" He smiles weakly.

"Just promise me that you don't think of me like any other courtier would, that I'll hate you if you dare to show me a bit of yourself. Yourself is what I love most. Promise that your affection for me is not forced or fake." Ricarda draws a ragged breath. "Even if I didn't want you so much, I don't want to take advantage."

A flabbergasted Leonidas says, "Okay." Clearing his throat, because Ricarda deserves better than that after that little speech, he clarifies, "It's not forced or fake. I don't think like any other courtier. And I am—flattered, that you feel so for me." Fuck, how do people do this? He's never had to deal with a conscious king before, one who sought to make things better. One who actually cared about him.

"Good. Now." Ricarda lies beside him again, scooting his head into Leonidas' lap and moving Leonidas' fingers to his curls. "Assuming I'll be elated with whatever you choose, because it's the truth, tell me what you would do with this day. Where you would have us go." He gestures in a sweeping motion toward the window, where the sunset begins to descend.

Taking a deep breath, leaning back against the plush headboard, Leo wonders for a long moment what to say. He's never been asked what he wants before. He's always thinking of his client, whether that's another monarch, one of his clients in the whorehouse, or even Herra.

It's always been someone else. He keeps himself too occupied to think about himself, what he wants, who he is. He just becomes a new name, a new face, a new style. He is nothing. He is no one. He is the Lover, now on his fifth name.

If Ricarda wants him to create a new life for them both, it's what he'll do. Because a monarch wants it of him.

Eventually, he does talk, half-hoping that the motions of his fingers in Ricarda's hair will lull him to sleep before he can overhear anything real. Leo outlines an evening alone with him in the mountains at the north of Mariosa.

"Why there?" Ricarda murmurs, not asleep. It's a fair question. Why there when beautiful cities like Allicé exist for public entertainment? There couldn't possibly be anything worth seeing in the countryside.

Leo almost says, *it's where I'm from,* but instead goes with the safer but still true, "It's where I was born."

Truth. The taste of it is strange on his tongue.

"I would take you to the lake there," he says, grinning as he pictures it. "I would make you take a swim with me, and I would splash you till you begged for mercy."

"Mm." Ricarda cuddles closer, nuzzling into Leo's hip.

"Are you trying to start something with me, good sir?"

"No, no, not at all. Not yet. Carry on, please, though I might murder you if you don't keep going with my hair. We're in the river."

"The lake."

"Naked?"

Leo rolls his eyes. "Sure, though if so, the rest of the story will be over fast, because someone will have distracted me."

"A price worth paying." Ricarda kisses his knuckles in apology. "We're partly clothed in the lake."

"You shut up." Leonidas slaps a palm over his mouth and continues, painting a picture of a sunset you can't get even here in Allicé.

"How long did you say you were there?"

Leo closes his eyes, wondering how he could be so foolish. "In the summers, sometimes I would go there," he says. "Escape the Mariosan heat. My mother was from there. She had some family remaining." *Shut up, shut up, shut up, you're only going to get yourself into more trouble.* He is a Marquis of Sartini, and his story depends on Ricarda not getting curious enough to check the facts. Leonidas is dancing with danger, playing with fire at the deepest level.

"Ah. I would love to go there sometime," Ricarda says, looking up at Leonidas with stars in his eyes and youthful joy in his voice. A man who has gotten everything he's ever wanted without any real suffering. A man who knows nothing of Leonidas in truth. A man charmed by a facet, an illusion, a lie. "I'll go wherever you go, as long as it's not here."

Leonidas has to shut his eyes to be able to bear the weight of guilt, as Ricarda drifts off to sleep.

THE DIPLOMATS LEAVE with soothed feathers. Allicé breathes a collective sigh of relief, and Aless steals the three of them away to his family's villa before it grows too cold to be out in a pool. Summer turns to winter in Allicé faster than you can blink, Leonidas has been told.

All he can think of are the miserable winters in Ele, kept thankfully warm in Edgorn's mountain towers or his bed. The winters in the northern forests were harsh. Mitzi has been a relief.

At least Allicé will remain sunny.

"I don't even want to think about all the engagements I locked myself into in those meetings. The leaving feast," Ricarda moans. "Art shows in Delain and banquets and a dance, I think—"

At the time, Leonidas was in his room writing Herra about his lack of success with Zera. At the time, he was eager for one night away from the chaos of court dinners, but now he's ashamed to have missed Ricarda fumbling his way into hell.

"Delainian art is beautiful," Aless cuts in. "The man who did our fresco had a Delainian mother, and his trips there gave him inspiration."

"There's about a thousand other things I'd rather be doing than attending a Delainian art show," Ricarda says, lifting his head from the sofa in Aless' sitting room and looking Leo in the eye. He must be feeling their two weeks of limited contact as keenly as Leonidas is. He's missed Ricarda more than he thought he could miss someone while still seeing them every day. It's uncanny.

"That's for future Ricarda to worry about," Aless says, patting Ric's hand comfortingly. "Nothing exists beyond this villa."

"For four measly days," Ricarda moans, hiding his face in the sofa behind a mess of curls.

Aless throws his hands up. "Alas, he is beyond my reach. Leo, you're on your own."

Leonidas laughs and joins Antonia on a sofa across the room, sitting up stiffly as Aless' parents walk in. They're dressed in finery and high collars, jewels sparkling as if they're at court. All the revelry in the room dies, and Ricarda scrambles into an acceptable position.

"Mother," Aless says. "Father. You're back early."

Leonidas looks between them, trying to puzzle out the relationship. Aless doesn't talk about his family much. Only that he comes here with Antonia, alone, when his parents are away somewhere else.

His mother is a woman of dark eyes and a deadly frown, who manages to turn it into a smile. "Alessandro." She bows deeply to Ricarda, then Antonia. "Your Majesty. Your Highness."

"Hello, Andrea. How many times have I told you to call me Ricarda?" His smile comes easier than Aless' for once. That smile helps Leonidas breathe when Madam de Rege turns her eye on him. She scans him, making sure he fits some set of unknown requirements, and he doesn't relax till after she drops her gaze.

"We are honored to have you all here, as always," her husband says with a noticeably warmer demeanor. He carries Aless' blond hair and blue eyes, and the same jovial smile, gripping his wife's arm firmly. He nods to Leonidas. "Marquis. We've heard so much about you from our son—it's a pleasure to finally meet you."

"And you." Leonidas flashes a smile. He's glad when those two take their leave to some other part of the villa after a few minutes' conversation, leaving the boys to collapse into the sofa and sigh in relief.

"You don't have to tell me they're emotionally exhausting," Aless sighs. "I know. I've had to live with them for twenty two years."

He and Ricarda dissolve into their usual mindless bickering, and Leonidas turns his attention back to Antonia and the brown skirts that threaten to swallow up her legs. The four of them have a lovely view of the yard and the setting sun, but he'd rather look at her and her green eyes. She's less tiring to be around than the boys. She's easy and calm and quiet like him, where their boys are loud and boisterous. They love them no less for it, but sometimes Leonidas needs that reminder of Mitzi, of Herra. Of peace.

Antonia's getting her healer's license soon. The negotiations got in the way of her training, but Leonidas is already privy to the ball Ricarda is throwing her in honor.

"You look lovely today. You wear gowns better than anyone I've ever seen," Leonidas praises. "And you make them better than almost anyone."

She pulls back in mock offense. "Almost?"

He smiles. "There's a seamstress in the south I befriended who could do things with beads you wouldn't believe. I wouldn't dare dismiss your talent, though, princess. Ricarda might throw me out of his bed then."

Antonia laughs. "We couldn't have that." She shrugs a little, looking down at her brilliant skirts. "They were the only thing that brought me joy when I walked every day through these halls and people mistakenly called me by the wrong name, the wrong gender. I knew so little of joy in life. They meant nothing by it because I hadn't told them yet. But they didn't understand, and it tore me apart."

She smiles and smooths out her skirts, watching them shimmer in the sunlight. "And then I did tell them all, though I swear I'd never been more scared. And of course, Ricarda was the first to run to our seamstress to ask her to make new dresses on my behalf. I didn't know the art then as well as I do now. Now, I make everything myself. It's a slow process and it can be a pain sometimes, but I wouldn't trade them for anything. All things dear to the heart take time to foster."

"For creative people, maybe. My heart doesn't require so much time, Antonia."

She looks at Ricarda and back at Leonidas, a glint in her eye. "Doesn't it?"

LIKE EVERY VILLA IN Mariosa, Grimitata has a pool and several balconies from which to overlook it and jump in if one is so inclined. Leonidas likes water—he wasn't lying about going swimming in the lake near his birthplace—but he's amused with just how much Mariosans enjoy it.

They watch Antonia shriek with laughter as Ricarda splashes her, chasing her through the crystal clear water. It's a scene Leo has witnessed countless times, and it never fails to bring a smile to his lips.

Aless shakes his head where he sits beside Leo, their legs hanging over the balcony edge. Leonidas hasn't seen a balcony with a railing since he's been in Mitzi. "I don't know how you put up with him."

"You've put up with him for far longer than I have," Leo says. "And anyway, I wouldn't say it's so much putting up with him as it is a pleasure and a privilege to have his affection."

"Don't let him hear you say that. He's like an eager puppy when it comes to praise."

Leo smiles. "He is the best of all my past lovers."

The moment he realizes his mistake, he feels Aless turn his head to lay eyes on him. "I wasn't under the impression you'd had many."

Leo shrugs as casually as his pounding heart will allow. "I never said either way."

Aless laughs. "You sly lynx, you. I need to give you more credit. Tell me, then." He elbows Leo in the side.

"There was one." Leonidas closes his eyes, knowing that if he's vague there won't be a problem. He pictures Edgorn's face the first night he saw him, his dark features and handsome face tainted with a scowl underneath the mustache. Leo only ever saw him smile twice. Once, he was the cause.

The other time, he was reading a report about Iliath's soldiers suffering heavy casualties. His mouth curled into a satisfied, dangerous smile. His beloved Cardamom had been sitting beside him, struggling not to be ill.

Leonidas murmurs, "He was charming, when he wanted to be. Handsome when he shut his mouth."

Aless snorts. "Ah, one of those. There were a few of those at the summit. Did you love him?"

Leo guffaws. He'd have to be as dull as an old blade for love to blossom between them. Any love he would've had with Edgorn would've ended in flames, anyway. Edgorn is destructive, and he destroys everything good around him without even meaning to.

"Gods, no. We were supposed to get married," he lies, wanting to make sure this isn't all truth in case Aless gets curious and smart. "I would've had everything I'd ever wanted. He bought me the finest clothes and jewels, showed me off as the jewel in his crown. His favorite pet.

"He went away often, and when I had those breaks from him and his temper, I convinced myself I could weather it. He got angry, but I was used to dealing with that. I would've been one of the most powerful men in Ele." He shakes his head. "And yet, inexplicably, I broke it off."

He realizes too late that he mentioned Ele, a foolish slip, but he can't take it back. "Gods, I was so reckless. I don't know why I broke it off." He laughs a little, ashamed as tears well in his eyes. "I could've had everything if I just decided to stand his temper when it came. I didn't even have to love him."

Aless doesn't reply for a minute. Leonidas doesn't dare face him.

"Maybe," Aless says at last, "you had some self-respect, and you wanted to find someone who treated you like you deserved. No unlawful temper, no unjustified anger. Someone who loved you and wanted you and could give you all of those riches as well as their love."

Their eyes find Ricarda in the pool. Aless quietly adds, "The fault is not yours. He is the one with the loss. And based on how you are with Ricarda, you couldn't have found everything you wanted in that Elen court anyway."

Leonidas smiles fondly. Ricarda is right there below him, but Leo still misses him, misses those warm eyes boring into him. Aless notices this and whistles down, drawing Ricarda's attention with all the eagerness of a puppy.

Leonidas, seasoned lover and master seducer, blushes hotly at the honesty in Ricarda's grin. Ricarda slicks his hair back from his eyes, waves jovially, and blows a kiss. Aless keeps his comments to himself for once.

"I didn't come to the Mariosan court hoping for love," Leonidas says, shamelessly ogling Ricarda's back as he turns, muscles rippling under the water.

Aless laughs. "I don't believe you."

"What?"

"The way you came up to the high table, your head held high like you owned the room. I thought you wanted him from that first instant."

Leonidas supposes he's right; he didn't come here looking for love—only Ricarda's love, not his own.

"Why did you come to court, then?"

The fantasy of Ricarda's body and his bright green eyes is shattered. Leo looks anywhere but Aless, certain he's going to see through the lies. He tries to shrug nonchalantly. "Because I wanted to see what it was like. Who wouldn't?"

"Many. The Ilyakan delegation couldn't wait to be out of here." Aless sighs. "I wonder if they hate us so much because we have one of their own chained in our dungeon."

Herra's letter about Zera swings back to the forefront of Leo's mind. Damn, he thought he'd be able to forget about that for at least a little while. Now he's back to wondering how much of this peace and poolside tranquility he can get away with before it'll be time to unleash that information.

Edgorn's army edges closer to Mariosa each day, and it's only a matter of time before Cadhan and Isabella show up. Only a matter of time before Ricarda is forced to join them; three against one. Being the Lover is too dangerous in unpredictable, unstable wartime. Leonidas can't be here then.

He always has to leave at some point.

What's most disturbing is that the possibility actually hurts, like a panic he can't wade through. He's always been so eager to leave before. What's changed now?

"All the things that prince said were true," Leonidas says carefully. He hasn't been able to get the words out of his head at night, when Ricarda is long asleep. Sleep hasn't come easily in a while.

"True enough." Aless switches the subject not out of sympathy, but apathy. He doesn't know that Leo has been reevaluating how he thinks of a country he's never really cared to think of before. He's never cared about anything but himself, but now he's starting to care about Ilyaka. "Have you ever met King Cadhan?" Aless asks.

Leo's lip curls into a smirk. "I have had that...experience, yes."

"Experience? Not pleasure?"

Leonidas lets his silence speak for itself. Aless hums in understanding. "I am glad he chose not to come to the recent summit. It was a near thing, though. Only the war kept his attention—and that of Queen Isabella's. The eastern forest queen, of course, never treats with others, and keeps her borders ever closed. Let's pray her mountains and her trees keep Edgorn out of her lands."

Leonidas doesn't care about the eastern forest queen when all he can think of is the possibility he overlooked that Cadhan or Isabella might've been here at the court, at the summit. All the great monarchs of the continent suddenly losing their lover is suspicious enough to the right person. It's why Leonidas takes care to make sure the fault is never his own when he leaves them.

Gods, what explanation would he have given the Mariosans if those monarchs had been here? Faking a sudden illness for two weeks, remaining in his rooms and turning away even a doting Ricarda? *That* would've been suspicious. This once, he'll thank Edgorn for starting a war.

"Yes," he says, "let's."

Aless eventually bullies Ricarda out of the water so he can sidle up to Antonia, fawning over every bit of affection she gives him.

The affection he gives in return is more genuine today, or maybe that's just because Aless has the comforts of home to give him some extra confidence. Instead of loud poetic proclamations, it's willful sighs in exchange for Antonia's soft words and softer smiles.

Leo remembers the day they were getting dressed for a ball, Aless' jittery nerves as he stood in that gown, Antonia's assurances calming him down. Leo wonders what Aless is really like when the two of them are alone, when he doesn't have to put on a show for anyone. He wonders if Aless has ever played his piano for her, soft and loving, just to watch her dance.

Leo looks at her middle finger again, the single ring resting there. He wonders why she doesn't seal things. Pride? Time? The running joke finally coming to an end? It doesn't take a genius to tell that she loves him too. If Ricarda is a puppy, Aless is a groveling kitten begging for scraps.

Ricarda, in turn, takes Aless' place on the balcony, arm thrown over Leo's shoulders. The two below amuse themselves, flirting and laughing, and Leonidas is happy to let his walls down and rest his head on Ricarda's shoulder. Soon they'll be cuddling in thick winter cloaks, although the furs won't be as warm as Ricarda's skin. The nights in the north are already growing chillier, but here in the south they're milking the last dregs of summer.

Ricarda gets up to fetch them a plate of grapes and fresh cheese. While he's gone, listening to the soft patter of his bare feet on the stairs, Leonidas allows himself to hope this could be real. If he were honestly the Marquis of Belimati and he met Ricarda at that table by coincidence, if he came to court because he wanted to experience it and ended up falling like Aless believes he has.

If he could look forward to this—vacations at Aless' villa before the cold hits, nights spent in Ricarda's arms after long weeks of meetings. A peaceful life. A good life.

"Did you know I was born here?" Ricarda asks when he returns.

Leonidas smiles up at him to cover the heartbreak seizing his chest. "What? The king of Mariosa, born anywhere but golden Allicé? Why, good sir, I'm ashamed on your behalf."

Ricarda tips his head back and laughs, his curls spilling back in a waterfall. Leonidas can only stare.

"So your parents and his have known each other a long time, then?" Leo asks. He doesn't know much about Ricarda's mother, Bella Donati, only that she died of an illness long before her husband. He's heard the rumors—Ricarda IV was never the same after death. He lost part of his mind with her, wasting away, trying to cope in others' beds. Leonidas doesn't know how true they are.

Ricarda smiles. "Oh, yes. You saw how Madam de Rege treats me."

"She didn't treat any of us with apparent kindness—respect to you and Antonia, maybe, but not even a warm smile to Aless." He recalls shuddering memories of his own mother, hardened by her impossible life and the struggle of raising a child she never really wanted. Leonidas felt it all too clearly.

"She's not the warmest woman," Ricarda agrees, "but she does harbor love for us all. I wish I had the freedom to be more like her without starting several wars. Instead, with a burden ten times hers, I must simply retreat away for a few days to curb my unhappiness."

"Oh, poor you."

"Mm." Ricarda buries his nose in Leonidas' neck and breathes deep.

My unhappiness. While trying not to lose himself in the insistent press of Ricarda's lips, wanting to think of anything but work, Leonidas forces himself to say, "Your unhappiness? You're really that miserable in your position as king?"

Ricarda stops his ministrations to Leonidas' relief/disappointment. Slowly, he says, "I'm dramatic. You know this. I don't—I don't hate being king. Not like you think. It just gets tiring and I like to complain about it. But truly, if it was ever taken away from me, I don't know what I'd do. It's all I've known all my life. My parents chose me to be king instead of Antonia, and I never thought about anything else in my life. I am content here, and you have only helped to improve my stance. But no one likes dealing with unhappy diplomats."

"Mm." Leonidas cuddles closer to him. "Have you ever thought about following in your father's footsteps? Becoming an emperor?"

Ricarda covers Leo's hand on his shoulder absentmindedly. "I would need an Ancient's approval, wouldn't I? But the Ancients died with my father. If we still had them, we wouldn't have Edgorn, the issue that made this summit so much harder than it usually is." He sighs and tips his head back onto Leo's shoulder; they've rearranged. "Damn him."

Leonidas hums in agreement again.

CHAPTER FOUR

L asilas has his head submerged underwater.

Arthur, resting in the pool nearby with his arms spread out to the sides, watches as he comes back up. Lasilas shakes his hair out, preening shamelessly when he catches Arthur staring. Arthur's heart stutters.

He makes a show of wiping the water off his face. "You're like a dog."

"Loyal, kind, and known for my beauty? Why, thank you."

Arthur rolls his eyes. They've stopped in a town with an old bathhouse. It's stunning, with marble ceilings that reach for the stars, painted with frescoes for them to gaze up at as they soak in steaming water. They're close enough to the Mariosan border for a fresco to be a common sight.

Arthur didn't realize how desperately he needed to relax his weary muscles until he sank into the hot pool and felt his tension melt into the heat. Steam rises up from the water in curls, and bars of soap lay in pockets along the outside of the large, circular pool.

The size of the building, big and open and airy, is almost the size of their average army camp. It's beautiful, serene. Lasilas stretched out along the pool's edge beside Arthur brings a sense of calm. Lasilas hasn't been himself lately, stressed and hidden and quiet. Different than typical campaign stress.

Arthur has been trying to determine the cause, to no avail. Perhaps the strain of growing closer to Alizima each day is finally getting to Lasilas. One can hardly blame him.

"The frescoes are beautiful, aren't they?" Lasilas sighs with more ease in his voice than he's had in days. "You could paint something like that, my dear captain."

Arthur's heart stutters. "Just because I'm a bit handy with a brush doesn't mean I could do a masterpiece like that, Las."

"Bullshit. You could paint anything in the world you like and it would turn out just like that."

Arthur laughs shyly, stunned by Lasilas' blind faith in him. "I thought you were the one criticizing our lofty faith of you."

"Yes. Your lofty faith of *me*. Not you. You, I can praise all I like, and I say you could paint the world. You belong in House Liele." He looks over with an easy smile. Gods, his eyes are so big and blue and bright. How is he so pretty just like this?

"There are only certain things in the world that interest me enough to paint. I cannot pick just any subject and have it end up like a Mariosan fresco." Arthur's heart does flips in his chest as he asks, "Would you—would you let me paint you?"

He fears Lasilas' response, likely a laugh of disbelief and gentle pity. Instead, he gets a radiant smile and the soft reply, "My dearest captain, I would be honored."

Arthur grins at his lap like a fool.

A foreign voice comes to shatter the moment. "Sir, if I may interrupt?"

Lasilas turns his head, his hair still stuck to his neck. Arthur watches the droplets of water carve a path down his skin and fights an unexplainable urge to trace the path with his tongue. "Yes?"

A messenger hovers above them. "There's a message, sir. I've been instructed to give it—"

"Only for my ears, yes, I know." Lasilas sighs and rises from the water with the grace of a god. Arthur knows if he tried that, buffoon that he is, he'd probably slip and fall on the wet tile. Waiting until he's certain Lasilas has a towel around his waist, Arthur cautiously glances behind him. It's the same messenger who interrupted his dinner with Lasilas. Apparently he did decide to change employers.

"Alright, then," Lasilas says with a sigh. "Let's have it."

"King Cadhan of Delain has announced a formal declaration of war against your army, King Edgorn's army, and any who fight for him. He has already deployed royally trained troops of his own to join the fight."

Arthur's stomach drops. It was only a matter of time, yes, but the truth of it rattles him all the same. Edgorn should count himself lucky to have avoided real resistance thus far. Although lucky is not the proper term.

Now, he is going to meet justice.

Lasilas sighs and tips his head back, muttering curses. Water continues to travel down his neck. "Thank you. Go see my guards for a coin, for your trouble. I don't have any on me." He smiles sheepishly. "So much for a man's attempt at rest."

"I'm sorry to ruin it, sir," the messenger says.

"You're far from the first. Think little of it." He crooks a finger toward Arthur, and all discussion of painting subjects and frescoes are put from his mind. With a swallowed sigh, Arthur rises to follow his general, as he always has and always will.

"AS MUCH AS IT PAINS me to ask you to put on clothes, my lord, I must ask: the green jacket or the yellow?"

Deciphering the words slowly, Leonidas looks over at his lover with fresh horror as the truth dawns. "Sweet gods, is this affair starting already?"

Ricarda pauses, looking at each jacket in his hands and chewing his lip. "I have opinions, if you'd like them."

"Yes, Ric, I know you do." Leonidas sighs and flops his head back onto the pillow of his bed, seriously debating going back to sleep. "I forgot it was today. I think this whole day is pointless and strange."

"You're pointless and strange," Ricarda retorts, climbing into bed with him and shoving his face against Leo's neck. "Do you know how many servants and chamberlains and even advisors anticipate this day all year? Mariosa's greatest holiday, they call it."

Leonidas looks at him fondly, stroking Ricarda's curls like he's silently begging for. "I'm already used to your affection and attention, my love. I don't need a holiday of superiors fawning over their inferiors just to receive it."

"Oh, come on. Don't you want a whole day of me fawning over you, attending your every whim? And don't say inferiors. That makes me sound like an ass."

"You are an ass." Leonidas kisses his cheek. "Subordinates, then. And no, that's not something I particularly want." He squirms away from Ricarda's ticklish curls, though he lets his lips roam where they will. "It's uncomfortable."

"By gods, you are so strange! Don't be like Aless and try to refuse your gift. Please."

Leonidas pulls back to look at him. "You're serious? You actually—want to do this? Dote on me today like our roles are reversed?"

"Yes, my love. It's always been my dream to take care of a lover like this. With the meetings and my weakness for your fingers in my hair, it's been you taking care of me, but don't you worry." He leans down to kiss Leo slow and sweet, leaving his lips tingling pleasantly when Ricarda pulls back. He's all that Leo can see, his face framed in a halo of curls. "Today is yours. I am yours. My only price is your aforementioned fingers in my hair, and your attendance at tonight's ball. Though that's probably a given."

Leo smiles. "I thought I was ruling today. I would much rather keep you here than have to share you out there."

Ricarda smirks with a heavy promise. "Tempting, tempting. But I am the king, so I have to be there, and I will not suffer it without you."

A knock comes at the door before Leonidas can reply. "Enter," Ricarda calls as they separate.

When he sees them, Aless promptly slaps his hands over his eyes. "Oh, gods. Do I want to know?"

"We're decent, it's fine," Ricarda says, sitting up.

"You two are never decent even when you're clothed. You should see yourselves."

"You're one to talk," Ricarda retorts. "What do you want?"

"My darling Antonia has requested the worst of me," Aless moans, sinking dramatically into an easy chair by the sliding balcony door.

"You asked for it by refusing to let tradition be," Ricarda says. He slings an arm around Leonidas' shoulder, absently playing with the thread on his collar. Leo's breath hitches at having him so close, so casual. "What did she want?"

"To make me rescind my request to ignore today's holiday. To wait on me this day instead, as *tradition* demands."

Ricarda and Leo exchange glances. "Isn't that what you're always saying you want, Aless?" Leo asks. "The affections of your heart, for you alone, or something like that?"

"Yes, but—" Aless flails his hands about. His golden hair follows. "It's supposed to be me! I'm supposed to lavish her with attention till she finally accepts my proposal. It is the right way of wooing. Unless she pushes me away and calls me an ass, I should dote on her, give her gifts, anything she asks."

"And you have," Ricarda says patiently. "You have done nothing but, my friend. Although she's too much of a coward to say it, she loves you too, so you might as well let her show it. Indulge her indulgence today. You've never been known to deny her before. Consider it fulfilling a request of hers if it makes you feel better."

Leonidas leans forward. "Aless, you deserve to be loved, too. For all that you give, you deserve to be treasured too. Relationships should never be one sided."

Hypocritical words from a hypocritical man. He won't think on them too hard.

"There you are!" comes Antonia's voice as she bursts into the room, wearing a slim fitting gown for once. She's said she prefers the ballgowns because they give her the illusion of the shape she wants, but she could never be persuaded against a dress of any sort. "Now, man, are you going to let me take you out, or are you going to run and protest some more? We've got all day."

"I could be persuaded," Aless replies, rising to his feet. "I have been threatened and cajoled."

"Good." She captures his hand like a prisoner and spares a glance for Leonidas and Ricarda. "I don't want to see you two before tonight."

"Likewise," Ricarda says, standing and pulling Leonidas along with him. "Come on, my love. Anywhere in the world you want to go. I'll take you anywhere you like, do anything you want, be whatever you choose."

Leonidas tilts his head, considering. He's been trying to stop thinking of Ricarda and more about himself in their encounters, though it's difficult. For years he's put others first. Such a habit is not easily undone, no matter how sweet Ricarda's words. "The library," he decides.

"What? It is your day, not mine."

"I know." He holds firm to Ricarda's hands. "I know what I said."

"Okay." Ricarda casts him a strange look but obediently tugs him along, pushing past doors they've entered dozens of times. This has become as much a sanctuary to Leonidas as it has to Ricarda.

"We're here. What next?"

Leonidas arranges them so that Ricarda's head lies in his lap on a settee in the room. One of Ricarda I's diaries sits beside them. "I know I said this was my price," Ricarda says, "but first of all, I was joking, and second of all, we didn't need to come here for this."

"Hush," Leo says, burying his fingers in Ricarda's hair and beginning the slow task, familiar to him by now, of separating the tangled curls, since he doesn't want to get his fingers dirty with the hair oil Ricarda uses. "I brought you here for selfish reasons alone, I assure you."

"Hm. I'll take it."

Gods, Ricarda is so warm. The warmth of him against Leo's thighs threatens to lull him back to sleep. "Tell me about Francesco," Leo says. "Where he was buried. Any hint about where that missing journal might be, or the ring."

"Ah. Well—we've walked by his tomb in the city many times. Are you thinking the journal would be in there with him? I'm sure one of my ancestors has checked. I bet my father did. It's not in there, though that's a good guess." He shoves his forehead further into Leonidas' hand and continues.

"One of the only references Ricarda the First makes to Francesco after he died in battle reads, 'I visited my love today in a field of pure, bright green, in the peace of nature, where he asked me to come. Where he could find peace, between two great oak trees that look down on a river that never slows. His body might be gone from this realm, buried in the earth, but I know his spirit floats around me still. I paid tribute and left the last pieces of my heart there with him.'"

Leonidas' eyes fly open from their sleepy haze with a warm Ricarda in his lap. That description matches his birthplace, the place where he spent his summers when his mother took a break from the whorehouse. He knows that river between the two oaks, the brightness of the grass that was something otherworldly. He sat there many mornings as a child, wishing for things to be different while staring at the reflection in the water.

The last pieces of my heart—

"I wonder where Ricarda might've gone," Ricarda murmurs, voice heavy with sleep.

"Yes," Leo murmurs, throat dry, utterly awake. "I wonder."

The subordinates' ball comes and goes in a blur. Leonidas hardly touches the liquor, another longstanding practice in his necessity of keeping secrets. He is alone in that practice, other than perhaps Antonia.

Aless plays piano at Antonia's request, and afterward those two stumble out of a parlor together for reasons that Aless swears aren't sordid. Leonidas is the only one who believes him, since he knows Antonia wouldn't want their first time to occur while Aless was even slightly inebriated. She would want him to remember it all, treasure it all, and she'd never want to take advantage. For all the honor he has shown her, she would return it.

After an hour of dancing on tables and making a fool of himself, Leonidas finally snags a hand around the sleeve of Ricarda's blue coat and drags him off. The crowd whistles encouragement. He doesn't even care, not when he has the king and future emperor of the continent hanging onto his arm and begging for a kiss like he's the one who has experience in seduction.

Future emperor. He wonders when he decided.

Leonidas wonders, as he slams Ricarda's back against the wall in the stairwell to kiss him, pinning his hands above his head, why he stays. Why he hasn't left to tell Herra that he's found her man.

Why was today the catalyst? Was it the ease with which Ricarda let himself be ordered around, giving up control just as easily as he takes it in that council chamber? Edgorn would rather be caught dead than be in Ricarda's shoes right now, even a modicum of control relinquished.

Ricarda pulls back from the insistent push of Leo's lips with a gasp. "Good gods," he laughs breathlessly. "I have been looking forward to this all day."

Leonidas smiles in the darkness of this corridor, looming ever closer. He realizes that with them as close as they are, Ricarda slouched a little, Leo comes out taller. Ricarda curses softly. "Let's—focus on getting to my chambers, okay? No distractions."

"No promises."

Despite that, Leo keeps his hands—mostly—to himself until they pass Ricarda's guards and make it into his chambers. They rarely come here, almost always defaulting to Leonidas' chambers, but Leonidas doesn't want to hide tonight.

He wants to face the fact that Ricarda's canopied four poster resembles Edgorn's a little too much, that the darkness of the room and the contrast of the bright yellow lights above takes him back to that night he left. The night he was busy dodging Edgorn's blows and vying for freedom. *You deserve someone who loves you,* Aless told him that day on the balcony, and Leonidas, dangerously, is starting to agree.

They trip and fumble their way to Ricarda's bed, where Leonidas puts himself in the moment by force. He's looking down at the most gorgeous man he's ever had the pleasure of lying with, curls splayed everywhere and green eyes looking up at him in wonder. It's a heady power rush.

"In what other ways can I be of service to you, my lord?" Ricarda murmurs demurely, looking at Leonidas from under his eyelashes, twining their hands together.

Leonidas smirks. "I can think of a few things," he says, and dives in.

"Darling," Ricarda gasps. "Let me—make a request."

"Anything." Leonidas doesn't care that this is his day. All he wants is to keep having Ricarda look at him like that. That is a treasure enough, a gift enough.

"Tell me you're mine," Ricarda says, "just as much as I am yours."

"I am yours," Leonidas says, like a line from a play. Whatever his targets ask of him, he does. Whatever they want him to say, he says. These particular words he has said three times before. But the words catch in his throat this time, and he nearly trips over them as they make it out of his mouth. His eyes start smarting, and he nearly falters. What the fuck?

"I am yours as you are mine," Leo says, a challenge to himself more than an indulgence of Ricarda. At least, that's what he intends, but Ricarda drinks up the words like water, and with a half sob he curls his finger around the back of Leo's neck to pull him in, cutting his next words off.

"I am yours," Leo says when he's allowed breath once again, though it comes shallowly. "I am yours, I am yours, I am yours."

It sounds less and less a lie, coating his tongue in something sour. He won't allow the sweetness to burst through.

"I love you," Ricarda says, and Leonidas closes his eyes and surrenders himself to sensation instead of thought for a while.

When their breath no longer comes short to their lungs, when the candles have burned low and the noise of the party downstairs is but a distant hum, when Leonidas stares into Ricarda's face as naked as he's ever been, he runs out of words. Because what could he say about the gentle crease of Ricarda's face, the softness of his smile that threatens to tear Leo's heart free? *I love you,* he hears in Ricarda's voice, whispered and shouted a handful of times in the past hour. More times than Leonidas has ever heard it.

"You are so beautiful," Ricarda murmurs, voice heavy and sated. His eyes shine still. His skin has the sheen of sweat, glowing gold in the low light. "Like something of old."

Leonidas smiles, he can't help it. He raises a palm tenderly to Ricarda's cheek, watching him lean into it. Ricarda is as desperate for any hint of his affection as Aless is for Antonia's, and it's almost more than he can bear. "I care about you, too."

Ricarda closes his eyes and drifts off to sleep, but it does not come to claim Leonidas. Oh, no. *I love you, I love you.*

It's not long before he's sliding out from Ricarda's red silk sheets and pulling a dressing gown on under the premise of getting a drink. He slips out the door that lets him go straight to the stairwell without passing the guards. It's a security installation for the king's convenience, and Leo has never appreciated it more.

He leans against the wall in the utter darkness and whispers his truth to the heavens, since he can whisper it to no one else.

"My name is Leonidas Sartini, and I am in love with Ricarda Donati. The Fifth," he adds after a moment's pause. He leans his forehead against the wall and says again, "I am Leonidas Sartini, and I am in love with Ricarda Donati the Fifth."

He pounds on the wall and repeats it, wondering why he feels so fiery from the inside out, enough to scream this out until his voice grows hoarse, but too crazed to care. So he screams it over and over again, trying to ignore the voice in his head hissing *liar liar*

liar as he says this name. He doesn't care that it was most unwise to scream that out, that Ricarda might wake. He should be worn out enough to sleep like the dead.

Leo flips around and presses his back to the wall, tilting his eyes up toward the dark ceiling. Tears well in his eyes and spill over onto his cheeks, rivers of sorrow. Leonidas can't hold them back for the world. Can't hold back his tears, can't contain his anger. Anger at himself for breaking the one rule of this job, at Herra for putting him here, at Ricarda for—for everything.

Please, gods, don't let Ric find me here.

The truth has found him and sunken its claws into the heart of him. It won't let go, no matter how many tears he sheds, no matter how long he spends against the wall with his head in his hands while Ricarda sleeps fitfully in the next room.

The day meant all for Leonidas. What a joke.

THE MORNING BEFORE the ball thrown to celebrate Antonia getting her medical license, Leonidas says, heart in his throat, "Ricarda, I have to tell you something."

"Mm? What is it, love?"

Leonidas almost says *fuck it, forget it* once again, but he can't keep doing this, hiding from the truth. None of his relationships or identities have ever been easy, ever lasted forever.

He's rehearsed this conversation in his head a thousand times since he received Herra's letter, but there never has been and there never will be a good way to say it. "I—you have to promise you won't hate me once I finish." That line hasn't been in any of his rehearsals, and it surprises him as much as it surprises Ricarda.

Ricarda's jovial smile morphs to a frown of concern, his brows knitting in worry, his eyes darkening as he wraps an arm around

Leonidas' shoulders. "Of course. I could never hate you. I love you. What is it? What's happened?"

He sits them down on the couch facing Leo's window, which almost makes this worse. Leo doesn't have anywhere to go. He can't pace to keep his nervous energy at bay. Extricating himself from Ricarda's embrace now would just make things worse, and he can't deny he likes the comfort of his warm arms. Leo buries his face in his shoulder and reminds himself that if Ricarda couldn't hate a bug, he won't hate his lover.

He hated Jona well enough.

Your monarchs all turned against you at some point, no matter how kind or calm you were.

How would you feel in his place?

Leo ignores that voice and starts speaking, leaving out the name of his source but including the validity of it. He outlines Herra's discoveries along with the fact that she has Zera in her captivity at this moment. Zera's confession, her admission of Jona's innocence, the reason for the murder, and the murder of House Catiana at Edgorn's hands to orchestrate the war years ago.

This is just a different person with a different name, the same crime. It shouldn't matter that much to Ricarda—right? As Leo speaks, he's turning over every word in his head, hoping it all comes out coherently, hoping Ricarda won't throw him out.

Ricarda says nothing the whole time, uncharacteristic of him. Usually, the three of them have trouble getting him to shut up. But he is quiet, and he is still, and Leonidas is terrified like he's never been before.

When he finally runs out of words to say, he looks at Ricarda for the first time. His brow is pinched in confusion, lost in thought.

His first question is, "Can I see the letter?" which sets Leo's heart sinking.

Leo swallows. "I'm sorry. I can't disclose her name. It's a confidential matter, but I swear to you on everything holy to us both that I'm not lying, Ricarda. Please. You have to believe me."

Ricarda nods slowly. "Come on," he says, standing up and pulling Leo with him.

Where are we going? The dungeon? Am I going to replace Jona for slander and insubordination? He looks out the windows at the sunlight they pass just in case. He shivers at the very thought of getting locked up in a cage like Jona's, brought out into polite society once a year to be laughed at and have rotten fruit thrown at his face.

Ricarda doesn't lead him to the dungeons. He leads Leo to the council room hallways he's become familiar with. The palace, for all its intimidating size, has become more of a home to him than he ever thought it would. There's nothing wildly different about this one compared to the other three, or to Herra's townhouse. So what makes this one home?

The people, come the whispers. *The people.*

Is Ricarda going to call a council meeting on just this? Leonidas swallows and prepares to be cross examined the way he's witnessed before, scrutinized under the unforgiving eyes of the councilors.

Ricarda doesn't take him to the council chamber. He takes him past it, through the hallways of mirrored ceilings and gold trim on the marble walls, to a private suite Leo has never seen before. Knocking on the door, watching as it slowly opens, Leo stands straighter and lets go of Ric's hand.

Inside stands Councilor Matteo.

"Ricarda," he says, surprised, as his eyes rake up and down them both. "Marquis. Come in. Can I do something for you?"

"Yes," Ric says, pushing his way in and dragging Leo with him. "Leo, tell him what you just told me."

Leonidas recites the story again, keeping his voice as flat as possible. Ricarda stares at Matteo until he's finished.

"Well?" Ricarda says when Leo collapses into one of Matteo's plush white couches. "Is it true, Matteo?" The silence permeates the room, fitting into every dark corner. Ricarda's voice takes on a pleading tone. "After my mother's death, no one knew my father better than you. Tell me what you know about this. What you never told me before."

Matteo sighs heavily. "Your father was found in his study in a pool of his own blood. None of us, not even me, know the circumstances. It is plausible that an Ilyakan killed him because the emperors of the continent have been less than kind to them, yes, although your father never did anything to hurt them the way other emperors have. That is the motive we could pin on Jona—"

"Where was Jona when you found him?" Ricarda has a hand to his forehead.

"Lurking just outside the study, head down, trying not to be seen," Matteo replies. "Why?"

"Like he might have been someone's lookout? Like he had never been in that study at all? The door was locked from the inside, right?"

"Yes, he probably locked it on his way out. Or whoever killed your father did." Matteo sighs. "Ricarda, even if this is true, what would it change? Why would it matter? Especially since they're brother and sister. It's not as if they're two completely different parties. Their motives were likely the same. They were likely in the league. If we have one, we have them both."

"What does it matter?" Ricarda marches, wide eyed, to the closest thing he has left to a father. "It would mean convicting a guilty woman and freeing an innocent man. It would mean doing what's right."

"Try convincing the public of that. It'd just be a hassle—"

"I don't care what the public thinks. I don't care how much of a hassle it is. I will do what's right, and blame the proper person. I will tell the truth. I am king." He turns to Leonidas. "Contact your informant and have her bring me Zera in exchange for Jona. Their meeting, their reactions, will determine the truth."

"I'll try." Herra won't be eager to give Zera up, even if it's to a lifetime of imprisonment. Especially not somewhere she can't follow on the transport journey. Leo will do his level best to persuade her.

"Matteo, what's wrong?"

Leo breaks out of his reverie to find Councilor Matteo's face drawn, exhaustion and sadness stitched into the lines of his dark skin. Leo notices all of the gray hairs in his long braids, wonder how many of them are premature.

"Nothing, dear boy," he says with a tight smile, reaching out to squeeze Ricarda's shoulder. "Old wounds that mention of your father brought to mind. Not your fault. Nothing you need concern yourself with."

"Matteo, you mean a lot to me." Ricarda holds Matteo by the arm. "If there is something wrong, I would like to hear it—if you honestly want to share. No one should have to carry any undeserved burden alone, however big or small."

Matteo sighs. "You're here, we're having this conversation—you might as well have some tea." He waves for them to be seated while he fixes them all cups of the cold tea Mariosans prefer. This is the only place Leo has ever had it, and it's delicious. He and Ricarda sit close, sides and legs pressed together on Matteo's white couch.

Matteo sinks into the one opposite them, facing the window that paints light onto his drawn face. He doesn't touch his tea, instead gesturing with nails painted an artistic gold—Mariosan through and through. "Your father and I were—close, when he died. I was his friend first and foremost, as always, but his death took a special toll on me."

Ricarda's eyes are blown wide. "Those rumors are true? I—don't take this the wrong way, Matteo, but I never thought—"

Matteo shrugs, smiles a little. "Your father was grieving and needed someone to fill the void after your mother died. I provided what he needed, nothing more. I was and have always been his closest friend, even before he met your mother. I was happy to serve his every want of me, always. I pretended like a young fool that anything he asked of me had any emotion behind it in that sense. I simply prayed he wouldn't find out the truth about my feelings."

"Are you saying that you felt—even before my mother—"

Matteo smiles again. Even Leonidas is enraptured now. "I would never have gotten in the way of them. I took what I could get when I could get it." He laughs a little. "Good gods. Your father's death and our affair disclosed in one conversation. That is not how I thought you would find out."

"Does Antonia know?"

Matteo inclines his head. "No, and I would thank you not to tell her. I will tell her myself."

"Of course."

Matteo smiles like it hurts him, so great is his love for the love of his life's son. "I only tell you now so that you'll both believe me when I say I understand the importance of discovering the truth. Your father...I suppose I let my own affection and rage blind me to the possibility that I had been wrong."

"I was blind, too," Ricarda says, looking at Leonidas.

Matteo chuckles. "There is no one more honorable in all of the continent to carry on his name and his blood than you. I know he'd be so proud of you."

Ricarda ducks his head, and this close Leo can see the tears beading there. He tries to see it through Ricarda's eyes, the source of his hesitance. Perhaps it has never before mattered who killed Ricarda IV or why, only that Ricarda had his father taken away from him. And that is not a wound that ever heals.

CHAPTER FIVE

Leo, to be perfectly honest, is scared. Terrified. He made the mistake of telling Ricarda his birthday, as if the treatment he received during the subordinates' ball hadn't been enough of a warning. He is a damned fool, doomed to an inescapable fate. The eagerness in Ricarda's grin spells nothing good as he leads Leo to Alessandro and Antonia.

Ricarda is a wild soul unleashed. His smile can be tender, gentle, and sweet, shown only to Leonidas in moments of peace. This particular grin is untamed, and often Leonidas finds himself just strung along for the ride.

"Before the mad horde have you for the night," Ricarda says, squeezing his hands, "we get to have you." Leonidas' life has been nothing but parties lately, but he finds himself enjoying them more than he did in any of the other countries he's visited.

"You wouldn't be Ricarda's lover if you weren't subjected to a humiliating, pointless, crazy party in your honor," Antonia says, smiling in her gown of deep blue and silver. Mariosans rarely wear blue, but she wears it well. The skirts swallow up her legs and much of Aless' on the settee, layers and layers of blue tulle on top of petticoats.

Ricarda makes a handsome figure in a long coat of pure white, with accents of gold on the stitching and the buttons. His half cloak is the same enchanting green as his eyes.

"Where's your gold half cloak?" Leo asks. "Isn't it something of a scandal to go without it? Royal honor and symbolism, and all that?" The ancestral sword is still strapped to Ricarda's hip.

"I forgo it today," Ric says, "in honor of you. Because you help me forget that I am king, and whisk me away to a world of tender, private sweetness." He drops a kiss on the back of Leo's hand, maintaining eye contact as he always does. Leo swallows, seeing the twist of Ricarda's smirk, the glint in his eye as his fingers fall away.

Aless groans. "Shut up," Antonia says, slapping his arm with her handkerchief. "You don't get to complain about them on Leo's birthday, just like they can't complain about us on my birthday."

It was the wrong thing to say. Aless' blue eyes light up like a fire in a dark room, his pout turning to a wide grin.

"Now you've done it," Ricarda murmurs.

"Leo," Antonia says, directing him to sit by her side, safely away from the boys and their antics, "this is just a small way to show you how much we love you. You've made our lives infinitely more entertaining since you showed up. Ricarda should be giving this speech, but he'd either start crying or get distracted in the middle of it."

"I would not!"

Her glare silences him. She tosses her hair with the confidence of a goddess and hands Leo a wrapped box, the bow tied as perfectly as the sashes on her gowns. "Happy birthday, love," she says, smiling.

Leo looks at it and freezes. He's never had anyone treat him like this before, but he can't very well tell them that. He remembers quiet nights as a child, his mother fucked off or fucked up somewhere. He'd be looking down at the little fire he made while the moon rose, the quiet wishes he'd whisper to himself. *Happy birthday.*

That was during his first name, when he'd never had cause to use another. Long before he had to use his seductive talents to make his way through life, through another day, month, year. Before Herra gave him a new purpose. His life was never simple, but those childhood birthdays were the only sense of innocence he's ever had.

"Are you going to stare at it until the moon rises or open it?" Ric teases, sliding onto the couch and pressing their sides together, linking their arms. Leonidas' heart clenches, his breath catches, and he tugs at the ribbon in this too-hot room.

Beneath layers of paper that could rival the layers of Antonia's skirts lies a necklace of sapphire and ruby, strung on a chain of gold links. He stares at it. It's so simple, so beautiful. It's different from the adorned jewelry he frequently wears, but it's more beautiful than anything he's ever owned in all his opulent courts.

"It's—I love it, thank you," he forces himself to say. "It's incredible."

"It's just a necklace," Ricarda chides softly, kissing his cheek. He fastens it around Leo's neck with utmost tenderness, his hot breath brushing his skin.

No, it's not. You don't understand. "I will keep it with me always."

"We're glad." Aless tugs him to his feet to hug him, the embrace of a true friend. The Lover doesn't have friends. He's not supposed to, anyway.

"Let's not keep the adoring public waiting," Ricarda says, rising smoothly to his feet and offering his arm formally to Leonidas. Trying to settle his fluttering, swooping heart, he links their arms and follows his new family out.

In the ballroom, in front of a crowd of cheering people all dressed in their finest, Ricarda raises his crystal glass. With his other hand, he raises Leo's. "To my wonderful lover, Leonidas Sartini!"

The room erupts into cheers—they don't really care about him, but they'll take any excuse to party, and they follow Ricarda's enthusiasm like a beacon. How many faceless people have they celebrated before just like this, raising glasses to good health?

Still, Leonidas smiles bashfully.

The party passes in a blur of sparkling lights and glittering conversation and champagne. He loses himself staring at the fresco until Ricarda's laughter pulls him free. The court of Mariosa has him bound utterly, and he feels himself spiraling into bliss further and further every day. That's not good. The Lover cannot afford that. Gods damn it, Ricarda is perfect, and he should just write and tell Herra that. But the possibility of leaving his position raises a primal sort of fear over him.

And yet he knows he'll end up doing it anyway. He cannot keep secrets forever. Ricarda expects differently of him now.

He dances in the center of the room with Ricarda and Antonia and Aless and whoever else will have him, wondering what Herra would think of him here. Though she scoffs at these parties, he wonders what her true feelings are. If she could find some joy in the spotlights too.

And then, like at the subordinates' ball, Ricarda whisks him away to kiss in a stairwell before too long. It's raining outside, the first true sign of the coming cold. Leonidas imagines it all: mornings cuddled close to Ricarda in bed, slipping out to get some water against Ricarda's protest, the arm he would throw over Leo's waist to keep him there with a moaned, "Leo, please, stay, it's too damn cold."

It appeals to him like the warmth of a fire in the dead of winter. It's a fantasy, a dream he can never keep. If he told Herra he'd found her perfect emperor, she might reveal his role in all this to Ricarda—or even if she didn't, Ricarda would work it out himself. He's not that dumb. He would be alienated, offended at being used the way he was. Leo wanted something from him just like everything else. The countless lies, the omissions, the unfair treatment...there'd be a price to be pay. And the Lover can't have that.

The Lover doesn't know how to do this.

Ricarda sighs at present, his nose buried in the hollow of Leo's neck. "Mm. I know it's your birthday, but I've been looking forward to this all day." A long, drawn out kiss, one that leaves Leonidas breathless and dizzy with want. Their arms are clutched tightly around one another, Leo's back to a window lit up with lightning and the rain pounding outside.

Leonidas pulls back reluctantly. He's been unable to stop thinking all day, everything Herra dragged him into, everything tying him down and everything tugging him away. "Ricarda, wait."

"Wait? That's not a request I thought I'd be hearing." Ricarda keeps kissing a path up his neck, and only a firm shove from Leonidas gets the message through. His brow furrows, and the sheen on his lips nearly makes Leo say *fuck it, forget it*, he'll address it another time. But he takes a deep breath and reins in his self-control.

"I'd like to talk about Zera."

That makes Ricarda fall still, then laugh incredulously. "Zera Musiek? That's who you'd like to talk about right now, on the night of your birthday? Not sure how I feel about my lover bringing up my father's murderer when we're about to—"

"Be serious for a moment. It's been weighing on my mind, and I can't relax."

That's all he needs to say. Ricarda's disbelief melts into concern, and he says, "What's wrong?"

Leo draws a ragged breath. "You're going to lock her up in the dungeons in Jona's place when she gets here, aren't you?"

"I—yes, what would you have me do? Let her sit on my throne and rule my kingdom? No, she's going to take her brother's place for punishment." He absently fixes his hair, curls falling effortlessly into place. Gods, he's beautiful. He's devastating.

Leo badly wants to bury this, but he can't. This festering wound will burst at a later date. This—this is the one flaw he's ever been able to find with Ricarda. No man can be perfect, and all relationships take work. Grievances must be aired. The Lover only knows how to leave at the first sign of trouble. He's never...done this before. Never encountered a problem he actually cared enough to work through.

Leo gives him a withering look. "I've always thought it was cruel how you treated Jona. I know what Zera did, and she deserves to pay, but that man—no one deserves to spend six years underground in total darkness, raised once a year to be a scapegoat in a cage."

"It's standard punishment," Ricarda protests, but they both hear the weak protest in his voice.

"When she gets here, grant her the release of death, at the very least," Leo cautiously says, his hands spread in plea. "If not because it is the kind thing to do, then because I ask it of you, and you love me."

Ricarda turns hardened eyes onto him, dark green in this light. Lightning illuminates them both.

"And what would you know about seeking vengeance for slain parents?" Ricarda snaps. "You never knew a father! You didn't have much of a mother to speak of, either! You know nothing of what it's like to lose the ones who guided me through life, one after another. You know nothing of the sweetness I felt when I finally had someone onto which to direct all my pain."

Leonidas pauses.

The anger on Ricarda's face falls and turns quickly into all consuming horror. "Leo, I'm so sorry, that was cruel." He reaches out, arms spread. Leonidas doesn't walk into his arms. He slowly backs up, away from Ricarda.

He's doing it. What he always does. The only way he knows how to do this. Run and flee when scared.

"I'm sorry, Ricarda," he says, voice shaking. "I love you. You're what I needed. I will tell you the truth someday."

Ricarda's expression only grows more destitute. The king of Mariosa, future emperor of the continent, has been reduced to a panicked mess. Other times it would be an accomplishment to be proud of. *I made the king love me so much he cried trying to keep me.* With someone like Edgorn, Leo would pay to see that.

Not this. Nothing has ever hurt more than this, like a knife tearing from his collarbone to his abdomen. The blade is Ricarda's voice, sharp and pleading, laced with whimpering hurt.

"Leonidas, love, wait. Fuck, stay. I'll do anything. I'm so fucking sorry, please, I need you—"

But Leonidas is already on his way, running far away, not looking back. Where he wants to be most, but can't. Not in this war, surrounded by monarchs who can never learn their lover was the same person. Not when Ricarda would hate him for the truth. Not when Herra needs him. Not when Zera is in question.

It had to end eventually. It always does.

He doesn't look over his shoulder, fearing what he'll see there. Ricarda's footsteps don't chase him down the dark hallway. Tears are running down Leo's cheeks now. Part of him wishes Ricarda would come sprinting down the hallway and pull him into his arms, into a kiss. That alone would convince him to stay. Leonidas wants to stay like he's never wanted anything in his life.

He can't.

The Lover discards his fifth name as he climbs out his second palace window in one year, a moonlit descent full of shame and sorrow. Tears down his cheeks herald his exit. The cold weight of the gold necklace rests heavily against his skin.

To nothingness he returns.

"LET ME GUESS. A MESSAGE meant only for my ears?"

The confused messenger stutters out an affirmation. Lasilas waves her on, impatient and tired after a long day of fighting Delainians. Instead of ragtag groups protecting little villages, the proper royal army has come to fight them now. Those battles have actually given Arthur a challenge, and he's little better than Lasilas right now. The only thing keeping him from completely collapsing into exhaustion is his armor.

The Coromodans will soon enter the field. Soon, Lasilas will lead the charge into Mariosa, where they'll have to contend with those vicious fighters. Worries for a future where Arthur has gotten some *sleep*.

Arthur, as always, hangs by his general's side. The messenger flinches at the stone cold look Lasilas gives her. "Can't you see I'm covered in blood? I'd like to go straight into that river and never come out, preferably as soon as possible. Get on with it, woman," Lasilas snaps. Arthur tilts his head, studying him. His snappishness is certainly new. Arthur's been trying to determine the source of his sour mood for weeks, but no theory has yet yielded results.

"I come from His Majesty King Edgorn of Ele, Emperor Presumptive. He summons you to a meeting in the tanstone caves in three days' time."

Lasilas frowns. "Did he say why? Three days, fuck. That's not long to get there." He sighs.

"No, sir. He didn't say."

"Ah, well." Lasilas smiles wearily at Arthur. "Better go see what the old bastard wants, hm?"

"He said to come alone, sir," the messenger interjects. "Not to bring your army."

Lasilas looks at her again, pale eyebrow raised. "Oh, did he? I didn't hear that part."

Despite the exhaustion weighing down his bones and his soul alike, Arthur smiles.

PART FOUR

THE HAMMER

CHAPTER ONE

A ugusta's voice, sweet and soft like honey, carries across the room as loud as thunder. Every eye in the Feathers house bar is drawn to her, listening with rapture to her enchanting song.

It's in Ilyakan, but no one cares. Augusta stands proud in the blue doublet Herra bought her, cheeks glowing, hair a sparkling mane under this light. She is flawless.

From the shadows, Herra feels a tickling pressure on the back of her neck; she's being watched. Twisting her head around, Herra spies Leonidas of all people lurking in the corner where none can see him but her. His arms are crossed, eyes low. He's dressed in golden courtly clothing, his hair much longer than when she saw him last. He looks—changed.

Normally upon his return he looks exactly as he did when he left, a statue, a perfect copy. The perfect lover molded to fit his target. Not this. This creature is different, whatever he is. It makes her curious.

It's not just the physical difference. Something about his posture, the look in his eyes, speaks of pain beyond what he'd ever express.

They lock gazes across the room. Leonidas raises an inquisitive eyebrow, daring her to question.

Herra gives him nothing in her returning glance, and after a few moments she tears her eyes away. She'll drive herself mad trying to work out why he's here. What made him leave. She wonders if it was another Edgorn, a sudden snap of the temper in Ricarda V. If it was his choice or the king's.

Knowing she can watch Augusta sing any other night of the week, Herra slinks away from the wall. With the melody of Augusta's song to cover her tracks and the crowd to hide her figure, she's not expecting Leonidas to be watching for her when she sidles up to him. He's smirking. "Hello, Herra. Long time no see."

"Why are you here?" she asks first and foremost. Better to know at the start if he's somehow added to the international crises. "No, you know what? Don't answer that. Let's go upstairs where we can have this conversation privately."

Leonidas—or, as she supposes she should call him now, the Lover—sighs with a heavy weight. "Let's stay and finish watching this girl," he says, gesturing to Augusta. "Leave the world behind for a moment. It's nothing that can't wait."

She says nothing, leaning against the wall beside him to watch. She slips into the foggy, familiar haze that Augusta's presence always brings about, like there is nothing else in the world but her. Herra feels Leonidas' eye on the side of her face, searching. Let him think what he will.

Augusta finishes her song with a last long, belted note, and the room erupts into cheers. So recently, those cheers would've been boos or threats on Herra's behalf. Following Herra's direction, the Feathers have turned to worship.

Augusta locks eyes with Herra across the room, grinning radiantly. She takes her bows and departs the stage, laughing away the demands for an encore. She saw the summons in Herra's eye.

Accepting a last shot from Ryn, the guest bartender here in the house, Augusta weaves through the crowd to Herra. A bard takes to the stage to replace her. Eyes drift away, and Augusta melts seamlessly to her place by Herra's side. Herra narrowly refrains from grabbing her wrist to pull her along. Not a dog.

"Who's this?" Augusta asks in Ilyakan. Although Herra is a reluctant student, they've started speaking a bit of it to give themselves an edge over others, a private way to communicate. Augusta glances at Leonidas. "Trouble?"

"No," Herra replies in Mariosan, trying to ignore the way Leonidas' eyes bug out of his head when he hears her speaking Ilyakan. Damn it, Augusta. Never been anything but trouble. "Come with us." Herra leads the way up the staircase, a polished railing of dark wood trimmed in gold. Utterly Mariosan. When she and Tasian redecorated this building to fit their needs, Herra snuck in some notes of Ancient architecture.

White fixtures, green accents for the traditional gardens they spend time in, color of all sorts sprinkled throughout. She's noticed with startling and disturbing clarity the similarities between Ilyakan and Ancient traditions. Augusta hasn't bothered hiding her smugness.

Herra leads them to her office and closes the door behind them. She leans against the door to ensure Leonidas won't be going anywhere until he answers all her questions—that is, unless he's started getting ideas like Augusta about jumping out of windows. He does have experience with that.

"Alright, spill," she says. He perches against her desk, confident like a cat, and eyes Augusta.

"I trust her," Herra says, scowling as Augusta stares. Gods, the entire sky and the ocean outside can be found in Augusta's eyes. "Speak freely. I'll explain her after you explain you."

He smiles. "So this is her. Am I finally going to find out the name of the companion from your letters?"

Herra rolls her eyes and gestures, trying not to let the weight of Augusta's unspoken questions get to her. She can hear Augusta's voice in her head. *What have you been saying about me, Ancient? Are they nice things?* "Augusta Tanner."

Augusta glares at her. "Augusta Grimash."

"Her brother's the exile prince of Ilyaka," Herra chimes in, earning another glare. "He's now the one leading Edgorn's army on an imperial rage through the continent, like I mentioned." In the court of Mariosa, he must've known all too well.

Leonidas' lips curve into a wide grin. "Oh? Is he my next target?"

Augusta tenses up, and Herra realizes what a mistake it was to let them meet. She works quickly to calm the waters. "No. Leonidas, tell me what happened. Shit, am I still calling you that, or just—"

"No," he says quickly, too quickly. "Leonidas. Please."

Herra raises an eyebrow. "What happened? Why are you here?"

"Nice to know I'm missed."

"No, you buffoon. I mean, what atrocity did you commit for him to throw you out?" She's explained the basics of his job to Augusta before, but making sure that she understands is not what Herra's concerned with at the moment. Augusta is smart, she'll put it together.

"It was nothing he did. Nothing I did. Well, I suppose it was me."

"What?"

Leo shrugs, too casual. What is he hiding? She remembers the flashes of pain she caught from his eye across the room. He is nothing if not good at protecting himself.

"What do you want me to say? He's perfect. He's your perfect emperor. Kind, popular, empathetic, smart, and responsible when stakes are high. Young. Handsome, should that ever, um. Be relevant."

He shrugs again. "Wise. Knows the duties of a king, though he leaves much of the work to his council. He's stepped up a lot more recently with the war, and though he hates diplomatic meetings—he's better on the battlefield—he can get it all done competently without anyone knowing how much he curses the foreigners out behind closed doors. He trusts easily. He listens to others. You can't wish for much more than that. In other words, perfect. Everything you could want."

Herra stares for a moment. He's serious. "Why are you here, then?"

Leonidas tilts his head—gods, that long hair is unnerving. It's to his shoulders now. "I thought the agreement was that I'd leave once I found the right person. It makes sense. I'm no longer needed. You'll appoint him and be able to interact with him directly. No more need for secrets on your end."

Leonidas cracks a strained smile, and she wonders what's on his mind behind his deep brown eyes. "We never discussed what I would do if I actually found the perfect emperor."

He's not wrong. He did the best he could in his circumstances, but still, white hot anger flashes through her. More and more common these days for her to be angry without reason. Taking it out on this man is something she's used to.

"You could've written," she grits out, stalking up to him and slamming him to the wall with one arm against his chest, "instead of leaving and jeopardizing our security in this uncertain time. In the middle of a war Mariosa is about to enter—for fuck's sake, you should've stayed!"

Something changes in his gaze then, fierce and fiery. Instead of brushing off her insults like the usual water on his feather, he sneers, "Don't tell me what I could've done to be happy. I don't need to hear it."

She raises an eyebrow, staring him up and down. She thought the tone of his latest letters was lovesick, but true happiness would not have been her first guess. "Happy? You were—happy?" She lets her grip on his chest slacken, and he slips out of her arms.

He raises his head. "Yeah."

Herra shakes her head. "You fell for one of your targets. I never thought I'd see the day when any of this became real for you."

She awaits sputtering denials, angry accusations, and paranoid deflections. All she gets is silence. Then, "Neither did I," with quiet resignation and a tinge of sadness so deep it scratches the soul. Her chest tightens.

He pulls something from beneath the collar of his shirt and runs his fingers over it: a necklace of gold links, sapphires and rubies alternating.

"Well, Herra," Augusta says, not letting them forget she's there, "you can fulfill your duty at long last, it seems. Fucking congratulations." She eyes Leonidas with the same sort of frightened fascination that she held for Herra when they first met.

Leonidas smirks at her. "Whatever, princess."

Augusta glares. "Just because my brother is a prince does not mean that I'm a princess. You obviously have no idea how Ilyaka works."

Leonidas raises his hands. "Wow. Okay. Jealousy noted."

Herra can almost see the steam about to come out of Augusta's ears, so she lays a hand on Augusta's arm and draws her eye. It's enough. That responsive touch of Herra's fingers has been drilled into her too thoroughly by now.

Augusta shrugs it off, and again Herra feels the pressure of Leonidas' gaze. Augusta turns to him and asks, "Why do you work for her?"

Herra glances at him, eager to hear his answer. She begins rifling through her desk drawers, searching for written rites she never thought she'd actually get to use, ones that have sat collecting dust for six years now.

He shrugs, effortlessly charming and endlessly mysterious. "She pays me. She gives me free room and board when I stay here."

"Oh, pah. You could get that anywhere with the right words and your—looks." Augusta gestures to him vaguely with a grimace. "I don't know, I'm not attracted to men. But she's told me you were a whore."

"True enough, all of that. But Herra lets me travel the land, find a use for my talents." He grins. "She has given me a purpose."

"You don't owe her a debt?"

"Not unless you count voluntarily following her out of the whorehouse where I worked as a debt." He casts Augusta an amused look. "I thought you Ilyakans were supposed to be the kind, merciful ones."

Herra laughs aloud at that. Augusta and her Grimash crest glare at her.

Leonidas says, "What if I told you she and I have simply grown to like each other, though she's loath to admit it?"

Augusta smiles. "Yes, she's like that, isn't she?"

Before Herra can protest that she's right here, Leonidas retorts, "You would know that, would you?"

Augusta sputters. Herra says nothing, hiding a smile and turning back to her work before the heavy gaze of Leonidas breaks her concentration again. She gets the sense there's something he's not telling her, something he won't say in Augusta's presence. She says, "This won't take long, Augusta, but I need a minute with him. Go downstairs and woo the crowd again."

"You only tolerate me for my talents and the coin it gets in your hat," Augusta says with no heat, squeezing Herra's shoulder on her way out. Herra barely notices it, barely hears her footsteps, so normal they have become.

"What is it?" she asks of Leonidas, thumbing through documents long stained and dirtied with tears. She copied the rites from memory soon after the deaths. Wasn't hard when her grandmother drilled the words into her at a young age, the most meaningful words she would ever have to say. They come back to her now easily as she mouths along.

Herra adds, "Nothing to say? Fine. I'll talk. You fell in love with your target. That's a first."

"You fell in love with a fucking Grimash." His arms are crossed where he stands in the doorway. "That's an impossibility."

They stare each other down for a few moments in silent judgment which dissolves into begrudging solidarity. The solidarity of two people who are utterly fucked.

"I am not in love with Augusta fucking Grimash," Herra says. "You don't know what you're talking about."

He smiles a bit. "I have watched dozens of people fall in love with me. Did you think I wouldn't know the signs?"

She doesn't back down. Leonidas sighs, and Herra hides her admiration for how long he's able to put up with her icy glare. That glare has sent others crying or cowering to their knees in the past.

"There is more," he says.

"Yes, it certainly sounds like it."

"Gods, you sound just like An—" He cuts himself off.

"Just like who?"

"Nothing. No one." Leonidas sees the look in her eye and sighs, knowing she won't let it go. "Just some friends I made there."

"You made friends too? Good gods."

He ducks his head, rubs the back of his neck. Is the great Lover actually blushing at that? My, my. So much has changed.

"No more about that," he huffs. "More about—anyway." He proceeds to tell her a winding story of Ricarda I's missing diary and his husband's missing wedding ring, Ricarda V's obsession with both, and the connection Leonidas discovered to his homeland with Ricarda V's unwitting help. "Oh, and another thing. Ricarda the Fifth wanted Zera there to stand in Jona's place. He said that if I could bring her to him, Jona would be released."

Herra laughs. "As if I'm letting her out of my sight."

"That's what I thought, but think about it. She would be getting life in prison. Isn't that what you want?"

She shakes her head. "You're already here. Your time in that court is over. It's already done. Anything else?"

Leonidas swallows down his obvious protests. "I am going to get the ring and diary from their northern hiding place, where I have a hunch Francesco is truly buried. I'll be safe out of sight from all the monarchs, away from the war. From Edgorn. You won't have to worry. I'll just fuck off, like you always want of me."

Herra looks up at his fallen face. "Augusta was right, you know," she says. "You are my friend. More than just my servant. More than my colleague."

A ghost of a smile graces his face. "You are, too."

"And you know I care for you. I don't despise you that much. I don't just want you to fuck off."

Leonidas smiles. "How much is it costing you to say this right now?"

"Don't push it. Augusta, get in here," she yells, knowing the girl is never far. She's probably been waiting just outside the door this whole time. Heat sweeps Herra's cheeks at the thought.

The door opens, and Augusta comes in with a dramatic sweeping bow. "I am but your humble servant, waiting on you every time you call on me."

"Shut up. We have a war to prepare against, and we can't avoid or deny our way out of it any longer. It's coming to Mariosa, to Ilyaka, and Edgorn won't stop until he has everything in his fist." She glances first at Augusta, then Leonidas.

"Do you think—" Herra bites her lip, wondering if it'll be a fruitless endeavor. Never hurts to ask, she supposes. "Would the Ilyakans listen to a call to arms from one of their own?"

Augusta is silent for a moment, then she breaks into laughter and points at herself. "Me? You mean me?"

"There's no other Ilyakan I could ask who I would willingly let out of my sight."

"Nice to know our relationship has progressed." Augusta is smiling with the levity of someone who thinks they're speaking to someone out of their mind. "In case you've forgotten, I left and never came back. I deserted and betrayed my country, my people. Many people said good riddance. I was a stain on Ilyaka, being the sister of Lasilas. I was the Golden Chisel, and I abandoned my duty.

"If I'm not instantly shot down upon my return, I certainly wouldn't be granted audience about a request as ludicrous as that. The Ilyakans won't be motivated to do something about Edgorn until he's right on our doorstep. Like I told you, we won't fight for an emperor. We won't fight for the king of Mariosa."

"But you will fight for your freedom," Herra counters, and watches something like hope flash through Augusta's blue eyes. It's gone quick as it arrived.

"What are you saying, Ancient?"

At some point, Leonidas slipped out, leaving Herra alone with Augusta's piercing blue gaze. "I'm saying," she says slowly, deliberately, "that if you do this, if you get the Ilyakans to fight before the entire continent falls and thousands of lives are lost, I will work with Ricarda to make sure he gives you your freedom."

Augusta draws a heavy breath, like she's dreaming of salvation and finding it too sweet to believe. "If you can't, there will be hell to pay."

"I know." Herra stares her down. Augusta doesn't flinch. "Have I ever broken a promise to you? I uncuffed you. I treated you differently when you asked me to. Zera is chained up in our dungeon, and you have the truth about your brother's banishment. More than that, I haven't harmed you since the first day we met."

Augusta says nothing.

"Ricarda the Fifth will be thanking me on his knees for making him emperor and saving his kingdom from ruin with the help of your army. The least of the repayments he can give me is Ilyaka when I ask for it."

The repayment will be the burden of her duty gone from her shoulders, but Ricarda himself will have little to do with that. Maybe she'll demand he gets Leonidas out of his head and back with him, wipe that sad expression off his face. That is not how the Lover is meant to look.

Augusta nods sharply. "Right. I'll ride for Ilyaka in the morning, then." She laughs like she can't believe she's saying it.

"We will ride in an hour," Herra corrects, reaching for her arm.

"What?"

"Do you think I would trust you not to run away if I sent you all that way by yourself?" The thought of Augusta being away for so long makes her itch, like she's missing a sense. "I need to make sure you don't dawdle. The journey is long, and we don't have a lot of time. We'll have to ride hard, no detours. Don't tell me you wouldn't be tempted," she says when Augusta casts her a long look. "This is your first foray back into your home after years away. Even I wouldn't have that self-control."

Augusta stares. "Yes, the woman who appoints the emperors that fuck us over, that is someone they'll want to listen to. The woman whose entire family we killed for that reason. That one. My best suited traveling companion."

"That was just House Grimash, though."

Augusta laughs. "Who do you think gave them the order? Gods, have I taught you so little about Ilyakan hierarchy? The houses, in theory, all work together. They're all intertwined."

Herra drops her arm. "You're not going without me."

"Possessive," Augusta mutters, but doesn't argue further, which Herra takes as agreement. Flinging open the door again, Herra calls for Leonidas and Tasian.

"You know," she says while she waits, "you'll be heralded as the hero of Ilyaka for bringing about its independence. You'll be revered and welcomed back with open arms. You'll be queen, or whatever the equivalent would be."

Augusta smiles, the corners of her eyes crinkling. "You know it doesn't work that way."

Herra smiles hopelessly back. "Yeah. I know."

Leonidas strolls in, eyes heavy with exhaustion both physical and mental. Herra reconsiders what she was going to say to him and instead says, "Good gods, Leonidas, find a bed and some soup downstairs and probably a bottle of alcohol. Go look for your ring with my blessing, but rest here a while first. Feel no rush while she and I are gone—we're going to Ilyaka. Tasian will tell you the details if you feel like asking." She waves it off. "Stay a while. You've been through a lot."

"I'm not the one who's been keeping my family's murderer prisoner," he says, but she can hear the relief in his voice. He slumps against the wall at just the thought of resting in a decent bed. Herra knows the long trips between targets and Mitzi are arduous enough, never mind the shitty inns. She has a fondness for how he looks once he comes back, quite literally like a starving man surrounded by a fine buffet.

Leonidas hasn't even mentioned dyeing or cutting his hair this time. So often people cut their hair as a sign of change. Perhaps this is a change, too. The Lover has always been in motion, always evolving and hardly ever taking a breath for himself. Sometimes it's good to clear the mind and just focus on one task, but too much and one starts to lose themself like he has. She doesn't know how to tell him that he *can* worry about himself, especially in his heartbreak. He is allowed.

She says, "You're too smart for your own good."

He grins, wolfish. "Not just a pretty face."

"No, a pretty body too. Presumably; I don't like men either. Now fuck off. Go find a bed."

As he leaves, Herra turns back to Augusta. She's shaking her head, eyes dark with disbelief. "I really am going back to Ilyaka to ask for a declaration of war," she mutters. "Fuck, the things I do for you, Ancient."

CHAPTER TWO

"No comments. Not a single one."

Herra grins widely, an expression that Augusta thankfully can't see since she's sitting in front on the horse. "Not even one?" Their horse clops along the well worn Amarinthine Pass into Ilyaka. During this busy wartime, Ilyaka has closed its borders. This is the easiest, fastest, and most plausible route.

Despite being a Grimash and the Golden Chisel, able to brute force her way through any combination of nature, Augusta chose the path of least resistance. Now she's paying for it. Well, she would be if she'd let a single word out of Herra's mouth.

"No. The pass is still not the only thing Ilyaka is good for."

"Well, so far, it has—"

Augusta twists around in the saddle and awkwardly claps a hand over Herra's mouth. Herra laughs through her fingers. "Okay, I relent. No comments."

Augusta grumbles and removes her hand. Herra takes a moment to actually look and appreciate the precious scenery of Ilyaka. For all they've talked about it, she never thought it would be a real place she could visit. Augusta's colorful descriptions made it seem like a place of fantasy, not somewhere people actually lived and worked.

It is, as Herra can see now.

Everything is so green. It's brighter than any shrubbery Herra has seen anywhere else, though to be fair, Mitzi is not known for its gardens. The trees here reach for the stars, their leaves thickly packed together to shade the trail. In the distance Herra can hear water rushing, reminding her of the Appointers' Court.

A waterfall was never far from home. The sound makes her ache for home. The rush of the ocean outside her window in Mitzi just isn't the same.

She still remembers the journey south she made from the Appointers' Court after the massacre. She was confused, frightened, yet determined, not knowing when she should stop or what her goal was other than the distant prospect of appointing an emperor.

Taking over her grandmother's task, carrying on her family legacy. She has often wondered what her family would think of her now, if they could see the terrible woman she has become. She is a scared girl of fourteen no longer.

Herra tries not to let herself feel the truth—that her parents, her aunts, her cousins, her honored grandmother would all turn their eyes away from what she has established in Mitzi. What she has done, the kindnesses she's forsaken to stay alive and in power. She needed it, once upon a time.

No longer. She doesn't need money, but she makes it anyway. She keeps prisoners in her dungeon and tortures them. She dawdled before finding and employing the Lover to start looking for an emperor. In her family's eyes, she would be a monster no better than the House Grimash murderers.

But they are not here to judge her, and she has not needed them for years. She puts them out of her mind and focuses on Ilyaka.

"Is there anything I should know before we meet your princes?" Herra asks.

"Oh, now she asks. Yes—it's inadvisable to bring Ancients along when you're trying to win your case."

"I don't have to be there for every meeting."

"You'll insist on it. And we'll be lucky if we're even granted a meeting with the princes." Augusta sighs heavily, tipping her head back to stare at the leaves. Herra imagines this must be quite the difficult reintroduction to her homeland. "We're lucky they're here right now."

"Where else would they go?" Herra's family never left Gina.

"Well, they just got back from that Mariosan summit," Augusta says, "and they like to ride around the continent together, immersing themselves in the way of others even if they look down on them like dog shit."

"Ah, perfect, idyllic Ilyaka."

"Hey, these are the princes appointed by the prince who exiled my brother, are you kidding? I have no love lost for them." She pulls the horse to a halt, sliding down off its back. "Fuck them. *This* is why I love Ilyaka so much. Why a part of me has always wanted to come back since the day I left." She wanders over to something like a shrine on the side of the road, a small clearing in front of an erected stone pillar.

"Augusta," Herra sighs, "we really don't have time for—" It's useless. Any attempt to drag her back onto the horse wouldn't work. It's better to just let Augusta have her moments. She'll be in a better mood.

"Come here," Augusta says, waving her over. She's kneeling on the ground in front of the pillar. "You're not Ilyakan, so I'm not supposed to do this, but I'm not supposed to be doing a lot of things. Fuck it. I hope the princes feel this in their bones." She gestures for Herra to kneel beside her, who does after a quick inspection for hidden dangers in the lush grass.

"This is a small, humble shrine to our gods," Augusta says, pointing to the nine flowers planted in the ground in a half-circle.

They're unnaturally bright, like the grass. The stone pillar seems plain in comparison.

"Our real temples are made of glass," Augusta says, "for an uninhibited view of the nature all around. Our gods' flowers are everywhere outside the temple walls." She smiles at the memory; it makes her look younger, without so much worry. "I haven't seen one since I left. They're exquisite."

"Which one would be my patron," Herra asks, "if I had chosen when I was a child?"

Augusta looks at her with a furrowed brow. She says, a little shaky, "The black lily, I think. Serenity, acceptance, respect, and peace. The emotions borne from a hard time, hardest to master."

She tilts her head. Herra watches the way her hair settles around her neck. "Or the white pansy—mine. Revenge and righteous corruption. Justice."

Herra looks at both flowers amongst the grass, the way the black lily seems to almost swallow the daylight. The white pansy is not as bright as one would think. It's rather dull in color, but that doesn't mean it's not still beautiful. "Opposites?"

"No. Quite the same, actually. Color theory has no meaning here."

"Only on my jackets," Herra says, nodding wisely.

Augusta's eyes catch on a purple violet, dark and demure and almost too strong to look at. It's like looking into the sun—a dark version of it. Herra has to blink. "What's that one?"

Augusta doesn't answer for a long minute. "Romantic love. It was the one Zera wore when I met her here. She was making a mockery of me for falling so easily. Her little joke, though I didn't see past her beauty at the time. What a fool I was."

Herra waits for her to stand up, shake it off, but Augusta seems trapped in the violet's hold, her eyes wide and her body perfectly still. Herra cautiously lays fingers on her arm, squeezing when Augusta jumps.

"What she did to you and Lasilas is not your fault," she says gently. "You were her victim, and Prince Heires'. Maybe it would hurt less if you hadn't been betrayed by your own people so terribly, but it does, and nothing will heal that. I know. But you cannot blame anyone for this but Zera. She was the one who used you, pretended to care about you only to commit premeditated murder for a sadistic warlord of a king. It was never about you. To her, Lasilas was just a pawn. Your people failed to see that. That is their fault."

"The people you asked me to come back here to bargain with," Augusta mutters, wiping her eyes. Herra goes quiet.

Augusta's face falls, and she takes Herra's hand in both of hers when she starts to pull away. "I'm sorry, Herra, fuck, I didn't mean that. You've done more for me than my own people did in the wake of the massacre. You're the first one who actually gave a shit, despite being my enemy.

"To everyone else, I've always been Lasilas' little sister, living in his great, bighearted, strong shadow. And then I was the Golden Chisel, but surely I couldn't be, because of the stain on my blood. Because I wasn't a fucking prince.

"You're the first one besides my brother to ever see me on my own, as someone worth something beyond him. Maybe that's only because you've never met him, but I'm grateful."

Herra nods, and they both slowly retract their hands. Herra's heart is hammering. She wonders why it's here that she can smell Augusta's scent the strongest—clean sweat and flowers and metal—instead of when they were on the horse.

"Can you pick them?" she asks, motioning to the flowers. "Keep your patron with you for good luck?"

Augusta laughs as they stand. "Gods, no. That would be like desecrating a painting or breaking a statue. You leave these alone. They're precious, physical manifestations of our gods. You've got to leave them for someone else to take comfort." She pats her white pansy crest. "That's what these are for."

HERRA IS ALL TOO AWARE of the time slipping away from them, the threat of Edgorn on the horizon. However, that feels like a worry for the distant south, not a concern of theirs up here in peaceful Ilyaka.

She can see why the Ilyakans don't want to involve themselves in southern affairs when they have this to retreat to. They have mountains and forests to protect them, much like the eastern queen. Every inch of the land is beautiful.

Beauty aside, their defenses just mean it'll be harder to get them to agree. Hopefully the taste of freedom will be too sweet to resist.

On their third day in Ilyaka, after countless meals of snared rabbits and picked berries, Augusta lets out a sudden gasp. Herra reaches for her bow, scanning for the threat. They've been blessedly alone so far on their journey, but that peace might be ending now. "What's wrong?"

"Nothing. We're at House Grimash." Augusta gestures at the distant house on the crest of a hill, peeking through a few layers of low hanging leaves. Herra squints.

"That's it?" From here, it seems like nothing more than a small cabin. Herra was expecting a palace, or at the very least, a mansion. This is the house of people who killed her family?

The reminder makes her grimace. This is the house of people who killed her family. She'll have to interact with them, perhaps look into the faces of people who stabbed and shot her family. Hopefully her ability to compartmentalize will triumph.

"What were you expecting?" Augusta asks.

"Something bigger, grander. More like a palace. Not just a house in the middle of the forest."

Augusta laughs. "Sweetheart, that's where all the houses in Ilyaka are. To the west, there are more clearings, but here you're not likely to see the sun through the leaves. I can't believe I never told you that."

"We're not going to House Catiana?" Herra asks as Augusta leads the horse boldly into plain view of the house.

"No. You need special permission to go there unless you're family. Lasilas is not a prince anymore, so I have no privileges. You certainly wouldn't. Remember the debacle with Zera?"

Herra gets chills. "Of course. I—sorry." Augusta chuckles, thankfully.

Herra barely has time to ask, "We're not going to be shot down, are we?" before Augusta is sliding off the horse and waving her hands up at the house. Herra sighs.

"I come in peace!" she yells in Ilyakan. Herra understands her—her skills have been improving. "I am House Grimash! See my crest!"

Herra hangs back, heart in her throat, while someone in a cloak as white as a cloud comes floating out the front doors. Herra gets a shuddering flashback of her mother stuffing her in a closet, telling her to stay there, it would all be okay. Her mother left with Herra's very bow in hand when she went to meet those white cloaked monsters.

Hours later, Herra picked up the bow from her mother's cold body, bleeding all over their wooden floor. It's strung across her back now.

Augusta is not shot down, and the figure in white doesn't notice Herra hiding amongst the leaves. As horrified as she is, there's something fascinating about seeing a full fledged Ilyakan in person, in their traditional garb.

They were as much myth and legend to her as the Silver Hammer is to them. A fairytale, a dreamy sight she thought she'd never see. Of all the stories her grandmother told her of other cultures, Ilyaka was always the one she found most fascinating. That is, until they desecrated her family and her ancestral home.

And now she is here, seeking their aid in war.

Augusta's conversation with the Grimash isn't pretty. Amidst shouting and gesturing, Augusta gets a harsh slap to the face that makes even Herra wince. But she is not otherwise harmed, and the stumped Grimash finally throws their hands up in defeat. With an overexaggerated bow, they gesture Augusta inside, the sleeves of their white robes falling around them.

The Ancients wore white too.

Augusta gestures for Herra to come out of hiding, which sparks another argument between her and the Grimash that rages on till Herra has hitched the horse and is standing beside them. It's all in Ilyakan too rapid for Herra to follow. She'll be at a disadvantage in more ways than one.

Once upon a time, she would've only relied on translations from Liss, her half Ilyakan Blue Feather. Once upon a time, she didn't trust a word that came out of Augusta's mouth.

She wonders what her past self would think if she saw Herra now, alone with Augusta in a strange land in the middle of a war. She would probably laugh.

The Grimash relents again under Augusta's sharp tongue, and Herra follows them inside the clan building. Herra fumbles for Augusta's hand, taken with hesitance in the darkness as they edge inside. Augusta doesn't slap it away—she squeezes it.

"Old Minyan, the language of the Ancients, is the closest living thing to Ilyakan," Augusta whispers to her. They've been speaking

Mariosan or Ilyakan the entire time they've known each other, and Herra thrills at the possibility of hearing her own tongue again. "I'll try to work something out."

The fact that she cares enough to do so instead of just translating the Ilyakan for Herra sets her heart ablaze. Augusta is on Herra's side even in the house of her own people, and that helps Herra smile and relax as she presses deeper into enemy territory. They haven't been asked to remove their weapons, thank the gods.

"This way, Grimash," says the Grimash member with the title spat out. Herra is busy recalling her old tongue, retired for six years, that she almost doesn't notice the way Augusta's hand tightens in hers.

They're led to a council room drawn in low light, the brown walls and brown tables and dark floors soaking it all up. Herra sits stiffly where Augusta bids, and a flurry of Grimash enter with their expressions as sharp as knives.

Augusta whispers, "Just think in Minyan," before she begins to speak to them, hands clasped on the table. Herra notices the way she proudly juts out her white pansy crest, as if reminding them *I'm Ilyakan too, you buffoons, and I have as much a right to petition you as anyone.*

Herra tries to follow along with the Ilyakan, but she doesn't understand more than a few words at a time. She hears the important ones: emperor, alliance, war, independence. Please. Augusta's tone translates the rest.

The Grimash aren't happy. They wouldn't be happy even if it wasn't Augusta delivering the message. Herra sits still and quiet, antsy, bearing the scorn they give her.

Finally, when Augusta's voice grows hoarse from explaining the same thing five different ways, appeasing them and answering every little question with still no give, Herra rises to her feet.

"House Grimash," she snaps in broken Ilyakan, knowing Augusta will translate what she can't say, "let's not pretend you have much honor. You slaughtered my family in cold blood because of what we might do to you as others had done in the past. But I am here, and I am willing to look past that, if you are willing to give me a chance.

"She does not lie when I say I will grant you independence. I will not appoint an emperor who does not agree to that. You will be free of the matters of the continent. There is no more to it than that. I want nothing from you other than your fight in this war. I offer you the pleasure of getting to slice a conqueror's head from his shoulders. Consider it, please." She draws a breath. "We will not leave until we have what we want."

Augusta translates quietly, a hush falling over the room. The Grimash who first met them outside grumbles, "We are never truly free," but the one who sits nearest him says stiffly, "We will deliberate. Thank you, Ancient."

It's not a total denial. It's not a curse or a threat. It's a chance. It's the best Herra can hope for.

She and Augusta lock eyes and nod.

CHAPTER THREE

A rthur hates caves.

They're dark and wet, for one, and holding a torch means he has one less hand free for self-defense. There has been no indication so far that he'll need self-defense, but he can't shake that feeling. These caves are so small, so cramped, making him check obsessively over his shoulder. Doesn't help that he's pressed almost chest to back with Lasilas' soldiers.

Lasilas' voice at the front is all that's keeping Arthur in the present and out of a blind panic. "Come on, folks, we're almost there, just keep going! Soon we'll be out of these nightmares and back under daylight, and this will be just another anecdote to laugh at."

At least Lasilas didn't bring his whole army down here. He left a few captains and divisions at the surface, guarding the entrance in case of an ambush.

Paranoid. That's the word for this. Arthur is paranoid, and maybe a little claustrophobic. He's large and his armor weighs him down, and he's not built for spaces like this. He'll blame it on his height.

"How are my captains doing back there?" Lasilas calls. "Regretting ever joining up with me?"

"Considering it, sir," Arthur calls back, earning a hearty laugh.

"We'll be the ones to drag your corpse out and give it a proper Ilyakan burial when Edgorn inevitably kills you," Nyer calls from the back of the line.

Arthur holds his breath, but Lasilas laughs at that too. "Why, Nyer, that's almost treason. I like it."

Arthur's chest tightens at hearing someone else make Lasilas laugh.

At long last, Lasilas says, "We've reached open cave, folks," earning a cheer through the ranks. Arthur is just focused on getting out of this hellhole as quickly as possible. This might be the thing that's tested his resolve most. *Lasilas, you're lucky you have my absolute loyalty.* Hopefully this meeting with Edgorn will be over soon and they'll get to the surface. He's already dreaming of fresh air, the cool night breeze against his skin.

Soldiers drop down one by one into the cavernous space below. Torches rest in sconces here, thank the gods.

"Now, I do have to go into the meeting alone," Lasilas says, looking at Arthur. "At least pretend to have followed his orders. Don't worry too much about me. It's just routine, though he could've picked somewhere more accessible than these dark caves." He shakes his head, pale hair shining in this orange light. "Ah, well. I won't be too long." His eyes sparkle as he backs away toward another entrance, sword in hand.

Arthur glances back at Lasilas' soldiers, finding his own thoughts mirrored on all their faces: a desire to follow, to protect, or at least to oversee. What is a general without a force at his back? Arthur quietly beckons a handful of soldiers to follow him, leaving Nyer and Callum to oversee the rest.

Inspecting the tunnels and the walls of this mighty cavern, Arthur finds a crawlspace high up. It's just big enough for himself and the others to huddle into and overlook the meeting room.

His height and muscle are required to boost the soldiers up to the opening. Finally, they're good for something.

Crawling up, Arthur sees Edgorn sitting at a table, splayed out in his red robes with a bottle of wine and two glasses. The room is lit low with torches, Lasilas standing silently at the entrance.

Edgorn raises a glass of dark wine. "General."

"My king." Lasilas bows low, the picture of polite obedience. The sight makes Arthur long to know what he was like in his princely days, the smiles he gave the people to calm them, the confident speeches he gave, the handsome figure he must've cut on a horse in full regalia. Arthur's breath grows heavier thinking about it, Lasilas in his element at his prime. Instead, Lasilas stands here as a shadow of himself with the man who reduces him to nothing.

"Sit down," Edgorn says. Guards in red stand in the shadows behind them, hands on their sword hilts.

Lasilas does, propping his boots up on Edgorn's table. He helps himself to the second glass of wine. "What can I do for you, my king? I must say, this is an unconventional location for a meeting. Is there something about my recent service that has displeased you?"

"I have changed my mind," Edgorn says, getting to the point. "I do not want you to lead the charge to Alizima and stake my claim there."

Arthur watches dozens of emotions flicker across Lasilas' face, but he presents a confused smile. "My king?"

"Instead, you will lead the attack on Ilyaka," Edgorn says, as gruffly and casually as if discussing a supply shortage. He sets down his glass to have a good look at Lasilas, whose expression turns to horror before he can hide it. Arthur presses his face closer, hearing little hitches of breath from the soldiers beside him.

"You will take the princes Catiana as your prisoners. The entire nation will be under your control. You will crush its resistance in your palm, and then you will join me in Alizima. As a reward for your ceaseless service to me, Ilyaka will be yours to govern under the shade of my empire. I will give you back what you once lost."

Lasilas swallows. "My king, I—"

Edgorn fixes him with a look, dark hair falling around his face to cast it in shadow. "You know what will happen if you disobey. My little weapon, as always, remains sharp and ready to attack. Her blade will all too easily find your sister's throat if you are not careful, or if you are too slow." He takes another long sip of wine. "Are we clear, General?"

"Yes, my king." Lasilas rises to his feet unsteadily, dipping into a bow. "Anything else?"

Arthur can hardly breathe, so great is his horror.

Horror turns quickly to anger that burns through Arthur's veins from head to toe. He can't let Lasilas do this. This is going too far. Arthur will desert if he has to.

Or, he'll go with the easier and better option, the one he should've gone with a long time ago. He hops down from the hole in the wall into the room below. His armor rattles and creaks when he lands. When he stands, answering creaks and rattles land behind him. Lasilas' soldiers followed. Arthur swells with pride.

They keep filtering in, not just from the tunnel in the wall but from the route Lasilas took, confident captains and their soldiers with their weapons all drawn. Lasilas is looking at them like he doesn't know whether to be grateful or angry. He's smiling with resignation, eyes dark and sad. Arthur wants to put fire back in his eye.

"What are you doing here?" Edgorn rumbles, not bothering to get up. He probably thinks he has a great and intimidating presence, but Arthur is not intimidated by him. He refuses to be. "Get out. This is a private meeting. The general apparently can't follow one simple instruction to leave his troops behind. He is only good for so much."

Lasilas' head lowers, and they can't have that.

"It sounded like you were just about finished," Arthur says, stepping forward, sword drawn. He stands tall and puffs out his chest, showing the might of the Silver Hammer.

Edgorn's mouth and dark mustache curl down in anger. "Get out, all of you," he spits. "Do your duty. Do not speak to me that way. I am your king. You are *mine*."

Arthur smiles. "We are not yours, Edgorn We are not loyal to you, but to General Lasilas." Arthur looks at Lasilas when he says it. "We are Ilyakans. We stick with our own, and we fight for no foreign king. We go where our commander bids us, nothing more. We are not like your other armies. We are independent. And we will not conquer our own country, just as I'm sure our commander would rather die than rule it in those circumstances. Because we, unlike you, have honor. Ilyakan honor."

King Edgorn shrugs, calm and collected instead of the infamous explosive temper Arthur expected. He stands and draws his sword, and every eye in the room follows the movement. "Very well." He reaches out and grasps Lasilas round the waist, dragging him close and wrapping him up in one fluid move. He's too fast for Lasilas to get his bearings or resist.

As Arthur steps forward, Edgorn's sword goes to Lasilas' throat, arm locked around his middle. Lasilas' eyes widen, but he doesn't move. Panicked eyes find Arthur's in desperation, pleading for aid.

Edgorn stands tall in defiance. "You fight for your commander. I control him. Do you fight for me now?"

One could hear a hairpin drop. Arthur looks at his fellows, astonished, but no one steps forward. No one even speaks. Bitter disappointment fills him up till he's nearly choking on it. Everyone else is too afraid of the consequences to act.

It's alright. He will stand alone.

"Not for you," Arthur shoots back. "Never for you. For him." He draws his sword, holding it with both hands in front of him. "The honorable Lasilas Catiana would never let himself be controlled by a man as odious as you. I will fight you for his freedom."

"Arthur, no," Lasilas gasps out before Edgorn's blade bites further into his throat, silencing him.

"Fine," Edgorn says, a smirk creeping onto his face. He signals to one of the guards he came with, releasing Lasilas into their care with a calculated dance. Arthur holds Lasilas' gaze the whole time, finding fear and fury for him as well as Edgorn. Arthur will not apologize for protecting the commander he swore loyalty to, no matter the risk to himself. This is his duty, his honor. His pleasure.

Edgorn puts his sword up, and Arthur's heart settles. All of this—the eyes on them watching with relief or hatred, the first clang of steel against steel—it all feels so right.

This is what the Silver Hammer was meant for. Not for slaughtering and conquering innocent people, not the bile in Arthur's throat every time he's fought. This armor demands righteousness, the walking emblem of the honorable blue carnation. The patron of soldiers, of protectors, of people like the Silver Hammer.

Arthur and Edgorn dance around the cave, the click of metal against metal echoing off the walls. At some point, Edgorn's crown of gold and rubies gets knocked off, and one of his guards picks it up before Arthur can smash it with his armored boot. Arthur slips in under Edgorn's guard once or twice, but it's never enough to gain the real advantage.

They're evenly matched, quick on their feet and in their minds, fighting not just for one man but for their respective reputations, for their countries, for their causes.

Arthur's armor sings in tune with him, riding that sense of righteousness. His sword swings before he's fully decided to, his feet move before he realizes Edgorn is lunging toward him. Edgorn spins and twirls, meeting his sword in some version of elegance that he has managed to brutalize like everything else around him.

Arthur's rage is his fuel. He has hated this man for years, but the hatred only intensified once they finally met in person. Edgorn sucks the life out of Lasilas, takes that glow from his eyes, the smile from his lips. Arthur will take all those things from Edgorn in return.

When they cross swords again, Edgorn glares. "Why do you fight for him so vehemently? You are just a captain. You would dare fight a king for your general? Why?"

A thousand responses come to mind, but not one of them includes the words that end up coming out of Arthur's mouth. "Because I love him."

The room falls into a hush. Edgorn falls still, and Arthur should be using that to press his attack, but he can't. The words tumble out, and he can't look at Lasilas to save his life.

"He is the most honorable man on this earth, righteous and brave. He has been corrupted by you and your wickedness. You would have him kill his own people—my people—and reign over the broken kingdom as your puppet. You think you have him snared so neatly, but I know Lasilas better than that. He would never."

Finally unfreezing, Arthur shoves hard against Edgorn's sword before Edgorn can take advantage. Arthur shuts his mouth before he says anything else detrimental and focuses on the fight.

It was Lasilas who taught him these moves when Arthur was a private in his army. Lasilas was ever patient, leading all the new recruits through repetitive drills until the movements stuck in their heads. They're instinct to Arthur now, but Edgorn is using techniques Arthur has never seen before. Dodging and ducking keeps Arthur on his feet, but it doesn't knock Edgorn off of his.

Drawing a breath, encouraged by the cheers of Lasilas' troops, Arthur charges in and knocks aside Edgorn's blade. Not with his sword, though. The Silver Hammer grabs it with his gauntleted hands and tosses it aside, towering over Edgorn in his full height and armor, six feet of Ilyakan might and myth. He is almost glowing, certainly the brightest thing in this torchlit cave.

Arthur remembers with shocking clarity that he is much taller than Edgorn.

The mighty king of Ele, emperor presumptive, looks up at his towering shadow with the first hint of fear in his dark eyes. Defiance and anger quickly return, and he bends to scoop up his sword again, but the Silver Hammer won't let that happen.

"Let him go now," he says. "We will walk out of this place alive, and so will you as long as Lasilas goes free. If not—" He smiles, holding both their swords in both hands. "I would relish the pleasure of seeing your head slip out from beneath your own blade."

Before Edgorn can answer, hands close around Arthur's wrists from behind. What feels like four pairs of hands lock his arms behind his back and remove the swords from his grip. He fights, curses, shouts, but the guards just hold on tighter. With a fresh boiling rage, Arthur realizes that Edgorn was just biding his time until he could let Arthur think he'd won, then capture him in turn. Like a fool, Arthur took the bait.

"No Ilyakan will be walking free today," Edgorn says, taking both swords. He inspects his blood splattered along the blade that hurt him and wipes it off on the tail of his robes. The evidence that Arthur ever touched him is gone.

"No," Arthur gasps. "You will let him go, you bastard. You promised. You really do have no honor."

Edgorn laughs, a harsh, terrible sound. "Did you really think I was going to let him go? My most valuable asset? The Ilyakan prize jewel in my crown?"

Gathering the last of his strength, Arthur growls, "He is not a prize, or an asset, or a jewel to be kept. He is not an object. He is a prince of House Catiana, wrongfully exiled, screwed over by every colleague he's ever had. And that tradition will end with you. You will not touch him."

Edgorn shrugs and walks across the room to Lasilas, deliberately running a finger from Lasilas' collarbone to his ear, tracing the line of his jaw, ignoring the way he flinches away. Arthur growls. In a bored tone of voice, Edgorn says, "Watch me."

"No," Arthur says, fighting like something wild in the arms of his captors. He is the Silver Hammer, dammit, twice as big as them and covered in twice as much as armor. Can he not break the hold of a few measly arms on him? Is he so useless? Fuck, this is when he's needed most, to protect, and he can't deliver. "No. You will release him right now!"

"Arthur, don't worry," Lasilas calls over the rising chaos, his troops pushing against Edgorn's guards and Edgorn himself to get to their commander. Lasilas and Arthur are dragged in different directions. "Don't worry about me! I'll be fine! Worry about yourself!"

Arthur and Lasilas call each other's names, crazed and furious, as they're dragged into tunnels of pure darkness. The sound fades out, muffled by the walls, and in comes the jingle of heavy keys. Far too late, Arthur puts the pieces together.

Edgorn held this meeting in a cave system for a reason. Caves come with dungeons.

CHAPTER FOUR

Arthur is pacing the length of his tiny jail cell. It's pitch dark like the night sky but without any of the brilliant stars or the cool air. This is cramped, dank, and musty, and he's been fighting rising claustrophobia with each passing minute. Removing his armor would probably make it better, and would at least cool him down, but he doesn't want to be caught off guard. He must be ready to fight.

He's been trying not to think about what Edgorn will do with him. Lasilas is the one Edgorn needs, but releasing the mouthy captain who made his loyalties clear wouldn't be wise. Arthur will probably be left here to rot, low on Edgorn's list of priorities, especially if the campaign succeeds and he has a new empire to contend with.

Fuck. So much for not thinking about it.

Footsteps approach the cell, and Arthur jumps to attention. He doesn't know how long he's been in here—a few hours, maybe? He wonders what became of the other soldiers, if the ones at the mouth of the cave system even know what's going on.

The door to his cell creaks slowly open, ancient metal scraping against the rock. Arthur vibrates with restless anger. The person barely fits themselves through the door before Arthur has an arm locked around their neck. He doesn't dare use enough pressure to actually hurt them, just enough to scare them, as he suspects they're a low ranking servant.

"Shh," Arthur says, listening to their gasps and whimpers. "Just stay quiet and don't fight me. Everything will be alright. You know he put me in here for a reason. You don't want to irk me."

"N-no, sir," the servant stutters. In the dim light, Arthur sees the tray of food they set down just outside the door so they could open it.

"Here's what we're going to do," Arthur says quietly, calmly. "You're going to tell me where General Lasilas' cell is, where I can find the key to it, and then you're going to bring that food in here. You'll leave quietly and lock the door behind you. You're going to pay no mind to where I go, and you're not going to say I slipped out. You saw nothing. You do that, and you won't get hurt. Understand?"

"Yes, sir. Please, sir, I have a wife, a pregnant wife—"

"Just follow my instructions, and I will have no reason to hurt you, like I said. Now, where is General Lasilas' cell? Do you know? Do you have someone you could ask who knows?"

"It's in the eastern wing of cells," they gasp. "The third one down once you come in. You'll know it, it's the only one occupied."

"Very good. And where is the key?"

"With King Edgorn."

Damn. As he feared. "I am going to let you go, and you're not going to scream. You're going to do exactly as I said, do you remember?"

"Yes." Arthur slowly removes his arm, his other hand ready to slap over their mouth if need be. They don't scream. Arthur releases his breath. "Good. Is there anything else I should know?"

"There are guards at the northern wing. You'll have to pass them to get to the eastern wing until you can melt into the shadows."

"Thank you." Arthur slips out the door, wincing at how loud his armor jangles in the dark. "May your wife deliver safely."

He creeps down the hallway before they can respond.

Arthur isn't made of shadows or smoke, but he sneaks past the northern guards easily enough. He holds his breath the whole time, darting past once they've turned toward each other. They reach out for each other in a moment of downtime. Guards, alone on a late night shift. They're thinking of other things than the hallway they're supposed to guard.

The eastern block of cells is identical to the western block where he was being held, except for a sliver of light. Arthur is quick, seeking out his goal quickly. Third down. His heart beats faster as he approaches the cell, fearing what condition he might find Lasilas in.

"Lasilas?" he whispers into the darkness, hoping desperately that his general will answer his call.

It takes a long, long while before he gets an answer from the darkness within. "Arthur?" Lasilas rasps.

Arthur nearly sobs at the hope in his voice. He is that hope for Lasilas. Him. "Yes, yes, Las, I'm here. I'm going to get you out, just hold on."

Lasilas creeps forward into view, kneeling down at Arthur's level and clutching the bars. His face is long and ashen, utterly hopeless. "You might as well give up. It was always going to come to this. Edgorn was always going to win over me."

Arthur's heart clenches. "Is that what you really think? That I—we—were just going to let that happen? That all of this was fruitless?"

Lasilas doesn't reply, his form meek in the darkness, his arms wrapped around his knees as he leans against the wall. He looks so small.

Edgorn made him this way.

Arthur swallows his rage for the moment and says, "Well, you're wrong. Edgorn is a piece of shit, and we are done working for him. We are going to fight for Ilyaka, against him, for what's right. But I am going to get you out of here first. I will duel him a thousand times if I have to."

"Arthur—"

"What language do we speak?" Arthur asks, then again when he gets no reply. "Tell me, Lasilas."

Lasilas raises his head to smile at him, amused and bashful and a little bit awed. He breathes the word like it's holy. "Ilyakan."

Arthur grins and switches to it, little though he knows. "That's right."

Lasilas laughs, a broken sound. "You're too good to me, my dear captain."

"You don't know your own strength, my prince." Arthur rests his fingers on the bars, waiting until Lasilas scooches forward to lace their fingers together. Righteous fury burns through Arthur's lungs at the sight of Lasilas locked away like this, turned meager and helpless. This is the last place he belongs.

"I will get you out," Arthur vows, knowing he'll keep that promise till his dying breath. He lays a kiss on the back of Lasilas' hand like they're courtiers.

"Promise me something else," Lasilas whispers, his eyes like bright beacons in this darkness.

"Anything," Arthur replies, the truth. He would do anything for this man.

"Promise me you won't sacrifice yourself for my sake, Arthur."

Arthur hesitates.

"I cannot lose you," Lasilas says. "You are my brightest star, Arthur. My brave soldier, my symbol of strength. Without you my world goes dark."

Lasilas can't say things like that. Words like that make Arthur want to do unwise things like yank these cell doors clean off their hinges and pull Lasilas out into his arms, hold him close with one hand while slicing off Edgorn's head with the other. Things that the Silver Hammer alone could do.

Instead, he swallows, but that doesn't prevent his voice from cracking. "I am not your only captain, Las, nor your only soldier. You would be just fine without me."

Lasilas shakes his head vehemently. "Not one of them is just like you," he whispers. "Not like you. Please, don't get yourself killed. It would break me. If we die, we die here together, or you let me die here and get yourself out."

Arthur squeezes the bars one last time. "I won't get myself killed. I will get you out. We will walk away free together, as long as you promise you will never work for Edgorn again."

Lasilas' hesitation breaks Arthur's heart. "You should've told me he was threatening your sister, holding you hostage," Arthur says. "I could've done something to help."

"How? Until recently, you didn't even know I had a sister. I don't know where she is, who the assassin is, and no clues about how to find her. There was nothing anyone here could do, and I wouldn't let you leave to look for her when I needed you most. Augusta can manage more than well enough on her own." Lasilas sighs. "I was such a fool. I promise you that I wouldn't have worked for him for so long had he not held my sister against me."

"You don't need to explain anything. Not to me. I will get you out," Arthur vows, standing up. "I will be back. Just you wait here."

Lasilas smiles at him. "Not like I have anywhere to go. I will wait for you, my captain. My bright star."

Arthur slips away into the darkness again.

Ten minutes later, he comes back with a rusty key in hand, startling Lasilas with a gasp as he unlocks the door. "How—what—you were just here—"

Arthur grins, trying to keep the noise down.

"Wasn't that key on Edgorn's person?" Lasilas asks.

"Maybe. Maybe not. I have my ways."

Lasilas shakes his head and takes the hand Arthur offers, pulling himself to his feet. "You are even more brilliant than I gave you credit for, my star. I suppose you have a plan for how we're going to get out of here, too?"

Against Arthur's better judgment, he pulls Lasilas into a hug. Words evade them both for a moment, and Arthur realizes belatedly that he's crushing Lasilas with his bulk and his armor. He loosens his grip but doesn't let go. The sight of Lasilas held captive is still stuck in his head. "Edgorn will never harm you again."

Lasilas smiles, giving Arthur a final squeeze with his endless warmth as he pulls back. "I'm your general. Aren't I supposed to be reassuring you?"

"We all need a bit of comfort sometimes. We can't all be expected to be a caretaker, wear a stoic face, lead an army without breaking. It's alright, Lasilas." Arthur takes a leap and strokes his thumb over Lasilas' cheekbone. "You have me."

Lasilas' smile is the only sunlight Arthur needs down here. "Again, Arthur, I don't know what I'd do without you."

Arthur forces himself to keep Las at arm's length. "I'll make sure you never have to find out. Now let's get out of here."

CHAPTER FIVE

"You are trying to get us lost in the woods."

"I am not getting anyone or anything lost in the woods! These are the woods I roamed every day as a child. I know them better than my own palm. It's just the hot springs I'm less familiar with. Usually they're an honor reserved for—"

"We're lost," Herra says. "You're lost."

"We are not—" Augusta sighs and cuts through another bundle of leaves in their way. Herra entertains the thought that she's leading them in the most roundabout path possible just to take out some stress on these branches. "Look, there! See the steam coming off the water?"

Grumbling, Herra looks over her shoulder. It's dark, and moonlight doesn't have the same power in a thick forest that it does in Mitzi by the waterside. "I don't see shit, Grimash."

"All that time indoors preparing to appoint an emperor must've ruined your eyes, Ancient. It's right there." Augusta presses on. Herra sighs and continues following, knowing she'd get even more lost trying to get back to the house in the dark.

Pushing through a last stubborn cluster of trees, Herra finally sees what Augusta assured would be worth the long walk in the dark. A system of hot spring pools, set deeply into the ground with lush greenery surrounding them. Holy flowers are sprinkled throughout the clearing, providing bright dashes of color.

"Fuck whatever I said before," Augusta says, stripping quickly in the dark. "This is what I missed most about Ilyaka. Gods, whenever I'd visit Lasilas at House Catiana, we would come to one of these. They're everywhere throughout the country."

Herra crosses her arms. "Why would we go in the dark? This would be much prettier in the daylight."

Augusta gives Herra a withering look. "Not like we had a lot of time today, if you remember. I didn't want to wait till tomorrow." She wades into the water, sighing. Herra tries to avert her eyes, but they're pulled toward Augusta's body anyway.

Augusta sinks into the steamy water up to her shoulders. She takes down her braid and says, "Get in or I'll splash you until you do."

Herra raises her hands. "Ooh, I'm so scared."

"I mean it! That lovely yellow coat, all wet!"

"You'd be doing yourself more of a disservice as the mistress of my wardrobe," Herra says, fighting a smile and giving in.

The water is hot and lovely, working wonders on muscles battered by long days of sitting on a horse. She puts her back to the wall of the pool and sits in silence, watching Augusta thrive, happy to hang back.

"Why are you so tense?" Augusta asks, settling and treading the water. The pool isn't big enough to swim in, but she's vibrating with energy that needs an outlet.

Herra sighs, wondering when Augusta started picking up on her mood changes so easily. "This—this doesn't feel right. We should be using every waking moment to prepare for the war, not lounging in hot springs. Edgorn isn't going to wait for us."

"Edgorn is not the end all, be all for us," Augusta counters. "No matter what happens here, me and my people get our freedom thanks to you." Her smile is brilliant. "Fuck Edgorn. He's no more dangerous to me than a fly."

Edgorn's not going to care whether you're technically free or not.
Herra doesn't say that, since it will go nowhere and get her nothing.

Instead, she chooses a safer topic. "If you could be anything, go anywhere, who would you be? Would you go back to your old life?" She sweeps her hand at the forest around them, at the steam rising from the pond.

"Or would you choose something different? You can rebuild your life into whatever shape you want. The possibilities are endless, Augusta. Your duty as a member of House Grimash doesn't have to be everything. There can be more than the Golden Chisel in her service to Ilyaka." Herra hears the spark of life in her own voice and wonders where it came from, why it appeared now. "You exiled yourself. That means a certain type of freedom. You can pick your own fate."

Augusta snorts, staring into the depths of the water. The same spark is present in neither voice nor eyes, and the way she hangs her head is not even despair—it's defeat. All her excitement quickly deflates. "You know people like us don't get choices like that."

"I always thought so too. But I look at Leonidas, who changes names and lives and identities on a whim, adopting wit and poetry and sensitivity, and I think—" She swallows, listening to how foolish she sounds. She hasn't thought like this, spoken like this, in years. How strange that a war would bring back her hope.

"He gives me hope. Hope that my life need not always be like this, survival and a distant dream of appointing an emperor. That there are things other than my duty. Or that it's a matter of completing my duty and then being free to choose."

She expects Augusta to laugh, but all she hears is silence. When she speaks, it's in Ilyakan, her accent thick and her voice rough. "We have a saying in Ilyaka. The wise sapling never grows far from his mother tree."

Herra puzzles slowly through the words. "The obedient one, certainly," she replies. "Keeps them easy to control. Adherence to the rules of the mother tree is how dreams die." She looks back in the direction of the house. White cloaked Grimash members either wait to assimilate Augusta back into their society, or pray for her to leave them once and for all.

Augusta won't meet her eyes.

When they get back, stumbling through the forest in the dark of night, the issue of beds is raised. Augusta leads Herra silently to her old room, untouched all this time. "No one would stain themself by sleeping in the traitorous Golden Chisel's room," she spits. They haven't been in this part of the house yet. Thankfully, everyone is asleep. Unfortunately, not a candle is lit.

"Are all Ilyakan houses this dark?" Herra grumbles, speaking Mariosan for the illusion of privacy.

"Are all Mariosan ones so bright?" Augusta counters, though it's a weak retort and they're both smiling when she pushes open the creaky door to her room. The smile fades then.

A layer of dust covers everything. The bed has the sheets pulled over it, and a large window lets moonlight in on the east wall. The walls are that same miserable dark, soaking up the light and the joy from the room. At least the carpet is soft underfoot.

Augusta lingers in the doorway, staring at everything. The adornments on the walls. The writing desk in the corner. The armor stands. The white robes hanging in the wardrobe. Herra looks her fill, getting glimpses of Augusta's life before exile.

"Fuck," Augusta breathes. "This is weird."

Herra grips her arm for comfort, hoping that will break Augusta's stupor. "Just as much a piece of shit as I imagined anything of yours would be," she says without heat. Augusta chuckles in the dark, approaching the bed. When she peels back the sheet, a mountain of dust explodes into the air.

Herra coughs, waving it away. "They could've at least given us new bedding, fuck."

The sheets underneath are thankfully dust free, and after a bit of whacking, Augusta declares the bed fit for use. "Do you mind sharing?" Augusta asks hesitantly.

"No," Herra replies, and that's that. Augusta's been sleeping on a pallet beside Herra's bed the entire time they've known each other, she doesn't see how this could be any worse. "As long as I don't find myself tied up again."

"You wish, Ancient." Augusta slips off her boots and climbs into the bed. Herra follows, her heart suddenly racing. Ilyakan houses are too small, too cramped, or maybe she's just gotten used to the airiness of the Blue Feathers house.

She's not used to being so close to Augusta. They lie side by side, facing each other. This close Herra can see every freckle on her face even with the meager moonlight. She's wide awake.

You fell in love with a fucking Grimash.

Herra has seen this girl covered in blood, anger ruling her face, crazed with revenge, feral with the fight. Herra has seen her amused and happy and infuriatingly smug. She's seen her heartbroken and despairing in the wake of Zera's truths. Today she was strong as she pled their case. However, Herra has never seen her soft like this, eyes hooded with weariness. Augusta's guard is nonexistent. It makes Herra's chest ache.

"What did they ask you today?" Herra murmurs. "I noticed some questions drew stronger reactions than others."

Augusta sighs. "Among other things, they asked if the Golden Chisel was going to make a return since the Silver Hammer has appeared in Lasilas' army. A lot of them are afraid he's going to be fighting against us instead of for us. They wanted to make sure I was on their side. As much as they hate to admit it, they need me, and they don't feel safe without one of their mythical protectors. Our mythical protectors."

"What did you tell them?"

Augusta breathes slowly. "I didn't really give them an answer. I didn't know the Silver Hammer had shown himself." Her voice is weak, weary.

Herra fumbles with the urge to comfort her. "Well, it's good that the Silver Hammer is around, right? You two are destined to work together, or something like that."

Augusta's laugh is a relief to hear. "Yes. Something like that."

HERRA AND AUGUSTA ARE called to the Grimash council room early the next morning. Herra has never been a morning person, and she drags herself to the meeting room with her mug of coffee clutched close. Augusta, infuriatingly, is as cheery of an early riser as always. Herra notices it all the more when they're sharing a bed.

Herra hardly slept a wink.

Augusta told her that Ilyakans don't like to take their time, they like to solve problems quickly and move on. However, Herra is still shocked when the Grimash members announce that they've reached a decision.

They say it flatly. Yes, we will provide warriors. We have contacted House Catiana about this. If you do not give us independence, there will be hell to pay.

It's so simple, so victorious, so damn early, that Herra doesn't know what to say. Thankfully, Augusta uses what diplomatic patience she has to thank them prettily.

Augusta leaves shortly after to buy supplies in town for their return journey, including an actual meal they can eat on the road instead of berries and rabbits at all hours. She insists she can handle it herself, that Herra should stay and soak up all of Ilyaka that she can. "You won't be assassinated or abandoned," she promises, which isn't all that assuring.

Herra takes the gentle *I want to be alone with my home while I can* for what it is and willingly stays, wandering around the Grimash house and being careful not to get lost in the forest.

One of the Grimash members—the one who first agreed to consider their proposal—sits beside Herra on the stoop of the house. It doesn't look so dreary in the daytime, lit up and surrounded by flowers and greenery. White pansies spring up everywhere Herra looks. "She is a wild one, isn't she?" they ask.

Herra smiles despite herself, puzzling through their thick Ilyakan accent. "Yes. She's unlike anyone I've ever met."

Rough laughter. "That's certainly true. We've all missed her."

Herra meets this person's eyes. "Tell her that."

Her companion looks away instead. "Look, Ancient." Herra gets the distinct feeling they were put up to this, perhaps by Augusta. "You know why we had to do what we did. You understand. No hard feelings."

Herra thinks of a thousand replies, a thousand curses she imagined in the long six years. How long has she dreamed of this moment? Reckoning with her family's murderers?

Instead, she replies, "Yes. No hard feelings."

When Augusta comes back, the lower part of her arm is swathed in a bulk of bandages. She keeps it close to her body, grimacing as she loads her packages into their saddlebags.

Herra hovers, trying to sneak a peek under the bandages. "Where the fuck have you been? Why the bandages?"

"I cut myself on a branch," Augusta replies stiffly, refusing to meet her eye. "Are we going?" Herra notices the way her eyes drift over the trees, drinking it all in.

"We'll be back," Herra says quietly. "This isn't goodbye."

"I know." Still, Augusta stares into the trees and the chilly sky like she's starving for them. Herra would kill to know what memories are circulating in her head, yet she knows that she can never know all of Augusta. Just as Augusta can never know all of her.

Herra hops up on the horse behind her, hugs her waist, and rides off into the future.

WHEN HERRA PUSHES THROUGH the door of her office exhausted to the bone, she finds Leonidas waiting for her. He lounges like it's his birthright, leaning against the wall with his arms crossed.

She wastes no time. She's never been one for pleasantries, especially not when she's dead tired. She sinks into her office chair with a sigh, longing to join Augusta in their room and sleep. Alas, duty calls. "Did you find them?"

Leonidas holds out his palm, showing off the stunningly beautiful ring. "In Francesco's tomb, where I thought it would be." He raises his other hand with the diary triumphantly. Herra whistles, looking at the ring—a diary is a diary, worthless to her. The ring is huge, a centerpiece with a giant emerald as the focal point. Little diamonds surround it. Inside the gold band, worn with age and time but still polished nicely, is an inscription. *To the one I love most.*

"Beautiful," Herra says.

Leonidas nods, turning it over and over in his hand. He's still wearing the gold necklace of rubies and sapphires.

"Everything alright?" Herra asks. "You—you know you can talk to me."

He smiles. "Everything's fine. The journey was slow. I did a lot of thinking. I might have lingered there a little longer than strictly necessary. Everything alright with you? Did you two meet your goal?"

"Yes. Ilyakan forces are on their way to Alizima to fight Edgorn as we speak. They're only concerned with themselves. Can't say I blame them." She lifts her shoulder. "In exchange, they get their freedom from the empire."

Augusta blows into the room like a storm. Herra's hand doesn't even go to her sword, so used to Augusta's explosive presence she has become.

"Hello to you too," Leonidas says.

"Ah, you got it. Good. Wait," Augusta says, taking the ring from him. She turns her head and squints, making a soft noise.

"What is it?" Herra asks.

"These are Ilyakan flowers," Augusta says, pointing to tiny little carvings on the outside of the ring, what could be mistaken for scratches. "Ilyakan goddess flowers are always depicted in the same style, there's no mistaking what those are. But how? Wasn't the owner of this ring Mariosan to his bones?"

"That has always been the story, yes," Leonidas says. "Curious."

Herra and Augusta exchange glances. The exhaustion fades from Herra's bones.

"Leonidas," Herra says slowly, "you wouldn't mind if we left you for a bit, would you? Entertain yourself with Tasian. Talk to Ryn. Gwyn. Liss. You have friends here."

He raises his brow. "With those looks on your faces? I don't want to know." He smooths down his new frock, the brocaded gold he favors. Augusta hands him back the ring. "Wouldn't want to get blood on my courtly clothes."

Herra smiles with a kindness she no longer has. "Who said anything about blood being involved?"

He chuckles. "It's always a possibility with you." Obediently, he slips away.

Herra fits her fingers into their spot on Augusta's arm and tugs her through familiar hallways, down to the place where they met once again.

CHAPTER SIX

The thunder of hoofbeats echoes in Arthur's ears. Wild Edgorn chases after them, but he's the farthest thing from a threat right now. Edgorn has only a handful of guards while Lasilas has an entire army escorting him away. Edgorn on his own against an army isn't intimidating, no matter what he'd like to think about himself.

Arthur laughs wildly. Lasilas is at his back, clutching his waist while they share a saddle. Arthur's hand is empty, as Edgorn still has his sword, but he was happy to give that up in exchange for freedom.

Only as the wind roars in their ears does Lasilas say, "Thank you for fighting for me."

Arthur's chest swells with pride. "It was my pleasure. The first truly honorable thing I've fought for as the Silver Hammer."

"The first of many." A pause. "You must think me a fool for fighting for him for so long. I certainly feel foolish, given how easily we just walked away. You had the courage to tell him everything I wish I had years ago."

"You're not a fool, Lasilas." Arthur can't tolerate any slander against him, especially if it comes from Lasilas himself. "You were his victim. Your sister was threatened, as was your life. Anyone could see why you'd do it. No more protesting," he adds when Lasilas' mouth opens again. "I will have none of it. The past is the past. We can only look to the future."

321

Lasilas smiles sadly when Arthur looks back.

"I'm sorry you got captured because of me in the first place," Arthur says. "If I hadn't fought him—"

"You did what I didn't have the courage to do," Lasilas stresses. "He is a bastard without honor, and he should've let me go. But I would never expect anything else from him."

Arthur breathes, his guilt assuaged. "Are you worried about your sister, now that you've done what you have?"

Lasilas sighs. "Of course, but I know she can take care of herself, no matter who he's going to send after her. Knowing that she's the Golden Chisel certainly changes things."

If Arthur leans back into Lasilas a little more than strictly necessary, well. Lasilas doesn't raise any protest.

THEY PITCH CAMP WITH Edgorn off their heels. Hopefully for once he's thinking before making a rash decision and realizing he won't catch them. The lower Minyan countryside doesn't lend itself to a pursuer.

Pitching camp is a routine, quiet affair, one that blurs across Arthur's senses as he fights the night's exhaustion. It was not so long ago that he fought Edgorn and won. That is no easy feat.

He settles down on a log beside Dainthi, warming his hands on the fire. Winter is fast approaching, and one can feel it more keenly here in the north. *I want you in Alizima by the time the first snowflakes fall.* What irony.

"You did so well," Dainthi says to Arthur quietly. "We're all in awe of you. You were incredible, and I'm ashamed of myself now for refusing to fight him. I was just—so—"

"I know," Arthur says quietly. "You don't have to be ashamed. You don't have to explain. I won't pretend like it was easy. I'm glad I had the opportunity to give him what's been coming to him for years." His blood is still singing with righteousness, his armor in tune with him. It's like a second skin. He'd sooner die than take it off right now.

"We're all glad to have you," Dainthi says gently. "But please, tell me what's wrong."

Nothing's wrong, he almost says on default, but stops and takes stock. He's shifting restlessly again without knowing why.

It doesn't take long for his eyes to stray to Lasilas, as they so often do. "I feel like he's avoiding me," Arthur says, staring with naked longing. Lasilas is sitting alone a few fires over, lost and small and quiet. Arthur wonders if he can solve Lasilas' problems the way Lasilas solves his. *Let me in,* he wants to beg. "Have I done something? Do you know?"

Dainthi shrugs. "Well, other than ignoring his flower, no. But that would certainly be enough to bring him down."

"What are you talking about?" He's in no mood for riddles. "The yellow flower he put behind my ear? Why, that was just a gift. A pretty thing. Something to commemorate our evening. Understandable if—if he's trying to court me." It aches all the more, knowing he somehow did something to screw that up.

He wants Lasilas so badly it aches. It's all the clearer after tonight, when he nearly lost him. Arthur is desperately aware of what he'll do to keep Lasilas in his graces.

Dainthi is quiet. "I thought you were just being dense," she says. "Being lovestruck tends to muddy the brain. But you're telling me that you actually don't know what it means?"

Her lover, a Mariosan named Nagalia, slides an arm around her shoulder. "It's understandable, my love," she purrs. "If he wasn't raised in Ilyaka. His mother might have overlooked some things or forgotten to explain them entirely."

Arthur is ready to scream. "Please, tell me—what does a yellow tulip behind the ear mean?"

Dainthi sighs and runs a hand down Nagalia's arm. "It means courtship. An offer in Ilyakan culture. He was asking if you'd consider being his lover. You were supposed to respond yes—if you wanted that—by tucking a purple violet behind his ear. The opposite ear."

"Inquisition, and romantic love," Arthur recites quietly. No wonder Dainthi and all the others looked at him so strangely when he came out of Lasilas' tent.

"Rather similar to the Mariosan tradition," Nagalia says casually. "Offering one thing, putting yourself on the line, then waiting for reciprocation. Except with flowers instead of rings."

Foreign yellow tulips weren't in season when they had that dinner. Lasilas couldn't have just strolled through the nearby fields and picked a yellow tulip on a whim. He would've had to find a merchant who grew and sold them in special conditions. The flower was planned. It was carefully thought out.

And Arthur knew none of it. No wonder Lasilas has been so snappish, so glum, so defeated lately.

All at once, Arthur feels like the greatest ass who's ever lived. The weight of it crushes him where he sits, making him bury his head in his hands.

He manages, "Thank you. Now if you'll excuse me, I need to attend to something." He barely finishes speaking before he's jumping to his feet, bolting toward the nearest horse. He hears Dainthi's chuckle. Arthur doesn't care if he seems eager. He *is* fucking eager. Lasilas' curious gaze follows him as he hops onto the horse, sending a shudder of anticipation up his back.

They always camp within an hour's ride of the nearest town, usually much closer if they're in friendly territory. Here, just inside the border of Minya, they made camp in a quiet field far from any city. It was partly Arthur's decision. Now, he curses it.

Fuck, where to find a flower merchant? An Ilyakan, no less?

He'll have to make do. Violets are not exclusive to Ilyakan gods, just like tulips aren't. They grow elsewhere, though never with the same vibrancy. Lasilas will understand. If he'll even forgive Arthur for waiting this long.

Arthur doesn't have to ride for long before he finds a line of merchants packing up their stalls—or maybe they're setting up, given the early hour of the morning. He stumbles off his horse and approaches the line of merchants along the main path. Blessedly, a flower merchant is among them.

Arthur buys his violet with shaking hands, eager to race back, but the old merchant's hands clasp around his own to still them. "Easy, my boy." These merchants aren't Ilyakan, but that doesn't mean this one smiles with any less kindness. "Steady those nerves." The old man winks. "Good luck with them, whoever they are."

Arthur forces himself to draw a breath. With murmured thanks, he presses a coin into the old man's hand more firmly than is strictly necessary.

The ride back is fast and hard, the violet clutched in a careful grip. Arthur apologizes to his horse for riding her so hard as he dismounts. He's been in motion for close to a full hour.

He runs toward the center of camp, shouting, "Lasilas!" with the flower in hand.

Every eye in camp turns toward him, including Lasilas'. Arthur doesn't care about the others. He's done being afraid of what others think, the weight of their gazes. He will do this, and he doesn't care if the whole continent is watching.

Running like a fool, out of breath, Arthur skids to a halt in front of Lasilas. They're standing on the crest of a hill in full view of everyone. Lasilas' eyes are so bright, so full of hope for the first time tonight. Arthur can't banish the image of Lasilas destitute in that cell, the sound of his defeated voice, but he can try to replace it with something better.

He reaches out to tuck the violet of midnight purple behind Lasilas' ear. While he can, Arthur tucks back locks of pale blond hair, looking a little too long into Lasilas' face. What does he have to hide now?

Judging by his achingly soft smile, the light in his eyes—good gods, those eyes—Lasilas doesn't mind Arthur looking in the slightest.

"I'm sorry it took me so long," Arthur whispers. "I'm sorry I made you think I didn't want you. I'm sorry I didn't know this was what I was supposed to do."

Something in Lasilas' face softens. "You didn't know? That was all?"

"That was all, my prince," Arthur laughs quietly, dizzy with relief. "If I had, I would've raced out of the tent to get you a violet in seconds."

Lasilas smiles bashfully. If not for the orange glow of camp torches, the red flush of his cheeks would be more pronounced, the same red as his crest. "Not a prince, anymore, Arthur." His voice is as light and breakable as paper.

Arthur smiles till he feels the corners of his eyes crinkle. "You're always going to be royalty in my eyes." He slides his arms around Lasilas' waist in a bold moment. It'll be daybreak soon. This has been the wildest night of Arthur's entire life, but he doesn't want to rest for a minute lest the brightness of Lasilas' eyes begins to fade.

I love you, Arthur thinks. *I always have.*

"What do you say?" he asks. "Shall we wait for Edgorn's army to come to Mariosa and defend it against him?"

"I don't know." Lasilas assumes a voice of faux concern, as if it's a decision he's at all debating. "We might be shot down by the Mariosans. I wouldn't blame them."

Arthur grins widely. "Still a better outcome than shooting them down ourselves."

Lasilas laughs softly. "Let's go, then." He touches the violet tucked behind his ear like it's the most precious thing he's touched in his life. Arthur nearly swoons.

He turns to the army, to his friends, his captains, his folks, and finds them all smiling.

Callum yelps as a shadowy creature appears before him, nearly knocking him down in its haste. Gasps and murmurs rise throughout the camp, weapons drawn.

It's a horse, Arthur realizes. A great black warhorse. It has determination in its eyes, and its mission is Arthur. He nuzzles into Arthur's palm, docile now that he's found his master. His beautiful coat is as black as the night sky they stand under. He might be freakishly tall, but he's the perfect height for Arthur.

"The Silver Hammer and the Golden Chisel will each have a trusty steed," Lasilas recites. "Congratulations, Arthur."

CHAPTER SEVEN

Herra and Augusta find Zera in quite a different condition than how they saw her last. Pride has been beaten out of her, and her once fine clothes are now stained and tattered. Her hair hangs in the same greasy locks Augusta's did the day she was Herra's prisoner. The parallels and ironies are not lost on Herra.

Defiant blue eyes fix on Herra, eerily reminiscent of Augusta the day they met. A glowing beacon in this darkness, this ugliness.

"Hello again," Augusta says. Herra gives quiet orders to the guards outside that they're not to be disturbed. "Time for us to play with you."

"Let's start with the questions," Herra says, laying a hand on her arm. Honestly, she should just let Augusta come down here and take her stress out on Zera whenever she gets on Herra's nerves. "Zera, have you thought about how none of your people have come for you or even noticed you're gone? Quite pathetic. Their loyalties are plain. A shame for you, isn't it?"

Herra has done her fair share of threatening to ensure nothing will come of Zera's absence, whipping the Ruby Rings into shape quickly. Like any group, without their faithful leader to hold them up, they crumbled. Her competition will remain intact, and she'll have nothing to fear from other gangs. "Your threats don't have so much heat now, hm?"

Zera doesn't dignify that with a response.

"Tell us what you know about Consort Francesco's wedding ring," Augusta says, crossing her arms.

That draws laughter. "What? I have no idea what you're talking about."

"I think you do." Augusta kneels before her. "Tell us more about how you worked for Edgorn."

"I told you; I'll never tell you anything. He'd kill me."

"And we already told you, you need to worry more about us than him. So, spill."

Zera sighs and raises her head, loathing etched into her eyes. "What do you want to know?"

"I think there's more about that ring than you're letting on." Augusta tilts her head and frowns. "Shall I go get a bucket of water? Make this fun?"

Zera flinches. "It's not me you should be torturing," she says. "It's Edgorn. He's the one who commanded me to get rid of your brother. He's the one who commanded me to kill the emperor."

"If he were here, we would—wait, what the fuck did you say?" Augusta and Herra exchange glances.

"Did you say Edgorn commanded you?" Herra smirks. "I knew there was some flaw in your motive. You're not righteous or honorable. You work for money, not morals. You wouldn't kill an emperor for the sake of your country, no matter how much you loved it. Of all the ways to get Lasilas banished, you chose the deaths of others. That doesn't speak of loyalty. No, someone would have to pay you to kill Ricarda the Fourth."

Zera looks murderous, probably most at herself. Herra's mind turns over and over with this new information. Ricarda IV, dead at Edgorn's command.

"How long have you been working for Edgorn?" Herra asks. "How do you two have such a close, longstanding relationship?"

Zera chuckles. All she needs in order to cave is the bleak reminder of her own situation—something they're more than happy to provide. "I broke into his study and went through his valuables."

Augusta says, "What the fuck? Where did you learn how to do that?"

Zera shrugs innocently. "I was born in and assigned to House Liele. The definition of artist is a broad one."

Augusta's mouth twists. "House of artists. I suppose you think that's funny?"

Zera laughs.

"Enough, you two," Herra says. "You can debate her loyalties later. I want to hear about how she broke into Edgorn's study and didn't wind up dead because of it."

"He was impressed," Zera says. "He recognizes talent when he sees it. Instead of punishing people for little transgressions, he uses them. He used me."

"He paid you to do his assassinating. There's a difference. Don't pretend you're innocent."

"Mm. Maybe. He sent me to steal something." She smiles. "A missing ring."

Herra demands, "Why would he care about Francesco's wedding ring? How would he know it existed?"

"If you would shut up, I would answer. Edgorn visited the library in Allicé as a boy, when Ricarda the Fourth was newly crowned. He read about what the ring once meant, and where it was buried. He knew that if he wanted to become emperor without an Ancient's approval, he would need that ring to prove his legitimacy. Even then, he knew he wasn't honorable enough to ever be picked by an Appointer, and nothing he could do on his own would keep him in power long."

"Explain."

Zera smirks. "So, you did think it was an ordinary wedding ring."

Augusta clutches her chin and forces her head up. "You're going to give us straight answers or nothing at all. Stop leading us around."

"Stop letting me." Zera jerks her head out of Augusta's grasp. "That ring holds the legitimacy of the empire as much as that one around your neck." She nods to Herra's Ancient seal ring, strung around a chain as it's been for six years. "Francesco was Ilyakan. He had a sister, and the ring was hers originally. She was an Ilyakan, and her lover was a Minyan.

"The Ancient seal ring first belonged to the Minyan who founded Gina—she was the first Ancient, as I'm sure you know. The Ancients and the Donati dynasty of Mariosa coincided. Franceso's wedding ring is more accurately known as the ring of Ilyaka. Both rings were meant to seal the emperors in place, instead of just one. Ilyaka would've had a say in who got to use the Amarinthine Pass, and for what. That system would've solved all the problems we've had of emperors abusing Ilyaka."

"What changed? Why don't we still have that double ring system?" Herra thinks of that ring in Leonidas' possession. So pretty, so insignificant. A symbol of romance, but nothing more. She wonders if her family knew about this system, if there were any records in Gina that detailed this long lost tradition.

Zera replies, "Franceso's sister and the first Ancient, her lover, had a falling out. They parted on bitter terms. Franceso's sister gave him her ring and told him to use it for the same purpose. It was the ring he put on his finger to accept Ricarda the First's proposal.

"He wore it on his finger every day, but he never used the ring to appoint another emperor alongside an Ancient. He never found one worthy enough, and the power of the Ancients was growing. His cries were drowned out. The tradition died with him."

"So, Edgorn wanted both rings to become emperor without dispute. He needed Lasilas to lead his charge and conquer Ilyaka skillfully." Herra tips her head back and sighs. "So, he asked you to kill Ricarda the Fourth, too? To clear the way for him?"

"No. He only asked me to steal Francesco's ring from Ricarda's office. The murder was an accident to cover my tracks. Edgorn told me above all else I could not be seen or caught stealing the ring from Ricarda the Fourth's office. I might have lied."

Herra's head hurts, trying to keep track of this all. "But the ring has been missing for—forever."

Zera shrugs. "Ricarda the Fourth had it. Precious weapons never change hands through pirates and thieves and the underground market? You are an underground dealer. Your people are thieves, Herra. You should know how this shit works. The emperor knew what it was, what it truly meant. He was well read."

Herra crosses her arms. "So, what really happened in there?"

Zera smirks. "I stole it. He walked in on me, tried to convince me to give it back. Tried to convince me that he would use it for its proper purpose if I gave it back. I didn't believe him, of course. Jona was my lookout. I killed Ricarda the Fourth and slipped out the window."

"And the ring?"

"I lost it in the brawl."

Herra sighs, clutching her forehead. "And how did Edgorn know where the ring would be? How did he know about the old system?"

"All he told me was that he visited the library of Allicé as a child and got lofty dreams. I assume Ricarda the Fourth took those kinds of records out as soon as he realized the damage that they could do."

Augusta and Herra exchange glances. "Is there anything more you're not telling us?"

"No. That is all to my story, I swear." Zera hangs her head. "But let me explain myself. I left Ilyaka because I never felt like I belonged. Not in House Liele, not in any other house. I wore my crest, but I ever connected with the gods. I was restless from the moment I was born.

"I didn't care about the honor they preached of. I just wanted to see the world. I thought I was dead when Edgorn caught me in his study, and instead he gave me a chance for a new life. Jona just never knew when to quit, when to leave me alone. He idolized me. He wanted to follow me everywhere. I tried to tell him no, but he never listened. That is his own fault."

Augusta kneels down and grips Zera's chin in hand, staring her deep in the eye. "You are the one at fault in all of this. You and Edgorn, no one else. None of your victims. For the sake of the love I once bore you, I grant you this mercy. And never forget that's what it is—a mercy."

Zera swallows, but nods within the grip of Augusta's fingers. "I will do better by you," she rasps, and kisses what of Augusta's hand she can. "I will repent."

Augusta's face twists into a smile as she runs a blade into Zera's heart. Herra hangs back, letting her have this moment. Augusta's eyes close, and a single tear runs down her cheek as she sheathes the knife. They are done with Zera at long last.

Augusta sighs once it's done, her hands covered in blood. "I only wish that the others she's hurt could've had a crack at her."

Herra asks softly, "What do you want to do with her body?" knowing it's not her place to decide.

"Burn it," Augusta says, accepting Herra's aid to her feet. "Give me the ashes."

"It will be done." Herra holds her bloodied hand longer than strictly necessary. Gods, what is it about an Augusta who's feral and violent that makes her heart race? She can hardly look at Augusta's face, the fire in her blue eyes. They walk out of the cell and back up to Herra's office, avoiding the Feathers. Herra conveys her orders with a murmur.

She doesn't realize she's gripping Augusta's wrist until Augusta jerks away with a hiss. The bandages Herra nearly forgot about are about to come loose.

"This was no branch, you're better than that," Herra snaps, reaching to pull them away entirely. Augusta's other arm shoots up to slap it away, but Herra has experience maneuvering around her. The effort is fruitless.

"No," Augusta says, crazed, but Herra doesn't give up until the bandages fall to the ground.

"You know, you should really change these more often if you cut yourself on a branch as you claim," she says. "I'm going to assume you know things about dressing...wounds...holy shit."

It's not a cut or a gash that awaits her under the bandages, but a tattoo. A tattoo of fingerprints on Augusta's wrist. Herra's fingerprints.

Herra slowly moves her fingers down Augusta's arm, careful of the still healing skin, and finds that her own fingerprints fit perfectly into the black lines. She doesn't even want to think about how, or more importantly why—she can hardly think at all when seeing that. Forget an Augusta who has freshly killed. Nothing has ever made Herra's heart race like this.

Slowly, she drags her eyes up to Augusta's, which are blown wide with fear and a wild spark of interest. Herra slowly squeezes, not too hard, just to hear Augusta's breath hitch. "What the fuck is this?"

Augusta struggles for a reply.

"This is where you were just before we left Ilyaka?" Herra snaps. "Getting a—a tattoo of my fingers?"

Augusta swallows. For the first time, she doesn't shrug Herra's fingers off. "Yes," she says, voice rough. "Ilyakan tattoo artists are the best. I wouldn't trust your Mariosan butchers."

They're just words to fill the air. Herra finds her breath harder to control, discovers that it won't come when she needs it. She asks the next obvious question. "Why?"

"Do you think I know?" Augusta snaps, still not drawing her arm back. Herra's grip keeps them close together. As they have before, she finds her eyes straying down to Augusta's lips. Augusta is gorgeous, angry, and untamable—just Herra's type.

Even if she were a stranger in the street, it'd be impossible not to notice her beauty. However, their past has encouraged Herra to ignore the mix of lust and something deeper that swirls in her chest each time she looks into Augusta's eyes. Each time she sings that mournful song, each time she shoots Herra one of those *provoke me if you dare* smiles, each time they find themselves on the same side.

Her fingerprints are tattooed on Augusta's forearm, a symbol that should represent Herra's distrust, their animosity, and Herra's desire to control her. Instead, it shows that Augusta feels something too.

Or so Herra hopes and prays as she steps closer, never taking her eyes from Augusta's face. Her scattered freckles, her bright hair, blue eyes like crystals that have always held Herra captive the way she held Augusta in the dungeon. She didn't know what she was walking into that day.

Herra doesn't know which of them moves first, mirroring each other's movements perfectly. They meet with Herra's hand still circling her wrist, Augusta grasping at Herra's shoulders like they're her only tether to this world.

Herra squeezes her arm tighter, trying to process the way her heart seizes as if she were touching some intimate part of Augusta. It's just her forearm. Her fingertips on Augusta's forearm forever.

Fuck. Herra gives in.

Augusta is just as wild in a kiss as she is in the rest of life, passionate and angry and fierce. She has a hold of the back of Herra's neck now, and—when did they end up with Augusta pressed against the wall, Herra pinning her wrist above her head? Augusta doesn't attempt to get away; rather she pushes closer. She hooks her leg around Herra's back, drawing her in, hot breath mingling.

They're panting into each other's mouths, and all Herra can focus on is the fact that Augusta makes her heart race and her body come to life like no one else ever has. Despite who she is, because of who they are to each other. She's fire, and Herra is caught in the blaze in a way she doesn't mind in the least.

She doesn't know when she went from dreading Augusta's presence to being unable to sleep without the sound of her breathing in her room. Her skin is itchy when Augusta's not there invading her space, driving her mad, obeying commands only if she feels like it.

She was Herra's prisoner, but she never followed Herra's every word. Augusta has been independent and fiery. Since the moment they met, she's been everything that's been missing from Herra's life.

She's brought Herra answers, peace, truth, *hope*—and now, with her fingers in Herra's hair, tugging at her messy braid, she brings desire and joy. Joy and safety are not things she should be feeling with House Grimash. Yet it floods Herra's veins as she lets Augusta's arm down. They stare at each other, regaining their breath. Augusta is the one to seize Herra's wrist and pull her toward the bedchamber.

If she's being honest with herself, this has been coming since the day they met.

HERRA STARES AT AUGUSTA'S bare back, admiring her newest discoveries. Freckles the same shade as the ones on her face. A gorgeous centerpiece tattoo—an eagle that covers most of her back, inked in lines of gold talons and a screaming mouth, wings flapping in anger. A moment frozen in time.

Herra asked if the eagle was an Ilyakan symbol. Augusta replied that no, it was her own choice, which makes it all the more beautiful to Herra. She wonders how it never came up in conversation before. A tattoo is the reason they wound up here.

The eagle and the fingerprints are not Augusta's only tattoos. On her ankle lies a small bird. On her left side is a poppy flower outlined in bold black, but not colored in. Augusta says it's the orange poppy, a goddess flower representing anger, passion, and lust. The patron she's been tempted to choose in recent years, since the white pansy holds too many bitter memories. Since it doesn't quite fit her anymore.

Herra would ask why she hasn't switched yet, but she knows better. She knows the answer. It'd be like asking why she still hasn't gone back to Gina after six years.

"Your eagle is beautiful," Herra says, pulling on an undershirt. She realizes belatedly it's Augusta's, but after a moment's thought, she doesn't bother changing it.

"Is this what we have shifted toward now?" Augusta asks, her accent thicker postcoital. She catches the shirt Herra tosses her and pulls it on, rolling onto her side as Herra crawls back into bed. "Pillow talk about my tattoo?"

Herra smiles, she can't help it. "What?" Augusta asks with a scowl, totally unaware of how bewitching her hair looks in this light. A thin stream of gold sunlight floats through the open window, letting in cool seaside air. Herra doesn't care if someone from a neighboring building looks in and sees them.

Now that she's allowing herself to look, Herra notices all the facets of Augusta's beauty she deemed off limits before. Augusta's hair lies strewn across Herra's pillow, her blue eyes caught in the light.

"What are you thinking about?" Augusta rumbles.

As if there could be any other answer than you, "You."

A ghost of a smile cracks across Augusta's face. Close up, Herra can see the dusting of freckles across her nose, the same red as her hair. It appears brighter in this light. Orange, like her poppy. "I'm thinking about you, too," Augusta whispers, her hand venturing out to cup Herra's cheek, pull at her hair. It came undone from its braid long ago.

"About what a great lay I am?"

The moment dies, Augusta scoffs, and Herra doesn't know how to feel. Her chest is tight. She doesn't know how Leonidas did this day after day, person after person. It wasn't real for him till Ricarda, she tries telling herself, but she could never imagine waking beside someone and smiling at them like this unless she meant it totally.

She means it totally.

"Please tell me now is not when you're going to spook and run away," Augusta mumbles. "I'm drowsy, and I'm not in the mood to tie you down to make you stay. The rope is too far."

"I thought I cleared all of that out of this room when you were on your tirade."

Augusta grins, wolfish. "I have my ways."

"I'm not going to run away," Herra says, sitting up. "I always thought that'd be you." She reaches a hand out. "Come with me."

Augusta dresses the rest of the way and follows curiously, holding her hand. Herra is tempted to hold her by the forearm again, her fingertips slotting into place, but she doesn't want to get distracted right now. She leads them through the house, ignoring the knowing stares the Feathers shoot them, and takes Augusta to the beach.

They sit on the sand close enough to let the water lick their ankles. Herra doesn't let go of Augusta's hand, pulling her own knees up to her chest. The ocean provides something simpler to stare at.

She just needed a moment to think, but she didn't want to leave Augusta alone. She never does again.

Leonidas finds them there and settles on the sand beside Herra, still clutching Francesco's wedding ring in hand. He has a faraway look in his eye as Herra and Augusta fill him in on everything Zera said.

"What is it?" Herra asks, knowing how he looks when he's wondering about a question.

Leonidas tilts his head, staring at the huge emerald on the ring. He has the diary in his other hand, running a thumb gently over its cover. "If she stole the ring, how did I find it in its rightful place in Francesco's tomb where it belonged, alongside the missing diary?"

"Hm. She said she lost the ring in the scuffle to escape the emperor's study." Herra grins as the truth dawns. "Oh. She was lying. She didn't want to admit that she cares about Ilyaka after all. That she did something nice. She brought the ring—and presumably the diary—back to Francesco's tomb instead of giving it to Edgorn."

They all fall silent for a moment. "That's one thing she did to subvert him," Augusta says.

"Does it redeem her?"

"No," Herra says. "Not really. At all."

Not in the big picture. But it's something, just one less piece of Edgorn's imperialism. One less pain in the ass they have to deal with.

"Herra." Tasian runs up to them on the beach, kicking up sand. Their arrival shatters the peace, snuffing the last embers of Herra's afterglow. "I just got the report from the king's scouts. They've been running through the city to warn everyone. Edgorn's army, led by Edgorn himself, just crossed the border into Mariosa. There's no sign of the army headed by General Lasilas yet." They draw a heavy breath. "They're coming to Alizima. Edgorn is going to stake his claim there."

Herra processes the words distantly, nodding faintly and thanking them with a word. Tasian runs away, calling out the warning to others, and Herra's breath leaves with them.

Herra falls forward onto her knees. She can't help it.

Mariosa is not her home. Home lies to the north in a forest village, but she has grown to care for this golden country despite herself. For gods' sake, she's been here for years. She's built an empire all her own while trying to build the one that truly matters.

She has made friends, enemies, allies. Now, a lover. She has the king of Mariosa almost in her pocket, her perfect emperor. Her duty is almost complete.

One man from Ele will ruin it all.

Leonidas, the Lover, sinks to his knees right in front of her. He takes her arms, a similar grief and love sliding over his face. His hands shake.

Herra leans forward and presses her forehead against his, holding his hands as her breath comes slow. The Lover closes his eyes.

"Herra." Augusta's voice shakes. She's not immune either. Maybe her knees will give out and she will join them, press her head to Herra's shoulder, topple them all.

Herra looks up at her, at a face knit with determination and grit.

There's a tight frown on her face. "I need my armor."

PART FIVE

THE CHISEL

CHAPTER ONE

King Ricarda Donati V of Mariosa, golden heart of the former empire, is putting on his armor.

It's a delicate process, a routine one, one he could do in his sleep. Not that he's ever fought in battle—it's one of the reasons his hands shake as he tugs on his gauntlets, newly polished after being buried in a chest for six years. The motions of his sword tutor are drilled into him as thoroughly as greetings for foreign ambassadors, the customs of his allies and his enemies, the proper way to sit on a throne.

The greaves sit like this. This is how the buckles securing your pauldron and your breastplate rest. No, not that way—put these on first. You see?

He follows the motions, recalling his tutor's voice like he's fifteen again, afraid of getting hit on the wrist with his own wooden sword in case it bruised. He was never brave. He has never been especially smart. Just competent, and studious.

Your father would be so proud of you.

Would he, Matteo? Would he believe in a son who's been abandoned and wrecked by another man, who has lost the will to go on without that man in his life? He went through life quite well for the first twenty three years without him, but now Aless' jokes and Antonia's smiles aren't enough. His lover's quiet look, his endless mystique, his effortless charm, and his seductive comments have left a void in Ricarda's heart.

Matteo is in the war camp, advising generals and helping with the small things a few tents down. Things Ricarda should be doing. As always, Matteo is helping clean up his mess.

The others have been broken up about Leonidas' departure too, torn about the suddenness of it, the utter unreason. They've tried telling Ricarda it's not his fault, but he remembers the way Leonidas went still in his arms after he said those thoughtless words. There was a change in his dark eyes.

Ricarda relives it every time he closes his eyes, wanting to reach through time and hold Leonidas close in his arms. He'd say, *I'm sorry, I love you, I'll never hurt you again. Whatever you do, don't run away again.* If Leonidas were here, all would be well.

No, that's not true. Ricarda's home is still getting invaded, and not even Leonidas could magically whisk that away. But he could calm Ricarda down, with the sweetness of his kisses like honey nectar. He ruined Ricarda like nothing else. He made sure he'll never love anyone else. He could get a thousand years with Leonidas, and it would not be enough. He would never get tired.

Some would, but he always remembers what his father said about his mother, about how he fell hard and fast. About how Aless is devoted to Antonia utterly and will be for the rest of his life. All Ricarda has ever wanted is his own Francesco, a kind person whom he could shower with affection and share his woes with, whether it be beautiful man or handsome woman.

He had it, and he lost it.

Next comes his sword belt, strapped on almost thoughtlessly. He wears it every day. It's ceremonial. The movement of his hands, the snap of the buckle, is familiar to him. Today is one of the only times in six years that he'll be taking it out of the sheath.

They say Edgorn snapped when his lover left him. The only thing that could keep him at bay was suddenly gone. His temper became unhinged, and a war started. If what Leonidas told Ricarda about the murder of the Ilyakan princes is true, then that sorry lover is not to blame for Edgorn's actions. However, Ricarda ponders it now.

He hasn't snapped into a murderous rage after his lover left him, but he can imagine all too easily how he could. He could cut off his emotions and scream about the unfairness of it all. He could strike with his sword, do anything to forget the fact that he fucked up the best thing he's ever had in his life. The thing he'd do anything and kill anyone to get back.

I'll tell you the truth someday. Those are the words that have kept Ricarda awake every night since Leonidas left, making him wonder about what he never told him.

Leonidas. What a beautiful, sacred name to have in his mouth, one he spoke in every tone imaginable. Ricarda only hopes he'll be able to say it again.

Commotion stirs outside Ricarda's tent, the canvas marked in unmistakable gold and white. The same shades as the half cloak he fastens above his armor now. Making fists inside his gauntlets, he plasters on a smile for the first face he sees when he turns around.

Gods give him the strength to defend his country and make it out alive to see Leonidas on the other side.

CHAPTER TWO

"**S**haring a horse is positively the worst idea you've ever had."

"Yeah, well you're the one who got my fucking fingerprints tattooed on your wrist."

"What does that have to do with anything? Horses are cramped and uncomfortable enough as is. I don't care if we share a bed, we should not share a horse. No one should."

Herra tips her head back and sighs; Augusta pulls the end of her braid. She twists around. "For gods' sake, let's switch places. If you dislike it so much, then you ride up front."

"How about we just get another horse?"

"Because we're too far into the fucking Minyan mountains for there to be any villages that would have stables!" Herra slides off the poor horse and tugs Augusta forward, climbing back up in the saddle behind her. "I've never liked horses in the first place."

"Any other complaints, Madam Ancient?"

Herra sighs and squeezes Augusta's waist until she gets the horse moving again. She thought sleeping with Augusta and establishing a tender peace each night might solve their endless bickering, but no. Peace only comes at the end of the night. The day is spent dealing with the same infuriating girl she's used to.

Another excursion into the north was not what Herra planned on so close after Edgorn's invasion. No one was more surprised than her when Augusta told her where the armor was buried. She offered to go alone, find her way there while Herra stayed where she was needed.

Herra made the selfish decision and insisted that Augusta couldn't possibly find her way by herself. Gina is hidden for a reason, much like House Catiana. Augusta stumbled across it on her way south by complete accident.

House Grimash found it no problem.

Augusta took her excuse for what it was. Herra is trying not to think about what awaits them back in the south.

Eventually, Augusta slides off the horse, pointing to a patch of grass near a dead tree stump that's as wide as Herra is tall. It's near the edge of the hill, providing a magnificent view from the mountaintops Herra saw every day as a child. It makes her heart churn and ache now that she's seeing it again.

Augusta kneels down and starts digging in the dirt with her hands. "This is the spot. I know it is. I buried it next to that tree stump, so I'd know where to find it, because it was so recognizable." Herra asked her why she buried her armor here at Gina, the most ironic place she could've chosen. Augusta didn't have a good answer.

Herra stands back and waits. She allows her eyes to wander, dredging up memories just as Augusta must've while staring at House Grimash.

A crazed expression comes over Augusta's face. She keeps digging in the dirt, pawing furiously, breathing raggedly, but she doesn't find it. There's nothing there in the ground. Sitting back on her heels, she growls, "No, no, dammit, where the fuck is it—"

Footsteps crack behind them, and they both whirl around.

"Both of you, turn your heads right now. Hands in the air, or I swear, I'll shoot you both faster than you can blink."

Herra scowls. Who dares desecrate her homeland a second time?

She freezes as she glimpses the figure standing up on the ridge, holding a drawn bow toward her and Augusta. The figure is dark skinned with only a thin tuft of hair, eyes the same dark ones she sees in the mirror. She scans him for several moments; sure she's been faced with a ghost. No, he's real. The man staring back at her, his mouth hanging open in equal shock, is indeed her father.

"Father?" she breathes, drawing Augusta's startled eye.

"Herra?" he asks, lowering the bow. "By gods, is that really you?"

"Is it really *me? What about you?* H-how are you here? I watched you go over a cliff."

Her father laughs wetly, leaning on his bow like a crutch. It is a crutch, Herra realizes after a moment's inspection. He's fitted it to endure the rocky mountain terrain, with both ends flat so he can rest his armpit on one end. The bow is as large as he is for a reason.

"I didn't say I was without injury," he says. "But I survived. Come up here and meet me, please—I can't climb down that way like I used to. I will tell you everything." His eyes cast uncertainly to Augusta.

Herra knows the path and finds it easily, even if it's overgrown with weeds and grass. Everything has fallen into disrepair here. The grounds are impossible for one person alone to take care of, and Herra's father was never known for his green thumb.

Gods, she can't believe he's here, alive. He is a dream, not yet real.

The moment she can, she runs into his arms. He clutches tightly at her back, and she feels tears drip onto her head. This is a dream, worse than a nightmare. She will wake up in Mitzi, her parents dead and no one but Augusta beside her to comfort her—

"Are you real?" her father murmurs, as if he can't believe it either. "Are you real?"

"Are you?" She pulls back to look at him, the face that has hardly changed in six years. A few wrinkles more, a long scar that cuts across his forehead, probably from a gash she doesn't want to ponder. But alive, alive all the same.

Herra catches her breath and pulls back from him enough to remember Augusta is standing a safe distance away, hovering awkwardly. "This is Augusta, by the way. My—" She hesitates on the word, but she doesn't want to keep secrets, and she doesn't want Augusta to think she means less to her than she does. "My lover. You can trust her and speak freely."

Her father raises an eyebrow, but nods. "There was a river below that cliff," he says. "Without it, I would have died."

"I didn't know."

"I know. Gods, I always told Maura we should take you out more, familiarize you with the terrain, but she never—" He purses his lips and lets it go. "Come with me, girls, please. I want to hear your stories."

"Are the houses still intact?" Herra asks quietly, walking beside him as he moves along on his crutch with an expertise gained over time.

Her father smiles. "Oh, yes."

Herra has a thousand questions, and she can't get them out fast enough. "What happened after you fell into the river?"

"I hit a rock, which didn't kill me but did shatter my leg. I don't remember much after that. A lot of pain." He points to his forehead. "Gashed my head open on a rock trying to swim out. I had to stay down there by that river for close to a year, fashioning a crutch out of every tree branch I could cut down. I scavenged on berries and lived off rabbit snares, but eventually I made it back up here." He smiles.

"I'm so sorry, Papa," Herra says. "I just left without even looking for you. I never thought to come back to check for any survivors—all the blood, I mean—"

"Hey. You listen to me." They stop so he can look her in the eye. "*I* wouldn't have believed I survived. As I was falling, looking into that bastard's face, I didn't think I would survive, even with the water under me. There was no reason for you to come back. Frankly, I'm glad you got out. I'm glad you didn't stay. Don't you ever blame yourself. I've done pretty damn well for myself, and I've been happy here. Alright?"

"Alright."

He smiles. "And no pity, either. I'm still your father, just as I've always been."

"Of course, Papa." She motions Augusta forward, though she sees the panic in her face. Herra takes her hand, assuring her with a smile that nothing will happen to her here.

"Enough about me," her father says. "I want to hear about you. Lovers, hm? How did you two meet?"

Augusta and Herra exchange glances, wondering if they should tell the truth. "I have done things, Papa," Herra says slowly, "that you will not be proud of. Some cruel things. Not always in the name of what's right."

Her father smiles. "It has been six years since we've seen each other. You've been elsewhere, clearly. Of course we would have changed. I will not judge you for making your own life out of the terrible circumstances you were given, A'ya."

She smiles at the old endearment. It's been so long since she's heard her own language like this. Longer than Augusta has been living on scraps of Ilyakan, longer than Herra's known Tasian and been in Mitzi. She didn't realize until this very moment how alone she has been.

"This is Augusta Grimash," she says, squeezing Augusta's hand, "member of House Grimash. She was here that day."

She waits for it to sink in. When it does, her father sputters and stutters, looking at Augusta in a new, scrutinizing light. "And you're—she's your lover?"

Herra never imagined a day would come when she'd be defending Augusta against her own father. "She was the only one who did not strike against us. She sees the fault in their ways, and I have hurt her too. We have been through many trials together." She casts eyes onto Augusta's face, true beauty and those eyes that swallow Herra whole. "She has learned. She is worthy."

Her father still looks stricken.

Herra adds, "She started out as my prisoner, if it makes you feel better."

Her father shakes her head. "Come inside, come inside. I'm still not sure I'm not hallucinating."

Herra pictures her father making his way back up the mountain trails, wandering back into the houses just to find the bodies of his loved ones turned to bone and dust in pools of long dried blood. She wonders how long it took him to scrub the stains away. She wondered how long it took him, because of both his new disability and his aching grief, to bury all the bones.

Herra still remembers the face of the bastard who put the crescent scar on her cheek. That day was the first in centuries where blood had been spilt on the holy soil of Gina, the blood of the Ancients, but it was also the first day Herra ever spilt blood herself.

She still remembers the way the sword cut into the man who gave her the scar, the surprising ease of it, the shock on her uncle's face when he barged in only to get stabbed in the back. The last he saw of her was her murder. Herra still bears the weight of that shame.

Her father has to wade through a pack of various woodland animals—squirrels and the like—as he enters the house. Augusta chuckles and says something soft in Ilyakan. "Hm?" Herra asks.

"Isiona. A myth we have about a man who attracts animals like fish to water. He has a way with them, a charm. It's more of a type of person than a singular myth, really." She smiles fondly.

"Your people have a lot of myths."

Augusta shrugs. "We are the oldest culture on the continent, along with you. We've had time."

Herra follows her father into the house, walking amongst ghosts. He asks, sitting down, "So what prompted you to return now, Herra, after six years' absence?"

Herra sighs and sinks into her mother's old easy chair. There's no an easy answer to any of his questions. "Papa, have you ever heard the Ilyakan myth of the Golden Chisel?"

"No."

She tells it quickly, adding the part about the Silver Hammer and trying not to notice the way Augusta's face falls. Just as Herra was alone as the only Ancient left in the world, Augusta is alone without her counterpart. Some fundamental piece of her soul is missing. Knowing he's around and alive is not enough.

"This woman here is the Golden Chisel, and she buried her armor here. We came to get it back."

Her father looks between them, mouth agape. "You're just one surprise after another, sweet gods. Why now? Why did you bury it in the first place?"

"Long story," the girls say in unison. Herra adds, "I promise, we'll explain everything as soon as we can, but right now there's a war waging throughout the entire continent that has us short on time. It's imperative that we find that armor first."

"I understand." He sighs. "I have felt guilty about shirking my duty of appointing an emperor. I'm glad to see you're taking care of it." That guilt shows on his face. "I am the next oldest alive, after all."

Herra's father, like many Ancient consorts, was chosen from the outside to be assimilated into Ancient culture to marry and prolong the bloodline. He's Coromodan in blood, but he has no memory of his heritage, since he was brought away from his culture when he was a baby. The Ancients choose babies that are abandoned, giving them a new chance at life and a home where they won't miss their old one.

Consorts, since they're not part of the bloodline, choose emperors only when no blood Ancients are left.

Herra rests a hand on his shoulder. "I have an emperor picked. Don't worry. He will be appointed shortly."

Her father's smile is one of pure relief. He covers her hand with his own, frowning at her scars. He's not the only one who has changed.

"I dug up the spot where the armor was," Augusta says, "but it wasn't there. Would you happen to know where it is? I buried it years ago." Her Minyan is rough, but the fact that she's trying at all is touching for Herra.

Herra's father smiles. "I found it a few years ago and was utterly stupefied. I don't know how I didn't notice you when you came here. Yes, I have it. I took it out and put it in a box for safekeeping." He stands. "Let me get it for you."

"No, Papa, let me," Herra says. "I'd be happy to."

"What did I say about no pity? I have managed for six years on my own."

"It's not pity. I just—" She pauses. "Want to see the house."

He nods, his tone softening. "It's in the attic, next to your mother's favorite broken lamp that I never got around to fixing. Probably covered in ten layers of dust by now."

Herra laughs, finding tears welling in her eyes again, and nods. She glances at Augusta, asking silently if she wants to come. With a shake of the head, it seems she'll brave the interrogation awaiting her.

The words, "So, you're a Grimash, hm?" are the first out of her father's mouth once Herra rounds the corner. She sighs and smiles, wishing Augusta luck as she climbs the stairs in the hallway.

Her feet still know the way like nothing's changed, although nothing is as pristine as it once was. Her grandmother would throw a fit, but Herra finds it homely. It's a marker of time, of history. Of survival.

The railing is made of the red wood that surrounds the entire Appointers' Court, like the dead tree stump outside. The painted gold detailing has faded, but Herra remembers the better days, the cleaning her family would do for parties and guests. The excitement Herra felt when she got to wear colorful new robes, the pride in her mother's face when she donned her own. The awe in her father's face, how he called them both the most beautiful women he'd ever seen.

The attic door is just as finicky and difficult to unlatch as she remembers, and the collapsing stairs nearly hit her in the face when they come down. She has a tiny scar on her nose from when they did.

She finds the box of heavy armor easily, under a window next to the lamp. One could make a wool blanket out of all the dust up here, but Herra blows it away, taking everything in. The window up here has never been clean, and little has changed since she was fourteen, when she was often sent up here to fetch something for her mother. She welcomed it as a break from her lessons.

She dawdles a while, swimming in memories, before carrying the box downstairs. Augusta isn't cringing away in fear, and her father isn't angry—they're both smiling and laughing.

"Were you exchanging embarrassing stories about me while I was gone?" Herra asks, setting the box down in Augusta's lap and sitting close to her just because she can.

"Maybe," her father drawls, leaning back in his favorite chair to watch Augusta lift the lid of the wooden box.

Safe within, it hasn't collected any dust. Though a polishing would do it some good, it's breathtaking just as it is. A pure, dark gold, like the color of a maiden's hair in a fairytale. It's almost too bright to look at directly.

Augusta smiles fondly down at it. "I've missed you, old friend," she murmurs in Ilyakan, lifting the pauldron out, then the breastplate. They're both embossed with designs of the sun, swords, grass, leaves, Ilyakan god flowers. The crest on the breast is not the white pansy, but the orange poppy. Augusta's breath hitches. Herra has a feeling it's different than when she last saw it.

"Thank you for keeping it safe for me," she says, unable to tear her eyes from her old companion. Herra contemplates the warrior she must've been in Ilyaka. How could anyone look at someone wearing that and think of them as a traitor, a disgrace?

Herra's father laughs. "That's not what I thought I was doing, but you're welcome, honored protector. Use it well. End this war of the continent."

"Oh, I plan to." She looks at Herra, blue eyes filled with promise. Herra gets a thrill that sets her heart pumping. Fighting with Augusta at her side has always been dangerous in its own way. It's intoxicating. Fighting with the Golden Chisel will be a whole new experience.

"We need to get going, Papa," Herra says, rising to her feet. "I swear on our gods that I will be back to tell you the rest of the story. Unless you want to come with us?"

"Maybe some other time," he says with a smile. "I'll sleep peacefully knowing that you're alive, and our duty will be carried out after all."

Before Herra can reply, Augusta gasps softly. "What is this?" She lifts an axe out of the box, pure gold with a handle of polished wood. It's long yet nimble, the blade wickedly curved and sharp. It's a thing of beauty, and it fits perfectly in her hand. "This isn't mine."

"Oh, that," Herra's father says. "I nearly forgot about that! I found it in an old storage box when I attempted to clean out the attic a few years ago. I don't know where it came from or what its story is, but I just lumped it in with that armor because I thought it matched."

It does. Augusta runs her finger lightly along the blade, testing it, and quickly draws it away with a hiss. This isn't dusty or in need of a polish. When she turns it over, Herra catches glints of light from the sapphires inset in the handle. It's beautiful and golden, and it looks like it was made for her. The Golden Chisel.

"I'll take this with me, if you don't mind," Augusta says slowly.

"Go ahead. It's not doing me any good up there." Herra's father smiles. "Do you really have to go now? You'd just be riding into the night. It's almost dark, and it's cold. Winter is approaching. Stay the night, let me cook for you, make you a fire." His dark eyes soften. "I'm not eager to see you go so quickly. I know you'll be back, but still."

Herra sighs, thinking of Edgorn and the war and every misery awaiting them. She glances at Augusta, finding the reluctance to leave mirrored on her face.

"Okay," she says. "Okay. Cook for us, Papa. She and I will stay in my old room. Is there anything I can do to help?"

Her father beams. "Wonderful. No, I have it handled. Why don't you go show her the lake at the retiree's cabin? Wash up?

You'll be living there soon anyway, Appointer." He winks. "I need a bit of time."

"Of course." Herra holds out her hand, finally getting Augusta's attention off the armor and that beautiful axe. "Let's see which is better—my lake or your hot springs."

On the way out, as they walk, a horse with a pure white coat strolls into their path from the forest.

"Look at that," Herra says with a smile, watching fondly as Augusta gasps. She walks up to pet it. The two of them fit together as if they've always meant to.

Augusta murmurs, "I thought your father said all the horses were gone."

"He did. I thought you said that the Golden Chisel and Silver Hammer both had mighty steeds."

"I did." Augusta continues petting the horse, stupefied in realization. Herra smiles.

"WOW," HERRA MURMURS, stunned breathless by the figure Augusta cuts on the white horse in her golden armor. It hugs her like it was indeed made for her, from the high collar to the way the helmet rests over her tight bun.

Watching her put it on this morning framed by the glow of the sunrise was like watching someone breathe. The motions were familiar to Augusta even after years, and she needed none of Herra's help.

And that axe—good gods. There's a brace on the back of her armor meant to hold a weapon, and the axe slots into place there perfectly. The whole of her sparkles and shines, starting with her smile and the crinkles in the corners of her eyes. She looks whole again.

Augusta bows her head, stroking the horse's mane, clutching her helm in her free hand. "Golden Chisel at your service, my lady. How may I serve you?"

Herra's breath comes short, looking into the sun like this. Oh, gods.

It's going to be a long journey back to Mariosa.

CHAPTER THREE

Mariosa is windy.

Arthur didn't know it was possible for wind to be this powerful. That could be due to the utter lack of nature in this strange country, the barren fields that stretch as far as the eye can see. Nagalia, the closest thing they have to a Mariosan representative, assures him that these winds persist even in the more urban parts of the country.

Of all things, the wind is not what Arthur should be contemplating. Therefore, it's what he focuses on, the way it blows over his buzzcut but tosses Lasilas' hair fiercely. Arthur breathes it in, uses it to calm his thundering heart.

The exhilaration of riding into Mariosa not to attack it, but to defend it, was like nothing he's ever felt. He's still riding the high—if he weren't, he would collapse from exhaustion. He can't remember the last time he slept, but sleep can come when Edgorn's head lies on the ground.

Arthur is thankful for the reception they received from Mariosans upon crossing the border—distrusting, but not outright hostile. The Mariosans accepted their assurance that they're fighting for Mariosa until they do something to prove otherwise. That's more than Arthur hoped for, more than they all deserve. The Mariosans might be a little naïve, but Arthur won't look that gift in the mouth.

The Silver Hammer in him sings to be sitting here on his proud warhorse of midnight black, borrowed sword in hand, armor shined and polished in preparation for the tremendous battle that lies ahead. The sense of rightness has returned.

Lasilas sits on a horse by his side, taking it all in. He hasn't removed the violet from his ear, and he's taken great pains to ensure it stays there. They lock eyes and smile.

"Isn't the Silver Hammer supposed to have a mighty sword worthy of the rest of him?" Lasilas asks, eyeing Arthur's borrowed blade. There's nothing wrong with it, and Arthur is thankful to have a weapon at all, but he agrees it doesn't match. It doesn't *sing*.

"Not everyone can be perfect," Arthur says with a little smile that disappears once he scans the horizon. "Shit, look."

He points to the horizon, past the lines of Coromodans and Delainians to the red armor of Elen invaders. The army is far from them, at the bottom of this hill. Lasilas and the other foreign units haven't been noticed yet. The Mariosan king's army is nowhere to be seen.

"Let's ride, folk!" Lasilas calls, raising his own gleaming sword. "Fight for what's right!"

His words draw a cry from deep within all of their hearts, guttural. It swells in Arthur's throat and draws heady emotion to the forefront. He rides beside Lasilas as the honorable Silver Hammer, righteous in mind and body.

Herra stands at the edge of the barren battlefield just outside Alizima, arms crossed, wind blowing through her hair. The seal ring strung around her neck has never felt heavier. This is where the armies of at least four countries are going to make their stand against Edgorn. Mariosa's is notably absent. *Come on, Ricarda, where are you?*

She doesn't need to be here, and it'd probably be better if she was out of harm's way. But like hell she's going to pass up a chance to watch the Golden Chisel work.

The very woman herself rides up beside Herra on her white horse, armor gleaming in the sunlight, axe in hand. There's nothing but them, the field about to flood red, and the golden sunlight bouncing off Augusta's armor.

The sight still takes Herra's breath away, even with the helm over Augusta's head. What a brilliant sight, the woman who has so wonderfully and totally upended her life.

Not even her hair is visible right now. Herra did her bun for her late last night by the light of candles. She needed no light, only the feel of silken strands under her fingers and the soft lullaby of Augusta's singing.

"Come here," Herra says, speaking Ilyakan without much thought. She steps into the stirrup—Augusta's feet hang loose—to tug her close, nearly upending them both.

"Gods, let me get my helm off," Augusta grumbles, always feigning tolerance and loathing just as Herra does. Neither of them mean it now. They haven't for a long time.

The touch of Augusta's lips, as Herra grips her forearm over her armor, sends tingles through her whole body. Augusta smiles when they part. She's gorgeously backlit by the sun. Herra squeezes her forearm, metal digging into her fingers.

"Have I ever told you how breathtaking you are when you're about to fuck someone up?" she breathes into the scant space between them. She gets the satisfaction of hearing Augusta's breath hitch.

"Let me go fuck some people up, then," Augusta says, her voice broken. "I see it will take very little to keep you by my side."

"So, keeping me is something you're concerned with?"

Augusta scowls. "If it makes you feel better, Ancient." She pulls the helm on again and shoos Herra back to the ground. She perches her axe over her shoulder. "Wish me luck?"

"You don't need it," Herra says, smiling. "Go fuck it up, Grimash."

"That's Chisel to you." Augusta digs her heels into the horse and rides away, thundering down the battlefield. An army of red armor crests over the hill Augusta gallops toward, a sea of dark hair and weapons flying Edgorn's flag. The Elen army.

Herra draws a slow breath, praying for Augusta's success. She looks around for the Silver Hammer, for the army headed by Augusta's brother. No one knows where they are, what they're doing, who they'll be fighting for. If they'll even be here today. Augusta has tried to hide how anxious she's been about the prospect of any and all of the above, but Herra knows her well, and it's hard to hide things in close quarters.

Among other things, Herra prays for the Tanner siblings' reunion today.

A stirring sound behind her makes her pause, hand going to her sword. A hand clamps over her mouth before she can draw it, before she can scream.

And then she's being dragged backward, her arms pulled behind her. "Not a sound," comes a growl, hot breath on the back of her neck that she longs to shake off. She fights, struggles with all her might, wondering who the fuck—how the fuck did they sneak up on her, there's nothing to hide behind here—

And then she gets a glimpse into the bastard's face, long black hair hanging around his face, mustache curled around a sneer, dark eyes burning with hate, red armor gleaming.

King Edgorn.

His face is the last thing she sees as he clamps a cloth around her mouth and her head fills with fog.

ARTHUR HAS BEEN IN dozens, probably hundreds of battles at this point, but none have felt as charged as this. The thunder of his warhorse's hoofbeats pound under him in tune with the thrum of his blood, the roar of soldiers and commanders all around him. He grips his sword tight in his gauntlet, flexing the armored fingers. His breaths come raggedly in his helm.

They ride amongst a contingent of the king's Mariosans in gold and white. The red Elens are brutal and ruthless, slaying person after person with quick strokes and slices. The kings on either side are nowhere to be found.

Lasilas' soldiers try to stick to their circle formation, but it's always harder to maintain in a big battle, always harder when they're on horses. Arthur is the Silver Hammer and needs no protection, nor any aid. He'd rather his squad go toward protecting Lasilas.

They've had a few kills so far, mostly against unsuspecting Elens from above. Arthur is lucky that the chaos means they haven't been fully acknowledged yet as Edgorn's traitorous army. He keeps an eye out for Edgorn himself, determined for his blade to find that blood above all else. Preferably while Lasilas watches Arthur's blade bite through his neck.

"Arthur!" Lasilas yells from inside his own helm, pointing with his sword toward a body. He hovers long enough to make sure Arthur sees where he's pointing, then thunders off, a circle of soldiers forming around him.

Arthur dismounts his horse with one hand firmly on the reins, though he suspects he doesn't have to fear this one spooking and running away. It's been in tune with Arthur this whole time, hardly making noise of any kind. Now, he grumbles gently as Arthur inspects the dead Mariosan Lasilas pointed him to, sticking close.

The dead lies on their stomach, limbs splayed out, golden armor splattered with blood. A mighty sword sticks out of their back between the chinks of plate. The sword tip is bloodstained but otherwise untainted. It's a thing of beauty, longer than a typical sword and wider in the blade. A green-blue gem is inset into the dark wooden hilt, an oval that gleams in the sunlight. The hilt is carved and flares out at the edges, sturdy wood that won't break upon impact.

Arthur pulls the sword free of the corpse, whispering a prayer for the poor soul. The blade is not too heavy in his hand, molding to fit his fingers perfectly. Its disproportionate length and width, like the horse, is perfectly suited for him.

The sounds and sights of battle fade out as he raises the blade to inspect it in direct sunlight. The tip catches light, pure silver, and reflects Arthur's smile back down to him as he mounts the horse again. Rightlight, he'll name the horse, for the righteousness and light Arthur finds in his midnight coat.

He rides off into the throes of battle again, fated blade gripped tightly in hand.

HERRA WAKES TO A BRIGHT overhead lantern shining in her eyes.

Edgorn is fluttering about the dark little room they're in. It has plain walls and no windows, no defining features. She begins struggling with her bonds, twisting every which way, but she's tied firmly to a chair. He looks at her.

"Ah, you're awake. Good." His smile is something ugly, his stare even worse. She squirms away from it. "Since you killed Zera, I had to do this myself. The stupid bastard got herself into that mess, but I won't lie; I don't mind doing this." He creeps closer to her, and Herra struggles all the more, pride thrown away in the face of survival. For a moment, she is fourteen again, nameless and just trying to survive.

"Zera? What does Zera have to do with you kidnapping me?" Herra asks.

Edgorn sighs and thankfully puts some distance between them. "She was supposed to seduce you," he bites out, "same as she did that Grimash girl. Get in your bed, in your mind, convince you that I was the one to serve. She was supposed to bring you to me, that seal ring held out in the palm of your hand. The Ilyakan ring would be in the palm of hers.

"It's mere coincidence that she was also my chosen assassin for the brat sister of Lasilas should he disobey me. Coincidence that the two of you found each other. I see now why Zera failed to carry out her orders."

Herra blinks. It all falls into place—why Zera let herself get captured and bound herself to Herra so easily, why she never tried to escape, why she answered their questions so quickly. She was the perfect pet prisoner, enduring torture and Augusta's revenge with hardly any pushback. Only enough that they wouldn't get suspicious of her complacency.

Shit—it must be why Zera established the Ruby Rings in the first place, a means of getting close to Herra. Nothing about her was a coincidence.

No matter her motives, she fucked up this job utterly. Herra remembers the exhaustion in Zera's voice in that cell, and wonders if at last grew tired of serving others at the expense of herself. Maybe she finally wanted to give up, accept the way out. The way to peace, now that she'd alienated herself from her home.

She could've gone to the eastern queen's kingdom, an independent asylum for many who want nothing to do with the empire. However, she never would've made it past Augusta.

Augusta was the one variable in Zera's plan, and things went as catastrophically for her as they could've.

Zera is—was—a twisted mirror of Leonidas, a servant without an identity of her own, only one task after the next. Herra wonders how one went so right when one went so wrong.

"Useless bitch," Edgorn mutters. "One failure after another. Couldn't bring me that ring, couldn't bring me you." He raises his head. "But I don't need her. I don't need anything. I will take it, as is my right."

"The only right you have," Herra says, "is to shut the fuck up."

Edgorn backhands her. That's a small taste of what's to come, she's sure. "You will make me emperor," he growls, "or you will die."

"I thought you were going to just take the emperorship by force," she says, tilting her head innocently.

"I will only ask you once more. Make me emperor, or you will die."

"I'm going to die here anyway. Doesn't matter much what I do before or after."

Edgorn hesitates, and Herra realizes what the problem is with a grin.

"You can't kill me," she says. "You can't rule the continent on fear and force alone, not after centuries of emperors appointed peacefully. That would be going too far. You would be overthrown faster than you could cut off my head. So, I suppose you'll send me back to Gina and make me stay there in exile my whole life under threat of death? Guarded by your soldiers?"

Edgorn doesn't reply, but his glare, sharp as lightning, is answer enough.

Herra tips her head back and laughs.

"Don't laugh, little girl," he murmurs. "Your life is a worse fate than your death. It means you will find no escape no matter what I do to get you to agree. And you will agree."

"I will never agree with you," Herra growls, straining against her bonds to look him in the eye. She would spit in his face, but she's not about to encourage him to draw her blood.

A door bursts open behind her, where she can't see. She tries twisting around in her tight bonds. Her heart pounds in her throat. The growled words she hears make her slump in relief.

"Get away from her," Augusta snaps, as Herra hears the metallic clang of a weapon being drawn.

She steps into Herra's line of vision, a bright beacon of gold metal and orange hair. Edgorn meets her eyes with darkness and hatred, but Augusta swings back her axe to take a strike. He backs away and pushes past her through the door she came in, a whoosh of wind at Herra's neck.

Herra twists around, wondering why Augusta doesn't go running after him, why she focuses on Herra's bonds instead. Augusta shakes her head. "Fuck him. I'll catch up with him again. There's a whole alliance of armies and monarchs out there waiting to see him dead. I'm not worried about him getting away." She slices through the last of the ropes with her axe.

"The Blue Feathers are here, by the way, just as you asked. They don't have much in the way of armor, but Tasian's doing a damn fine job of leading them. They have the might and strength to make up for their lack of flair. I would fear for Edgorn if they got him in a room alone." She chuckles weakly. Her hair is disheveled, strands flying every which way.

Herra stares at her gold savior, a little stupefied by Augusta's flushed cheeks and blue eyes. "I—thank you. Thank you." She's rattled and her heart is still pounding, so she goes with the first logical response: hugging Augusta as tightly as she can.

Augusta flounders for a moment, but Herra doesn't let go, remembering the first time Augusta hugged her after receiving that blue doublet. Augusta's arms, warm through the hard plate, come up a moment later. She seems just as relieved to find Herra in one piece as Herra is to find her. She releases her breath and realizes in a moment how desperately she can't afford to lose Augusta.

"Don't die today, whatever you do, whoever you kill," she breathes into Augusta's neck. "I—I need you."

Augusta's breath stills, then releases. "I will protect you, Herra. I will do better by you."

Herra pulls back and kisses Augusta's bloodied face. "Just stay alive," Herra whispers. "Just stay alive."

CHAPTER FOUR

The Silver Hammer tears through ranks of red, the new sword in his hand slicing through them like paper. His blood pounds, roars and rings in his ears. He has one eye out for Edgorn at all times. He's sure the king of Ele would announce himself, but the desperate can be unpredictable.

The Silver Hammer is ruthless. He is an inspiration to the rest of Lasilas' army, to the rest of the battlefield, providing life where it falls away in some other places. He reaches down to help the fallen to their feet, he saves others from near death with one effortless swing of his sword, he dodges all blows with a gentle nudge of his horse to the side. He, his blade, his horse, and his armor act as one, moving like the wind. The life of the battlefield.

Arthur pauses in his carnage, squinting at a line of new soldiers in the distance. They wear plain chain-link armor under colorful cloaks, special crests embossed onto their left breasts. They're caught in combat with Elens, ignoring the green armored Coromodans and blue Delainians and golden Mariosans. King Ricarda's army has finally arrived.

This mysterious army turns away any who tries to give them aid or demand their attention. They work completely on their own.

His breath hitches. An—an Ilyakan army? Here? Fighting Edgorn? Arthur certainly wasn't expecting that. He spots the princes at the head, Heires leading a charge, and grits his teeth.

He will deal with Heires after.

Arthur gets separated from Lasilas' army, drawing blood under the blazing sun. Eventually he dismounts the horse to have better mobility on the ground. He doesn't fear for its life. It will find safety somewhere and wait for him.

Still no sign of Edgorn, but Lasilas is never far from Arthur's sights. They both separate from the scuffle to pull towards each other. Arthur can't tell which side is winning, if the Elens are getting pushed back or if they're advancing toward Alizima. He can see the outline of it in the distance, towering spires and high walls protecting it.

Arthur's legs finally buckle, and he kneels for a moment, just to rest. Lasilas crashes to his knees beside Arthur on the ground, dropping his bloodied sword at their sides. His hands are shaking, but as they cup Arthur's cheeks, they fall still. They're nearly close enough for their chests to touch. Not a single part of either of them is not covered in blood.

Hints of Lasilas' blond hair peek through the sea of red, strands of it falling in his face. Arthur wipes the blood away from Lasilas' brow and nose, tucking back the hair from his sweaty forehead.

The sun blazes down on them both, making them hot in their armor, but Arthur only cares about the crystal blue of Lasilas' eyes. Covered in Elen blood, Lasilas Catiana has never looked more beautiful. That damn flower is still tucked behind his ear, crumpled and broken though it might be.

Lasilas breaks into a smile, teary eyed and breathless as his thumb strokes Arthur's cheek. Dried blood cracks under his touch.

The sounds of battle are distant, the clang of swords and screams of soldiers a faint buzz in their ears. The field around them is trampled and bloodstained, but the only thing that exists is them. Them and the bodies of the Elens they've killed, framing them in beautiful and joyous destruction. Lasilas and Arthur caused that together—vengeance, finally. It sends a rush through Arthur, a heat.

Their breath mingles, both of their hearts slowly coming down from the fight. Arthur couldn't tear his eyes away if the whole world depended on it.

Arthur observes the sharp line of Lasilas' jaw. He's always wanted to lick it, to bite it, before he even realized what that meant. Hope starts to blossom in his chest that perhaps he can now. It's only natural that the next moment ends with Lasilas filling that last bit of space between them, pressing together their lips with a slight tilt of his head.

Lasilas is so strong, so solid, but in Arthur's hands and against the insistent press of his mouth he's so soft. He tastes sharp, like blood and metal, and it's better than Arthur ever imagined it could be. Arthur's hands don't know where to go, drifting from face to shoulders—gods, those shoulders—to back.

Arthur always forgets he's bigger and broader than Lasilas. It's easy to forget when Lasilas is who he kneels to, but he realizes like a brick to the head that he could fold Lasilas into his arms. Push him back and blanket his narrow shoulders and keep him safe, keep him all to himself. Arthur wants to be Lasilas' whole world.

That sharp jaw works well, turning and breaking the kiss for a moment's breath. Lasilas stares down at his lips, sick with hunger, and reconnects like he can't get enough. Little noises take Arthur's breath as quickly as it comes. Throughout it all, Lasilas' hands never stray from his face.

I love you, Arthur thinks. *With my whole soul, I love your golden heart. You are so good, and you have no idea.* And yet it is he that Lasilas slumps against when he breaks for breath. Arthur who Lasilas pants against, Arthur's neck that he hides his face in. Recovering breath turns into nosing at his jaw, pressing idle kisses to bloodied skin.

"My sweet, sweet soldier," Lasilas half sighs, half laughs into his neck. He pulls back and grips Arthur's face again, smiling with watery eyes. "You are so beautiful. My blunt Silver Hammer. My weapon of destruction and revenge and justice." He strokes Arthur's temple, follows it with a kiss to his forehead that makes Arthur tingle down to his toes. "Go on, go, do what you need to do. Go kill Edgorn. Go with my blessing. I will rest here for a while."

Arthur is reluctant to leave him, but the Silver Hammer knows his duty. "You have the honor of a thousand men," he says, kissing Lasilas tenderly one more time before rising to his feet. But before he can walk two steps, Lasilas makes a wounded noise behind him. Arthur whirls around again, sword raised faster than he can blink. No one and nothing will hurt Lasilas ever again. Not as long as Arthur is around to protect him.

But Lasilas isn't wounded, isn't bleeding, and there's no one close enough to be considered a threat. The fighting has moved east, past them. In their daze, they didn't even notice.

Arthur scans the horizon and finally lands on the object of Lasilas' wonder, a figure in golden armor as pure and bright as dying sunlight. They're riding a horse as painfully white as Arthur's is black. Loose hair flies out into the sunlight, lighting them up from behind.

A mighty axe rests in their hand, raised to catch the light. Arthur knows them just from a glance. From behind their visor, the two of them lock eyes, and the closer they get the easier Arthur can make out the embossing on their armor. It's identical to his but for the poppy crest on their breast instead of his daisy.

This is the Golden Chisel here in the flesh, myth and legend coming together. Is this how it feels to look at him in battle? Like looking into the face of a god, into the sun, too bright and ever powerful?

Lasilas says something soft and mournful in Ilyakan. If this is the Golden Chisel, then that means they're—she's—

Arthur steps toward her. She hops down from her horse, shadowed by a brown skinned figure with a messy black braid. Arthur hardly pays her any mind, only interested in the Golden Chisel the moment she pulls her helm off. She glances at him, eyes raking down his armor. It takes only seconds for Lasilas to run into her arms.

They both make noises straight from the heart, arms clutched so tightly around each other that bones might break. Lasilas is sobbing, speaking Ilyakan mindlessly. The girl—Augusta—clutches him close, pulling off her gauntlets to get her pale hands on his bloodied face. She's asking if it's his, he's shaking his head no, and they can't stop spinning. Arthur stands, sword at the ready to defend them and make sure they get the reunion they deserve.

His heart seizes at the way Lasilas clutches Augusta like she's his most precious jewel. Arthur knows what it's like to be held like that now. Arthur can still feel the flicker of Lasilas' warmth over his arms and chest, trapped under his armor.

Augusta and Lasilas are a reunion years in the making, years too late. Two souls royally screwed over by foe and friend, separated across countries and armies and sides in a war.

Arthur gets a glimpse at Augusta's face when Lasilas pulls back, noticing the similarities and the differences. They share the same small, round tipped nose, she has freckles, he's an inch taller than her. But the eyes—that same clearwater blue, like the world's clearest sky or deepest pool.

Arthur glances at the woman Augusta came with, the fierce looking thing with a beautiful bow strung across her back. In a roughed up jacket, strands of hair fly wild around her face. She shakes too-long black bangs out of her eyes.

She gives him a nod, and he returns it. Whoever has kept Augusta safe and treated her well is a friend of Arthur's.

"Herra," she says, extending a hand. He pulls off his silver gauntlet to shake it.

"Arthur di Mars, Herra." He speaks Mariosan. "I am the Silver Hammer of Ilyaka, and Lasilas' captain and protector. You have a second name?"

She hesitates. "Of the Ancients. I am an Appointer. Don't worry," she adds quickly in response to his horror. "I don't work for Edgorn, and neither does she. I work with Ilyaka, not against it. Long story. Ask her when you get a chance."

Arthur nods. By now Lasilas and Augusta have let go of each other long enough for Augusta to get a look at Arthur. While Lasilas and Herra introduce themselves to each other, the Golden Chisel approaches Arthur.

Arthur clasps her arm, watching their gauntlets slot into place against each other. The embossing lines up perfectly. All the more confirmation that they were meant to be together. "Sister," he says, looking into her eyes.

"Brother," she returns. "I feared I'd never find you. That I'd never get to meet you at all."

"I feared the same. It is the fortune of the gods that the same man brought us together." He looks fondly over her shoulder at Lasilas, now shaking Herra's hand.

She says something in Ilyakan too fast for him to understand, and Arthur's stomach drops. He says, "I'm—I'm sorry. I wasn't raised in Ilyaka. I know some of the tongue, but not all. Lasilas and I don't speak it often."

His cheeks turn to flame. The Silver Hammer, mythical symbol of Ilyaka's strength and might, and he can't understand the language in full? The things Lasilas has said about being Ilyakan in full no matter where he was raised...they refuse to stick. Whispers of doubt wash over him.

"I'm used to it," the Golden Chisel says in Mariosan with a little smile, looking at that dark haired Herra again. Her eyes stray to the violet tucked behind Lasilas' ear. "She didn't know a word of it before I began teaching her, and I almost had to tie her down to get her to learn at all. I hadn't heard my own language spoken in years."

She shrugs. "There are Ilyakans who have never set foot in Ilyaka that still worship the gods, claim our culture, identify with the houses. You're the fucking Silver Hammer. You're the most Ilyakan one could be."

Arthur smiles bashfully, nodding at Herra to take the attention off himself. "Someone to you?"

Augusta chuckles, releasing his grip. She looks at Herra with the same shine in her eyes that Arthur sees when Lasilas looks at him. "Yes, something like that. And you?"

"Hm?"

She smirks like Lasilas would if he were more of a bastard, meaner and truer. "I saw you two on the ground. This battlefield is an open place, you know. Should I be worrying about your intentions with my brother?"

Arthur smiles. "I'm the Silver Hammer. Let's let my reputation prove my character."

"Very well, very well. For now." She winks. Arthur bets she's a fiend in and out of battle, a fierce creature who's wicked with that axe.

"Let's go find that bastard Edgorn," he says, "and kill him for what he has done to my general. For what he has done to this whole continent."

"And for what he means to do to Ilyaka," Augusta says, extending her arm once again. They lock gauntlets and nod goodbye to their companions. Helms pulled on, weapons in hand, they hop back up onto their horses—Arthur's was waiting for him when he turned around—and thunder away. Side by side, as they were always meant to be.

LEONIDAS DOESN'T KNOW why he's here.

He's not a fighter. He's not a medic. He's not a messenger, nor an elderly commander too frail to fight but needed to run things from the sidelines. He is estranged from Ricarda. There is utterly no reason but idiocy for him to be here on this battlefield needlessly risking his life.

And yet he rode up with the Blue Feathers anyway, assuring Tasian that he'd watch his own back. There was no need for them to give a single fuck about his wellbeing when they had a small army to run themself.

He's told himself that he wanted to see the action, that everyone he knows will be here, that sitting alone in the Blue Feathers house would do him no good. He'd have to wait days for news from the north. Herra was coming. It's going to be a momentous day in history books. It made sense for him to come.

Still, he avoids the truth.

Something compels him to turn from his hiding place by the healers' tents, safe from the bloodshed. Only a handful of wounded rest there now, since few have been brave enough to venture onto the battlefield to whisk them back here. They'll come in a flood soon.

When Leonidas turns, the face he finds there is the last he ever expected to see. King Edgorn, his ex lover and the tyrant of the continent, stands there with his helm off. Leonidas smiles, strangely. His heart is calm. Edgorn cannot hurt him, not when Leonidas has nothing left to lose.

"Hello, Edgorn," he says. "Remember me?"

Edgorn's eyes widen with a satisfying degree of fear. Leonidas looks different than the Cardamom he remembers, but not terribly. Edgorn should recognize him.

Edgorn fumbles for words before landing on, "H-how—you—"

"Yes, your sweet Cardamom. Not so sweet, nor so special. I was never who you thought I was. That man was one I made up for your pleasure. You were far from the only one."

If there's one thing Edgorn hates, it's to be told he's unremarkable. That he's just a bully like any other.

Leonidas laughs. "Go on, Edgorn. There are thousands here waiting for your head. Go walk into their arms. I will not mourn you. No one will. The throne will fall happily into your niece's lap."

Edgorn clutches his helm tighter and runs like a scared child away from a ghost. Leonidas chuckles, watching the man who has ruled his mind dissolve into the farthest thing possible from a nightmare.

Strolling a little further along the line of tents, he spots Antonia and Alessandro walking by. Their voices raised, their hair up, they're arguing. Antonia is exasperated, and she heaves a sigh, putting a break in Aless' tirade. What are they doing here? Leonidas would've thought Ricarda would tell them to stay in the capital under pain of death. She has her medical license now, but it must've taken a monumental effort to convince Ricarda to let her be here.

She turns toward Aless. "Less—"

Aless throws his hands up. Leo wonders how this started. Probably the jitters of being on a battlefield in the first place. He dearly hopes that his departure didn't erect some rift between them. "You know, I'll just go, since I'm not wanted—"

"Less!" she snaps, and shoves her middle finger in his face. An affronted remark looks like it's on its way out of his mouth, but when he sees what's there, really looks, he stops.

Above the gorgeous ring he gave her rests a second ring, smaller. Its gold band glitters with sapphires and silver details. It sparkles just as brightly as the first, and the two fit well together. Antonia is nothing if not a stylist.

Leonidas grins, observing the two of them from afar. He gets to watch the moment it dawns on Aless, the shocking truth. She certainly chose an interesting time to make this leap. Perhaps it's because she's afraid of losing him. Perhaps she wants to make sure he'll take care of himself, for her sake. It's a perfect tool for resolving arguments, clearly.

Aless makes a wounded noise and gathers her into his arms, sweeping her up with pure adoration in his eyes. He murmurs, "Can I?" and Antonia nods before he lays their lips together, his eyes closing, her arms sliding around his neck. They're not soft about it—it's the desperate kiss befitting battle.

Leonidas turns away to give them their privacy, grinning to himself and leaching off their joy until he can mend his own.

Fuck it. Ricarda is why he's here. Leonidas will do anything to get him back.

He wanders as close to the battlefield as he dares, knowing his man in gold is out there somewhere. He wrings his hands, careful not to let Aless and Antonia see him, though he's probably the last thing on both their minds right now.

"Ricarda!" he calls, turning round and round, calling into the sea of armor and blood. "Ricarda!" But no matter where he turns, where he looks, Ricarda is nowhere to be found.

AT LONG LAST, ARTHUR sees his target.

Edgorn races onto the battlefield like something crazed, something wild. His sword is held high as he hops onto the first horse he comes across.

Arthur and Augusta lock eyes through the slits in their helmets and clutch their weapons a little tighter. They grip their reins and thunder toward Edgorn, who is surrounded by a group of Mariosans that part once they see the Hammer and Chisel approaching. Arthur doesn't hesitate.

Axe and sword bite through Edgorn's neck as the Chisel and Hammer approach him from either side. Time seems to slow around Arthur, leaving room only for the splatter of blood and the settling of the body as Edgorn's head flies off. His sword goes flying, and Arthur is winded from the blow he takes to the stomach, but Augusta picks up the slack. The Golden Chisel is sliding off her horse to pick up the prized head.

Time resumes, and Arthur breathes, looking into the fixed eyes of the man most wicked. The man who would have conquered the continent and thrown Ilyaka into his crown as a jewel to be admired, good for nothing more than vanity. The man who had no problem locking up his most loyal general when Arthur refused to let him fight.

In the distance, on a horse of deep chestnut brown, is a woman with a long dark braid over her shoulder. She's wearing silver armor trimmed in Elen red. She is Iliath, Edgorn's niece, the usurper and rebel he thought he pushed back enough to focus on his imperial dreams. He was wrong.

Arthur gives her a curt nod from afar. She returns it, clutching her helm under her arm, her healthy army at her back.

And then, Arthur does what he vowed to do.

With Edgorn's head safely off his body, Arthur collapses to the ground and falls asleep.

CHAPTER FIVE

The cry goes up throughout the ranks, reaching Leonidas where he stands near Antonia's healing tent. *Edgorn is dead. The would be emperor, the Scarlet King, is dead. The battle is over. Rejoice, all, rejoice!*

Leonidas has been watching from afar, careful not to let Alessandro or Antonia notice he's here. He's been discreetly searching for Ricarda, and even now, he can't stop his heart pounding at the thought of a different would be emperor lying somewhere dead. Even if he went out looking in the sea of wounded, Leonidas wouldn't have much luck finding Ricarda. Chaos occupies every inch of Alizima's outskirts, no matter that Ricarda is king.

Ilyakan forces headed by princes in house colors pass Leonidas without giving him a second glance. They're only here because of Herra and her lover.

From what Leonidas has overheard, the biggest news on the battlefield is about General Lasilas' army. Namely, how they switched sides and won them the battle. The famous Silver Hammer and Golden Chisel won them the war. There's talk that the two of them killed Edgorn, but that news is distant for now. Ricarda is priority, and the Mariosans won't care who killed Edgorn as long as he's dead.

Somewhere here are Cadhan and Isabella, supervising their own generals while staying safe inside their silk tents. His heart races at the thought of seeing them. Their reactions might be surprising. The monarchs might be flattered to learn why he infiltrated their courts. Still, better to lie low until Ricarda is crowned.

Leonidas steps cautiously out of hiding and moves into the flow of Ilyakans. Looking both ways, he hopes no one who recognizes him will spot him sneaking away from Antonia's tent.

"Leonidas? Is that you?"

He winces, inwardly cursing, and turns to face Alessandro. He braces for shouting, shoving, threatening.

When he turns, he finds Aless grinning at him.

Leo sighs. He doesn't know why he expected anything different. Nothing could ever banish the joy from Aless' face.

"It is!" Aless laughs. He slaps Leo's shoulder like no time has passed. "By gods, I never thought I'd see you again. I've missed you. We've all missed you. What the hell happened? Why are you here, of all places? I thought you were just as hopeless with a weapon as me."

"I'm not here to fight," Leonidas says, unable to tamp down his own smile. "I—I owe you so many explanations. I'm so sorry for deserting you all like that."

"Don't apologize to me. Apologize to Ricarda."

Leonidas' heart leaps in his throat. "He's alive?"

"Yes. He's right in there." He gestures to the tent behind them. Leonidas wondered how he missed it when Ricarda was brought in. "He's injured, but he's alive. Relax, wipe that look off your face—gods, good to know nothing has changed in your heart. Ann's been taking care of him. She's alive too."

"Yes, I know. I saw you two."

A newfound grin spreads across Alessandro's face, electric. "Yes! Gods, I knew it was only a matter of time. Can you believe it? I love her." He sighs dreamily.

"Yes, I know that too. I'm happy for you." The thought of their love sours his mood when he thinks of who's lying in wait for him in the tent. Ricarda probably hates him. How could Leonidas blame him?

Aless jerks a thumb toward the tent. "For the love of gods, please go do something about him. He's been an utter and complete wreck since you...since it happened. There are only so many times a man can change his shirt after his king cries into his shoulder. Besides, a wounded Ricarda is a whiny Ricarda. Unbearable. You should go talk to him before Antonia murders him."

Before Aless can move on, Leonidas catches his arm and pulls him into a tight hug. Aless' arms hover by his sides, and Leo worries that his hug is unwelcome, that Aless hates him after all. But then those arms come up and lock around him with an aching desperation. Alessandro's hugs are tighter than Ricarda's, unafraid of breaking anything. The air is squeezed out of Leo by the arms tight around his shoulders.

"I'm sorry," he says. "For everything."

Aless smiles a watery smile. "You did what you had to. You did what you thought was right. What more can any of us do than that?"

Leo thumps him firmly on the back and lets him go. "Go back to your beloved, where I'm sure you're needed. Sorry, your soon to be wife."

Aless grins brighter than the sun. "Go, go! Put him out of his lovesick misery, please, for all our sakes." He shoos Leo toward the tent where Ricarda lies wounded. Leo steels himself with a breath, squares his shoulders, and puts one foot before the other.

He's faced three monarchs and their viper filled courts, endless days of fear and general discontent, days before that where he was nothing but a means to others' pleasure. He has looked Herra of the

Ancients in the face and did not flinch away from her glare, or from the glare of the Golden Chisel. He made the journey to Francesco Donati's coffin alone and brought back the fabled ring, the key to the empire.

He can face this.

The soft swish of the tent fabric peeling back pounds in Leo's ears as he slips inside. Ricarda lies there under the lamps on a cot, his arms crossed over his breast. His armor lies strewn across the nearby tables, bloodstained and dirty. Ricarda himself is covered in white bandages that make Leo's heart stutter just to look at. He's breathing smoothly. Leo lingers in the doorway for a moment, watching the candles burn. "Ricarda."

"Leo." Ricarda says his name with far more ease than Leo expected. He doesn't lift his head from the pillow. "I am dying."

Leonidas pauses, his stomach falling. Ricarda evidently does hate him that much. Fuck.

"I would not be hearing your angelic voice unless I were dying," Ricarda moans, turning his head. "Antonia! Antonia, get in here, I'm dying."

Leonidas fights a spike of panic. Fuck, a man can only go through so many emotions so fast. He rushes to Ricarda's bedside, narrowly stopping himself from taking Ricarda's hand. "You are not dying, Ricarda Donati, damn you. I am not a phantom."

Ricarda fumbles for his hand instead, gasping. His grip is warm and strong, giving Leonidas life in turn. "Oh, gods," he breathes. "Leo. It's really you." He raises his head, staring at Leo with those brilliant green eyes, grinning like a fool. Probably the painkillers adding to the fog.

"Yes," Leonidas says, smiling despite himself. "I'm here."

"You're here because I lost you in the first place." Ricarda sighs and lays his head back. "And it's no one's damn fault but my own."

"Ricarda." Leonidas lays a hand on his shoulder. He's warm and alive. "My leaving had nothing to do with Jona or Zera or you, truly. Nothing at all. You mustn't bear that guilt. You did nothing wrong."

A spark returns to Ricarda's eyes—hope. "Nothing?"

Leonidas shakes his head, desperate to restore that hope in full. "He was just an excuse. I was planning to leave whether we had that fight or not. *That* is the truth."

Ricarda's eyes grow hazy and lost for a moment. Leonidas takes a deep breath and accepts that they're doing this now. He takes a seat at Ricarda's bedside and steels himself.

"Let me start from the beginning. I have nothing more to hide, and I told you someday I would tell you the truth. If you would be courteous enough to listen." Leonidas barreled in here and assumed Ricarda would be a willing saint, forgiving and kind. So far, he is, but Leonidas hardly believes that's all there is to it.

Ricarda doesn't stop him. He's still staring at Leonidas with a dazed expression, so Leonidas goes on. "I am known as the Lover. I have had five significant names in my career, though I've had dozens in all. People made up names or called me by the name of whoever they pictured they were with.

"I haven't had an identity of my own since I was a child. You've been the first to give me a true sense of belonging, of purpose. A life I want to keep. I've tried on dozens of them, but my life as Leonidas in Mariosa has been the best."

Ricarda grips Leo's collar, dragging him close. Sharing space like this again, Leo finds it hard to draw breath. "Your name is not really Leonidas."

"No. I'm not a Marquis, either. Lady Filipa is safe and alive. I have utterly no relation to her. My identity was all a lie." There's something freeing in saying it, though a pit of fear still opens in his stomach. *Wrong, wrong, wrong,* his instincts scream, but he shoves them down and gives into the warmth blooming in his heart.

Ricarda stares at him openly, without judgment. It's more than Leo deserves. "What was your original name, then? Your first."

"Malcolm," the Lover replies, heart beating out of his chest. "I was born as Malcolm."

"Malcolm." Ricarda puts the name in his mouth. "It's—strange. I've never heard it before. What was your surname?"

"Didn't have one." Leonidas smiles. He never thought he'd see the day where he'd be discussing his names with Ricarda. "Neither did my mother. My sire was a one night stand from the profession I took after her. She never saw them again after that night."

Ricarda takes only moments to work it out. "You were a prostitute?"

"Eh, yes. Do you—do you have a problem with that?"

"Of course not," Ricarda quickly says, covering Leo's hands with his own. "When I said I wanted to know everything, I meant it. Tell me. Hide nothing. What were your five names?"

"Malcolm. Henry, when I was the lover of King Cadhan. Aleksander, when I was the lover of Queen Isabella. Cardamom, when I was the lover of King Edgorn. And now Leonidas with you."

Ricarda wrinkles his nose. "Aleksander is far too close to Alessandro. He is not who I want to be thinking about when I'm with the man of my dreams."

"Good thing I don't want you to call me Aleksander, then," Leonidas says, squeezing his hand, riding the high of those words. "Call me Leonidas, like always. It is the name I have liked best, and the name I want to keep. The one I want to be known as. Marquis Leonidas Sartini, beloved of King Ricarda. If you'll have me."

His heart pounds. "I don't know if you could ever forgive me for the way I hurt you, the way I deceived you, but I meant what I said that night, Ric. I love you, and you are perfect, and I would be honored to live my life at your side. I understand if you want me to go—"

He's being pulled down into a kiss before he can finish. It's—gods, it's so good. He's missed this so much. He has little capacity for thought beyond that.

"And you had the nerve to leave on your birthday," Ricarda murmurs into his mouth. Leonidas chokes on a laugh.

"There's more."

"Tell me." Ricarda says it with the same soft fondness that he speaks about his ancestors, with which he recites poetry. "Tell me."

Leonidas tells him all of it. His involvement with Herra, what it means, what he did in the other countries. Ricarda shakes his head as if it's just dawning on him now that Leo was Edgorn's lover. "I can't imagine how hard it must've been to bear his abuse."

"I was happy to see him get his. I knew he would. The most difficult part was fearing that I would be discovered as the same ex all the monarchs shared. I am lucky they're somewhat dimwitted."

"Ah, yes." Ricarda kisses his hand. "You said you were Queen Isabella's lover, but I thought you weren't attracted to women that way?"

"I'm not. But Herra didn't care to mold my targets to my preferences, and none of it was supposed to be real anyway. None of it was real, until you." He smiles.

"Isabella was kind, and a good friend. If I were attracted to women, we might have...anyway. But I gave her what she needed, kept her happy. Her little cloth trader from the east. That was my persona. I knew she could tell I didn't feel the same things she did. I quietly slipped away in the night, out her window, after a conversation where neither of us said what we were thinking aloud. She didn't look for me or raise any alarm. She had no reaction at all, which was the best I could hope for."

"You'll have to tell me all the things they did wrong," Ricarda says, "so I can know all the things to do right."

"Anything you have done wrong is fixable. You are human, Ricarda. That means you make mistakes and grow from them like everyone else."

Ricarda laughs a little, waving that statement away in disbelief. Leonidas will devote his whole life to helping Ric understand how he's changed Leonidas, how he's made him want to keep one of his lives and thrive in it like no one else ever has.

"You answer one of my questions now," Leonidas says. "How did you get injured? How bad is it? Did you kill the bastard who did it?"

Ricarda smiles. "Yes. I didn't get much of a look at their face, but their sword grazed my side. Not too deep, nothing serious. Going to scar, though. I'll be absolutely fine, I assure you. Gives Ann a chance to dote on me, if she can tear away from her beloved long enough." He clutches Leonidas' hands tighter, pleading. "I have an ask of you."

"Anything."

Ricarda looks nervous. Leonidas is still riding the high of *he knows, he knows, he loves me and he forgives me still.* Ricarda is more than Leo could ever deserve in his wildest dreams, yet he has him. Ricarda should know that he has nothing to be worried about.

"You're still wearing the necklace," Ricarda whispers, noticing it hanging around Leo's neck.

"Yes. I never took it off, just like I said I wouldn't. What were you going to ask?"

Ricarda says, "I would be honored if you would make me your husband, call me yours for the rest of our lives. I don't have a ring to place on your finger, which I am deeply sorry for, and I know—" Ricarda gestures. "Me, the one obsessed with marriages and rings, should've had this figured out. All my plans kind of went to shit. You left and I went to war."

Leonidas chuckles. "I'll forgive you."

Ricarda looks up. "Please say something? I just realized you haven't said something."

Leonidas silently procures Francesco's wedding ring—the seal ring of Ilyaka, another story he has to tell—from his pocket and shows it to a stunned Ricarda. In his other hand, he presents the missing diary edition. "I was hoping to ask you the same thing. Consider the diary an engagement present."

One couldn't put a price on the look on Ricarda's face. "Holy shit. Holy shit! You are the most perfect husband I could ever want in the whole continent, good gods. Come here and kiss me."

Leonidas grins and complies.

CHAPTER SIX

Herra leans against the wall to watch Augusta rain destruction.

Herra's not technically supposed to be here, but Augusta isn't going to shoo her out, and Herra won't alert anyone to her presence. She remains in the shadows.

Augusta stands in full regalia at the head of a table. The princes of Ilyaka take up every seat. Prince Heires hasn't taken his eyes off the Golden Chisel since she bullied him into this shack on the edge of the battlefield. She didn't want to wait till they got into Alizima to have this discussion. She said Heires would evade justice no longer.

"Let me make myself very fucking clear and not waste anyone's time," Augusta says with a nasty smile, leaning forward to brace her hands on the table. "You will forfeit your throne or your life, for the crimes you have committed against my brother. Please choose."

Heires glares up at her. "Who do you think you are, you little swine, to tell me what to do with my own fucking country?" He says something in Ilyakan that makes even the most stoic prince gasp. *Filthy exile.*

One doesn't say that to the Golden Chisel lightly.

Augusta slams her hand down. "I am the Golden Chisel," she snaps. "I killed your would be conqueror for you, and this is how you repay me? Repay us?" She jerks her head at Lasilas, who has stayed tactfully quiet in the back of the room. Being the Golden

Chisel is perfect for her—she gets to rain terror onto whoever deserves it most. She makes a fitting mercenary.

As always when watching Augusta torture or threaten, Herra's heart beats a little faster. Augusta adds, "Show us some respect, then maybe we'll get somewhere."

Heires doesn't flinch from her, but it's a near thing. He looks at his fellows, the subordinates he appointed, and finds no support. With a heavy sigh, he says, "My resignation is my choice. Who would stand in my place?"

Augusta slings an arm around Lasilas' shoulder and propels him forward. His eyes widen. Lasilas was likely hoping to see Heires brought to justice, not expecting his own reinstatement.

Heires is lucky that the Silver Hammer is sleeping off his exhaustion and recovering from his minor injuries in the princess's tent. If both of Ilyaka's mythical protectors were stacked against him...gods, he wouldn't last a minute.

"He will retake his rightful place in this council of princes," Augusta proclaims. "He was wronged by Prince Heires and Zera Musiek, as I have been telling you since the day of the murders." She allows herself a small smirk, a moment to relish the recognition she and Lasilas are getting after all this time.

"Do you have this Zera Musiek here as a witness?" one of the princes asks.

"No," Augusta replies. "I killed her."

"Convenient," Heires sneers.

She tilts her head, draws a breath. Herra braces for the storm before it comes.

"I know Heires handpicked you all for a reason, and some of you will only ever believe him because you're damned fools. But hear this. You are all Ilyakan. We are Ilyakan. Look down at the crest you wear on your breast. Face the judgment of the flower. The carnation values honor, yes, but also honesty and truth.

"Look into your hearts and do the right thing. Believe what I say. Welcome Lasilas back with open arms. Be honorable. Leave this snake behind." She gestures to Heires, her arm of gold gleaming. "If not for me, do it for the Golden Chisel, for Ilyaka, for our gods. We criticize emperors for overlooking us, for treating us like shit. But we treat one of our own the same for a crime he did not commit, all because of one man's jealous agenda."

Augusta squares her shoulders. "Furthermore, I will not serve you as the Golden Chisel any longer unless you agree to my demands."

That sends shocked silence throughout the room. Lasilas stares at her, horrified, but Augusta is firm in this. She and Herra lock eyes. *I hope you know what you're doing,* Herra thinks, though Augusta's smirk does not waver.

"We cannot afford to lose you again, Golden Chisel. The protection of Ilyaka is too important. Consider yourself a prince again, Lasilas Catiana," Prince Lydia says with a little smile. "Heires, consider yourself a Catiana no longer. You will take the title of exile in Lasilas' place for the crimes outlined by the Golden Chisel, for turning against one of our own and poisoning the rest of us against him."

Herra exhales.

HERRA HAS AN ENERGETIC Augusta to contend with in the wake of victory and Lasilas' reinstatement. Augusta pulls Herra by the collar into the Blue Feathers' tent, where she gives orders for them not to be disturbed. Despite the teasing and whistling, Herra wears herself out in ways she thoroughly enjoys, doing her best to finally make Augusta settle down.

Hours pass before Augusta succumbs to the unfortunate human need for sleep. Finally, Herra is free to wander the Mariosan part of the war camp. Wander is a strong word, implying that she doesn't have a goal, a target in mind.

Tasian and the Blue Feathers are gathered around King Ricarda's tent like his personal vanguard. The sun has set, and the sky above is a mass of twinkling stars and blessed cool. The lights of Alizima shine in the distance. In the morning, the wounded will be moved there to formally heal, and King Ricarda will be given proper accommodations.

"Herra!" She turns toward the sound of Leonidas' voice, light with glee. He strides up to her. By the look on his face, she'd wager his reunion with Ricarda went well. She hasn't ever seen him this happy. It's rather infectious to watch, even fresh off the high of Augusta's affection.

"Leonidas. Good evening. I'm going to go meet your beloved," she says, jerking a thumb toward the king's tent.

He nods, then pauses. "How did you know?"

"Look at you! Not a moping mess anymore. Not toting around that ring like a fool." She punches his shoulder, walking backward toward the tent. "Go celebrate. I can hear several parties raging on. Soon we will all be smelling the bonfire smoke. You of all people have something to celebrate tonight."

"You, too," he says. "I'm certain that you and the Grimash could be heard as far as Ele." He waggles his eyebrows. "Now go. Fulfill your duty." He jogs away, the tails of his gold coat fluttering behind him. Herra draws a breath.

It's time.

She peels back the tent flaps and sticks her head through the gap. "Your Majesty?" Her voice is weaker than she hoped.

"Yes?" King Ricarda Donati V raises his head from his cot. There are dark circles under his eyes, yet a spark of life is present in the emerald eyes Leonidas waxed poetic about. His short brown curls threaten to swallow up his forehead.

Herra enters and bows to him. "Pleased to meet you. I have heard much about you from Leonidas, the Lover."

He raises an eyebrow at her. "Are you the friend he mentioned?"

"Herra of the Ancients," she says, extending a hand. "Pleased to meet you. He spoke highly of you, projecting his love across the entire continent with just his voice. He didn't have to say it."

Ricarda smiles. "I know. He gave me this only a few hours ago." He holds out the Francesco wedding ring adorning his middle finger, sighing dreamily and leaning his head back. "We are to be married."

"Congratulations. I'm happy for you both." Leonidas, the sly dog. He certainly didn't waste any time. "Treat him well, or I'll be forced to commit regicide. I don't care what war it would start."

Ricarda nods. "You *are* his friend, then."

"His closest one, apart from the people he met with you."

"Ah. I'm glad to hear that there are others who care for him. I suppose you're here to discuss what he told me? Everything he revealed was a whirlwind, and my wounds have me tired. Normally I'm livelier than this, my apologies." He smiles and raises himself up on his elbows.

"Please, Majesty, you don't need to put on decorum for me." She takes a seat in the chair beside his bedside, imagining Leonidas sitting there hours before to propose.

She's lucky that Ricarda hasn't banished her so he could rest, but she isn't about to leave without being asked. She's never been that type. Many others would undoubtedly say *oh, no, it can wait, I'll let you heal and recover in peace, anything to please you, my king.* But he is not Herra's king.

"I'm here for not what you can give me, but what I can give you." Augusta extracted a promise out of her before she let Herra go tonight. *Promise me you'll honor what you said. Make him give Ilyaka independence.*

Have I broken my word to you yet? was Herra's reply, earning herself another kiss.

She smiles at the memory, and at Ricarda's expectant look. "How would you feel about following in your father's footsteps, Majesty, as emperor?"

ARTHUR NEVER THOUGHT there could be any disadvantages to having Lasilas as his painting subject, but he was wrong.

The man won't stand fucking still.

"Lasilas, please, just a little longer," he pleads as Lasilas squirms and moves his legs again. "Good gods, you ride around in battle all day without issue, but you can't stand still for an hour?"

"Exactly the problem," Lasilas says, tilting back his head. Arthur has been staring at the back of his blond locks for the past half hour while Lasilas has had his head to the wall, artistically posed at Arthur's request. Yet Arthur can't help but stare. There's not a part of Lasilas that's not bewitching. "Staying still. In battle, I'm allowed to move around."

"May I remind you that you're the one who offered. You're the one who wanted to do this!"

"Yes, like many of my decisions, I didn't think this one through."

"For fuck's sake. I'm almost done." Arthur lowers his brush. "We can take a break if you really need to."

Lasilas sighs. "No, carry on. I'm just being a bitch." He adjusts his arms where they're placed on the wall above his head. Not as if he's waiting for them to be tied, but braced there in brackets, like he's trying to learn the wall's greatest secrets. Arthur can't say what inspired him to pose Lasilas that way, in the dark corner of this little shed with only the window to bring the painting to life.

Arthur's brush resumes its path on the canvas while they fall back into easy silence. Arthur would kiss him for consolation, but that would probably have the opposite effect.

It doesn't take long for Lasilas to grow bored again. "My captain, can I ask you something?"

Arthur smiles. Lasilas hasn't stopped calling him that, and he frankly doesn't want him to. Not when it sends tingles up Arthur's back to hear it in that soft voice. "Yes, of course, my prince." Now, Lasilas can't say he's no longer a prince. The thought still makes Arthur grin.

They've been lingering in Mariosa, enjoying their first taste of freedom in years. Enjoying the festivities, the preparations for the coronations, staying to clean up in the wake of the war. Soon they'll depart for Ilyaka, where Arthur will get to watch Lasilas reclaim his rightful place.

Arthur will get to experience his home—truly experience it—for the first time. He will see each House, perhaps join one. House Liele, as Lasilas said, is the house of artists. Arthur has written to his mother about it and asked her to join them for a short time. He revealed to her the truth of his nature; he's yet to hear back.

He and Lasilas will take a tour of the Ilyakan countryside, restoring peace and confidence and assuring the people of the truth. Lasilas will get to tell the truth and *finally* be heard. The idea makes Arthur giddy.

Lasilas takes a while to voice his question, and Arthur doesn't pressure him. Arthur fills in the shadows in the corner of the painting, caressing Lasilas' ankles and wrapping around his trousers, the edge of his right side. Every space that licks up Lasilas' body, Arthur paints into color. He paints an ode to Lasilas' colors, the shine from him, the light. He brings it all to light.

"When you told Edgorn that you loved me, how did you mean it?" Lasilas sighs raggedly and leans his forehead against the wall, but Arthur doesn't chastise him this time. His brush pauses.

Lasilas' wavering voice tugs at the very heart of Arthur. Lasilas looks up at the ceiling like he's trying to gather the courage to turn and look Arthur in the face. "Please, put me out of my misery. It's been driving me mad since you said it."

Arthur swallows down all the emotions begging to slip out. The brush sticky with red paint is set down. "Lasilas, please look at me."

Lasilas turns his head, his face twisted in an agonizing mix of emotions.

Arthur says, "I love you as my general, the most honorable commander and the best warrior I've ever had the pleasure of serving under. I love you as the prince of our country, the finest leader we could ever hope to have protecting us. I love you as the most caring and understanding friend I've ever had, the one I could share anything with. I could come to you with any problem and emerge with it solved." His voice shakes. Lasilas makes him weak.

"And I love you as the man I want to spend the rest of my days with, the one I will walk over hot coals and through bloody battlefields and into the mouth of damnation to save."

"Arthur," Lasilas groans. Arthur stills, hardly dares draw breath. "What?"

"You can't just—say things like that."

Lasilas' voice is destroyed, tortured and yearning. Arthur's heart pounds. "Why not?"

Lasilas looks at him then, eyes burning and full. "Permission to abandon the wall and kiss you till I can't breathe?"

Arthur's breath catches at just the thought. "Fuck the painting," he whispers, rising half out of his chair as Lasilas meets him halfway.

LEONIDAS STANDS BESIDE Ricarda with his heart in his throat, watching Jona Musiek's cell door slide open.

This is happening far too late. Ricarda should've freed Jona while Leonidas was away, or better yet the moment they found out he was innocent. There is no good reason for why he was not freed sooner, but Leonidas has held his tongue on the matter. At least it's happening now.

They're accompanied by guards who lurk in the shadows, ready to protect in case Jona—rightfully—decides to take some revenge. Leonidas is not sure he should be stopped, and he would say so if it weren't his fiancé in the line of fire.

But Jona steps out of the darkness with a calm breath, taking a glance at the stairway that leads up to the ballroom. His sister is dead. He's been told.

"Jona," Ricarda says, breaking the terrible silence. Leonidas marvels at how much Jona resembles Francesco Donati's portrait, with red hair so bright it's almost orange. "Jona, I—sorry does not even begin to convey—"

"It's okay," Jona says, smiling thinly as he looks at the man who kept him in that dark hellhole for six years. All the wickedness went to Zera and all the good went to him. "I would have done the same. We take family very seriously in Ilyaka, though it looks far different than family here. I—I cannot say I forgive you, but I understand. I will be okay if I can leave this golden country. I have never gotten to feel its light myself. Maybe that is where my prejudice begins."

His words cut through Leonidas like a knife.

Ricarda lays a shaking, bejeweled hand on Jona's shoulder. "I will never be able to atone for all that I have done, but if there is anything you can think of that will make this even slightly better, please tell me. No boon is too great. I am to be emperor now. I have great power."

Jona chuckles. His Mariosan flows smoothly out in the thick Ilyakan accent that Herra says Zera never had. Always a traveler, she was. Ambitious. Jona's only crime was idolizing her, following her when he should've run for his life. "You always have."

He bends over to pick up the necessities he's been given in the face of his freedom, hoisting them in his arms. He turned down all offers of a carriage ride or servant. Ricarda has offered him titles, lordship, land anywhere in the empire, anything he could want, but Jona has refused it all.

"What can I do?" Ricarda pleads. "Tell me." *Tell me how I can sleep at night.*

Jona rights himself again, his new life grasped firmly in his hands. "Treat everyone with kindness. Even with Ilyaka out of the picture, don't let anyone abuse their station in the empire. Let the rings guide you, not your own greed and power." He gestures to the ring on Ricarda's finger, smiles, and walks away.

UNDER A GLOWING SUNSET in Mitzi, Herra pours two drinks.

She's seated on an easy chair on a balcony in the Blue Feathers house, a marble table between her and the other chair. The liquor poured from its decanter is a rich amber color with all the taste of poison. Herra recalls early days of truces and tentative trust as she hands a glass to Augusta, who is sunken back into the other easy chair. She's too proud to sit in Herra's lap.

"I'm going to miss this city," Augusta sighs, holding the glass firmly. Herra thinks of fabled queens of old, the raw beauty and poise they held. She takes a minute to soak in Augusta's sheer beauty in the sunlight before the words register.

"We'll be back," Herra says. "I would miss the water too much. And the sun." Tasian is taking over the Blue Feathers in the wake of Herra's temporary retirement, both from the gang and from Appointing. She and Augusta will go away to Gina for a while, to Ilyaka, to the forests and the mountains.

Their paths will take them back to Mariosa, but perhaps not for some time. Still, Herra knows the Blue Feathers and the Ruby Rings—also under her purview—will be here for her whenever she's ready to return.

After the coronations, Herra will be free. It's a strange prospect. Francesco's ring, the ring of Ilyaka, will choose emperors in joint with the Ancient ring. As it was meant to be, even if Ilyaka is now parted from the empire. Ricarda V agreed to it easily.

Herra's only remaining task is to appoint a successor to inherit the rings. That is a task for another day, however. Herra allows herself to settle back into the chair.

"Traitor to the north," Augusta says in Ilyakan, winking. Up in Gina it's probably snowing miserably right now. Herra's mind drifts to her father, waiting out the winter alone. They'll be up soon to join him. Maybe Herra will convince him to come with them to explore Ilyaka and the continent at large. The horizon is limitless to Herra now.

"My beautiful warrior," Herra whispers, the Golden Chisel and Augusta Tanner Grimash melting into one before her.

Augusta returns, soft, "My brave B'uoya."

Herra can now say she knows many Ilyakan words, but not that one. "What does that mean?"

Augusta smiles. "God chosen."

"I am not god chosen. Only my bloodline is. I am not special."

"Yes, you are. You're the only one who listened. You're the only one who's been willing to change."

Herra stares at her.

"Don't look at me like that," Augusta says with a scowl, turning her head as a red flush consumes her cheeks. That's new, something Herra has taken deep pleasure in drawing out every chance she gets.

"I'm not doing anything." Herra adjusts her grip on the glass in her hand. She watches the way Augusta stares at her fingers. "I've done much worse to you than just look. Our relationship started with me torturing you in the dungeon."

Augusta shrugs. "Comes with the territory. My surname has a reputation."

"Your surname is Tanner."

Augusta cracks a smile, ducking her head. "I never should've told you that."

Herra smiles hopelessly back. Gods, to think she could've ever wanted this girl dead. She's so much more interesting alive and free. "No, you shouldn't have. Why did you?"

"I thought honesty would get me somewhere."

Herra throws her head back and laughs, feeling the way Augusta's eyes dance over her throat. "It's like you've never worked in the unsavory world before."

"Would you believe me if I said I found you quite annoyingly beautiful, and I was trying to get somewhere?"

Herra snorts. "You must've thought me a dolt if you thought I'd go for that. You were my prisoner."

"Yes, but Zera's goons just nabbed me off the street and passed me to yours. I thought there'd been some misunderstanding. I didn't know I was dealing with a fucking Ancient. The only remaining fucking Ancient, at that."

Herra peels back the collar of Augusta's shirt, exposing the scar she gave Augusta that first day. "That changed quickly enough."

Augusta snorts and clinks her glass against Herra's, holding her eye as she takes a drink. Her sleeve falls, exposing the damn tattoo. It still takes Herra's breath away.

"Scars, a tattoo, the recovery of your armor," Herra murmurs. "I wonder what other marks I've left on you."

Augusta offers vulnerability in her blue eyes. "The marks you've left on me go far deeper than the surface."

Choosing to give a little, Herra admits, "For me, too."

Under the sunset, Augusta laces their fingers together.

CHAPTER SEVEN

Arthur has never felt so awkward in his entire gods damned life.

Riding into battle on a warhorse in full armor and sword in hand, risking his life for thousands of others, kissing his beloved for the first time while they were both covered in blood on the battlefield—no problem. He would much rather be sleep deprived and slicing Edgorn's head off than here dressed in silk, praying for Lasilas to come rescue him.

As happy as he is for the new couple and the coronations, Arthur doesn't know what to do with himself. The bastard that Arthur is now lucky enough to call his lover is occupied with the Ilyakan princes across the room, far away. Lasilas is having a joy of a time, since he was blessed with social graces on top of everything else. Arthur would be happy for him if he weren't so jealous.

"Parties not your thing either, hm?"

Arthur turns, pushing off the wall where he'd plastered himself, finding himself face to face with Herra of the Ancients. Her posture is just as stiff as his. Her hair is loose around her shoulders, thick and black and wavy, perhaps at the behest of the Golden Chisel. She's dressed in formal clothing, same as him.

Gods, Arthur wishes he could've worn his armor, retained some sense of familiarity. At least he's allowed his sword.

"No, they're not. I mean, the setting is gorgeous"—he points to the breathtaking fresco that he barely managed to tear his eyes from—"but this place is foreign to me." The Alizima royal hall is just as intimidating and stunning as he'd expect.

Herra nods and takes her place at the wall beside him. She crosses her arms and presses one foot to the yellow wall behind her. "It's been six years since I've been to a civilized party with respectable people. I had to remember my manners and my etiquette. Augusta made me polish my boots. I feel dirty even though the point is that I'm clean. I don't know how Leonidas did it for so long."

Arthur chuckles, trying and failing to recall the details of the famous Lover's exploits. The story of the emperor to be getting engaged the day of the battle has been floating around everywhere. Arthur doesn't much care about the details as long as everyone he loves is safe and the man he hates stays dead.

"Let us take peace in each other, then." Lasilas slings an arm around a tipsy Augusta's shoulders, raising the glass in his fist to make a toast. Arthur chuckles.

Though this is a royal wedding, one that's apparently been in the making for years, the ceremony was private like all Mariosan weddings. To compensate, the Mariosans have a huge and rowdy afterparty, but the happy couple are yet to be seen. That didn't stop Lasilas and Augusta and countless others from dipping into the drink early. Mariosans are strange.

As Lasilas comes sidling up, sliding an arm around Arthur's shoulders, an announcement from the soon-to-be emperor takes their focus.

"Lovely folks of the continent, I would like you to welcome my esteemed sister, Mariosa's new queen." Ricarda V sweeps an arm toward the crowd as cheers and applause erupt.

Arthur joins in as the grand doors at the back of the room slowly open and the new queen walks out. Hair the same chestnut brown as Ricarda's is done into a twisted updo of braids and sparkling diamond pins, arranged so that a crown would fit perfectly on her head.

She smiles brightly at the crowd, and waves with light pink nails. Against her white skin lies the most gorgeous gown Arthur has ever seen. Not that he's seen many in his life, certainly not those of a queen.

Pale pink, it sparkles from bodice to skirt with gold thread and detailing. It's strapless against her flat chest. Against her collarbone rests a golden locket, and she proudly displays her two courting rings with a wave. The skirt of the gown is as wide as she is tall, a thick sort of tulle that she carries effortlessly. Arthur hears whispers that she made it herself.

"Where is her husband?" Arthur asks of Herra. He's been her companion more than once in the past days, since their lovers are siblings.

"Mariosan weddings dictate that one person makes an entrance by offering some form of entertainment to their partner—singing, playing an instrument, reading poetry." She shrugs. "Leonidas told me. He's already daydreaming about being emperor's consort."

From the glimpses Arthur has gotten of them, that's not why Leonidas Sartini dreams of marrying the emperor. He has the same aching warmth in his eyes that Arthur sees when Lasilas looks at him, something he's still trying to get used to.

The applause continues until Antonia Donati sits down. Ricarda stands in front of her to make her queen. He has a crown of gold leaves and sparkling diamonds in hand, which he places on her head. The room hushes.

"I pass down to you the crown," he says, his voice carrying across the whole room, "the throne, and the honor of Mariosa. Antonia Bevelia Donati, do you swear to uphold the values we all treasure until you pass down this crown yourself, or until it falls from your head in death?"

"Yes." One simple word carries the gravity and might of a queen. The room shivers.

Ricarda unbuckles the royal sword and hands it to her. He bows to her and kisses her hand. When he stands, he smiles with aching pride. Mariosa's doctor queen. Mariosa's seamstress queen. "Then I crown you queen of Mariosa and wish you the best of luck keeping its chaos under control." He sweeps an arm out at the crowd again as thunderous applause erupts in the room.

Antonia smiles, wearing the crown like she was born to it. She is being crowned because, unlike their father, Ricarda V doesn't want to rule a kingdom and an empire at once. He will focus on the broader picture. She will focus on Mariosa. They will undoubtedly work together for the strength of it all.

When applause dies down again, Ricarda says, "Now you shall meet your lover as your husband for the first time." The king turns back to the crowd.

"Before we welcome the queen's husband, may I introduce the woman that we all owe our lives, our countries, and our dignity to—" He cuts off as Leonidas whispers something in his ear. "Well, half of the reason, but my point is that the Silver Hammer doesn't have any singing talent, or so I'm told."

Chuckles rumble through the crowd as Arthur tries to hide his face. Gods, to be able to sink into the floor. Ricarda adds, "He's welcome to come up and join if he likes, but for now, we have Augusta Tanner to sing in companionship to Alessandro's piano. Oh, and welcome to Alessandro de Rege, the queen's consort and beloved husband. Probably should've said that first."

LEONIDAS WATCHES WITH rapture as the doors open for Aless. Not a soul breathes in the room.

Aless walks out wearing a smile more nervous than any Leo has seen on him before. His golden hair is braided over one shoulder, blue eyes warm as ever, and he waves to the gasping crowd. What the crowd is focused on is not his expression or his hair or his pink nails. It's his gown.

It's a full ballgown, the skirt as wide—perhaps wider—as Antonia's, a dark and dusty rose that perfectly complements hers. Thick straps over the shoulders are the only part not beaded with gold and red. The front panel has gotten the most attention, a beautiful mosaic of gold and dark pink that looks as stunning as if it were done by Antonia herself. It's perfectly tailored, perfectly accessorized. For all his nerves, a gleam of joy sparkles in Aless' eye.

Antonia's jaw drops.

Leonidas grins. He and Ricarda have been waiting for her reaction since Aless nervously told them about this, whereupon they both whooped and hugged him. Leo gave him tips for walking in a ballgown skirt without tripping. Aless wears it just as well as he did the day they caught him trying on Antonia's gown before a party, so long ago. Their encouragement was the last thing he needed to throw nerves to the wind and embrace it.

"Less," Antonia breathes, when she can finally form words. "Less." She breathes his name like it's the sweetest breath of rosy air. They both do, in fact, smell like roses.

Aless is still frowning, his expression radiating nerves. Her opinion is the only one that matters to him, and he waits impatiently for it. Leonidas wants to tell her to stop ogling him and tell him that she's ogling him lest he mistake her stare for disgusted shock. He holds his tongue.

"Ann," Aless says. His voice is the trigger she needs. She leaps up from her chair, ballgown skirt and all, to fling her arms around his neck and plant a kiss on his mouth.

"You like it, then." He wraps his arms unsteadily around her, a grin breaking onto his face. "Oh, good gods, you like it."

"Now we've done it," Ricarda mutters into Leo's ear. "We'll never hear the end of this. Now it will be two people talking about their gowns in progress instead of one."

Leo chuckles, watching them kiss like they're alone. Antonia places a crown of gold onto his head, the true consort. Alessandro fawns over it. "Will you wear something like that on our wedding day?"

"My love, I will do anything you ask of me and you know it," Ricarda replies with a grin. "You are welcome and invited to abuse that privilege."

Leo rubs his back over his long velvet coat, delighting in the way Ricarda pushes back into it. As if he can't help accepting Leo's affection. "How does it feel, finally seeing them get married off?"

Ricarda shrugs. "They were always going to end up together. I had resigned myself to being Mariosa's most eligible bachelor for the rest of my days, always trailing after them as the unwanted third." He smiles and intertwines their fingers. "And then I met you, and I fell at first sight."

Leo scoffs. "No one actually falls at first sight. That's bullshit that foolish poets like Aless make up."

Ricarda pulls him close with an arm around the shoulder. "Oh, but I did."

Leo's heart stutters. He can have this, as openly and truthfully as what Antonia and Aless have. He can have this. Ricarda wears his courting ring on his finger as proudly as Antonia. The three of them don't hate Leonidas for what he hid. They all forgive him. Ricarda loves him, and Jona is free.

Leonidas is living a dream.

"You're supposed to be serenading her with the piano, you idiot!" Ricarda yells at Aless. The cheers are still going, explosive and wholehearted. Aless is getting all the support he probably dreamed he'd never have.

"Yes, yes, right," Aless says, stepping away from her and smoothing out his skirts. He grins at the little act of being able to do that. Augusta Tanner, dressed handsomely in a sky blue doublet with puffed shoulders, sings in Mariosan as if she was born to it. Aless plays with all the enthusiasm he usually does until Antonia is laughing and the whole room is clapping.

Before the festivities can truly begin, there is one more appointment to make: Ricarda's. Herra of the Ancients steps up to fulfill her duty. Leonidas smiles widely as Ricarda shoots him a nervous grin.

"Go on," Leo shouts, though it's barely heard over the crowd. "Go assume your position."

His own duty is fulfilled, and once Herra places that crown on Ricarda's head and names a successor, hers will be too. Who knew duty would end up with Leonidas finding his place in life, the man of his dreams, the name through which he has found himself?

The Lover with five names will take only one name more: Donati.

Acknowledgments

THIS NOVEL WAS AN AMBITIOUS behemoth of a project. It was crafted through pages upon pages of notes, late nights untangling plot, and discovering new ways I could misspell common words...but it would not be what it is without some outside help.

To all of my wonderful beta readers: this book was made leagues better because of your advice. I appreciate your dedication, your honesty, and your time. Sincerely, thank you.

Thank you to my writeblr crew for always encouraging my flights of fancy. Sometimes, those flights turn into books like these. What began as a 'male femme fatale falls for his target' novel morphed into a political fantasy beyond the scale of anything I had attempted before, largely because of your enthusiasm.

And lastly, to my readers, my friends, and anyone who has ever left a kind word on my work: thank you. I write because of you. Without you, these books would never leave the prison of my mind.

About the Author

Lila Mary has always craved fantasy romance books where queer characters exist just like everyone else—so, she writes them! When she isn't daydreaming in fantasy worlds, she can be found entertaining her cats. She was born and raised in California. The Lover with Five Names is her second novel, after The Red King's Mystical Suitors.

She can be found at:

lilamarybooks.com

lilamarybooks on Instagram

Also by Lila Mary:

The Red King's Mystical Suitors

Milton Keynes UK
Ingram Content Group UK Ltd.
UKHW010629150124
436059UK00001B/107